common grounds

ALLIE SAMBERTS

Editing by Megan Carver

Cover Design by Jillian Liota, Blue Moon Creative Studio

Artwork and Chapter Art by Lorissa Padilla

alliesambertswrites@gmail.com

www.alliesamberts.com

To anyone who has ever fought like hell to hang on to something special.

To anyone who has ever felt stuck in a rut with no way out.

May these pages bring you hope.

Author's Note

Every time I write a book, I start with one goal: That my readers finish the book happier than they started.

This book... This. Book. It has had me bursting with happiness from start to finish. It is sweet and joyful and funny in a very different way from my other books, and I'm so proud of it. I can't wait for you to dive in.

But, I am who I am. These characters, like all my others, have pasts with grief and trauma. Specifically, the death of one character's grandfather and father are a big part of the story line. Their deaths do not happen on the page, but they are discussed often.

Two of my other characters—sisters—have parents who don't accept them; one, because of her divorce, and the other, because she married a woman. This also happens off-page, but is discussed throughout the story.

There is also an emotionally abusive ex, a little bit of violence, and a very brief mention of IVF (though not related to infertility).

And, as you've probably come to expect from me, my characters use profanity and are intimate. There are three explicit scenes for you to look forward to (or avoid) in chapters 6, 25, and 30.

If any of these things could affect your mental health in a negative way, you might want to put this one aside and come back when you're ready.

I truly hope you enjoy this book, dear reader. It was so fun to write, and it was a labor of love. These characters are near and dear to my heart, and I know they will worm their way into yours.

Welcome to Baker's Grove.

Artwork by Lorissa Padilla

srećo

(s/r/-eh-choh) | **noun**

Happiness. Luck. Something Sweet.

Chapter One

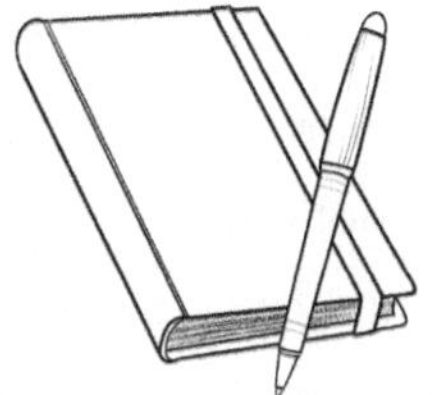

Emery

I WALK-RUN DOWN THE street, my high heels clicking rhythmically against the concrete. My purse slips down my shoulder, and I shove it back where it belongs. I'm sweating in the early-August heat, but I run anyway because I'm late.

I hate being late.

When I finally reach the diner, I pull hard at the heavy door. It opens enough that I slip through and pause in the entryway to catch my breath. I scan the maroon booths and shiny Formica tabletops as I wait for my eyes to adjust to the relative darkness. The diner is dingy, and it looks like someone put it in a time capsule and preserved it for fifty years, but I love it here. It's my comfort place.

Once my eyes adjust, I spot my younger sister, Cassandra. Her blue-black hair that perfectly matches my own shines in the dim lights. I breeze past the hostess with a wave and a smile and slide into the booth across from her. I pinch two fries off the massive plate in front of her and shove them into my mouth as I sit.

"You should never keep a pregnant lady waiting." She glares at me as I steal two more fries.

"I'm pretty sure that's not a thing." I hold the two fries together and bite off the tips of them.

"Pregnant women make the rules," she insists.

"I'm pretty sure that's also not a thing," I counter.

She scowls at me. "You know what? It is a thing, and now you have two people to apologize to, not one."

I press my lips together in mock sympathy. "Oh, poor you and baby, waiting for me with a plate of fries the size of your head. You have it so rough."

"God, Emery. You're such an asshole." She folds her arms high up on her chest, right above the bump that has seriously popped in the past week or so. "I had a craving, okay?"

I suppress a smile as I slide out of my side of the booth and into hers. I throw my arm around her shoulder and pull her close. "I'm sorry, Cass," I say, not at all sorry. Then, I reach my free hand to rub circles on her belly as I lean close to it. "And I'm sorry to you, too, little baby." Cass groans, but I lean further in to plant a kiss where I imagine the baby might be. She shoves me so hard I almost slide off the booth.

"Dammit. No. Keep your hands and your mouth to yourself." She scoffs at me, though she's hiding a smile. "My body is not public property just because I'm pregnant."

I chuckle, returning to my side of the booth. "I know it's not, and I really am sorry I'm late. I almost missed my deadline today, and I don't need Randall riding my ass any more than he already is."

Cass tilts her head and gives an over-exaggerated pout. She must feel bad for me, though, because she pushes the plate of fries to the middle of the table in an offering. "What does he have you working on now? A story about some old lady rescuing fifty kittens from the alley behind her home?"

I huff. "You're not far off. It was two corgi puppies that were found at the carnival last weekend."

"I hope you at least got to interview the hot firefighter who found them?" she speculates, her voice tipping up at the end of the sentence in hope.

"I did get to interview the rescuer," I admit, and she perks up. "But he was a sixty-year-old man with onion breath." I sigh deeply, resigned. With the stories Randall keeps forcing on the writers, you'd think Baker's Grove was a town with a population of three thousand rather than a bustling metropolis. Sure, it's no Chicago or Indianapolis, but it's big enough for some real journalism.

Cass grimaces as if reading my mind, then pops a fry into her mouth. "You can't keep writing these garbage stories. You used to write such interesting stuff at *The Gazette*. Why does he still have you on these fluff pieces?"

I sigh heavily, taking five fries off the plate. She frowns as I eat all of them in one lump together, but I deserve to eat my feelings when I start thinking about how far I've fallen. "Randall doesn't care what I did at *The Gazette*. As far as he's concerned, they laid me off for a reason. And, besides, an online local lifestyle magazine isn't really the place for hard-hitting material." This isn't exactly true, and Cass knows it, which is probably why she's prying again. Randall will run edgier pieces if he thinks the readership will be interested in them, or if the feel-good stories start to get a little too sugar-coated for his liking.

"*The Gazette* was acquired by a larger publication and made cuts. That's the reason. And maybe *Baker's Grove Living* would get some more traction if he let you do something that's actually interesting."

I shrug. "I'm on this feel-good bullshit for the foreseeable future. Ray-of-sunshine reporter for *Baker's Grove Living* is not the career move I thought I'd make, but here we are."

Cass grunts and covers her mouth with her hand to hide her smile. No one on the planet would ever call me a ray of sunshine, and we both know it. The irony of surly old me writing cute and fuzzy stories for any publication isn't lost on either of us.

"Hey, Em. How are you today?" Our waitress interrupts us.

I brighten as soon as the owner of this diner, Donna, sidles up to the table. Her gray hair is pulled into a wispy bun on top of her head, and her weathered skin crinkles around her eyes as she smiles at me. Cass and I have been coming here since we were in high school, and Donna—not only the owner, but the namesake of Donna's Diner—has been a mainstay the entire time. She has always been a sort of second mother to both of us, from checking in on our homework to keeping tabs on us as we've grown into our careers. She was at both of our weddings, and when my marriage fell apart, she was there to help me pick up the pieces when my own parents decided they were too disappointed in me to offer much support. When our parents were disappointed again after Cass announced she was marrying a woman—my childhood best friend, Violet—Donna was there to pick up those pieces, too. She has shown us nothing but unconditional love and support. Cass and I barely have a relationship with our biological parents anymore, content with Donna making up the difference.

"Hi, Donna. It's so good to see you!"

"I told your sister here I hope you two are staying out of trouble." There's a warning in her tone, but her smile gives her away. She not-so-secretly loves living vicariously through our adventures, even though she tries to hide it.

"Well, this one had to go and get herself knocked up, so one of us has to be the responsible one." I grin at Donna, who chuckles and playfully smacks her little notepad at me. Cass simply raises a perfectly manicured eyebrow, unamused.

The truth is, Cass didn't get herself knocked up and everyone knows it. She and Violet looked meticulously for a sperm donor for years before undergoing two rounds of IVF. Cass has wanted to be a mom since we were kids, and she was determined not to let a little thing like marrying a woman stop her.

Violet, speak of the devil, sneaks up behind Donna and wraps her arms around Donna's ample middle, putting her chin on her shoulder and whispering, "Boo!"

Donna jumps, but quickly realizes who is behind her, and then it's Vi's turn to get a swat with the notepad. Vi just giggles and slides into the booth next to Cass.

"Oh, you girls keep me on my toes," Donna mutters, flipping her weapon to a blank page and clicking her pen. "What can I get you?"

"It's cute how you pretend that we aren't going to get the same thing we've ordered for the past twenty years." I tease.

Cass raises her hand. "I'm not. I need red meat, Donna. A huge burger. With cheese. And pickles." She says the last part of her order dreamily. Violet and I exchange glances, both of our eyebrows raised.

"You got it, honey. Milkshakes for the two of you?" She indicates Vi and me. We both nod vigorously. "Coming right up," she says as she wanders away to put our order in.

Violet slouches in her seat, wrapping her arm around Cass's shoulders and nuzzling her nose against her temple. Cass practically melts into her, her eyelids fluttering closed briefly, and her shoulders relaxing away from her ears. She sighs and rests her head on Vi's shoulder, settling into the embrace.

They've always been like this. Completely in love and absolutely perfect for each other. That is, after they finally told me about their relationship. They hid it from me as long as they could, worried that I'd be upset my best friend was dating my sister. To be fair, I was worried it would fundamentally change our friendship. But only for, like, a minute.

I love how much they love each other. Seeing them together all those years ago was one of the first clues I had that my marriage wasn't working out. Well, it would have been, had I been ready to admit it to myself. Now, as a thirty-seven-year-old divorcée, I've come to terms with the fact that I'm not meant to have the kind of shared moments these two have. I have my vibrator, and when that's not enough, Vi makes a great wingwoman.

I grab another fry off the plate in the center of the table and use it to point between the two of them. "Why aren't you giving Vi shit about being late, too?" I punctuate the accusation by popping the fry in my mouth.

"Because she's not late. She told me she'd be here at five-thirty. You said five." Cass breathes, her voice sounding like she's sinking into a warm bath rather than sitting in a dingy diner booth with her wife.

Violet tips her head back and forth, eyeing me. "Yeah. At least I'm accurate in my estimation of arrival times."

I pick up a fry and throw it at her. She catches it and eats it, smiling. Suddenly, her smile turns to a grimace. "How much salt is on these? Jeez, Cass. You're going to skyrocket your blood pressure with these things."

Cass groans, her eyes still closed as she leans against Violet's shoulder. "Don't start. It's not my fault you don't like flavor."

I chuckle quietly as Violet scowls. If it were up to her, all food would be free of seasoning, sauce, and spice. Which is ironic considering most days she dresses like the spiciest girl at the ball. Today, her hair is bright purple—a little too on the nose, if you ask me, but to each her own—which matches the purple horseshoe lip ring she's sporting. She's wearing a flowing, emerald green, cotton dress paired with her ever-present black combat boots. It's a look only Vi can pull off. She's like a deadly butterfly. Gorgeously colorful, perfectly coordinated, but lethal.

"Besides," Cass continues. "Baby gets what baby wants. And baby wants salt, red meat, and pickles." She wiggles in her seat in excitement at her upcoming meal.

Vi's scowl turns into the cheesiest grin I've ever seen, and it completely transforms her face. Her blue eyes light up, and the normally harsh lines of her mouth disappear. She puts a hand on Cass's belly and kisses her forehead. A soft smile plays at Cass's lips.

"Oh, come on," I moan, completely ruining their moment. "You're not going to give her crap about touching your belly either?"

Cass opens one eye to scowl at me. "It's Vi's baby. She's allowed touch." She closes the eye again.

"I'm the auntie!" I protest.

"Don't care," Cass sighs irreverently.

Violet shoots me an apologetic look and shrugs the shoulder Cass isn't leaning on. I shake my head incredulously.

Just then, our food is delivered. Cass practically bounces up and takes a huge bite of her burger, ketchup sliding out the other side of it and plopping onto the plate. She lets out a moan that sounds vaguely sexual. Vi's cheeks turn a bright pink, and she coughs on the sip of her milkshake she had just taken. A corner of Cass's mouth turns up as she looks at Vi suggestively, licking a bit of ketchup off her bottom lip without breaking eye contact. Vi turns even more red.

My eyes dart back and forth between the two of them. "Y'all need some privacy?" I ask. When Vi's expression changes from horny to horrified, I cackle.

Vi groans. "You're the absolute worst," she says on a grimace. Cass, as usual, is completely unbothered by my teasing. Violet, however, is adamant that it's always going to be a little weird to be my best friend and be married to my little sister. It doesn't really bother me, but I also try not to think about it too hard.

Vi clears her throat. "So, Em, do you still want to grab drinks later?"

"She definitely needs a drink or two after that story she had to do about Onion Breath and his two new puppies," Cass says around a mouthful of hamburger.

Violet looks at me questioningly, but I shake my head. "Not worth explaining. Yes, drinks would be awesome. I'll swing by at around eight?" I ask.

"She probably means eight-fifteen," Cass interjects, taking another huge bite of her burger.

I roll my eyes and sigh. "I'm late one time, and you can't let it go?"

"Hmm." Cass pretends to think about it, then drops her chin toward me, her eyes serious. "No."

I shake my head, then glance at Vi, who only has eyes for Cass again. She's basically a purple-haired, heart-eye emoji with a lip ring. The way she looks at her is as sickly sweet as the milkshake I'm sipping, even as Cass takes another massive, inelegant bite of her hamburger.

I swirl the whipped cream topping with my straw and lick it off before taking a long draw of vanilla milkshake through it. All conversation has halted while my two companions clearly play footsie under the table. Vi uses her tongue to fidget with her lip ring. Cass's gaze snags on the movement, and then it's her turn to blush.

I'm happy for them. I really am. And I'm not jealous. I came to terms with my divorce pretty much as soon as I threw his cheating ass out of our apartment. Their kind of love just isn't meant for me.

But it might not be a bad idea to charge my vibrator for when I get back from the bar tonight, either.

Chapter Two

I'VE BEEN OVER THESE numbers a hundred times. Maybe even two hundred. The situation never changes. Unless there's some kind of miracle, we have two months tops before we're going to have to shut down Baker's Blend Coffee Shop.

It's a good thing I believe in miracles. Otherwise, I'd be completely lost.

I'm not one to lose hope, but things look pretty dire as I bend over a worktable in the tiny office-slash-kitchen in the back of the shop, staring at the spreadsheet I have practically memorized. Red numbers line the sheet, getting blurrier the longer I look at them. I know they don't have to be literally red, but what can I say? I like a little drama.

"Hey, Boss?" James sticks his head between the double doors with an apologetic look on his face.

I pinch the bridge of my nose as I look up at him. "How many times have I told you to call me Trevor?"

"Oh." He straightens slightly, opening the door wider. "Um, a lot."

James is a nice kid, but he's probably—no, definitely—another reason we are losing money. I hired him when his mom begged me to give him a job so he could get out of the house and start making some money. I guess I'm a sucker for a good cause.

Right now, he's standing there, staring at me. It's starting to get awkward.

I sigh. "Did you need something, James?"

"Yeah, Boss." He cringes. "Um, Trevor. Your buddy is here." He shrugs and leaves the back room, letting the door swing closed.

Very carefully, I snap my ancient laptop shut. One of these days, it'll probably turn to dust under my fingers, and I don't need another added expense. I stand and stretch before sighing deeply. Staring at these numbers isn't going to make a miracle appear, anyway. Might as well walk away for now.

I push the door to the serving area open to see Mike, my best friend, standing on the other side of the laminate, L-shaped counter. He brushes a crumb off one of the empty, well-worn oak tables sitting sad and empty behind him. Despite the emptiness, I grin. Mike and I have known each other since college. He even used to work here on breaks, and he still tries to stop in as much as he can.

"Hey, man. How's it going? Can I get you anything?"

He smiles back. His eyes flit to James as his expression turns mischievous. I know before he even says it that he's going to order something complicated as a test. "An oat milk latte would be great."

Could be worse. Could be the hot flat white with a triple shot of espresso, nonfat milk, and extra foam he ordered a few days ago. We stand there for a moment, then I swivel to James, raising my eyebrows expectantly. Surely, he can handle a simple nondairy latte?

James looks behind him as if there is someone else there to pass the order on to. There's not. There never was. Once he finally figures it out, he pulls out the whole milk to start making Mike's latte, showing no small amount of trepidation as he approaches the decades-old espresso machine on the counter. It faces the barstools where patrons used to sit and sip their tiny coffees. I clear my throat, then clear it again louder because James didn't hear me the first time.

"He said oat milk," I remind him.

"Oh, shit," he curses, then covers his mouth, his eyes wide. "I'm sorry, Boss. Wrong milk. No swearing. I got it."

He does not "got it." This is how he's been for the past six months since I hired him. I cock my head then shake it before bumping him out of the way so I can take over.

"Let him, Trev. It's fine," Mike says, leaning over the counter and grabbing my arm before I can make it too far. "Seriously." He reaches for his wallet and pulls out a $100 bill.

I eye him up and down, frowning. "It's on the house."

He scowls at me, then glances around the empty shop, letting his gaze linger on several of the empty, wooden chairs that surround the tables. "Can you afford to give away lattes?"

I shrug. "Your seven dollars is a tiny bandage on a very large bullet hole, friend." I glance down at his hands. "Besides, we don't have enough cash in the register to break a hundred, anyway."

I pass the still-full pastry case as I come around the counter. Mike's scowl deepens as he puts his money back in his wallet, but I catch him throwing a twenty in the tip jar when he thinks I'm not looking.

I slump into one of the smaller tables near the huge windows that line the front of the shop. This view is one of my favorites, the Baker's Grove skyline visible just above the shops that line the other side of the street. The buildings are shiny and tall, but several older shops like mine are still interspersed at regular intervals. Passersby come and go on the sidewalk outside the window, and the hustle and bustle is palpable. I really wish some of that energy would make its way inside here.

I'd miss this view if the shop goes under.

I love this place. When my grandfather came to America from Croatia after World War II, he found a community of Croatian immigrants, realized they needed a coffee shop, and opened it. Croatian coffee culture is a major thing according to his stories, and that didn't change when they immigrated to America. People from the community would come and sit for hours, sipping espresso and chatting. Going out for coffee was an event, and the shop did well for a long time.

Eventually, with the rise of flavored lattes and plastic to-go cups, my grandfather decided to step back—though never did so completely—and my dad stepped up. He made changes to the menu which brought in some new clientele. But when my grandfather and father passed away within a few years of each other, the shop became mine.

At first, it was fine, but ever since the big box coffee shop opened down the street, business has trickled out. A few customers that were my grandfather's age remained, and they'd still come in and sip their espresso for hours. But new high-rises had started popping up in my childhood, and our bread-and-butter had been the people who worked in them. Much to the chagrin of my grandfather's friends, these newcomers would stop in for their giant, to-go coffees, but they bought enough that we continued to turn a profit. Once that store opened down the street, though, we couldn't compete with their speed. Or their prices.

For a while, our loyal regulars made sure to throw in an extra muffin or two to help, and we made do. But they're aging and have started to venture out less. Some, like my mom, have moved to milder climates than northern Indiana, and some have sadly passed away. We greet fewer and fewer customers each day now, and not only are we making less money, we're also losing it on the expired food and coffee we have to donate at the end of each week.

I sigh deeply as I tear my gaze from the window to look at Mike.

"I take it you're having a great day." His voice is dripping with sarcasm. He sits across from me with an annoying smirk on his face. His back is straight and his forearms are pressed against the table. He's always so proper, wearing freshly starched, button-down shirts and perfectly pressed slacks every single workday. There's never a smudge or a pit stain in sight, even in this sweltering summer heat. He almost looks out of place against the earthy tones in this cozy shop.

I know without looking that my green shirt is rumpled and there has been a coffee blot on my tan chinos since ten o'clock this morning.

"Yeah, awesome. We've had a line out the door since morning rush. This is the first time I've been able to sit down all day."

James brings Mike's drink over to the table and sets it down next to him. "That's not true, Boss. Mike is only our third customer today."

I don't bother expending the energy it would take to glare at him. Mike snorts, then sips his latte and coughs.

"Not oat milk?" I ask.

"Probably soy," Mike answers.

"Dammit. I'm sorry, Mike. I can make it again? I swear I'll get it right this time." James pleads.

Mike pushes the cup an inch or two toward the center of the table and leans back in his seat. He folds his arms and smiles, his movements smooth and languid like they always are. "It's no problem. I love soy milk."

James slumps a little and lets out a quiet breath as he shuffles back behind the counter.

I cock an eyebrow at Mike. "You hate soy milk."

"I also don't need a latte at five-thirty in the evening. We both know I'm not coming in here every night for a caffeine fix."

I shoot him a bland look, then glance out the window to the sidewalk. It's a hot day. There's not a cloud in the sky, and the sun is golden where it hits the sidewalk between the taller buildings. A beam of light illuminates the pink flowers and bright green leaves in the planter outside the window, and I wonder briefly if I remembered to water them this morning.

"I'm not closing the shop." My voice is barely audible over the acoustic coffeehouse playlist coming from the speakers.

"That's the spirit," Mike says sardonically.

I turn my attention back to him. "I'm serious. I'm not doing it. Something has to work out. This place is too important to fail."

"You're not a bank, dude. There isn't some bailout coming, and you can't keep sinking money into this place," he insists.

"I know, I'm not an idiot. I just think…" I trail off and look out the window again. People are starting to walk past in earnest, probably on their way home to families or out to meet friends for dinner and drinks.

Baker's Grove is about an hour and half outside of Indianapolis. It's the perfect cross between suburb and city, with some new buildings mixed with older shops in the heart of the downtown area. The juxtaposition of the old and new is what made my grandfather decide it was the perfect place to open this shop, naming it Baker's Blend Coffee Shop as a nod to the town that had given so much to him.

It's a nice place to live and work—there's a decidedly urban feel I still struggle to explain to people who aren't from here. The best way I've ever heard it described is the biggest small town, which encompasses both the chatter and warm familiarity of the downtown area and the sharper steel of the more modern buildings surrounding it. Small enough that you don't have to drive for forty-five minutes to get to the other side of the town, but big enough to enjoy some anonymity if you want it.

I, however, have been enjoying too much anonymity as of late. I haven't had a social life to speak of in a long time. The stress of the shop has been almost too much to bear. If I'm not here, I'm in my tiny studio apartment across town, lying awake most nights thinking of ways to save this place.

Mike is looking at me as if I'm one of those abandoned puppies in those late-night animal adoption commercials. I take a deep breath and let it out slowly. "Where there's a will, there's a way."

"Don't you think if there was a way, it would have appeared by now?" Mike asks.

A woman running down the sidewalk catches my eye. She's wearing a light pink blouse, a black pencil skirt, and shiny, mile-high heels. Her blue-black hair trails behind her as she weaves in and out of the growing crowd of people on the sidewalk. I track her progress for so long that Mike swivels in his seat to see what I'm looking at. When she disappears around the corner, he slowly shifts his gaze to me, looking positively amused.

"She was hot."

I groan and scrub my cheek with my hand, my palm catching on the stubble I'm too preoccupied to shave. "Lay off."

He leans back, a self-satisfied look on his face. "Face it. If you had someone in your life, you'd spend a hell of a lot less time worrying about this shithole—"

"Watch it." I shoot him a warning glare.

"My bad. This *establishment*. You need a lady in your life, man."

"Says the man who is chronically single," I grumble.

He looks at me pointedly. "Single by choice. I know you've always wanted a partner. Maybe it's time to get back out there. Your love life has really fizzled out since you took over this place."

"I'm forty years old, Mike. Don't you think if there was a woman for me, she would have appeared by now?" It's one of my favorite things, parroting his words back at him. It grinds his gears, and I'm rewarded for my efforts by his heavy sigh and low growl.

"You know," he says slowly, "if you spent a little more time out there, and a little less time in here, you might find a woman worth your time."

I roll my eyes. He's always on me about this, and it's not worth a response.

"Listen," he says, angling toward the table. He spares a glance for the coffee cup on the table, grimaces, then pushes it to the side so he can lean in fully. "A few of my buddies from the office are going out tonight—"

I hold up a palm to stop that train of thought before it leaves the station. "I have zero interest in grabbing drinks with a bunch of software engineers."

He genuinely looks offended, even though we've been down this road a thousand times before. "What's wrong with software engineers?"

One would think this particular profession would be full of a bunch of soft-spoken nerds, but the startup Mike works for is somehow populated by guys just like him. Maybe like attracts like. Or maybe the company's ping-pong table in the break room attracted them. Either way, when you get a little alcohol in them, they get rowdy and obnoxious, which is not the crowd I want to spend my Friday evening with.

"Fine." Mike leans back in his chair with finality. "Spend another night in your sad apartment by yourself worrying about what else you can sell or downsize to keep this place open. Sounds super fun."

"You make a great point. Even if I wanted to come out with you tonight—which I don't—I couldn't afford it, anyway."

He flashes me his blindingly white, mischievous smile. "I have it on good authority that these software engineers you have such contempt for make a ton of dough. Drinks are on me. You know that."

I press my lips into a fine line as I regard him. "Are you going to let this go?"

His grin gets impossibly wider. "I'll put it this way. I'm more determined to get you to come out with me tonight than you are to keep this place from bleeding your bank account dry."

"You're a funny guy, you know that?"

He stands, coming around the table and clapping a hand on my shoulder. "See you in a few hours." He makes his way to the door, resting a hand on the doorknob and turning to face me again. "Oh, and stop at home first and grab some clothes that don't have coffee splatter all over them, huh?"

I throw a wadded-up napkin in his direction, but it falls short as he cackles and leaves.

Chapter Three

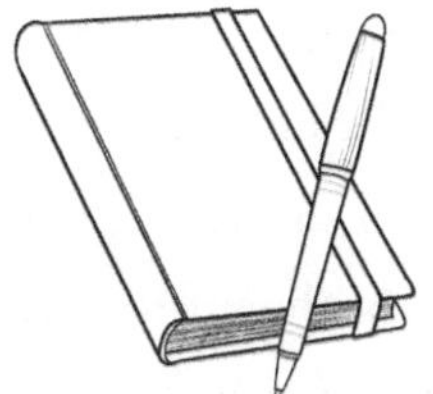

Emery

Vi and Cass live in an adorable two-story on the outskirts of Baker's Grove with a view of the downtown skyline in the distance. Not that it's much of a skyline. I mean, sure, there are some cool buildings, but the city is too small to be of any real interest, in my opinion. And yet, their real estate agent sold it to them as a home with a view, which worked, I guess. Their perfectly manicured yard—Violet's pride and joy—is framed by beautifully tended rose bushes and a cobblestone walkway from the sidewalk up to their house. Vi is an excellent gardener and uses most of her spare time to tend to their landscaping.

I spitefully shove their front door open just before eight o'clock and step into their dark entryway. "Vi? Cass?" I call, flipping on a light.

"Shhhh!" Violet comes around the corner, shushing me. "Cass is napping." She's changed her dress to one with dark, moody florals. Her short, purple hair is curled and frames her face perfectly.

"Isn't it generally called 'sleeping' when it's this close to an actual bedtime?"

Vi rolls her eyes. "She has a conference call with some investors in China or something in a few hours."

"These middle-of-the-night calls can't be good for her." I frown.

Violet gives an exasperated sigh. "If you want to try to get her to slow down, be my guest."

I huff a laugh. No one on the planet can get Cass to slow down, and we both know it. "Sorry, pal. She's your problem now."

Vi pulls on her boots and shakes out her dress. When she stands to check herself one last time in the mirror next to the door, I can see her face over her shoulder. She flutters her eyebrows suggestively. "'Problem' is not the word I'd use." She turns her attention back to the mirror and gently adjusts the necklace she always wears. It's a tiny charm with both her and Cass's birthstones on it. Blue topaz for Cass and aquamarine for Vi. She always says they were meant to be because the stones are both blue.

I level a glare at her, but the corners of my mouth from turn up slightly all on their own. "You two are so fucking cute."

She turns around, grinning as she ticks her head toward the door. "Cute and thirsty. Let's get out of here."

We walk the half-mile or so to Violet's bar of choice, The Tipsy Geezer. As the name might suggest, the place caters to an older demographic. The music is loud, but not blaring. There aren't any flashing lights or dance floors. It's a dimly lit, cozy pub which makes it a great place to get a beer and chat with a friend.

As soon as we enter, though, we stop in our tracks. A group of about ten raucous men are either crammed in or standing around our favorite booth in the back corner. Vi grumbles something under her breath, but I chuckle. For someone who frequently experiments with wardrobe choices, she's surprisingly attached to her habits, so I know she's annoyed by the unavailable booth. The fact that it's currently occupied by a bunch of annoying dudes only adds salt to the wound.

I slip my arm around her waist and gently lead her to the bar. "Come on. We'll have the first round over here, then hopefully they'll leave, and we can move over there. Okay?"

She grumbles again but slides onto one of the high bar stools lining the butcher block counter. I plop onto one next to her. The bartender comes over to take our orders. He must be new here because I've never seen him before, and I know without looking that Vi is flaring her nostrils in frustration at another new curveball this evening.

He leans on the bar and flashes Vi a grin, his biceps popping. She pins him with a look that could kill, then orders us a couple of beers in a tone that conveys absolutely zero interest in whatever else he's offering.

"Cass told me Randall is still humiliating you with these feel-good assignments," she says as the bartender shuffles away to get our drinks, his ego clearly wounded.

I tip my head back and groan. "It's not even close to writing real news. One of these days, the journalism police are going to come and confiscate my degree," I intone.

"You gotta pitch him something heavier, Em." Apparently, she doesn't want to engage with my dry humor. "Wasn't there a story about the misallocation of school funds you were trying to get off the ground?"

The bartender comes back and deposits our glasses in front of us. I take a deep pull from mine, savoring the balance of the bitter hops with an undertone of bananas. I can't resist a good wheat beer on a hot, summer night. I wipe the remaining foam off my upper lip before responding. "Yeah, but Randall's not going to be interested in something like that. Or, if I pitch it and he likes it, he'll probably assign it to Brett or someone he thinks is better suited to the important stories."

"By 'better suited' do you mean—"

"A man? Yes, that's exactly what I mean."

"How much longer are you going to work for that pig? You were doing such great stuff at *The Gazette*. There's so much untapped potential here. I can't believe Randall doesn't see it."

I shrug. I've been over this issue a million times, both in my head and with Vi and Cass. I don't have an explanation or a solution. What I have are bills to pay and soon, a new little baby to spoil. And frankly, *Baker's Grove Living* pays really well. I knew I'd be lucky to find any kind of job in my field after I got laid off. As a feature writer, I thought I might be safe at *The Gazette*, but no one was. Well, no one except the most senior reporters and, because it was an election year, the political reporters. News, it would seem, is a dying art. Unless it's about corgi rescues, apparently.

I try to change the subject. "You know what's better than talking about my sad excuse for employment?"

"Literally anything?" Vi smirks as she raises her glass to her lips. She winces as a round of particularly thunderous laughter comes from the group at the back of the bar.

I snicker at her discomfort. "Well, yeah. But specifically, how you're feeling about baby Darlis-Jacobson making their arrival in a couple of months. How you hanging in there, Mama?"

Since I've known her, Vi has been all hard edges and blunt force. Her love language is punching your nemesis in the face—literally. We became best friends in fourth grade because she shoved Davy Jenkins on the playground for teasing me about my outfit. But when I mention the baby, she melts. Her blue eyes search mine, full of earnestness and hope and unfiltered joy.

"Em, I've never been this happy in my entire life."

"You're getting soft in your old age," I tease.

"You take that back." She reaches over and shoves my shoulder so hard I almost topple over.

I laugh again, rubbing my upper arm. Vi looks behind me, and her eyes catch on whatever she sees, so I twist slightly to check it out. A man has appeared next to me, an empty glass resting on the counter between his corded forearms as he leans against the bar. He has thick, golden-brown hair that has been styled but still falls over his forehead, and stubble that looks disheveled but purposeful. His cheekbones are high and prominent, and I swear they could actually cut glass. His shoulders are broad, but he's lean in that hipster kind of way, with a dark t-shirt that clings to his torso and skinny jeans that show a little ankle above his flat sneakers.

I slowly turn my back to him and glare at Vi, whose eyes are flashing with mischief as she notices the same thing I just did: this guy is sexy as hell.

"Hi there," she says suggestively. I widen my eyes and shake my head almost imperceptibly. I hadn't meant for her to be a wingwoman tonight, but she's undeterred. "Come here often?"

"No, actually." Shit. His voice is gravelly and deep, and I can almost feel it rumbling through me. That voice singlehandedly pulls me to face him.

"I'm here with some buddies," he says, then reconsiders. "Well, I'm here with a buddy and his friends." He tips his chin, indicating the group of over-loud men in the back corner.

"You're with them?" I recoil. It comes out of my mouth before I have the chance to stop it, but he's so calm and casual, which is completely unlike the rest of those men with their bravado we can all hear over the music.

He laughs, the skin around his eyes crinkling. "Uh, sort of?" His gaze lands on me, and he blinks rapidly a few times, then his eyebrows pinch together slightly. He quickly looks me up and down, his smile changing into something genuine and welcoming. "I'm Trevor," he says, his eyes never leaving mine.

I'm silent for too long as we both apparently can't take our eyes off each other. Vi clears her throat, extending her hand around me for a handshake. "I'm Violet. This is Emery."

He spares her a glance to shake her hand, but then his gaze meets mine again. His eyes are a smoldering amber color, even in the dark lights. They rival his cheekbones to win the most striking facial feature award. "Emery." He says it like he's trying it on, and the glint in his eyes would suggest he likes what he hears.

Violet kicks me under the bar and I yelp. "Shit, Vi. That hurt!" I reach down to rub my shin. "You're wearing combat boots, for crying out loud."

She shrugs. "Sorry." It's totally insincere.

Another man sidles up on the other side of her. He is all smooth pretense and suave attitude with his slicked-back hair, pale blue shirtsleeves unbuttoned and rolled up, and dark wash jeans. "Hey, ladies. I see you met my friend Trev. I'm Mike."

He slides another inch closer to Vi, and her shoulders tense. I snort into my beer glass, and I notice out of the corner of my eye that Trevor has cocked an eyebrow as if he's mostly curious how this is going to go. The guys from the booth in the back get up to leave, and Mike gives them a wave on their way out before addressing us again.

"Can I buy you lovelies another round?" he asks as the bartender deposits another drink in front of Trevor.

Vi defers to me with a questioning look. I eye my half-empty glass. "Sure," I say, mostly because I want to see what happens when this Mike guy hits on my friend.

"Oh shoot," Violet says, pulling her phone from her pocket and glancing at it as the bartender puts my beer in front of me. "My pregnant wife needs me." She punctuates the words clearly, probably for Mike's benefit. "I'm going to have to pass this time." She stands, clapping me on the shoulder.

"You said she has a conference call with someone in China tonight." I narrow my eyes at her.

"Well, you know your sister." She chuckles good-naturedly. Then, for good measure, she adds in a singsong voice, "Never argue with a pregnant lady!"

Mike catches Trevor's eye over my shoulder and raises his eyebrows in question, but I can't see Trevor's silent response.

"Sounds concerning. I should probably come with you," I say. I know she's full of shit, so I try to stand, but she tightens her grip on my shoulder.

"Not concerning at all. Happy wife, happy life. You know the drill," she says through gritted teeth as she presses down on my shoulder almost painfully.

"You know what?" Mike says, slapping some money on the counter. "I'll walk you out if you don't mind."

"What happened to your plan to stay out all night and have a good time?" There is a taunt in Trevor's voice that is sexy as hell. I knew I should have charged that vibrator.

Mike fakes a yawn. "I'm not as young as I thought I was, man. It's late."

"It's nine-thirty," I say drily.

"Well past my bedtime, too." Violet stretches her arms out dramatically.

"I thought Cass needed you." I take a smug sip of my beer. I doubt I can get her to stay here, but I can at least give her shit for her inconsistent lies.

Vi shrugs, walking quickly toward the door with Mike on her heels. "Yep. She needs me. In bed." She makes a vaguely sexual hand gesture, which makes me almost spit out my beer. "See you later!" She practically giggles as she holds the door open for Mike, then rushes out behind him.

I stare at the door for a moment before looking at Trevor, who is studying me with a soft smile on his face. He indicates the drinks in front of us. "Seems a shame to waste these," he suggests.

"They did this on purpose."

He sighs, running a palm against the stubble on his jaw. I suddenly and inexplicably want to run my own palm against it, to feel the coarse hairs scrape against my skin.

"They definitely did." He faces me fully, leaning one arm on the bar. "I completely understand if you want to get out of here. I have a feeling you didn't come out tonight to get hit on by some guy."

I tilt my head and arch an eyebrow. "Are you hitting on me?"

He leans a few inches closer to me, his eyes practically glowing. "Not yet." His voice drops an octave when he says it, and it's dripping with sinful promise.

My toes curl, and warmth pools low in my belly. He's right; I did not come here to get hit on, but there's something about his self-assurance that is wildly attractive. I cross my right leg over my left so I'm angled toward him, then nod at the stool behind him.

He grins, and his eyes crinkle adorably at the corners again. It's the smile of someone who often finds joy, and it melts a little place in my cynical heart.

He drags the stool closer so he can sit. It's so close to me, in fact, that his knees brush mine under the counter. He flushes and turns his gaze to his beer. It's so charming, that pink hue of his cheeks. It strikes me as so incredibly genuine, and for the second time tonight, I want to reach out and run my hand against his jaw. He fidgets with the glass on the counter, twisting it this way and that and looking at it through his long, gorgeous lashes.

Dammit. He is really cute.

He clears his throat, then smiles sheepishly, still not looking at me. "I'm sorry. I don't... This isn't something I do often."

"Have a beer with someone at a bar?" I tease.

He eyes me sidelong. "Well, that too, actually." He takes a long sip of his drink, and I do the same. He swallows, then rushes to add, "I'm not a recluse or anything. I'm just busy."

Apparently, his self-assuredness is gone now that I've asked him to sit. His nervousness is actually more attractive than his confidence. I squeeze my thighs together under the bar. One glance at his hands where they're resting on his beer glass has me wondering what they might feel like on me... In me...

Holy shit. Where did that come from?

He raises his gaze to meet mine, clearly hopeful I'll pick up the conversation. Words. I can do words. It's basically my job, after all.

"What keeps you so busy?" I ask.

"Work, mostly."

Oh, boy. Never mind. This is going to be painful. It figures the cute one would be the hardest to talk to. I take another huge gulp of my beer, hoping to hurry this along. "And what do you do for work?"

He looks conflicted for a second, but it's gone too fast for me to linger on it. "I own a coffee shop," he says finally.

"You *own* it? As in, it's *yours*?" I sound impressed because I am. I would have definitely guessed based on appearances alone that this guy worked somewhere like a coffee shop, but never in a million years would I have thought he owned one.

He nods, a corner of his mouth tilting up. "My grandfather opened it about seventy years ago, and it has kind of been in the family ever since."

"That is so cool." I rest my chin on my hand. "So, it's a family business, then. How awesome of you to take that over. Was it always something you wanted to do, or were you forced into it?"

"I love the shop. I grew up there, more or less." He chuckles as he runs a long finger over the rim of his glass. "Coffee is in my veins. My first memory is running my hands through piles of coffee beans. My mom used them to help me learn math. My first job was grinding the coffee for people who wanted to buy it by the pound. I learned about money and making change from working the register. The espresso machine we still use today is the same one my grandfather bought shortly after he opened the shop." He seems to catch himself being whimsical because he pauses and sips his beer. He avoids my eyes when he says, "But I didn't take it over until after my father and grandfather passed. It's a special place."

"Sounds like it," I say gently. It's my job—or, at least, it used to be—to read people. To find the right angle to get a story out of them. Trevor is clearly done talking about this for now. I decide not to ask any further questions about his livelihood, even though I'm beyond intrigued. I haven't felt that kind of passion for a job—or a place, for that matter—since I was burning the midnight oil at *The Gazette*, poring over interviews and piecing together facts. A twinge of nostalgia hits me, and I wince slightly.

"So... your friend you came here with?" Trevor ventures, bringing me back to the conversation.

"Violet," I remind him.

"Right. She's your sister-in-law?"

I laugh, twisting my beer glass around on the counter in front of me. "Yes. She's also my childhood best friend. We grew up together, Vi, Cass and me. Cass is my sister," I add for his benefit. "Vi and I went away to college, and then she spent a few years abroad exploring and working odd jobs and the like. When we came back, Cass was all grown up, and Vi fell hard."

Trevor's light brown eyes searching mine. I could get lost in those eyes. They're crystal clear as they glimmer in the dim lights of the bar. "Was that weird for you?"

"Not as much as you might think. I'm glad they're happy. I've never felt like a third wheel with them or anything. And I'm very excited to be an aunt." I beam at that. I can't help it. I've never wanted kids of my own, but that doesn't mean I don't want to spoil this baby rotten when it gets here. I'm going to be the best aunt ever.

"Do you have any other family around?" he asks.

It's an innocent question, and one I would expect from someone making small talk with a person they just met. I feel my smile fade all the same. "Our parents live nearby. We grew up here, in Baker's Grove. But they..." I trail off, not sure how much personal information I want to divulge with someone I met only minutes ago. "They don't agree with some of our life choices," I say simply.

Trevor nods in a *say-no-more* fashion, and I'm glad he doesn't press for more information. I'm also unexpectedly pleased that he doesn't seem to pity me for my family situation. There's not much worse than that sympathy from people when they find out my parents essentially estranged their children. I don't need their pity. I don't even feel bad about it. I'm not the one that has anything to feel bad about, and neither is Cass.

Luckily, I don't have to dwell on that for long, because he looks at me, his eyes dipping to my lips then back to meet my gaze, and I'm turned on all over again.

"What do you do for a living?" He changes the subject, his face eager and almost boyish with interest. Just when I thought he couldn't get more attractive, he smiles this brilliant smile. I almost don't want to look at it for too long; that's how bright it is. His teeth are so white and straight, and his mouth creases at the corners under his stubble. I am somehow, yet again, desperate to feel it under my hands.

I cough, and my foot starts wiggling under the bar. Since our knees are still touching, he must be able to feel it, though his expression doesn't change. He just looks at me expectantly.

"I'm a journalist," I finally say, though I'm also not offering any more information than that.

"No way!" he exclaims. "Have you written anything I might have read?"

"Um..." I trail off, looking around the bar. My eyes snag on a bright blue bottle on the top shelf behind the counter as I avoid his gaze. "Not unless you make a habit of reading online local lifestyle magazines?" I raise an eyebrow, fully expecting the shake of his head. "I don't blame you." I let out a bitter laugh.

"Not your first choice of employment?" he guesses.

I take another sip and shake my head. "Not the first, second, or third. Probably not even the thirtieth. I used to work at *The Gazette*, but I was a victim of the layoffs that came after they were acquired." It's not usually something I talk about, let alone with someone I met mere minutes ago, but the words sort of fall out of me. Maybe it's the beer, or maybe it's the way Trevor's knee keeps brushing against mine under the bar, or the way his eyes light up with each piece of information I give him. It could be addicting, this singularly-focused attention he's turned on me.

I *really* wish I had charged my vibrator before I left.

I don't offer anything else—not because I don't want to. It's because I'm lost in the feel of his leg pressed against mine and the intoxication of the way he's hanging on my every word.

Thankfully, he comes to my rescue. "Sorry about Mike. He's a good guy when you get to know him, but I know how he comes off."

"How long have you known each other?"

"Since college. So..." he winces, and that's really cute, too. "Over twenty years, I'm embarrassed to say."

"Embarrassed because you are still friends with that guy after twenty years, or because you're old?" I ask without thinking. My hand flies to my mouth, and my eyes go wide. I really need to slow down this beer. That was a shitty thing to say.

Thankfully, he laughs. It's a low, rumbling sound that vibrates through me. "Both?" he asks.

I hum, then pretend to do some mental calculations. "So, you're, what, forty?"

"Bingo," he says.

"I'm thirty-seven." I shrug. "Though, that still feels weird to say. In my mind, I'm still in my early thirties."

He nods, understanding. "The 90s were ten years ago, and no one can convince me otherwise."

I chuckle, and his eyes flash again. I lift my beer to my lips but am sad to see it's empty. Not that I wanted more to drink—I definitely don't need it, considering the woozy feeling in my belly. But I kind of like being around him. My cheeks hurt from smiling, which hasn't happened in a really long time.

"Do you... uh..." he starts, then runs a hand through his hair. "It's a nice night. Would you want to take a walk, maybe?" He spits out the question as if he's afraid if he doesn't get the words out fast, he won't say them at all.

"That sounds nice, actually." I also say it quickly, before I can think better of it.

His face lights up in surprise. That was clearly the answer he wanted, but not the one he was expecting. He jumps off his bar stool and slaps the counter. I try to hide a smile as I slide to my feet more slowly and follow him out the door.

Chapter Four

TREVOR

SOMEHOW, I AM STROLLING through the streets of downtown Baker's Grove with Emery, who I am absolutely positive is the woman I saw running in heels past the shop earlier today. She's even more beautiful up close, her hair shining as we pass under streetlights and her cheeks flushed in the warm, summer night.

Gone are the pencil skirt and heels from earlier; she's replaced them with a white linen tank top tucked into loose-fitted jeans and sparkly, flat sandals. Even without the heels, she's almost as tall as I am. I'd guess she's about five-ten. She carries her height with a grace and confidence I'm not used to seeing in taller women.

We walk in silence for a few minutes, our steps slow and aimless. It's clear neither of us know where to go, but we don't want the night to end, either. I'm trying not to walk too close to her, but the sidewalk must be slanted or something because I keep finding myself inching closer. When my shoulder brushes hers, I sidestep quickly.

"Sorry," I mutter, even as my hand flexes of its own volition at the desire to touch hers. A shoulder tap isn't going to be enough tonight. I already know this, but I'm not sure what the next move is. Forty years old, and I've been such a recluse lately that I don't know how to initiate contact with a woman. She doesn't seem to mind it, though, if her shy smile at my apology is any indication.

She's stunning. She's funny and sexy and way out of my league.

"So," she breaks the silence. "What inspired your grandfather to open a coffee shop? Was he always a coffee connoisseur or..." she trails off, waiting for me to fill in the blank. "Unless it's hard to talk about him for you? You said he had passed. I'm not trying to bring up hard memories." She's babbling, and it's so perfect. I want to run my fingers along her jawline, cup her cheek, and watch her eyes settle on mine.

I don't usually talk about my grandfather. Not because it's hard, exactly. I miss both him and my father terribly at times, especially now when I want to ask them things like what the best move for this shop would be or how to talk to a pretty woman. I've seen the old photos. Both my grandma and mom were lookers back in their day. My mom used to tell stories about how my dad charmed her. Surely, they'd have some tips for me.

Most of the reason I don't talk about them, though, is because I don't need to. The only people I talk to are Mike, who knew them well, and James, who didn't know them at all. I'm out of practice.

I clear my throat. "No, it's totally fine," I flash her what I hope is a reassuring smile. "I like talking about them. A coffee connoisseur... yes, in a way. He has stories from his youth about cafés and coffee houses and the community they fostered in Croatia before the wars. He told me of coffee bars where people would sit and sip their drinks and talk and do business. Croatians do everything better than Americans, according to him." I smile slightly at the memory of his pride in his country. It was never-ending, that pride, and he had so many stories.

"What brought him to America?" Emery asks gently, drawing me out of my memories and back to the conversation.

"He immigrated here with my baba—my grandmother," I add for her benefit, "shortly after World War II. Europe was pretty devastated at the time. America was prospering." I huff. "Tale as old as time, I suppose. He was always good at talking to people, you know? He could read a room like no one else. I think the shop was a way for him to be part of a community here. See people and foster connections. And live the life he thought he'd have before the war made everything harder." I shrug as if it's no big deal, but it is. He was proud of what he did here, but he missed his country, and he was never able to go back, even for a visit. Travel was expensive. While the shop did well, it didn't do afford-a-trans-Atlantic-flight-in-the-seventies well. And being two generations removed from his, I've always felt left out of this connection he had to places of his past.

The back of Emery's hand brushes against mine as we step in time with each other. "That's beautiful," she says softly. Then louder, "Just when you stop believing in the American Dream, you hear a story like that. It gives you hope, in a way. Where was he from in Croatia?"

"Dalmatia. Right on the sea. He used to talk all the time about how beautiful it was there." I let my hand brush against hers again, welcoming its warmth and softness.

"You've never been?" she asks. I shake my head.

She turns her palm toward mine in silent question. I trail a gentle finger down it, then curl my fingers into hers as my heart beats like a middle school boy on his first date. Her hand settles into mine like it was meant to be there. I squeeze, and she squeezes back as she laughs lightly.

"Seems a shame for him to leave the sea for land-locked Indiana." She chews on her bottom lip for a moment, considering. "Wasn't Croatia part of Yugoslavia after World War II?" she asks.

"Impressive," I say. "Yes, it was, but the Croatian identity is a strong one." I pause, but I have to know. "You carry around knowledge of Croatian history with you to, what, bust out at parties or something?"

She laughs again, heartier this time. "It's a great party trick."

"I can only imagine you and your purple-haired friend sitting around waxing philosophical about the annals of eastern European lore and debating which country belonged to which empire and when."

Her laughter is still bright, but it turns a little bitter at the edges. "With Violet? No. Not her scene." She swings our arms between us as if she's trying to fake an air of nonchalance. "I... uh... I used to run with a different crowd."

"Historians?" I venture.

"Political reporters," she answers, and from the way she won't meet my eyes, I can tell that's where this conversation ends. Fair enough.

I turn us off the main road, and we walk a little more in silence until we come to a pedestrian bridge over one of the many little streams that weave their way through Baker's Grove. She stops and looks out over the water. Her fingers relax in mine, and I reluctantly take it as a hint to drop her hand. I lean my forearms against the railing of the bridge, clasping my hands together in front of me to keep myself from reaching out to her again. She, however, leans backward against the bridge, her elbows resting on top of it and her shoulder meeting mine.

Her eyes are dark, which I noticed in the bar, but when she turns her face toward mine out here, they're night incarnate. Deep pools of mystery, shining in the moonlight that's glinting over us in the absence of the lights that line the main street.

My breath catches. A corner of her mouth lifts. It's a taunt, maybe, but it's soft. I can't make myself look away from it. It's a challenge I want desperately to accept.

She takes in a deep breath, and her eyelids flutter closed. "You smell like coffee," she whispers. Her eyes fly open, wide as saucers. "Oh, I didn't mean to say that out loud."

I chuckle, pressing myself closer to her. It's her breath's turn to hitch, and it brings me no small amount of joy to know I'm having the same effect on her as she's having on me. "Job hazard," I tease, and I'm rewarded with a soft laugh.

"I like coffee." She drags her bottom lip through her teeth, her eyebrows raising slightly.

I don't have words. I'm too smitten with her, and too awkward to know what to say, so I take a chance. I reach up to tuck a strand of hair behind her ear. It's hard to tell in the moonlight, but the bashful curve of her shoulders suggests she's blushing. I take another chance and drag my finger slowly down her jaw like I wanted to do earlier. She shivers, her eyes closing again. Her chin tips up, and her lips part slightly.

That's it. That's my sign.

I close the distance between us.

Chapter Five

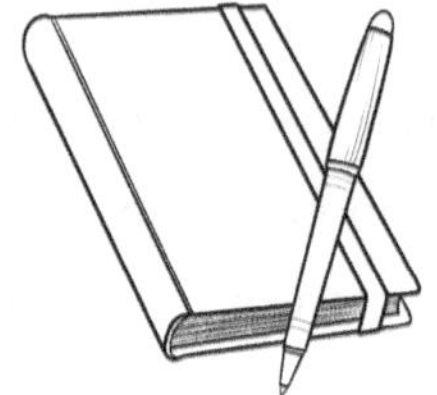

Emery

THE MAN IS FUNNY, charming, adorably awkward, and hot as hell. The scent of coffee mixed with sugar and vanilla practically comes off him in waves. It's a heady scent that could leave me breathless all on its own. And he's a good kisser, I realize as his tongue slips between my parted lips, the warm heat of it sending a wave of desire through me.

It's criminally unfair, how much this man has going for him.

For the first time in a long time, I regret the fact that I'm no longer a relationship kind of girl.

But when he slides a thigh between my legs and presses his chest to mine, his hand skimming my jaw on its way to weave his fingers into my hair, I don't care. I can't care about anything but the way his body feels against mine. The way his tongue teases mine. And, oh god, the delicious sting when he nips my bottom lip with his teeth.

He swallows my moan with another kiss, and I snake my arms over his broad back, taking my time feeling every inch of his lean frame through the thin fabric of his t-shirt. He shudders.

And then he breaks the kiss.

I want to cry out in protest as I fully register the absence of his mouth on mine, but I don't. My body and mind are buzzing, alive in the moonlit evening as we stand, still pressed together on a bridge over a creek. Our breath mingles in the minimal space between us, both heavy with unspent desire.

His eyes glint in the moonlight as they bounce back and forth between my own. Is he... checking on me? Making sure I'm okay with this?

Shit, that's hot, too.

He must approve of the results of his search because he smiles. It's a small smile, but it changes his features completely. Where his concern brought out his hard, masculine edges, his joy shows a softer exuberance. The shift in him is thrilling in a way I can't quite describe.

"Are you hungry?" he asks, then his smile turns sheepish. "That was a weird question. I just want to spend more time with you, and I was thinking—"

"Yes," I cut him off, though his rambling is endearing. He wants to spend more time with me, and I would not mind more of his mouth on mine. And I'll never turn down food.

Trevor's wide eyes suggest he wasn't expecting me to say yes again, which—dammit—is even more cute than it was in the bar. He trails a feather light touch down my arm and over my palm, leaving goosebumps in its wake. It's my turn to shudder, even though the summer night air is still warm and sticky. He doesn't break eye contact with me as he intertwines our fingers again. I can't seem to catch a full breath.

"Good," he says, and tugs on my hand for me to walk with him.

We walk for a few more blocks until we come to the area where the late-night food trucks usually congregate. It's an empty cul-de-sac that's brightly lit with both streetlights and hanging lanterns. There are several trucks lining the street and a few tables spread out in the middle of the dead-end. Some kind of industrial building used to be here, but it was abandoned a long time ago. The city eventually razed it, and the food trucks took over.

It's a little early yet for the bar-hoppers to be ready to soak up their alcohol before heading home, so there are plenty of empty tables. I veer immediately toward the waffle truck, Trevor's laugh rumbling deeply behind me as I lead the way with our intertwined hands.

"What's so funny?" I ask, getting in line behind two women who look much younger than me. They're sporting crop tops and miniskirts, and by the way they're giggling, their evening is just getting started.

I glance at Trevor, worried these two might have caught his eye, but he's smiling at me like he doesn't even notice the hotties standing in front of us.

It's interesting that I'm worried about it, and interesting that he's not looking at them, but he answers me before I have a chance to process. I file it away for later.

"I never thought of waffles as a late-night food," he says as he squeezes my hand. It's such a natural movement. One that would suggest the comfort of years together rather than the newness a couple of hours.

I gape at him in mock offense. "You take that back," I warn. "Waffles are an anytime food. Plus, it's the only sweet truck here tonight."

Trevor looks around, assessing the other options. "You've got a sweet tooth?" he asks as he turns back to me.

"You could say that." I eye the menu as we talk, though I know I'm going to get the same thing I always do: chocolate waffles with whipped cream. "But feel free to get whatever you want. I'm only judging you a little bit."

He squeezes my hand again as he leans in, his breath tickling the shell of my ear as he says, "Waffles are great."

Awesome. Now I'm turned on by talking about waffles.

Luckily, I can't melt into a puddle right here because it's our turn to order, and now that I've been promised waffles, I will stop at nothing to get them. I place my order, and Trevor gets the cookies and cream waffles, which is also a solid choice. We wait for the food, then carry our giant waffles on flimsy paper plates to a table on the outskirts of the cul-de-sac.

As I'm lowering myself into my seat, I scoop some of the whipped cream onto my finger and lick it off. Trevor is too busy looking around for something to notice, which is probably for the best. I hadn't meant it to be suggestive; I just really like whipped cream.

"What are you looking for?" I ask.

"Utensils," he says, distracted.

"Oh, no. Sit. I'll show you." I wave at the seat across from me. He eyes me warily as he lowers himself into it.

I carefully break the waffle in half and put one side on top of the other, smooshing the whipped cream in the middle like a sandwich. I take a bite, careful not to let too much whipped cream shoot out the sides, and I motion for Trevor to do the same.

His light brown eyes sparkle as he follows my lead, and he nods with approval as he chews. "It somehow tastes better this way," he says.

"I know. It's the perfect treat," I respond.

We eat in silence for a bit, neither of us looking at each other. I'm thinking of a thousand questions I'd like to ask him, but all of them seem too invasive for a man I just met. Chalk it up to years of interview experience. You can take the woman out of feature reporting, but you can't take the feature reporting out of the woman, I suppose.

Luckily, he breaks the silence first. "Do you have any pets?"

I shake my head. "I used to be gone too often. You?"

"My apartment is too small. What do you mean you used to be gone too often?"

I don't really want to ruin this evening by talking about the career I thought I'd have by now, so I simply offer, "My old job at *The Gazette* had me working long hours across the state."

He studies me for a moment before asking, "Why journalism?"

I take another bite to buy myself some time. How do I convey that the job was everything to me? Meeting people, digging for information, putting pieces together—it was exciting. It was magic. But now, it's just a paycheck. I'm bouncing from one miserable feel-good story to the next with nothing to look forward to and no one who really cares about anything I'm writing. Why journalism? I'm trying to figure that out myself right now.

"I've always been a writer," I start slowly. "Words were kind of my thing from a very young age. And I liked people a lot, too, you know? But I could never be a teacher or something like that. Journalism felt like the best way to put words and people together. I liked finding things out and telling stories people needed to hear. It was fun."

If he notices my use of the past tense, he doesn't let on. He nods in understanding, and he must be adept at reading the room, because he quickly changes the subject. "Do you go to The Tipsy Geezer often?" He takes another bite of his waffle while he waits for my answer.

I tilt my head back and forth. "Sort of," I say. I used to go there all the time. It was our weekly hangout, back when Derek and I were still married. Back when Cass and Vi first started dating. We celebrated their engagement there. We used to slide right into that back booth Trevor and his friends were occupying earlier tonight and toast to pitches accepted and jobs acquired and anything else we felt worth a drink. I remember Derek and his arm slung loosely around my shoulder, Cass and Vi snuggled up on the other side of us. Everyone laughing, completely unaware of where our lives were ultimately headed.

But I can't say any of that now. I may not be the relationship type anymore, but I don't want to scare this poor guy off, either. I wouldn't mind more of whatever that was on the bridge. More of his mouth on me. More of his hands on me. Just for tonight. Just... more.

I realize Trevor is gazing at me. He's not annoyed by my silence, or impatient for me to talk, or judging me. He's just looking. Expecting. Maybe wanting, but that could also be wishful thinking. Heat rises to my cheeks the longer we hold eye contact, so I break it to take the last bite of my waffle. Trevor collects my plate, and his fingers brush mine in the process. My skin tingles where he touches it, and that sensation makes its way all the way to my core. I'm suddenly feeling much warmer in the humid, summer air. I stand, just for something to do.

But when Trevor comes back to the table, his hand touches mine again. I turn toward him, and we're only inches apart. His gaze dips to my lips and back to meet mine. My body is on fire, and I'm feeling bold enough to take one step into him and press my lips to his. He presses his hands to my lower back and draws me closer. The length of his desire presses against me. He catches my moan with another kiss.

He says quietly, suggestively against my lips, "My place isn't too far from here."

I might not need that vibrator after all.

A corner of my mouth turns up even as the dial also gets turned up on that heat in my belly. "Lead the way," I say.

"I told you my place is small," he says as we start walking. We're walking away from the way I came, to the other side of town. "Really small. Studio small."

"That sounds like a disclaimer," I tease as I match my stride to his, which isn't difficult. We're almost the same height. But our pace is faster now. Not hurried, exactly, but anticipatory. Excited.

"That's because it is."

I shrug. "You're a single guy. How much space do you really need?"

"Right," he says, accepting my explanation.

He wasn't kidding. His place is really close to The Tipsy Geezer. He stops in front of a door on the outside of a beautiful, old, brick building. He fumbles with his keys, then leads me up two flights of stairs where he stops to unlock another door.

I brush past him as he holds the door open for me. His entryway, like the rest of his place, is cramped. As I pass, my hand brushes his, and his fingers almost instinctively close around mine.

My eyes widen slightly as I face him. My chest brushes against his, and my breath quickens. He doesn't let go of my hand.

Then, not wasting any time, our lips meet again.

Chapter Six

TREVOR

I DON'T KNOW WHO moves first, but before I can process any of the good fortune that has befallen me in the past couple of hours, Emery and I are kissing in my cramped entryway. And while I know this is exactly what we came here for, I still can't believe it's really happening.

Emery. It's a beautiful name. She's a stunning woman. And we are making out in my apartment, which somehow feels more monumental than making out on a pedestrian bridge.

It doesn't take much movement for me to press her up against the wall behind her. She gasps sharply, then closes her mouth on mine again. My tongue teases at her lips, and she opens for me. She tastes of chocolate and cream and sugar—a heady flavor that has me wanting more.

My hands rest on her hips, though I want to use them to explore every curve of her body. My fingers itch to drag themselves under her shirt and over her breasts, but I force myself to leave them where they are.

When I slide my thigh between hers as I press her further into the wall, I'm met with her soft, warm center. I press my lips to her collarbone and am rewarded with a bright, cucumber scent from her hair on a long inhale.

She moans and grinds her hips against me, and any restraint I was trying to exercise crumples. I press my thigh upward, and based on her quickening breath as she continues to move her hips against me, I hit the right spot.

My hand slides underneath her shirt, and my thumb circles over the thin fabric of her bra. Her nipple hardens underneath my touch.

"Oh, shit," she breathes. I press kisses down her neck, sucking and exploring, pulling another moan from her. The sound goes straight to my dick.

I move slightly again, sure from her next intake of breath that she can feel my hardness pressing against her thigh. I pull back to look at her. Her face is gorgeously flushed, her lips swollen and hair mussed.

"I want this if you do," I say, and I hope she can hear the question in it.

There is a glint in her eyes, and a corner of her mouth turns up a bit. I soak up this tiny grin. I don't know her very well, but I get the sense that her smiles are guarded and hard-won.

"Trevor." My name is a hum on her tongue, like a song she's singing only for me. "Don't stop." She circles her hips against me again, and I can feel my cock pressing painfully against the fly of my pants. Happy to oblige, my lips crash into hers again, and somehow, this kiss is even hungrier and more urgent than the last.

I turn us and walk her backwards toward the bed, which isn't very far from the entryway, shedding my clothes on the way. She follows suit, pulling her shirt over her head and sliding out of her jeans as we walk. I inhale deeply and catch that vibrant scent from her hair that sends another wave of desire through me.

The back of her legs hit the edge of the mattress, and they buckle, bringing us both down on the bed. She loops her fingers around the waistband of my boxers and pulls. I do the same with her underwear. Her skin is silky smooth, and I trace a line from her breasts all the way down her torso, cupping between her legs.

She lets out a breathy moan as I drag a finger through her center, then press one inside her. Her eyelids flutter closed as I touch and tease. I thought she was gorgeous in the bar, but that was nothing compared to seeing her like this, her skin flushed in the moonlight streaming in through the window next to the bed, and her chest rising and falling heavily.

"Trevor," she whispers. "Please."

I curl my finger upward, and she squirms underneath me. "So, you're begging now?"

"I will if that's what you want," she breathes.

I chuckle darkly. "Not tonight." I use my thumb to find where she's most sensitive. I make small, lazy circles as my finger works inside her warmth, and I'm rewarded with a gasping shudder when my thumb passes over a certain spot.

"Oh my god," she moans as she bucks her hips against my hand.

I remove my finger from her and use her own wetness to circle her clit. "You're beautiful like this, srećo. I want to see you come apart." I don't know what makes me use that name for her. It's one from the recesses of my past, but it seems to fit.

She shakes her head, swallowing heavily and grabbing my forearm, her nails digging into the skin there. "No, I need... more. You. Please?"

"I don't generally make a habit of turning down a pretty lady," I tease. She huffs.

I tear myself away from her to fumble around in the nightstand for a condom. When I finally find it, I rip open the foil and roll it on. I line myself up with her entrance and pause. "This okay?"

She bucks her hips toward me. "Yes. Please. Yes."

And then I'm inside her.

Being inside Emery is heaven. My hard edges meet her soft ones as I thrust a few times before I'm fully seated. She is warm and slick, and I have to force myself to take it slow. The gasps and moans coming from her tell me exactly what she likes, and once I think I've figured her out well enough, my mouth meets hers again.

At first, my hands don't know where to go, but it seems that she likes when I grab her hips the best, so I do that, pulling her even closer to me as we move in perfect sync with each other. She drags her hands up my back, then digs her nails into my skin. I shudder at the delicious thrill of her nails leaving their marks on my back. I thrust forward a little too hard, and she cries out.

"Sorry," I breathe into her neck.

"Don't be," she pants. She presses her nails into my back again. "Harder. Please."

I plunge deeper into her with a few hard, fast movements. "I already told you, you don't have to beg tonight."

"Oh. Trevor, I..." she curses softly, and then I feel her come undone beneath me. I press a kiss to her jaw as I pull her close, pumping a few more times inside of her and following her over the edge.

***

"You mean to tell me"—Mike sips his nightly latte on Monday— "that you banged that girl from the bar on Friday night before you even bothered to get her number, and when you woke up in the morning, she was gone?"

I drag a hand over my face. "Can you be a little less crass about it, please?"

Mike lifts his hands from his sides, looking around the empty shop. "There's no one here."

I sent James home early when Mike came in, promising to pay him for his hours, anyway. I had been too embarrassed to call my best friend over the weekend, but by the time five o'clock rolled around on Monday, I had been over and over it in my head so many times that I jumped at the chance to talk to him. I know, at eighteen years old, James is *technically* an adult, but I didn't feel right talking about this with him around. And, besides, it's not like we're packed with customers anyway.

"It's not the company. It's the principle. She was nice. I thought we were having a great time." I know I sound sad. I probably look sad, too. I can't believe I never got her number, and I don't know what I could have done wrong for her to leave while I was asleep.

My eyes widen as I look at Mike. "Do you think she was... I dunno... unsatisfied?"

Mike tips his head back and howls his amusement. I can feel my face heating as the room fills with his over-dramatic laughter, and I slink even further into my seat.

"No, man. I don't think she was 'unsatisfied.'" He says it like he's mocking me. "I'll try to be less vulgar, for your sake, but you know what it feels like when a woman comes, surely."

I bang my head on the table and cover the back of it with my hands. "Kill me now," I groan.

"Okay, listen." Mike's tone has become placating, which makes me think he feels bad for me. Mike never feels bad for me; he only ever gives me shit. I lift my head from the table to shoot him a wary glance, but he continues. "You're pretty sure she's the hottie we saw running past here the other day, right?"

"What does that have to do with anything?"

"Well, if she was running past this place and going to The Tipsy Geezer on the same day, there's a good chance she's local. So, maybe you'll see her around," he suggests.

I slink even further into my chair. "Doubtful," I mumble.

"Hey. Nuh-uh. Nope. You're the guy who is always talking about miracles and holding out hope for impossible good news. Where's that characteristic Trevor optimism?"

When I don't say anything and my eyebrows pinch even further together, a corner of his mouth tips up sarcastically. Which is how I know he's about to say something cutting to try to break me out of my funk. "You have a better shot at seeing her again than you do at saving this place."

I glare at him, still slouched in my chair. "That's low. I'm going to figure out something for this place. I just haven't landed on it yet."

"There he is. My ridiculously optimistic friend," he teases. "Hey, worst-case scenario, you had hot sex with a hot woman. I say you've won either way."

I roll my eyes at his logic, looking out the window and scanning faces in the crowd of people passing by. But no matter how hard I look, none of them are her.

Chapter Seven

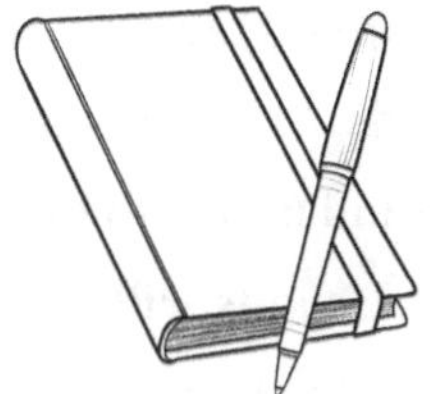

Emery

RANDALL POUNDS ON THE conference table. Hard. I arch an eyebrow at Ethan, a staff photographer and my closest work friend, who is sitting to my left. He scratches his pen against a pad of paper and tilts it toward me so I can see.

I wonder if his wife forgot to make the coffee again this morning.

I hide a snicker behind my hand and slide the notepad closer to me. I write, *I'd be cranky, too, if I had to drink the shit in the break room.*

"Our numbers are down for the third week in a row. I saw a video on some app that said those damn Millennial twenty-somethings are killing the news industry, and I'm seeing it with my own eyes." Randall is half out of his seat now, yelling and pressing his palms into the table, his tie dangling down in front of him.

Ethan scribbles something else on the pad of paper: *Who's gonna tell him* we *are the Millennials?*

I look sidelong at Ethan and tap my nose—not it. He huffs.

"Darlis." I straighten as Randall calls my last name. My turn, it would appear. "We need something happy." *Sreća*, I think, completely unprompted. And, probably for the millionth time since a week ago Friday, I wonder what it means. I'm a journalist. I could look it up. But something in me likes the mystery. It's not like I'm going to see him again, anyway. I left as soon as I heard his breath deepening, because that's what you do with one-night stands. And that's all it was.

I shake my head and remind myself to focus.

"We need something these kids will want to click on." Randall is punctuating his sentences with the palm of his hand against the table. "They're sick of the doom and gloom. What do you have for us?" He has returned fully to his seat, but his beady eyes are boring into me from across the conference table. Ethan drags the notepad back to himself and flips the page over, just in case Randall's evil eye can see that far across the room.

I clear my throat, forcing myself to come fully back to the conversation. "Well, sir, the corgi story is live and doing decently well—"

"We need better than 'decently well,'" he interrupts.

I take a deep breath to gather myself, and a beat to remind myself not to jump across the conference table and strangle him. "Right. Okay. There's a beauty pageant taking place at a local nursing home—"

"Millennials don't want to read about old people. Next."

"I could cover the kitten adoption at Pawesome Pets—"

"Did that two months ago. Next."

"Maybe the local honeybee farm—"

Randall whacks the table again, and I jump. Ethan, the five other reporters, and the three editors in the room all wince with sympathy in my direction.

"We need something better. Something more cutting-edge. Something with some teeth," Randall insists.

"Those kittens sure had teeth," Ethan mutters, rubbing his forearm at the memory of being bitten by one when we were there covering the adoption event at the start of the summer.

I sigh. "With all due respect, sir," I start carefully, then eye everyone sitting around the room with their shoulders slumped, trying to make themselves smaller to avoid his scrutiny.

Each meeting this summer has been progressively worse, with more and more insinuated anger and violence. As far as I'm concerned, the table-smacking condescension has gone on long enough. Someone should say it, and I'm just about miserable enough in this job to be the one to do it. I clear my throat and start again, louder this time. "With all due respect, asking for a fluffy story to also be cutting-edge is a bit of a paradox, don't you think?"

Randall goes completely still. "How so?" he asks deliberately.

Ethan raises his eyebrows at me in a look that clearly says, *Now you've done it.*

But it's too late. I've started, and I intend to finish. "What you're asking for doesn't exist. You want a story with some teeth. You want it to be new and exciting. Stories about puppies and animal adoption and happiness in a nursing home are not going to be any of those things. If you want something with some teeth, you have to go for the grittier stories."

Randall regards me for a moment.

Then another moment.

And another.

The silence stretches on so long, it starts to press in on me, but I refuse to slump my shoulders and make myself smaller like everyone else in here. I'm right, and we all know it.

Well, everyone except Randall.

He steeples his short, blunt fingers in front of his thin lips. "And I suppose you have an idea for one of these grittier stores?" His voice is scary quiet.

I try not to gulp. Now is not the time to show weakness. "I do, actually. The local school district is facing allegations of misusing school funds. This is something the community would care a great deal about, considering it's their tax dollars at play. And with layoffs at the local news outlets that used to cover this sort of thing, we could make a name for ourselves by adding these types of stories to the site."

Randall presses the tips of his fingers into his lips and stares at me, unblinking. Everyone else around the conference table avoids my eye contact like they're afraid to be associated with me. I fight to keep my gaze on Randall. He's the type of man who does not like to be questioned, but he appreciates when someone is unwilling to yield. So, I try not to yield.

Finally, he narrows his eyes into slits and takes a deep breath. "I'll tell you what, Darlis," he says as if he just devised the best, most evil plan to take over the world. I fight against a shudder as I wait for him to continue. "You bring me a pitch for a—how did you put it? A fluffy story. One that will bring in the readers. Then, you write it. One million clicks. You get that, and the school funds story is yours."

Holy shit. He's giving me a chance. A slim chance, but a chance, nonetheless. I straighten even further in my chair and try hard not to smile.

"But," Randall continues, and any triumphant grin I was trying to hide is forgotten. "If you don't get me my million clicks, you're on letter-to-the-editor duty for two months."

Ethan gasps, and I take a gamble with a look at him. His dark skin is ashen, and his brown eyes are wide. It's well-known that formatting and responding to letters to the editor is where journalists' careers go to die in this place. My gaze flicks to Josie—the current resident of the letters-to-the-editor black hole—across the table. She's looking straight at me, her expression a mix of sympathy and relief.

One million clicks? Is that even possible for a tiny, local web magazine? Surely, if there's anything this Millennial knows about the internet, it's that anything can go viral if it has the right combination of emotional pull and public interest. Can I make something like this go viral?

But then, I wonder, does it even matter? Responding to letters to the editor or writing this garbage—what's the difference? My career is dead already, anyway. At least if I take this shot, there's a possibility of digging myself out of this hole.

I nod once, resolute. "You've got yourself a deal."

"Excellent," Randall purrs. The Cheshire-cat grin that spreads its way across his face is probably meant to be foreboding, but the joke's on him. I've already decided I have nothing left to lose.

***

A few hours later, as the workday is winding down, Randall slinks out of his office and down the hall to the elevator. As soon as the doors close behind him, Ethan peeks over my cubicle wall above my computer monitor. "How's it going, Madame Stone Ovaries?"

I grimace. "That's a terrible nickname."

"Yeah," he agrees, "but I don't know how else to describe what you did in there today."

"You could pick something that sounds less like I'm running a seventeenth-century brothel," I grumble.

Ethan chuckles. "I'll keep thinking." He folds his arms on top of the cubicle wall and rests his cheek on them with a sigh. "But you standing up to Randall was sexy as hell."

I cock an eyebrow. "I'm not your type."

"I might not be interested in the ovaries, but I can recognize how objectively sexy a good pair of them is," he counters. "And don't think I missed that excellent writer pun. Well played."

I tilt my head at him in thanks.

Josie's red head pops up to my right, and she has a wicked smile on her face. "I am also taking great pleasure in this deal." When I frown at her, her eyes widen. "Oh, I'm rooting for you, for sure. Even the promise of leaving letters to the editor behind me isn't shiny enough for me to wish for that over you putting Randall in his place for once." Then, she smirks. "But, this is a win for me either way."

I look back and forth between their giddy faces. "Don't get too excited. I have no idea what to pitch tomorrow. I've been sitting here all day, trolling the internet for the latest viral feel-good pieces, and nothing seems like it's good enough to strike gold twice."

"You can't redo a viral piece," Ethan scolds.

"Not the same piece, exactly, but I was hoping to latch onto something similar," I say. "Ride a trend."

Josie frowns, her little button nose scrunching her freckles together. "That's what everyone does. They try to jump on a viral trend, but it hardly ever works. You need something fresh and new."

"Cool, cool. No pressure. Thanks," I deadpan. She shrugs.

Ethan jumps in. "She's right. But you're in luck, because my date canceled tonight, so I have nothing but time to help you come up with something spectacular. And, honey, I can go all night long." He raises his eyebrows meaningfully.

I groan and make a disgusted face. "Never say that again, please," I plead.

"I'm in, too," Josie offers. We both look at her questioningly, and she shrugs. "I told you, I want to see you win this thing. It'll be good for morale."

I check my watch, then slump in my chair. "I can't right now. I'm supposed to meet my pregnant sister at the diner in thirty minutes, and she hates it when I'm late." It's been a week and a half since I've seen her, and I know she's been anticipating this diner date ever since my best friend betrayed me and told her all about leaving me in the dust with a hot guy at the bar just over a week ago. She has bugged me every day for the juicy details, but I felt like it wasn't a conversation I was willing to have over the phone. She hasn't said so, but I'm sure Vi will tag along, too, since I haven't talked to her about it either.

"Donna's? I love Donna's," Ethan states matter-of-factly as he grabs his satchel and brings the strap across his chest.

"Best milkshakes in town," Josie says, shouldering her purse.

"Oh, no. This is kind of a... sister thing?" No way am I taking these two busybodies to meet with my sister. She won't care who's sitting there; she'll just dive right in and ask, and then I'll have to face the workplace teasing about a one-night stand I'd rather keep under wraps.

Ethan purses his lips and dips his chin, looking at me as if I'm a complete idiot. "When were you planning on coming up with an excellent pitch for Randall, then? Did you think you'd happen upon one in your sad, lonely apartment at midnight tonight? Or maybe that it'd come to you in a dream?"

I narrow my eyes at him, then turn to Josie for backup, but she just shrugs. "He has a point," she says. Traitor. Maybe if I can jump in and explain to Cass what's going on, she'll take the hint and realize this is more important than me dishing about some guy I'll never see again. It's not like it's some secret that I'm not looking for a relationship. It's been five years since Derek and I split, and I have made it pretty clear that my intention is to avoid another disaster relationship at all costs. It will never stop the sisterly teasing, but she might recognize the hierarchy of importance if I can explain fast enough.

I sigh, resigned, and push my rolling chair away from my desk. "Fine," I say, standing. "But once we come up with an idea, we are all going our separate ways. This isn't social hour; this is work."

They both agree, and we make our way outside, where we are met with cloudy skies and a few droplets of rain starting to fall. I look upward, grimacing. "I didn't realize it was supposed to rain today," I mutter.

"Me either, but it looks like it's going to open up any minute. We'd better hurry," Ethan suggests. We all take off at a power-walk pace toward the diner. My legs are longer than the two of theirs, so I try to hold myself back while they scramble to catch up. Anyone who might be watching us would laugh at how comical this looks, me with my navy slacks and red kitten heels leading the triangle, with Josie and her red curls bouncing on her shoulders and Ethan sweating in his sweater vest and loafers just behind me.

We make it the four blocks to Donna's right as the downpour starts. Cass and Vi are waiting under the awning where it's dry, Cass with her arms folded on top of her baby bump, and Vi with her arm around her. When I get a little closer, I can see Cass is pouting.

I take a guess at what the pout is about. "Hey, Cass. Sorry I had to bring these two along. I can explain inside." I reach to pull the door open, but it doesn't budge.

"Donna's is closed," she whines.

"Closed?" I ask, incredulous. That explains the pout. "What do you mean closed? Donna never closes."

Vi points to a note on the door. "Looks like half the staff came down with the stomach flu, so they can't open."

"Oh, darn," I say, though it's clear from my tone that I am not all that sad. If Donna and her staff getting sick gets me out of this awkward conversation with my sister and Vi, I'll take it. Sorry, Donna. "I guess Josie, Ethan, and I will have to go back to my place to work."

"There's that coffee place across the street," Cass offers. We follow her finger to where she is pointing. The shiny, relatively new establishment that's about the size of a small warehouse stands on the corner, all sleek black edges and mile-high windows. There is also a line around the outside of the building, everyone standing resolutely under their umbrellas.

"How is there a line around the outside of that place in a downpour? Who needs coffee that badly at five-thirty in the evening?" I ask, incredulous.

"Must be coffee hour," Ethan chimes in. When we all turn to look at him, he shrugs. "You buy a pastry, and they give you a free coffee. I've been a few times when I'm on deadline. The pastries are good."

Cass nods approvingly, and I can see her numbers-loving brain calculating. "That's genius. Get rid of the old pastries and get people back in the door to spend some money before closing."

"Ok, sure," I say, "but that still doesn't solve our problem. I'm not waiting in *that* line in *this* weather. So, I guess we raincheck, Cass, and these two can just come to my place to finish what we were working on." I all but tug on Ethan's arm to get him out of there.

But Josie has to open her mouth with another suggestion. "There's a cute little hipster coffee shop the next street over," she offers, pointing. I frown at her, and she knits her brows together. "What?"

"What is with everyone and coffee today? I'm not trying to be wired all night," I protest in one last feeble attempt to break up this little party so we can come up with a winning pitch, and I can avoid talking about sex with my little sister.

Cass loops her arm through mine. "Get a decaf, then. Come on, I want to hear all about"—she looks at Josie, then Ethan— "a lot of things, apparently."

Thoroughly defeated, I allow Cass to pull me into a run—well, in her case, it's starting to become more of a run-waddle—down the street where we turn, then turn again at the next block. Josie leads us up to a storefront with floor-to-ceiling windows with a huge logo painted on them indicating this is, indeed, a coffee shop. Josie pulls open the big, heavy, wooden door and holds it for us all to rush inside.

Once safely out of the rain, we all shake off, dripping onto the mat by the door. Cass looks around. "This place is cute," she says as we all take in the space. There are a couple of tables lining the window with an excellent view of the street outside. The tables are old but loved. Worn wood that looks comfortable and warm. The counter has some bar-height seating, too, and on it is an espresso machine that looks like it could have been made in the 1960s with over-polished chrome and art deco lettering on the side. Tiny, adorable espresso cups sit overturned on top of it in two neat rows. There are also some high-top tables that line the space in front of the other side of the L-shaped counter.

"I must have passed this shop a hundred times on my way from work to Donna's, and I never knew it was even here." I'm in awe that this adorable coffee shop has been hiding under my nose since... maybe forever, if that espresso machine is as old as I think it is. Something about that tickles my brain, like it's a fact I should remember something about, but I can't put my finger on it.

Looking around, it would seem that I'm not alone in my ignorance. Unlike the line around the corner at the place down the street, there is only one man in here, sitting with his back to us at a table near the window, and a teenage boy in a coffee-stained apron behind the counter.

The man does not turn to look at our group, but the teenager's eyes just about pop out of his head when he sees us coming toward the counter. "Are you all…" he trails off and swallows audibly. "Do you all want drinks?"

Ethan chuckles. "Uh, yeah, that's why we're here."

The boy nods vigorously. "Cool. Cool cool. Let me go get someone to help, okay?" He shuffles as fast as he can through the back door, leaving us all to stare at each other, wondering how this kid survives working in a coffee shop if making drinks for five people is too much to handle.

A moment later, the door swings open and the boy comes back out, avoiding our eye contact. He's followed by a man who has his head down as he hastily ties an apron across his midsection. He's wearing a mustard yellow beanie and a white t-shirt, and when he finally looks up, I can see his golden-brown stubble. His high cheekbones. And that's when his striking eyes land right on me and his jaw drops in surprise.

Before I can tell myself to play it cool, I gasp loudly, and everyone turns to look at me.

"Trevor."

Chapter Eight

Trevor

"Trevor," she gasps, and I'm having a hard time not remembering a week and a half ago, when she was gasping my name underneath me in my bed.

I can't believe it. I stepped into the back room for five minutes to take a call from the bank. Then James came in telling me there was a group of people here, and he needed help making drinks. I couldn't believe my luck then, and I certainly can't believe it now because Emery is standing in the center of a group of people, her dark eyes wide with surprise.

But maybe she's thinking the same thing because her olive complexion is turning a deep pink. Her dark blouse is wet and clinging to her curves in all the right places, and fuck, she's even more gorgeous than she was at The Tipsy Geezer.

I recognize her friend with the purple hair from that night, and she slowly turns her head to Emery, a shit-eating grin on her face. She chuckles darkly, and the pregnant woman whose shoulders her arm is slung over, looks up in confusion. That must be Emery's sister, if I'm remembering what she said correctly.

Who am I kidding? Of course, I remember correctly. I ate up every word she said that night and locked it away in my brain for later.

"Uh," James steps up to my side. "Boss?"

I clear my throat and shake my head vigorously. "Right. Hi. What can we get started for you?"

Emery's friend with the purple hair—Violet, I'm pretty sure, though that seems too on-the-nose with the hair, so maybe I'm wrong—hums. "Oh, no way. We're not going to acknowledge this at all?"

Emery whirls on her, practically shooting daggers with her eyes. "Acknowledge what?" she asks through clenched teeth.

"That we just happened upon your one-night stand's place of employment?" The question is innocent enough, but hearing her call me Emery's one-night stand hurts more than I expect it to. That *was* all it had been, after all, even though I had maybe wanted more.

The man standing on the other side of Emery makes an "ohh" sound that devolves into a gleeful laugh. She shoots her dagger-eyes at him next, and he rolls his lips together, indicating he's trying to keep his opinion to himself. His dark complexion reddens with the effort.

Emery sucks in a breath. "Dammit," she mutters, closing her eyes. When she opens them, she looks resolute. "Fine. Everyone, this is Trevor. We, uh, met at the bar the other night." She says it quickly, as if she's trying to get it out of the way. "Trevor, you remember Vi. She's currently canoodling my sister, Cass. And these two are Ethan and Josie, my coworkers." She shoots a warning glance at Vi and her sister, then pointedly asks, "We're good now?"

Cass's grin matches Vi's as she says, "Nope. But I'm going to need some sustenance before I thoroughly interrogate you." She turns to me. "What's good here, Trevor?" She says my name like she's taunting Emery with it, and Emery turns an even darker shade of red. To her credit, though, she stands tall and doesn't cower from embarrassment.

Her stoicism is incredibly hot.

"Hey, Lover Boy, the lady asked you a question." It takes me a second before I realize Mike has joined the crowd. I groan internally. If I know Mike—and I definitely do—his presence is only going to add fuel to this fire.

When I don't immediately say anything, Mike answers. "The blueberry muffins are my favorite. Trev makes them from scratch every morning."

"Mmm," Cass hums. "Yes, please. Two of those." When Emery scoffs, she says, "Hey, I'm eating for two over here."

"That baby is the size of a papaya," Emery grumbles. Cass shrugs.

Everyone else places their order, then Emery stalks to the corner that's the absolute furthest she can get from the counter. Everyone follows her, though Vi shoots me a sympathetic smile before she turns around. I get started making everyone's drinks while Mike slides himself behind the counter.

"Employees only," I say, pointing at a sign hanging on the wall.

"Get the fuck out of here with that," he says, then washes his hands quickly in the sink and starts plating the muffins. "I might as well still work here, and you know it." Then, he drops his voice so Emery and her friends can't hear him. "The girl of your dreams walks into your shop, despite the fact that you were sure you'd never see her again. What are you going to do, man?"

James glances curiously at me, then wisely grabs two cups and walks to the other side of the counter toward the coffee pots. I resist the urge to drag my hand down my face. It would only mean I'd have to wash my hands yet again before making the rest of these drinks. I focus on the steaming milk in front of me, contemplating my next move.

"She won't sit there forever, Trev," Mike warns.

I turn my attention to him. He's leaning against the counter, his arms folded and three blueberry muffins on plates next to his hip.

I point to them, trying to stay on more solid ground. "She only ordered two."

He shrugs. "Talking about them made me hungry. Quit evading."

I sigh. "I don't know," I whisper, grateful to the milk steamer for masking the sound of our voices. "You saw that whole exchange. She doesn't want anything to do with me."

"That's not the impression I got," Mike insists.

"What do you mean? She couldn't get away from me fast enough just now. Over a week ago, she left my place while I was sleeping. How many more hints does a guy need?" I pour the steamed milk over the espresso, finishing it off with a Rosetta on top.

"That's not what I saw," Mike insists.

I glower at him as I grab two of the plates and balance them on my arm while also carrying two lattes. I glance at James, who is coming behind me with the coffees he poured, and I send up a silent prayer to the universe that he doesn't drop them or otherwise mess this up. Just this once.

The universe must be listening, because he doesn't drop them, though he does put them in front of the wrong people. There's some shuffling of drinks on the other side of the table as I set Emery's and her sister's orders in front of them.

Did I reach my arm between them to get closer to Emery? Maybe.

Did I notice her throat bob as she caught sight of my forearm within inches of her cheek? Definitely.

She doesn't dare look at me as I deposit her order—a decaf hazelnut latte—in front of her, but her sister catches my eye, and the only way to describe the look she gives me is impish. I give her a quiet smile back.

She nods before turning her attention back to Emery, and I feel a little warmth at the solidarity.

Emery, though, is sitting with her back ramrod straight, and it is clear she is doing everything she can to ignore my presence. She sits with her back to the counter, so I take the hint and turn on my heel toward Mike. His arms are folded and he's grinning smugly.

"Out," I bark, pointing to the table where he was sitting when the group walked in.

He gives me a mock salute and follows the order. I join him at his table, squeezing myself as close to the window as possible. Of course, Mike sat with his back to the door so I'm forced to face out into the room, where I can see the side of Emery's face perfectly.

It's such a beautiful face. I'm having a hard time not staring at it.

"You are majorly screwed," Mike notes.

I scowl at him, then out the window at the rain still dumping from the darkening clouds. "Yep," I say.

Chapter Nine

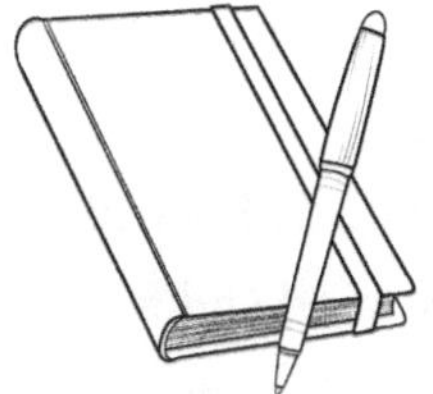

EMERY

IF I THOUGHT THIS evening couldn't get any more embarrassing, I would be wrong because Cass takes a bite of her muffin and moans in pleasure. It's not just any moan, either. It's so overtly sexual, Vi can't even resist reaching out a hand to grip Cass's knee under the table as she uses her other hand to toy with her necklace. I almost ask them if they need a room alone with their baked goods, but Cass rolls her eyes into the back of her head. As if this all wasn't bad enough, she addresses Trevor. I would rather ignore him, and she knows it.

"Wow, these *muffins*. Trevor," she calls across the room. "You make these yourself?"

"Yeah. It's my dad's recipe," he returns.

"Holy shit, Em. You've gotta try these." She breaks off a piece and hands it to me, but I shake my head and press my lips together.

"You're going to deny yourself the absolute joy of these pastries because you banged the guy who made them?" Cass asks, incredulous. And entirely too loudly. I resist the urge to turn and see Trevor's reaction.

Ethan squeals in delight again, and my jaw drops. "Shut up," I hiss.

"Seriously." Cass shoves the piece of muffin at me like she's going for a wedding cake smash at my mouth. "Try it."

I reel back and shake my head again. Violet breaks off her own piece and pops it into her mouth, staring me down as she does it. Then, her expression changes to one of genuine surprise. "Damn, Trevor. These *are* really good."

Ethan and Josie rip their own pieces off. "Oh wow," Josie says around her mouthful. She turns around and rests her arm over the back of her chair to address Trevor. "Can I get one for myself?"

What is with these people talking to the man I really, desperately need to ignore? I feel like I'm going to either explode or rip someone's head clear off their shoulders. Do they not understand that my job is on the line here? We are so far away from the purpose of this meeting that I don't even know if I see a way back to it.

The teenager deposits Josie's muffin in front of her, and she immediately takes a giant bite.

"You're really missing out," Ethan says, reaching to take a piece of Josie's muffin. Josie smacks his hand, and he pouts.

"I'm good," I insist.

"Suit yourself," Cass sings. "So, if we aren't going to talk about the elephant in the room, can someone please explain why your coworkers joined us this evening?"

Ethan sits straighter and leans forward. "Oh, this one's a good story. Randall was in *a mood* at our pitch meeting today."

"Yeah, it was like his wife forgot to make his coffee again." Josie grimaces.

"That's what I said!" Ethan shouts in triumph.

I grumble, but now we're making headway. I can't waste this opportunity to move on from talking about the man sitting behind me. "Yeah, well he was going on about what Millennials want to see in their news—"

"The man still thinks Millennials are teenagers," Ethan adds.

"What a moron," Vi says, and everyone at the table nods in agreement.

"Anyway," I continue. "I pitched a few cutesy ideas he didn't like, then finally told him if he wanted something cutting-edge, he'd have to let me write a story with some teeth."

Cass just about chokes on her food. Vi pats her back unhelpfully. When she's gained control of herself, Cass says, impressed, "You finally did it."

My face falls. "Don't get too excited. He basically challenged me to write a feel-good fluff story that goes viral. If I can do it, I can write my school funding piece."

"And if she can't do it, she has to respond to letters to the editor for two months," Josie says, a little gleefully.

"Oh, shit," Violet says, her eyes wide. "Isn't that, like, the worst assignment?"

"Sure is!" Josie giggles. "Sorry, Em. I really am rooting for you." She gives me a little simpering pout.

"I know." I sigh deeply.

"So that's why we're here. We offered to help Emery come up with a viral pitch so she can shove this in Randall's stupid face," Ethan says smugly.

"The only problem is it's next to impossible to predict what will go viral." I deflate slightly. I'm nervous about this, but I can't show weakness now, even to my friends. Whatever I decide to write about, I need to approach it with confidence. "He wants one million clicks on the article. I don't think anything this magazine has ever published has had one million clicks."

The whole table hums sympathetically, then falls silent. The teenager, who has been poking around on his phone throughout the entirety of the conversation, finally takes off his apron, hangs it up, and makes his way to the back room, presumably to grab his things. The sound of a chair scraping against the floor comes from behind me, but I still refuse to look.

"I liked the nursing home beauty pageant idea," Josie mutters. Cass snorts.

"I'd click on that just to see the pictures," Violet says.

I point at her, an eyebrow raised. "See? It could have worked."

The table falls silent again, the only sounds coming from Trevor, who I can see from the corner of my eye is starting to close up shop behind the counter.

Suddenly, someone clears their throat pointedly behind me. Mike, I'm pretty sure his name was, speaks up.

"I have an idea," he says slowly. Everyone gives him their attention. Josie and Ethan swivel around so their backs aren't to him. I turn, too, and try not to scowl.

"I couldn't help but overhear about your little dilemma. I think there's a story right under your nose that could be..." he trails off, pretending like he's thinking of how to phrase what he wants to say. "Mutually beneficial." He grins at Trevor, his eyes gleaming.

A pit of dread starts to grow in my belly. This is going to be bad.

"Our friend Trev, here, is having a little trouble with this shop." He's still looking at Trevor, who is standing there dumbly, clutching a towel.

"What do you mean?" I ask cautiously as I admittedly have to tear my gaze away from Trevor to look at Mike. There is something incredibly sexy about a man in an apron holding a towel. It's an objective fact. It's not like I'm thinking about what he might look like wearing *only* an apron, and what he might be able to do with that towel.

Thankfully, Mike's voice pulls me out of that particular thought. "Last I heard, our buddy here is about two months away from having to shut this place down. He can't compete with the big guns down the street."

Is that true? If so, it's a shame. I will probably never come back here because of the circumstances, but it's a cute place, and the coffee is admittedly delicious. I arch an eyebrow at Trevor, who shrugs. Must be true, then.

"How does this help me?" I direct the question to Mike.

"You said your target audience is Millennials? If I know Millennials—and I think I do—there is nothing they like more than a damn-the-man situation. Fight the corporate power and all that. What if you did a story on Trev's little shop here? Encouraged people to stop by. Shop small. Support a local business." He turns to Trevor, then, the expression on his face saying, *Not a bad idea, huh?*

"It would help me out," Trevor says with forced nonchalance. He goes to lean against the counter but must misjudge the distance and stumbles into the air. Mike shoots him a look like, *Real smooth.* I have to press my lips together to avoid laughing.

Ethan suddenly gasps, and I jump. I had completely forgotten he was there.

"You could do a series. Randall said a million clicks on one pitch, but he didn't say it had to be only one article. One post per week, with the history behind this place, a profile of this *very photogenic* shop owner." He winks at Trevor, and I cringe at the blatant objectification. He carries on, "All culminating in coverage of..." he trails off, considering.

Josie snaps her fingers. "An event! A grand re-opening after a refresh. Your articles will lead up to this event, drumming up interest and publicizing it." She looks around the table. "Oh my gosh, it would be so fun." She's practically vibrating with hope as Violet and Cass nod.

Can I let this happen? It's not a bad idea, and Randall might even go for it, but can I really write about my one-night stand's coffee shop for weeks on end? Does anyone on the planet actually think this is going to end well?

One glance at Trevor, and it's clear from the set of his jaw and the light in his eyes that I found the one person on the planet who does.

"I don't know," I say slowly. "Randall isn't the type to give more space to these fluff stories than one page."

"Because everyone hates writing them, and no one has ever pitched one like this. But you totally could. He wants something fresh and new. Why not also use a new format?" Ethan suggests.

I tilt my head back and forth, humming. I hate that it's such a great idea, and I don't have much time to come up with a better option. When I shoot Trevor a questioning look, it appears he's barely breathing.

"Do you want to do this? It wouldn't be... you know..." I swallow heavily, looking around at the table of people staring at me. "Awkward?"

Trevor's features slowly stretch into a smile. It's warm and comforting. Soft, like the night we met. I'm almost embarrassed to have everyone watching. There's no way they can't tell that smile is special for me. It makes my heart flutter in my chest.

"Maybe," he admits. "But I could use the help with this place."

I rub my suddenly-sweaty hands on my thighs. This could be exactly what I need to get out of this funk and kickstart my career back in the direction I want it to go. That is, if I can keep a tight lid on whatever feelings his smile is giving me.

"Okay," I say slowly. Everyone in the room breathes collectively in excitement. "I'll pitch it tomorrow, but there's no guarantee he'll go for it."

"At this point"—Trevor waves, indicating the otherwise empty shop, then settles his intense gaze on me—"I'll take my chances."

Chapter Ten

TREVOR

ONCE IT'S DECIDED THAT Emery is going to be writing these articles, everyone clears out at the speed of light. Her sister chipmunks her second muffin in her cheeks, mouthing around the crumbs that she'll call Emery later. Vi and Emery's male coworker have twin twinkles in their eyes as they all file out the door, with the young woman taking up the rear.

Mike steps to the counter and leans in, mumbling, "You can thank me later." I grumble at him under my breath, but he leaves just as quickly.

And then, we're alone.

Emery is standing in the middle of the shop looking lost. Well, no, she doesn't look lost, exactly. I can tell she's trying her hardest not to show any signs of uncertainty. But she's clenching her jaw a little too tightly, and her movements are stiff as she watches me come around the counter.

I try to smile comfortingly at her, but she seems to freeze. I guess that wasn't the right move, then.

"I'm glad you ended up here," I say quietly. The truth would be closer to me being ecstatic. Elated. Overjoyed. But she looks like she wants to bolt, so I don't want to overdo it.

She clears her throat and rummages through her bag, eventually producing a small notebook and pen. She sets them on the table and sits as she says, "Yes. Well. I'll need some information from you for my pitch if that's okay." She flips the notebook open to a new page and writes something at the top, all while avoiding my eye contact.

"Oh." I don't mean to sound disappointed, but I'm afraid it comes off that way. I push off the counter and walk toward the front of the shop. "Sure. Of course. Let me just lock up." I can feel her eyes on me as I walk toward the door. I flip both the deadbolt and the sign and take an extra second to collect myself, rubbing my palm against my yellow hat, shifting it slightly on my head.

When I turn back toward her, she quickly looks back to her notebook. But from the flush of her cheeks, I can tell she had been looking at me. Maybe checking me out from behind?

Hey, a guy can dream.

I cross the distance to her table but remain standing, resting my hand on the worn wood of the chair across from hers. When she realizes I'm not going to sit down, she looks up.

"Can I get you another drink? Or a muffin, maybe?" I offer. Then, I smirk. "We don't have the appliances to make waffles, but we do have whipped cream." A little teasing never hurt anyone, right?

She arches an eyebrow, and my mischievous grin deepens. Her face remains stone as she taps the mug still sitting in front of her, then waves at the chair wordlessly.

I let out a low whistle as I sink into the chair. "Not one for words tonight, srećo?"

Her eyes snap to mine, but her expression still gives nothing away. "I just need to know a few basic things about your shop, and then I'll be on my way," she intones with absolutely zero emotion.

I pinch my eyebrows together slightly and study her for a moment. She sits straighter under my scrutiny and presses her lips together. I tilt my head, then figure I might as well address the unspoken. "Did I do something to make you mad?"

She blinks rapidly several times, the first sign of visible emotion I've seen since her friends left. "No. What makes you think that?"

"Seriously?" I raise my eyebrows. When she doesn't respond, I blow out a puff of air and shift my beanie back and forth on my head again. "You're... Okay, I don't mean any offense by this, truly." I raise my hands, palms out. "Which I know means I'm about to say something offensive, but you're acting like you wish you didn't know me. And you *definitely* know me." My voice unintentionally drops a register. I try to own it with a grin, hoping it comes off as sexy and not awkward.

She frowns. "Are you trying to flirt with me?"

Well, not anymore. My smile falls, and I'm sure I'm staring at her with a dazed look. "Uh," I stutter. "I thought—"

"Look, I didn't mean to come in here today. I think you probably caught that. I had no idea this place was even here let alone that you owned it." She chews on the end of her pen. "I'm fully aware that your friend probably suggested this in part to throw us together like he did at the bar the other night, but the pitch is not a bad idea, and if my boss goes for it, it could really help me out."

"If it does go viral, it could be a miracle for me," I say earnestly.

"Exactly. And I know we can't pretend the other night didn't happen, so let's just acknowledge whatever it was and move on." She punctuates this statement by tapping her pen on her open notebook, her eyes tracking its movement.

I can tell by her finality that she thinks this is the end of the conversation, but I have to know. "What was it to you?" I ask gently.

She meets my gaze, and studies me for a moment. Her eyes roam over my face, snagging on my lips and jawline as they move slowly back to mine. When she swallows thickly, I know for certain she's fighting a war with herself about what she wants to tell me.

"It was fun," she admits.

Fun. I can work with fun. The corner of my mouth ticks up. "Yeah, it was."

"But I have a job to do here now. It's…" She sighs through her nose, biting her lip. "There's a lot riding on this for me. And for you, too. It's best if we focus."

She might be right, but her mood has shifted. It's subtle, but there's a question in her words. Maybe a little desperation, too.

"You spoke so beautifully about your career the other night." I wave, indicating the notebook in front of her. "I'm not getting the impression you feel like this is 'the best way to put people and words together.'"

She stiffens, her grip on her pen tightening. "You remember what I said?" she asks, and from the way she snaps her mouth shut, those words came out before she thought better of it.

"Of course I do," I say gently. And then I push a bit further. "That whole night is pretty much cemented in my brain."

Emery softens a tiny bit, but it's all my heart needs to water the tiny seed of hope that was planted the minute she walked into my shop. Maybe Mike is right. Maybe I'm stupidly optimistic, but I want to believe we were thrown back together for a reason. I *need* to believe it.

"I need this, Trevor." For a second, I think she's echoing my own thoughts. Until she says, "I'm not happy at this job, and this is a way to get back to doing what I love again. And I…" she trails off, looking around the empty shop. "I want to help you too. Please."

I can't avoid the image that bubbles its way to the surface of her laying under me, throwing her hips against mine, whispering, *Please, Trevor.*

But she looks almost anguished now. As much as she's shown any emotion all night, anyway. And I'm suddenly struck by the realization that I will do anything this woman asks of me, even if it means tamping down my desire.

I nod once. "Got it. Yes. We both need this, and setting this boundary would be... wise."

"Right," she says, equally resolved. "Okay. So, tell me about this place."

Chapter Eleven

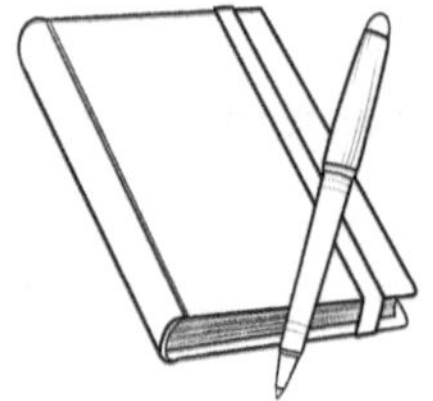

Emery

I GET WHAT I need from him and get out. Randall is only ever interested in two-minute pitches, anyway, so I don't need much. And staying there any longer than absolutely necessary would be foolish considering the sparkle I catch in Trevor's eyes every time I look up from my notebook.

I like that sparkle. A lot. And that is a very dangerous thing. I need to keep him at arms' length, both for the job and for myself. The way he walked with me last week, how he teased me about waffles tonight, when he remembered my exact words about my job, those times we were both clearly thinking about tumbling into bed together...

He's a good man. I can tell. I don't want to drag him into my disastrous relationship track record.

I manage to dip out of there before he asks me for my number. I keep waiting for it the whole time we're talking. I suppose it would be reasonable, under the guise of needing it for the story. Frankly, there's a fifty-fifty chance *at best* that Randall accepts this pitch, anyway. If he doesn't, it's a moot point.

I really, *really* hope he does. And not because I want to see Trevor again, which I refuse to let myself admit. In fact, I'm almost positive I can do at least half of this without even talking to him, which might be better for both of us, anyway. I can write these innocuous articles in my sleep.

About halfway to my apartment, my phone starts rapid-fire buzzing in my purse, and I groan. I know it's Cass and Vi before I even click on the screen.

> Cass: Em. Come over NOW.

> Vi: Or, you know, when you're done at the shop.

> Cass: Oh, she's done. You know she bolted as soon as possible.

Then Cass, again:

> Cass: I did not hear nearly enough about Hottie McHotterson. You cannot deny a pregnant woman this type of information. I need to live vicariously through you.

> Vi: Hi. I'm your wife. Can you maybe avoid talking about living vicariously through your sister's one-night stand?

> Cass: *eyeroll emoji* You know he's not my cup of tea.

Vi: He's not your TYPE. Missed opportunity for a journalism pun.

Cass: Ahh, but I did not miss the opportunity for a tea pun, which is close enough to coffee to count.

Vi: Shit. Well played.

I watch the messages come in on my screen, barely even a breath between them. Do I even need to be here for this?

Emery: I beat you to the journalism pun earlier today. Are you two sitting next to each other and texting?

They respond simultaneously.

Vi: No.

Cass: Yes.

And then Cass again:

Cass: Come over.

I trip over a crack in the sidewalk, my kitten heels click-clacking erratically as I try to right myself. I decide texting and walking isn't much better than texting and driving, so I hit the call button next to Cass's name. She answers on speaker.

I start talking before she can say anything. "As much as I'd love to come over, I can't. I need to work on this pitch, and then I need my beauty sleep."

"Bullshit," Vi says. "Randall doesn't ever listen to more than a two-minute pitch, and you put it together before you left the shop."

I silently curse them both for knowing me so well.

I run through all the other possible excuses I could make to not engage in this circus tonight, but my brain is fried. Bumping into your one-night stand at a coffee shop and not running away screaming takes a lot out of you, apparently. "What if I just don't want to?" I cringe, but it's the best I can do.

"You don't want to see your pregnant sister?" Cass whines.

"I literally just saw my pregnant sister, and I don't want to talk about running into my one-night stand," I correct her. "And you really need to stop using your pregnancy as a bargaining chip for everything. It's getting old."

"What's the point of pregnancy if I can't use it to get things I want?"

Everyone is silent for a moment, and I can picture Vi staring at her, trying to assess if she's kidding.

"The... baby?" Vi says, incredulous.

"Ugh, fine. Don't come over here. But if Randall accepts this pitch, you two are going to be together for the next few weeks whether you like it or not. You can't hide from this forever, Em."

She knows me well enough to know, when it comes to men, avoidance is my middle name. Challenge accepted.

***

The next morning, Randall pulls all of us into the conference room again. Usually, he reserves the group setting for Monday pitch meetings only, but based on his sinister smile as he stands at the front of the room, he's probably gathering us all in here so they can watch him tear me apart.

Ethan flashes me a thumbs-up under the conference table. Josie shoots me a grin that looks more like a grimace. Randall lowers himself carefully into his chair, his eyes trained on me like there's a target on my face.

This does not bode well.

He tents his fingers, then makes a noise as though he wants to gain the attention of the room. Which is pointless because no one has made a peep.

"Okay, Darlis. What do you have for us?"

I take a deep breath and smooth my hands down the tops of my thighs. It's now or never.

"I'd like to do a piece on a local business that's in danger of failing—"

Randall's voice is measured and scarily quiet as he cuts me off. "We are not doing a story about a business going under."

I drum up some of the confidence I had yesterday and say, "All due respect, sir, but I'd like the opportunity to finish my pitch. If you'll hear me out, I think you'll see it could be a great story."

He studies me for a second, his beady eyes squinting at me, then waves for me to continue. The room collectively exhales.

"Thank you. As I was saying, there is a specific local business that is in danger of closing, and I'd like to do a piece—well, a series of pieces—about the establishment. I want to start by introducing our audience to the shop and its owner, get them invested, and then establish the shop as an important part of the community, culminating in a grand re-opening of sorts."

Randall pushes himself back in his seat and makes a frustrated noise. "One million clicks on one story, Darlis. That was the deal."

But I'm ready for this one. I knew he would say this. "You're right," I say. This seems to placate him as he leans forward over the table again. "But I think the heart of our deal was to drive more traffic to the website overall. And not only that, but to foster an investment from our readers. Readership isn't built on one single viral story. It's built from a community of people who care enough to keep coming back. Right now, with our one-off stories of various odds and ends, our readers don't have anything to sink their teeth into. They don't have anything to look forward to, to come back for. I want to give them that. Which is why I'm willing to write a four-article series for this, rather than just the one article you were expecting."

I'm a writer. It's my job to turn a phrase—to persuade people to think and believe things they wouldn't otherwise. But Randall was a journalist in his day, too, and I pray to the universe that he doesn't see right through my insinuation that this is a service to the magazine rather than a loophole in our deal.

He regards me for a long moment, and everyone in the room stills again. He takes a loud breath in through his nose. "What's the business?"

I've almost got him.

"The Baker's Blend Coffee Shop on Main and Chestnut."

Shockingly, Randall's features smooth out. It's gone again quickly, but it was unmistakable.

"I didn't know that place was still open. I thought it shut down when that warehouse of a coffee place opened up down the street," is all he says about that. Interesting. He must have frequented Baker's Blend a long time ago. I file that tidbit away for later.

"It's still open, but barely. The current owner took it over from his father, who took it over from his grandfather, but he's struggling to compete with the big box stores popping up in the area. Which is why I think this is the perfect story. Millennials love nothing more than sticking it to The Man. They want to see local businesses thrive, and they're willing to let their money talk. They'll not only be invested in this series, but they'll come out for the grand re-opening. I can guarantee it."

Randall hums, narrowing his eyes further. I almost wonder how he can even see me when he squints like that.

"One million *unique* clicks over four weeks. Repeat readers don't count. One story per week," he counters. "And we will be a named sponsor at the grand re-opening."

In name only, is what he means. No way is Randall footing the bill. No matter. If he wants a banner with the magazine's name on it, he can have it. I can work with this. How hard could it be to get one million unique readers over four articles?

"Sounds fair." I nod.

Randall stands, but on his way out of the conference room, he stops near Josie and says, loud enough for me to hear, "I'd start cleaning out your desk if I were you. I think there's going to be a new Letters writer by the end of the month."

It takes all my effort not to growl. Fuck him.

Once Randall leaves the room, most everyone else files out after him. Ethan and Josie hang back. They're both wide-eyed with excitement, and Ethan is practically wiggling in his seat.

He pops up from his chair, slinging his camera bag over his shoulder. "I am going to head over to the shop right away to snap some pics of that tall drink of water for the first article. You coming, Emery?"

"No. I need to start writing."

Josie's face falls slightly, and Ethan gives me the side-eye.

"You're not planning to write all of these articles without even talking to him, are you?"

"What do I need to talk to him for? It's a coffee shop. No one goes there. Save the small business. Whoo-hoo." I make a circling motion with my finger in mock excitement.

Josie stands and walks toward the conference room door. "Yep, I'm going to go start packing up my stuff," she says on her way out.

"Thanks for the vote of confidence!" I shout to her backside, but she ignores me.

Ethan purses his lips and looks me up and down, then sighs. "I'll do the best I can to get some eye-candy pictures to post, but there's only so much I can do to help you, honey. If you want your readers to be invested, you're going to have to get invested, too." He turns on his heel and leaves.

I'm left alone in the conference room, feeling like I've been punched in the gut. The last time I got invested, I got my heart ripped out of my chest and handed to me on a platter. Twice, if you count the layoff. Getting invested is exactly what I'm trying to avoid, and I silently vow to stay as far away from Trevor for as long as I can.

Really. How hard can it be?

Chapter Twelve

TREVOR

No one is coming in for coffee at noon on a Tuesday, so I send James out to water the flowers in the planters outside the windows, and then I ask him to grab more milk from the store. We don't need milk, but I also don't need him around while I nervously reorganize, waiting for some word about this scheme.

Sometime before lunch, my phone buzzes, and my heart stupidly jumps into my chest thinking it might be Emery. But it falls again when I remember she doesn't have my number. When I pull it out of my pocket to answer, I see *Mom* at the top of the screen.

"Hi, honey," she greets me.

"Hey, Mom." I try not to sound too dejected, but she's known me for forty years. She can see right through me.

"What's wrong? You sound a little sad."

I sigh. "Nothing. I was just waiting for a call."

"Not my call, I take it," she teases. "Maybe a call from a nice woman?" My mom isn't pushy about my relationships or lack thereof, but that hasn't ever stopped her from hoping. And there is a distinct note of hope in her question.

I scrub my hand over my face. "Not exactly," I hedge. "Well, sort of. But we're working together. She's a writer, and she's doing a few pieces about the shop to help me out."

My mom hums as if she doesn't quite believe me. Then she's silent for a moment before she says, carefully, "Don't turn down an opportunity for something deeper just because of that place." It's not disdain for "that place" in her voice, exactly, but it's not endearment either.

"It's complicated. You know I want to keep the shop open, and this could really help."

"It's okay if you close it, you know," she offers gently. "Your dad wasn't too far from shutting it down before..." She trails off, unable to finish the sentence.

"I know," I reply quietly. Then, I take in a deep breath. "I don't think she's interested, anyway."

My mom's response is bright, as if the heaviness of her previous statement has been thrown off by her love for me. "Who wouldn't be interested in you? Everyone is interested in you."

"Mom, stop."

"Okay, okay. I'll let you go. Just think about what I said about the shop, okay? When one door closes, another opens and all that," she parrots.

We say our goodbyes, and I'm left alone again, pondering her words. Would I ever close this shop? Could I really walk away from a place that means so much to me? One that holds so many memories?

No, I don't think so. And I'm filled with a renewed hope that Emery can pull this off.

***

By the time one o'clock rolls around, I'm cursing myself yet again for not getting Emery's number. I kind of figured she'd ask for mine last night as part of her work on the story, but it must have slipped her mind with everything going on.

Slipped her mind. Right. Even I can't fully believe the lie I'm telling myself.

I wish I had a way to reach her to at least ask how the pitch went. I don't know a thing about how online magazines work, but it seemed like there was a possibility this wouldn't happen at all, and that would be disappointing on a number of levels.

I'm kneeling on the ground, shifting bags of coffee and tea around on the shelves underneath the appliances for the third time when the chime above the door rings. I try to stand up so fast that I hit the back of my head on the lip of the counter.

"Shit!" I cry out, covering the spot with my hand and rubbing.

"You okay?" a man asks. I try to keep my shoulders from slumping. I jumped up hoping it was Emery and banged my head for nothing. I guess at least I don't have to be embarrassed in front of her. Again.

"Yeah. The counter jumped out at me. What can I do for you?" I turn around, still rubbing the back of my head, to see the man who came in with Emery last night standing there, a small smirk on his face.

"Sorry to disappoint you." He swallows his laughter. "Ethan," he reminds me, offering me his hand.

I shake it over the counter, mustering up all the good cheer I have left. "Not at all. It's good to see you again."

"Sure." He clearly doesn't believe me. "I have good news and bad news. Which would you like first?"

"The good news," I say without hesitation.

Ethan frowns. "You're supposed to want the bad news first so the good news ends the conversation on an upswing."

I tilt my head, my brow pinched. "Why did you give me the option if you knew what you wanted, then?"

"Because no one ever asks for the good news first."

"I do."

"Okay, well, the bad news is Emery isn't coming."

I stare at him for a moment, blinking a few times. This might actually be the strangest conversation I've ever had.

He sighs deeply, as if I have exhausted him beyond his capacity for human interaction. "The good news is her pitch was accepted. Sort of. She has to write four articles about this place in four weeks and drive one million unique viewers to the website in that time."

"That's great!" I exclaim.

Ethan makes an "ehh" noise and tilts his head back and forth in a maybe-maybe-not motion.

"I thought you said this was good news." I raise an eyebrow.

"Okay, well, you've got me there. It's *better* news. It might be great news for you and your little shop here. But one million unique views over four articles is..." He grimaces. "Let's just say she's going to have to work very hard."

The corners of my lips turn down in thought. "But it's not impossible."

Ethan looks at me as if I'm a rare animal he's never seen before. "Are you, like, always this unfailingly optimistic?"

I huff. "Pretty much. It takes a certain level of delusion to think I can turn this sinking ship around, anyway." When he continues to gape at me, I clap my hands. "So, what can I do to help? Does Emery need more information from me? She wasn't here for very long last night—"

"I don't know if Emery is going to be here very often. Or maybe at all. That's probably a blow to your self-esteem, but she's not really interested in dating." He holds his hands up and shakes his head as if to stop me from asking why, which I wasn't going to do. "I'm not going to go into it. That's her story to tell. But suffice it to say, she's still got some open wounds from the last guy she got serious with. I can't tell you more, so don't even ask."

"Okay..." I draw the word out.

"Seriously. Don't," he insists.

"I'm not."

"Good. Because I'm just here to take some pictures." He sets his bag down on the table and opens it. He pulls out a camera and a lens and attaches them together. Then, he lifts the camera and takes a few shots, adjusts some settings, and takes a few more. "Okay. Do something... coffeeshop-ish."

I rub my chin. "Like what?"

He gives an exasperated sigh. "How should I know? Something that will look good above the fold on the first article. Make a latte or something. Roll up your sleeves and show your forearms. Ladies love that."

I raise my eyebrows but comply. "I'm feeling a little objectified," I say as I start rolling up my shirtsleeves so my forearms are exposed.

"You'll be fine," Ethan says dismissively as he clicks his camera a few times. He pulls it back to look at the pictures, his tongue sticking between his lips as if he's deep in thought. "Yeah, great. The lighting in here is perfect. Really highlights your cheekbones."

I balk at that. It's not the blatant commentary on my looks that bothers me, exactly. But I wonder how seriously he's taking this if he's only here to catalogue my features. "I fail to see what my looks have to do with my coffee."

"So go ahead and make some coffee, then. A hazelnut latte, maybe."

I lean forward slightly. "Do you want a hazelnut latte?"

Ethan clicks the camera a few times. He hums approvingly when he checks the photos, then brings it back up near his face. "No." He eyes me over the camera. "But Emery might."

I can't help it. My smile stretches across my face at the thought of her drinking something I've made her, and Ethan conniving to make sure she gets it. I get started on the drink to the soundtrack of the camera over the ever-present folksy music coming through the speakers.

By the time I slide the paper cup across the counter, I've probably heard the camera click at least fifty times. I hope Ethan's got something good. From the self-satisfied look on his face, I think he does.

He packs up his camera quickly, then shoulders the bag. He grabs the coffee and tilts it to me in mock cheers.

"I'll probably be back next week for more pictures." He takes a few steps toward the door, but then turns back. "Emery's a tough nut to crack. I want to see you both succeed, so I'll do what I can, but..." He trails off as if considering how to proceed. "Just be patient with her, okay?"

I nod once. Ethan looks as if he wants to say more, but he doesn't. He just turns on his heel and walks quickly out the door.

Patient, huh? Patient, I can do.

***

Actually, patience can fuck right off.

I'm trying. I really am. But when Friday rolls around and Mike strolls into the shop with his laptop under his arm, I've taken to biting my nails to keep me from incessantly refreshing the magazine webpage as we wait for the article to be posted.

"She didn't tell you when it would go live?" Mike asks sometime around ten o'clock.

"I haven't spoken to her since the night she wandered in here with her friends."

He stares at me for a second while he processes what I've just said. "Wait. Really?"

I slump into a chair and put my head in my hands. "Really."

Mike sits across from me, setting his laptop between us. "You must have really messed something up if she can't even see that talking to you about these stories is practically a necessity for this thing to work."

"Thanks, Mike. I hadn't thought of that," I groan into my palms.

He chuckles, then sits up straight. "Oh, check it out. It's up."

I straighten and grab the laptop out of his hands despite his protests. Sure enough, there I am under the headline *LOCAL COFFEE SHOP IN DANGER OF FAILING.* I click on the title to open the full story as Mike scoots his chair around to read over my shoulder.

I skim the story. It's fine, but that's probably all I can say about it. It's nothing special, that's for sure. The whole thing basically repeats what Emery and I talked about on Monday night. Straight facts with absolutely no flair. I push the computer away and lean back in my chair, folding my arms.

"This isn't going to do anything for me," I mumble.

Mike takes the computer back and scrolls to the top. He eyes my picture and lets out a low whistle. "The article leaves something to be desired, that's for sure, but look at you, buddy." He swings the computer back to face me, my picture taking up almost the entire screen. "You're, like, objectively hot."

I scowl at him, then turn my attention back to the picture. I have to admit, I do look really good. My eyes are lit up, and I'm smiling as I steam milk. My forearms look pretty nice, too. Ethan may have known what he was talking about.

"I need to get that guy to take new pics of me for my dating apps," Mike muses. I scoff, but Mike just shrugs. "Hey, think of it this way," he continues, scrolling down the page once again. "You might not save your shop, but maybe you'll get a girlfriend out of it."

I give him the side eye. "Look who's full of optimism now." My voice is dripping with sarcasm.

He shakes his head, pointing at the screen. "Not optimism. Facts. Look at these comments."

I lean in so I can see what he's pointing at. There are three comments, and all of them say something about me.

Ooo, hello. Is he single?

Hey Coffee Shop Hottie. I'd let you make me a hot drink any day.

Check out my profile, Trevor. I love coffee and steam.

"Woah." My eyes widen more with each comment I read.

"I know, right? This is awesome." Mike's eyes are gleaming with mischief. "Do you think I could be in the pictures for next week's article?"

"No."

"Why not?"

"No."

"The only thing better than one piece of eye candy is two." He taps his temple. "Think about it."

I shake my head incredulously as I turn my attention back to the computer screen. I guess if my picture gets more clicks on the article, it's not a total waste. But from the smile on my face, I have a feeling Ethan snapped this picture right after mentioning he'd give Emery the drink I was making. And knowing she wants to do this whole thing without so much as talking to me leaves a hollow feeling in my chest I can't quite shake.

LOCAL COFFEE SHOP IN DANGER OF FAILING

Emery Darlis

Welcome to a special, month-long feature of a local establishment, Baker's Blend Coffee Shop. It's a hidden gem in the heart of Baker's Grove. Sitting just off Chestnut Avenue and Main Street, this quaint little shop brings a bit of that old downtown feel to the modern landscape. Come in and enjoy a cup of coffee while seated in a well-loved chair with a view of the bustling street outside. Or enjoy the shop's free Wi-Fi as you get some work done.

Owner Trevor Kovacic holds the shop close to his heart. "My grandfather opened this place when he immigrated here in the 1950s, and my father took it over from him. Now, I run everything, and there's no place I'd rather be," he says. It's no wonder this adorable shop is family-owned; you can feel the love that has been poured into this place over the decades as soon as you walk in the front door.

"These are the best muffins I've ever had," one patron said around a mouthful. Indeed, the Kovacic family blueberry muffin recipe has a reputation that precedes it, and these tasty treats are a must-have if you come by. While you're at it, try a beverage.

My personal favorite is a steaming-hot hazelnut latte. Yes, even in summer! But, rest assured, anything you order will have your mouth watering.

The shop has had trouble competing with other, larger coffee shops in the area, and it's no wonder. Over the years, more and more big box stores have chosen sleek modernity over old-world charm. We all know how hard it is to compete with these large corporations.

But they don't have the family investment that Baker's Blend has. And they certainly don't have Kovacic's muffins. If you're looking to support a local shop that has been a staple in down-town Baker's Grove for generations, then you should check out this diamond in the rough. Tell them Emery sent you! And click back next week for more on this endearing place.

Chapter Thirteen

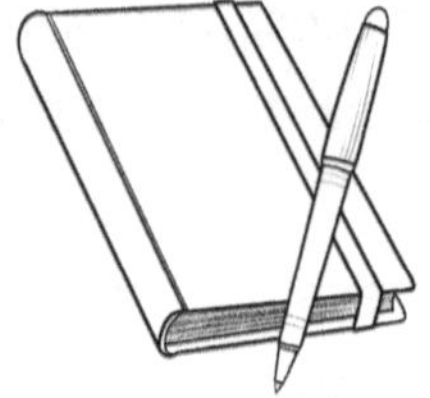

Emery

"Well, that was a less-than-stellar showing." I stab my milkshake with the straw a few times before pushing it away, uninterested.

"Fifty thousand clicks isn't nothing." Cass pops a fry into her mouth. She tilts the plate toward me, offering me some. I scowl, and she shrugs, taking two more.

"I know we're trying to be positive here," Vi says around a bite of hamburger, "but you've got a long way to go."

"Thank you," I intone. "I'm aware."

Cass takes the hamburger off Vi's plate and takes a huge bite. "You might still get some more visitors to the site over the next few days." She takes another bite and hums her approval. Vi starts to protest, then resignation settles on her face as she waves Donna over instead.

"I won't get enough visitors to get to a quarter of a million," I grouse. "They'll already be on to the next thing."

"You want growth with each article." Cass points at me with a fry. "You don't necessarily need a quarter on each."

"No, but it'd be nice." I sink lower into my seat as Donna sidles up to our table.

"Can I get another hamburger, Donna?" Vi asks. "Mine has been acquired by my wife."

"Sure, honey," Donna says warmly as she starts to leave. She thinks better of it and turns back. "Are you girls talking about Emery's article from today?"

"We sure are." Cass perks up.

"Baker's Blend has been around almost as long as this diner. I sure was sad when Marko passed. And then his son, too. Such a shame to lose them both so early. They put so much heart and soul into that place. But I always was a little glad Marko retired before that big store opened up across the street. If the cancer hadn't gotten him, trying to compete with that place would have. It did a number on my sales, and I'm not even a direct competitor."

I sit up a little straighter in the booth. "You knew the previous owners?"

"Oh sure," Donna says. "Watched that boy practically grow up in the shop, too. Wasn't sure what he'd do after his dad died, but I was glad he tried to keep the place going. He works so hard, but he's been fighting a losing battle." She stops talking and taps the end of her pen against her lips, then takes a breath. "A downtown needs a diner and a small coffee shop. It just does. It's not about the food or the coffee. It's about the community." She nods once to punctuate her statement, then turns to leave in a flourish. "I'll be right back with that burger for you, hun."

"Hmm," Cass hums with her mouth full again as we all watch Donna swing open the doors to the kitchen and walk through them. "Who knew she felt so passionately about that little place?"

"I definitely didn't." I drag my bottom lip through my teeth, thinking. "But it makes sense. The diner has been here forever. We've been coming regularly since we were teenagers, and it was old even then."

Vi nods thoughtfully. "You know, if Donna remembers that place in its heyday, it's not out of the question that other people of the previous generation do, too."

"I wonder if I could lean into the nostalgia while also appealing to a younger audience. Our generation is more likely to share things," I muse.

"I don't know." Cass's mouth is finally free of food. "People Donna's age sure seem to spend an awful lot of time sharing links on social media."

"Sure," I concede. "But they're not going to push a story to a million clicks."

"No, but a thumbnail of 'Coffee Shop Hottie' attached to the link they share might get the attention of their kids or twenty-something grandkids," Vi suggests.

I've seen the comments. I know what they say. There was a rush of them at first, all women ogling Trevor in the picture Ethan submitted with the article. And I'm not surprised. That smile coupled with those forearms is the fatal combination that had me jumping into his bed the night we met. Those comments *should* have given me hope that Trevor's objective attractiveness could help drive viewers to the articles.

But, instead, a pebble of white-hot rage burned deep in my gut each time my computer pinged with another one. Which is ridiculous. We slept together once, and I'm not interested in anything more than that. Even if the sex was amazing. And even if that smile of his does things to my insides I've been trying desperately to ignore since Ethan showed me the photo options on Wednesday.

My brain joins my body back at the table, and Cass is studying me intently, her head tilted to the side. "I can't tell if you're pissed or turned on."

"That's just Emery's resting bitch face," Vi provides helpfully.

I point at her. "RBF, definitely," I insist.

Cass looks unconvinced. "I've been looking at your resting bitch face since I came out of the womb, and that's not what it looks like. You're thinking about Trevor." She says it like a schoolgirl teasing her friend on the playground.

"I'm not," I insist. Cass thins her lips and raises an eyebrow in skepticism, so I continue. "And even if I was, it doesn't matter. We're working together now."

"You're not working together. He's working, and you're avoiding him," Vi chimes in.

"Whose side are you on?" I ask.

"We're both on *your* side, Em." Cass's voice is suddenly empathetic, which makes me suspicious. "It's just been a while since you've taken an interest in a guy."

Something in her tone makes me pause. Our sisterly default has been jabs and sarcasm our whole lives, so her sudden compassion is out of character. But I also don't want to go any further down this rabbit hole with her. Trevor is off the table.

Vi squints at me as if she's looking for whatever Cass sees. Suddenly, her eyebrows shoot up her forehead. "You *are* kind of interested in him, aren't you?" she asks with a note of surprise.

What is going on with these two today?

Thankfully, whatever is happening is interrupted by Donna delivering Vi's burger. Cass steals a fry off the plate before it even hits the table. Vi makes a noise of protest, but Cass stares at her.

"I'm growing eyelashes and fingernails right now, and I'm starving." Her voice is a challenge that Vi quickly—and wisely—decides not to accept.

"Hey, Donna," I call. She faces me expectantly. "The story that came out today is the first in a series about Baker's Blend, actually. Any way I could interview you for the next piece?"

"You're really going to do anything you can to avoid talking to Trevor, huh?" Cass scolds.

Donna takes a few steps back toward the table. "Why would you avoid talking to Trevor?"

"They have a history." Cass waggles her eyebrows on the last word. I groan.

"History makes it seem expansive," Vi points out. "It was only one night."

"Dammit. That's *private*," I hiss as I sink back down into the booth and try to hide my face with my hand.

Donna chuckles. "Oh, I see. Can't say I'm surprised. That boy is a heartbreaker."

I shoot upright again, vindicated. "See! That's what I'm trying to avoid. Heartbreak." I grab a fry off Vi's plate, suddenly voracious.

"Oh no, honey. I wasn't being literal. Certainly, a professional writer such as yourself can recognize figurative language when you see it. I meant he's a looker." She chuckles to herself again as we all gape at her. "I may be old, but I'm not blind!" she calls over her shoulder on her way back to the kitchen.

My sister and best friend—or maybe *former* sister and *former* best friend—are trying so hard not to laugh, their faces look like tomatoes. I flatten my lips into a harsh line as my gaze bounces back and forth between them. "You know what? Go ahead. Let it out. Laugh at my expense. I'm over here trying to respect my own boundaries where it comes to men and dating, but laugh it up." I steal another fry, but now it's to piss Violet off.

She schools her face by coughing and lowering her eyebrows. "We would never, Emery," she insists. Cass snorts, belying Vi's words. Vi shoots her a look, and Cass turns her head away, pressing her lips together to keep the rest of her laughter in.

"We wouldn't," Vi repeats, with more conviction this time. "We know a thing or two about the importance of not crossing boundaries."

Cass's face almost instantly turns into a pout as she whips her head to Vi. "If you're talking about a boundary around dating your best friend's sister, need I remind you we're now *married* and about to be *moms*, so I think crossing that particular boundary worked out pretty well for us." Her eyes glint silver, making her look like she's about to cry.

Violet slings an arm over Cass's shoulders and pulls her close as she plants a kiss on her temple. "I know, babe. I'm just saying we get it. Everyone has to define their own boundaries, and Emery has every reason to want to protect hers."

Cass snuggles into Vi's side and nods as if this is reasonable. "That's fair. I suppose if it were me, it'd take me forever to trust anyone again if we split up."

"Not gonna happen, babe," Vi insists, snuggling her closer. They only have eyes for each other, now, and both are completely placated.

I, on the other hand, am incensed. "Are you suggesting I have trust issues because I'm divorced? Because I really wish people would stop tiptoeing around that part of my life. I'm not embarrassed about it. I'm not sad about it. Good riddance to Derek and everything he stood for."

Vi turns her gaze to me, raising an eyebrow. "We know that. But you're lying to yourself if you think your divorce has nothing to do with your refusal to even talk to Trevor about a job that could literally change your life just because you fucked him one time."

My eyes widen, and my jaw drops. I open and close it a few times before saying, weakly, "That's not what's going on here."

"Liar."

"Writing these stories has nothing to do with sleeping with Trevor." I lean forward, ready to prove her wrong. "In fact, *we* decided to keep it professional because of these articles." So there.

"Who decided?" Vi asks. She's all about the hard truths today, it seems.

"We did."

"I doubt that. I'm very sure you told him you two should remain professional, and he didn't know what else to do, so he agreed," Vi counters.

I run through the events of Monday night in my head. I was definitely the one to bring it up. But I saw the resolve in his face. He knows how big of a deal this is for both of us, and he agreed pursuing anything between us would be foolish. I'm sure of it.

At least, I *was* sure.

A self-satisfied smirk settles itself on Vi's face. "If you're positive you're both on the same page about it, it shouldn't be any problem to visit him next week. For work." She all but air-quotes the last two words.

She's right. If we're both on the same page, it shouldn't be, but I can still remember the angry knot in my stomach at all those comments, and the subsequent gooey feeling I had at the memory of that picture-perfect smile against my skin.

I grumble something incoherent and grab another fry, but for the rest of the evening, I can't shake this feeling that Trevor is about to become a much bigger problem than a one-night stand.

***

"Dammit, Ethan. Not you too," I moan into my hands on Monday morning.

"What is that even supposed to mean?" Ethan whines over the cubicle wall. "All I did was ask if you wanted to go with me to the coffee shop to take pictures today."

"Well, I don't."

He disappears below the divider, then walks around to my side. "You sound like a child whose parent told her to read for ten minutes before she could watch television. What is wrong with you lately?" He leans his forearms against his knees and tents his fingers between him. Since when did he turn into my therapist?

"I don't want to go with you. I don't want to go to that coffee shop at all. I don't want to see Trevor." He's right. I do sound like a petulant child.

"Emery," his voice goes deep and soothing, like he's talking to a toddler throwing a tantrum. "You need to at least talk to the man."

"I don't want to," I say into my hands, punctuating each word.

"I know, sweetie." Okay, he's definitely toddlering me now. "But you have to. You can't do these stories justice without him, and you know it. Come on, love. Let's go. You've had harder assignments than this."

He's right. Writing about puppy adoptions and senior center antics isn't hard, but it is definitely more monotonous than anything I'm going to have to do for this series. What would be harder still is writing these fluff pieces until I retire. But I'll probably die of boredom first.

I sigh deeply and flare my nostrils. "Fine," I say, resigned. "But I'm only ever going when someone else is there with me so it's less awkward, and only for thirty minutes a week, and only for the story."

"That's the spirit." He makes a fist and swings it over his chest, mocking me.

We grab our bags and laptops and head out, opting to walk instead of drive because it is a rare, perfect summer day in Indiana. Usually, August is miserably hot and humid, but there's plenty of sunshine and a nice breeze today.

On the way, I fill him in on my plan to interview Donna and focus on what it means for the community to have a place like this downtown. He reiterates that Trevor needs to be involved in every story, but begrudgingly admits it's a good idea.

When we arrive at the coffee shop, Ethan pulls the door open wide and gestures for me to go in first. I give him the side-eye. He never opens doors for me. Ever.

"Ladies first," he says between gritted teeth.

"You've never given a shit about chivalry before this very second." My voice is low so anyone inside can't hear me.

"Age before beauty, then." He gestures again, but more harshly this time.

"Are you calling me old?"

"If the shoe fits." He kicks the door with his foot, then shoves me—gently, but still a shove—through the door. I stumble, but thankfully catch my balance before looking up straight into Trevor's stunning brown eyes. He looks amused as he wipes his hands on a towel that's threaded through the waistband of his apron. He has on a blue-and-black plaid button-down shirt that's rolled up at the sleeves and a black slouchy hat that somehow seems to accentuate his sharp jawline lined with stubble.

I know what he looks like. I've seen him before. I stared at the picture on the first article for longer than I'll ever admit to anyone. And yet, I'm still taken aback by how handsome he is.

My stupid heart skips a beat as his smile widens.

"Um, Emery?" Ethan says behind me. "Care to move out of the way?"

I realize I'm blocking the doorway and quickly step to the side to let him through. Trevor's gaze lands on him, and his grin turns almost chummy. He tosses the towel over his shoulder—why is that such a sexy move, and what the hell is wrong with me today?—and comes around the counter, extending his hand for Ethan to shake.

"Hey, Ethan. Good to see you again."

For a second, I wonder if I'm chopped liver next to Ethan, but then those light brown eyes meet mine again and, nope. I'm sure I'm the only person in the room he cares about. Trevor is just really... nice.

"Emery." His voice is a register lower. "I'm glad you're here."

Dammit. That voice does things to me I'm not proud of.

And, you know what? This is exactly why I wanted to stay away from this place.

I clear my throat and stand a little straighter. "Hi, Trevor. I'm here to ask a few questions, and then I'll be out of your way."

His smile falters a little at that. He sweeps an arm to the side, encompassing the space. "You're definitely not in anyone's way." He's not kidding. There's not a soul in here. Not even his employee seems to be present.

"Has anyone been here all day?" I ask before I can think better of it.

"A few regulars this morning, but no one since ten." He says it as if the fact doesn't bother him, but I can tell from the tick in his jaw that it does.

I hold myself rigidly tall, taking in the reality of the situation. "That article did absolutely nothing for you." It's a statement and not a question, but he shrugs in response anyway.

"Honey, that article did absolutely nothing for anyone," Ethan mutters as he walks around me to set his bag on a table.

I know that article wasn't what I wanted it to be, but fifty thousand clicks should have generated at least some business for him. I guess just because someone clicked on the headline doesn't mean whatever was there resonated with them.

And then it hits me. I really messed this up. In trying to put a wall up to keep Trevor out of my personal life, I ended up keeping *everything* out of this project. The result was a shit article that, as Ethan so rudely pointed out, did nothing for anyone.

To add insult to injury, Ethan is right. I hate it when Ethan is right.

But my personal—and very conflicted—feelings about Trevor aside, it's not fair to him. I saw the hope plainly written on his face when he talked about what this could do for him. He told me himself that it's a special place to him the night we met. And, from what Donna said, he practically grew up here. It must be like a second home.

I glance around and catch something glinting in the sunlight on top of the back counter, almost like the sun is reflecting off glass. I take a few steps toward it. "What's that?" I ask, shielding my eyes as I step right into the glare.

Trevor hums sheepishly. He walks over and pulls out two eight-by-ten-inch frames with pictures inside. One is a black-and-white picture of a man in front of this shop. He's standing with his arm around a woman, and his chest is puffed out. He's smiling, and I have to do a double take. I look at the picture, then back to Trevor, then back to the picture again. It's Trevor's smile, but that's not him in the picture.

"This must be your grandfather?" I ask.

"That obvious?" he grins.

I run my thumb over the glass right above his grandfather's lips. "You have the same smile," I say quietly.

Ethan's camera clicks a few times, pointed right at me. I shoot him a warning look, but he just shrugs and walks away.

I flip to the next picture. It's a color picture of a young man wearing a light blue button-down and jeans. He's smiling, too, but what's striking about this one is his eyes. Intense, amber pools peer up at me through time and space and film. They're Trevor's eyes. I meet his gaze over the photos. His smile has softened, and his own eyes crinkle at the corners as if he can read my mind.

"This is your dad?" I ask quietly.

He swallows hard. "Yeah."

I can see the pain written plainly across his face, even though he keeps his lips trained in a smile. It wavers almost imperceptibly. He misses them deeply. He must feel close to them here. This is not just a second home. It's a place that houses the memories of his family.

I look back at the picture in my hands. "People always said I have my mom's eyes," I say quietly. I'm not sure why I even say it. I'm not one to openly share information with anyone.

And, suddenly, I can see her eyes—our eyes—narrowed in disappointment, darkening in anger when I told her I wouldn't be running back to my ex, nor would I go back to *The Gazette* and beg for a job that didn't even exist anymore.

It's a far cry from the pride on the face of the man in this picture.

Ethan's camera clicking has conspicuously stopped, as if he's afraid to break the moment. Trevor takes a step closer to me. "You said you don't talk to her much anymore?"

"Not at all, actually," I admit. "She..." I trail off and inhale deeply. My gaze meets his again. He's closer to me than I expect, and my breath hitches.

What am I doing? This isn't about me, and I certainly don't need to be getting all personal with a man I am trying my best to stay away from.

But he tilts his head, his expression open and patient. My parents' rejection of me and Cass isn't something I'm ashamed of, but it is something I'm tired of carrying around. I don't know why, but it seems like sharing this grief with Trevor—even though it's different in a lot of ways—might feel good.

"She didn't agree with my relationship choices," I say, leaving it open-ended enough for him to come to his own conclusions. My parents being assholes is one thing, but my divorce is another. That's not something I'm ready to just blurt out in the middle of his shop. "My sister's either," I add. I can feel Ethan's mouth gaping. He knows how private I am, so it must be a shock to hear me say it out loud.

Trevor nods, but I don't give him a chance to speak. I walk past him to the counter and set the pictures back where I found them. I look around more slowly, taking in the space with this history in mind. I'm aware of Trevor's gaze on me and Ethan's camera clicking through more test shots as I do, but I take my time, letting myself linger on the dark, well-worn laminate on the counter, the warm lights of the display cases housing muffins and bagels, the cozy tables and chairs that were clearly selected and placed with love many years ago, the tin ceiling tiles that a vintage enthusiast would love.

Now that I've let myself see it, I can't unsee it. This really is a perfect space. People should be in here right now, working on homework, listening to their podcasts while watching passersby, reading a good book with a muffin and an iced coffee. It should be the space people meet for conversations.

It shouldn't be empty.

Donna was right. A space like this is a cornerstone of a community. It'll never make sales like the big coffee shop on the next block, but it should have a steady stream of regulars and new customers who are after a different vibe than that place provides.

I was supposed to help with that. And I didn't.

"Right," I say, crossing to a table by the window and setting my own bag down. "It's not too late to turn this around. The next article needs to do better than the last one, and I have some ideas. Trevor, do you have a few minutes to chat with me?"

Trevor gives me a wry smile as he looks around the empty shop, then back to me. "I've been in here all morning playing around with flavoring whipped cream." He purses his lips against a larger smile at what I'm pretty sure is an inside reference to my love of the topping, and I have to try hard to ignore the flip my stomach does at the memory. "I have pretty much nothing but time."

Ethan sweeps by me, camera in hand, and mutters as he passes, "There's that fire you've been missing."

I clench my jaw because he's right.

He starts taking pictures of the ceiling. Clearly, he noticed these details, too, which is why I love working with him even when he's pointing out my flaws. He often knows what I'm after before I do.

I pull out a chair and motion for Trevor to sit across from me, which he does. I tap my pen against the open page of my notebook for a second, thinking. I watch it bounce up and down and tell myself it's not to avoid looking directly at the man sitting with me.

"Okay," I finally say. "Can you tell me a little more about what this place means to you? I mean, I know it was your dad's, and your grandfather's before that, but I'm after something deeper."

Trevor takes a deep breath in through his nose. "We're going to get personal, then, huh?"

That's when I finally meet his gaze, and I shouldn't be surprised to find his eyes already on me, but somehow it unsteadies me nonetheless. I quickly try to regain my balance. "I think we have to, right? I mean, let's be realistic. You're never going to make big box sales." I raise my chin in the general direction of the newer store. "But you shouldn't have to. Yeah, they're a competitor, but your shop is different. It's got a different vibe, and it has a history that place doesn't. So, tell me about that."

"Well, my grandfather opened this place in 1954—"

I shake my head vigorously, cutting him off. "No. I know that already. That's just a fact. Tell me something I can't find on the internet."

Trevor leans back in his chair and scrubs a hand over the top of his head, which shifts his hat back so I can see his hairline. The hair there is a shade darker than his stubble—almost bronze. He readjusts the hat so it's back where it was as he tilts forward again, and a secret smile graces his lips.

"Okay, I've got one. See that spot on the wall next to the door to the back room?" He motions to an area behind the counter. I squint at it and shake my head slowly as I scan the area for what he's talking about. All of a sudden, I see it. It's a patch that's slightly raised, but if Trevor hadn't pointed it out, I never would have seen it.

"Oh, what is that?" I ask. Ethan turns his attention to the space, as well, walking a little closer to it and taking some pictures along the way.

"That," Trevor says with a grin, "used to be a hole that my dad made in the wall when he was a teenager. I don't remember how it happened. He was careless or something. Nothing dramatic. But my grandpa made him patch the hole and match the paint. Now, mind you, this was the seventies, so there weren't computers at home improvement stores to do paint matching for you. Dida sat him down with buckets of brown paint and made him mix up the perfect match. Wouldn't let him see his girlfriend until he got it right."

Ethan squints at the spot, leaning in. "He definitely got it right."

Trevor chuckles. "Yeah, well, he really wanted to see his girlfriend. And my grandfather was an exacting man. He wasn't going to settle for anything less than perfection."

"How long did it take him to match the paint?" I ask.

"The way my dad told it, it sounded like it took months, but Dida said it only took about a week."

"A week that felt like months, huh?" I say, and, against my better judgment, a smile rides my lips. "She must have been some girl."

Trevor's smile turns soft. "She was. Turns out she was my mom."

We're silent for a moment, looking at each other. Color starts rising on his neck, and I realize he's embarrassed telling me that story. I don't know why; it's a beautiful story. I try to smile reassuringly as Ethan says, "Well, if that isn't the sweetest fucking thing I've ever heard."

That knocks me back into the present enough to remind myself to jot down a few notes. That is actually one of the sweetest things I've ever heard, and it'll make great material. Community and family—that's what I need. Tug on the heartstrings a little.

"Where's your mom now?" I ask without thinking as I finish writing my note.

"She moved to Atlanta." His expression hasn't changed, but I think he sounds a little sad. "She has family there, and they always talked about living there in retirement. After Dad died, she couldn't be around here anymore, you know?"

I do know. It's not the same at all, but after I kicked Derek out, the first thing I did was pack up all my stuff and find a new apartment. It has been five years, and I still can't go to the restaurant where we had our first date or sit on the bench in the park where he proposed.

But Trevor doesn't need to know any of that, so I just nod. I tap my pen to my lips, considering, before I finally ask gently, "How did your father die?"

His gaze drops to the table as he takes in a breath. For a moment, I'm sure I've lost him. It's a fine line in reporting, asking the questions you need answers to without pushing your subject too far. I wasn't sure if I should even ask. He hasn't offered the information yet, and there must be a reason for that, but it was bound to come up eventually.

There's a notable lack of camera clicks, but I don't dare tear my eyes away from Trevor to see what Ethan is doing. When Trevor finally speaks, his voice is soft, and he doesn't meet my gaze. "My grandfather had cancer, and that's eventually what took him."

I nod, even though Trevor isn't looking at me. It doesn't escape me that this isn't the question I asked. He's working his way up to an answer, and I don't want to interrupt whatever inner war he's fighting.

When he does look at me, his eyes are so full of unrestrained sadness that it stalls my breath in my throat. It's been a long time since I've been around someone who is so open about their pain. Usually, people try to hide their grief, at least outwardly. They make it smaller, shove it down, steel themselves against it. Not Trevor. Not right now. *Not with me*, my brain seems to scream. Or maybe it hopes. And my sudden desire to pull him to me and hold him until it passes catches me completely off guard.

He swallows hard but doesn't break eye contact with me. "Dad had a pulmonary embolism three years after my grandfather passed. I had just left their house. He seemed fine when I left, but..." He trails off, then shrugs.

"I'm so sorry for your loss," Ethan says quietly. "Both of them."

I nod, unable to speak. Sorry doesn't seem nearly enough, and now I'm not sure where to go from here.

"Thanks," Trevor says as he scans the shop. I look, too, with a new appreciation for what this place means, not only to Trevor, but to generations of people who must have loved this family. The smiles they must have exchanged over cups of coffee and bites of pastry. The good-mornings and have-a-good-days they must have shared. The comfort they must have found in the warmth of a beverage and the presence of a neighborhood friend.

When my gaze lands back on Trevor, he's looking at me like he wants to ask me a question when I hear a couple of clicks directly to my right. I whip my head to Ethan, who is pointing his lens at us.

"I'm not in any of these pictures, am I?" I ask tersely.

He looks at me over his camera, the portrait of innocence. "Of course not."

I narrow my eyes at him. I'm definitely in those pictures, but I decide not to push it. I can always crop myself out later.

I turn my attention back to Trevor, deciding to move us back on topic. "Thank you for sharing that. I know it couldn't have been easy." Understatement of the century. "Anything else you can tell me that's similar to the story about the hole in the wall?"

"There's probably a million just like that." He smiles brightly, and his previous sadness is completely erased as if these warm and happy memories want to come pouring out of him. As if he wants to share them with me. There's something about it that wakes up a place in my heart that has been dormant for a while. I rub my chest as he asks, "How much time do you have?"

"About ten more minutes if you were serious about that appointment at eleven-thirty." Ethan pointedly looks at his watch, clearly referencing my initial thirty-minute time limit.

I chew on the side of my lip. "I think we can spare a little more time for the sake of the article."

"For the sake of the article. Sure."

I don't appreciate Ethan's sarcasm, but I can't snap back without being obvious, so I let it go. As much as it pains me to do so.

"It's okay if you have to go," Trevor draws my attention back to him. "I'm just glad you came at all."

I do want to get all my notes typed up to start drafting tomorrow. But more importantly, I know if I stay here any longer, I'm going to fall right into Trevor's smile and not be able to climb back out. And my heart hasn't quite stopped aching for him.

"I should actually probably go." I wince apologetically.

"Seriously, it's fine." He starts to stand. "Can I get you a drink before you go?"

"Oh, no, that's—"

"An iced matcha would be divine," Ethan interjects.

Trevor beams. "Coming right up." He shifts his gaze to me. "You sure?"

His hazelnut lattes are the best I've had in a long time, if I'm being honest. They're creamy and not too sweet, and I've been thinking about them since Ethan brought me one last Monday.

I sigh. "If you're making Ethan something anyway, I guess..."

Trevor beams yet again, as if making me a latte is the highlight of the day. Ethan snaps a few more pictures.

"Hazelnut, yeah? Coming right up." Trevor slings his towel back over his shoulder. God, this man is going to be the end of me.

"Can you make it iced, actually?" If I take a sip of a hot drink, I might melt. Ethan shoots me a sidelong glance.

"It's not that hot out today," he whispers pointedly. I reach over quickly and pinch the back of his arm. He yelps and jumps out of my reach, rubbing his tricep and scowling. Serves him right.

He starts flipping through some of the photos on his camera, but when I try to peek over his shoulder, he tucks the screen against his chest and looks at me, offended. "You know you don't get to see the rough drafts, Emery," he scolds. "You see what I want you to see when I want you to see it."

I lower my voice so Trevor can't hear. "I know I'm in at least a few of those. They are not to make it to print, understood?"

He salutes. "Yes, ma'am."

I don't know why that bothers me so much that he was taking pictures of me, aside from the fact that the conversation felt private in a way I can't quite put my finger on.

"Here you go." Trevor comes around the counter and hands one cup to each of us. I waste no time taking a sip. I have to force myself not to moan. It's even better cold than it is hot.

"Thanks for stopping in. I can't wait to see Friday's article." He looks so eager that I have to take another sip to keep from grinning right back. A little piece of me is glad my last dud of a story didn't disappoint him too much. An optimism like Trevor's is rare, and I certainly don't want to be the one to strip him of it.

I set my drink down and rummage through my bag for some cash.

"Oh, no. On the house," he says.

I shoot him a skeptical look. "Can you really afford to be giving away free drinks?"

He huffs. "I've been asked that before. Maybe someday I'll learn my lesson."

"If you want to turn this place around, you'll learn that lesson today," I insist, pressing the money into his hand.

He looks at it thoughtfully, then nods. "Let me get you some change."

"Keep the change." I grab my drink off the table. Ethan waves and leaves. I start to follow him out but turn to face Trevor again before I can think better of it.

"I'm sorry about the first article. I know it wasn't great. I let my personal issues get in the way of doing a good job, and it won't happen again."

He tilts his head, regarding me, but before he can say anything, I rush out the door.

Chapter Fourteen

TREVOR

THE ENCOUNTER WITH EMERY leaves me full of questions for days. I don't understand what she could possibly have to feel sorry about. I mean, sure, that first article wasn't great, but it was something. It was more than anyone has done for me in a long time, and if her expression during our conversation is any indication, she's invested now. I know she's going to find a way to succeed. And my heart dares to hope that she's not writing these articles only for herself. She's doing me a huge favor. All I can offer in return is a latte, and she wouldn't even let me give it to her for free. I can't get her clicks on these articles. It sure feels like one of us is doing the heavy lifting here, and it isn't me.

When Mike walks in for his afternoon dose of caffeine on Thursday, the night before Emery's next article is going to be posted, half of my brain is filled with thoughts of her—how stunning she looked on Monday with her hair in a messy bun and her flowy skirt showing a perfect amount of skin. The inexplicable desire I had to lightly run my fingers over her thighs just under the hem of her skirt. The number of times

I had to remind myself that she was very clear nothing could happen between us, and I need to keep myself in check when she's nearby.

The other half is a jumbled mess of worry and concern over the state of my business. I'm standing in the middle of the shop, one arm folded in front of me, and my other hand on my chin. I'm sure I look like a cartoon, scowling at the tables and chairs and walls, but I don't bother to put on a happy face when he walks in. Mike doesn't say anything; he just stands there, staring at me.

After a few minutes, he breaks the silence. "This is weird."

"Yeah," I agree.

"What are you doing?"

"Looking."

He's silent for a moment, and I can feel waves of confusion coming off him. "At... what?"

I sigh and drop my arms, sliding my hands into the pockets of my jeans. "The shop," I say, turning toward him. "I'm trying to figure out what it must look like to someone who has never been here. Who didn't grow up in here."

Mike's face is blank. "Why?"

I shrug. "I don't know. Is the space not welcoming enough? Is there a reason people don't want to come in?" I look around again, scrutinizing. "I'm worried I've kept things the same for too long, and I'm letting my nostalgia get in the way of progress."

At that, Mike takes a look around the shop. He walks over to the counter and runs a finger over it, inspecting it. "It's clean," he says, unhelpfully.

"I know it's clean. I'm not trying to get a health code violation on top of everything else." My voice has an edge to it that's new for me. My frustration is showing.

Mike must hear it because he raises his eyebrows at me. "Okay... What's going on here?" He slides into the nearest chair and motions for me to sit.

I sink into the chair across from him. "Well, as you know, Emery was here earlier this week." He nods, shifting forward in his seat a little, and I carry on. "It's nagging at me how she apologized for the first article. Which got me thinking that she's the one doing all the work here. I should be doing..." I trail off, looking around helplessly. "Something."

"What, exactly, do you feel like you should be doing? And what does that have to do with you standing in the middle of the shop looking constipated?"

"Jeez, Mike—"

He throws his hands up in surrender. "I'm just saying. You're not your usual, glowing self today. Something's got you stuck. Obstructed. Stopped up—"

"Please. Stop." I'm used to his antics, but right now, the only thing I want is for him to stop talking. He takes the hint, folding his hands in front of him and leaning forward on the table, waiting.

I look around the room again. "The ultimate goal is to get people in here. And for Emery to get what she needs out of this endeavor," I add. "But the only part I have any control over is getting people through the door."

"And yet," Mike starts, "If you could have done that, you wouldn't have needed Emery in the first place."

I nod slowly. "True. But maybe this thing with Emery is the kick in the pants I need to find some motivation to change things up a little."

"You love this place, though, just the way it is," Mike protests.

"Yeah, but it doesn't seem anyone else does." I look around at the well-worn tables and the chairs that have eroded from people sitting on them over the years. The brown laminate counter has a distinct 1950s vibe, but not in a cool, hipster way. The display cases for food are clean, sure, but look like they've seen better days. "I think I might have been a prisoner of my own nostalgia all these years," I admit. "Dad didn't want to change anything after Dida died, and I fell into the same trap."

Mike takes in the space, too. "What are you thinking of doing to the place with only a little time and even less money?"

I blow out a long, defeated breath through puffed-out cheeks. "I have no idea."

We sit in silence for a few minutes, not looking at each other. I think about asking Mike if he wants me to make him a drink, but we both know he's not coming in here for the caffeine.

I sag lower and lower in the seat as the weight of reality sinks in on me. This place isn't going to make it. 50,000 clicks on an article should have produced at least a few new customers. Maybe a couple of people checking in out of curiosity, or some people who haven't been here in a while would be reminded that I exist. Instead, I got nothing. Zip. Zilch. Nada.

"You could stand on the corner with free samples and try to bribe people to come in here," he suggests, and I can't tell if he's trying to be helpful or be an asshole. Then he adds, "You do love giving stuff away for free."

Asshole.

I don't bother justifying that with a response, though it's not a terrible idea. Maybe if people tasted my muffins, they'd at least come in for those. I happen to think I make a mean latte, too, especially when people like to try unique flavors. Not that anyone has been in here to order one in a while. I've been left to whip up random flavor combinations out of boredom and taste-test them on my own.

Mike snickers. "Maybe Emery has some ideas since we're fresh out," he suggests sarcastically.

I know he's teasing me. He's well aware of how much I've been thinking about her. I texted him on Tuesday asking if he thought she might stop in again. He sent back a laughing-while-crying emoji.

So, I know what he's doing here. He's trying to get my goat. Or, rather, he's trying to get me out of my funk about the shop by bringing her up. Little does he know, part of this funk was brought on by trying to distract myself from thinking about her. Constantly.

I violently push myself to standing, which causes Mike to startle in his seat. "I can't sit around here wondering when she's coming back," I say, mostly to myself.

Mike responds anyway, seemingly not thrown off by the change of subject. "What other option do you have?"

"You said I should give away some samples, right?"

"I was kidding. Obviously. That's a stupid idea." He looks at me as if I've lost my mind.

"But what if it's not?" I ask, making my way behind the counter and pulling out milk and espresso. "What if I could see her *and* pass out some samples to entice people to come in at the same time?"

Mike leans forward, his concern obvious. "Trev," he starts slowly. "I think we should maybe get you home."

"I'm going to bring drinks to her office." I start up the milk steamer before he has a chance to respond.

"How do you know how many people are there? Or what they like to drink?"

I pause to consider this for a moment. "Good point. I'll clear out the baked goods and bring those in. But I'll bring a hazelnut latte for Emery."

"Do you even know where her office is?"

"I can look it up on the internet."

"It's late," he says once the steamer has finished. "How do you know she'll even be there?"

I shrug, pumping in some hazelnut syrup. "She's got to be doing some final work on the article that goes live tomorrow, right? And what better way to burn the midnight oil than with her favorite latte?" I wiggle the cup in his direction. "And if she's not there, I'll hand these out to people on the way."

"Yes, because people are going to take muffins from some random hipster on the street," he says sardonically.

I shrug it off. It doesn't matter. She'll be at the office. She has to be.

"Okay..." Mike says slowly, standing as if I'm a wild animal he doesn't want to spook. "I'm going to take off, then."

"Oh, no you don't," I caution, eyeing him over the counter. "I'm bringing food for the whole staff. You're going to have to help me carry it."

***

As I make the drinks—a hazelnut latte for Emery, an iced matcha for Ethan, and an extra cappuccino just for kicks— Mike begrudgingly searches for the address of the magazine's office. It's not too far, but he insists his designer shoes can't handle the walk and forces me into his car. I'm grateful for it; walking with three drinks and huge bags full of pastries in this late-afternoon heat wouldn't be fun.

He parks, and I look up at the five-story building. Somehow, it looks more imposing than a five-story building should. The office is on the fourth floor, at least according to Mike's internet sleuthing.

"We're here," Mike announces after a minute, clearly trying to spur me on to action since I've been sitting here, staring up at what I imagine are the windows to Emery's workspace.

"This is stupid," I mutter. What was I thinking?

"Well, yeah." He shrugs. "But we're here, and you have three drinks and a shit ton of blueberry muffins in bags in the back seat, so we should probably at least get rid of them."

I take in a fortifying breath through my nose. "Yep. Let's do this." I spring out of the car before I can second guess myself. I grab the drink carrier and the bag of muffins from the back seat of the car. Mike takes the other bag and motions for me to precede him into the building. Right. My stupid idea, so I go first.

My heart is pounding as I cross the parking lot and open the front door. I look around for a security desk or something but, seeing none, I walk to the elevator and punch the *up* button.

I don't know what I expect when the elevator doors open onto the fourth floor, but the absolute silence that greets us isn't it. I thought newsrooms the night before a deadline would have a hum of activity. The energy in this space is almost dead.

The elevator dings shut behind me as I scan the space. I find Emery almost immediately. She sits in a barren cubicle with gray walls and a white desk, her dark hair shining in the overhead fluorescent lights. She's slouched over her desk. Her face is within inches of her computer monitor, and black glasses I've never seen on her before are sliding down her nose. She's wearing a blouse the color of dark honey paired with navy jeans. She's the only vibrancy in this drab space, and seeing her here makes me inexplicably sad. She always seems so tough and vibrant, but she's out of place here. It's almost as if the space takes some of the shine off her.

I study her for another moment before she sighs deeply and leans back to stretch her arms overhead. She tips forward again, resting her chin in her hand and gazing at something on her computer screen I can't make out from this distance.

Mike nudges me with his elbow, but it's not impatient. When I look back at him, his expression is almost sympathetic, knowing. Like everything I was just thinking was written plainly on my face.

Ethan's head pops over the cubicle wall in front of Emery, and he rests his arms, elbows out, on top of it. He looks down at her, but before he can say anything, he notices me and laughs lightly.

Emery clearly sees the expression on his face and turns slowly to follow his gaze. For a second, I could swear her eyes light up, but it disappears as quickly as it started. She leans back in her chair and folds her arms. "What are you doing here?" Her voice isn't cold, exactly, but it's not warm either. It's mostly curious.

I'm so engrossed in her at this point that I can't even speak. Luckily, Mike the wingman steps in.

"We thought you all might be burning the midnight oil, so we brought muffins."

"And a latte," I add uselessly.

At that, a few more heads pop up above the cubicle walls. Emery turns back to leave her glasses on her desk, then comes over to me. My feet are planted to the floor, and I'm grinning like an idiot. She stands close enough for me to smell her cucumber scent from her hair. I want to bottle it up.

Shit. I'm a goner.

"That was really decent of you," she says, her dark eyes meeting mine. She's so tall, we're basically at eye-level, which is super sexy.

"Well, I'm a decent guy." I give her what I'm sure is a doofy, lopsided grin. I'm trying—and failing miserably—to play it cool.

She studies my face, her eyes bouncing back and forth between mine for a moment. Then, she smirks and raises an eyebrow.

It's not a smile, but I'll take it.

I hand her one of the cups I'm holding. "This one's for you," I say tenderly.

I might be dreaming, but her smirk actually widens. She doesn't break eye contact as she lifts the lid and smells the contents. Her edges loosen as her eyelids flutter closed.

"Hazelnut," she breathes, her lips parting as she takes a sip. Her cheeks flush ever so slightly.

She's so gorgeous; I can't help myself. I lean in closer, my voice low. "I know what you like, srećo."

Her eyes fly open. I'm worried I've made her angry, but there's a sparkle in them that wasn't there before. It's almost mischievous. She licks her lips, and I have to force myself not to stare at them.

I'm beyond infatuated with this woman. And I'm in deep trouble.

"Step right up," Mike calls, shaking me out of my Emery-induced stupor.

"Do you think he was trying to be punny?" Emery mutters to me.

I furrow my brow in confusion. "What do you mean?"

She eyes me sidelong and raises an eyebrow. "Step *write* up?" she suggests. "Because we're writers?"

I chuckle. A smile *and* a joke? I must be dreaming.

"How about photographers who make hot coffee shop owners look good?" Ethan calls from where he's still peeking over the cubicle wall.

"I got you," I call, waving the other cup in his direction. "Matcha, right?"

Ethan hums in delight as he glides over to me to take the cup. "You remembered." He sounds genuinely touched.

"Why are you doing this?" Josie asks, digging through the bag for a muffin. I glance at Emery, who looks as if she's also very interested in my answer.

"Just trying to drum up some business," I say as casually as I can. Mike relieves me of the bag I'm carrying and makes his way to a few people sitting in desks off to the side of the office.

"Interesting tactic." Josie's mouth is full of muffin, so I can't tell if she's being serious or sarcastic. She walks back to her desk before I can ask.

"This place is kind of dead," I say to no one in particular.

"Yeah, most everyone turns their articles in by noon so they can get out of here early on Thursdays," Emery explains.

"How are you supposed to write fun pieces for a local lifestyle web magazine with a work environment like his?" I ask.

She gives a loud snort. "I frequently ask myself that question."

"You frequently ask everyone that question," Ethan chides as he walks back to his desk. Emery shrugs as if to concede.

A door opens to my right, and an older man walks out. He is easily a few inches shorter than me, with salt-and-pepper hair that's thinning a bit at the top. He wears a white, short-sleeved button-down and black slacks. By the way everyone hushes at his presence, I assume this is her boss.

He approaches us, his eyebrows raised. "Darlis, what's this?"

"This is Trevor Kovacic, sir. From Baker's Blend Coffee Shop." She speaks without an ounce of trepidation. It's clear he doesn't intimidate her like he does some of the other people who slink back to their cubicles. "Trevor, this is Randall Skinner. He runs the magazine."

I extend my hand, still awkwardly holding the extra cappuccino. "Nice to meet you, sir."

He shakes my hand gruffly. "What are you doing here?"

"He was dropping off some extra muffins and coffee. For research," Emery jumps in.

"Cappuccino?" I ask, holding out the drink.

"Hmm. Don't mind if I do." He takes it from me and takes a long sip. He lets out a satisfied hum, and Emery raises her eyebrows in surprise. "Good stuff. Thank you." As he starts to walk away, he calls, "Darlis. Don't you have an article to submit?"

"Yes, sir. I'll have it in on time," she calls back. She looks at me the corners of her mouth pulling down and eyebrows still raised, impressed. When we hear another door close on the other side of the office, she says, "That was the nicest he's been to anyone in a long time."

"Coffee will do that for you," I suggest.

"Hmm, maybe." She frowns in his direction and stands silent for a while.

"You're not done writing the article yet?" I break the silence.

I watch as a tug-of-war plays out over Emery's features. She clearly has an answer to my question and she's debating whether or not to tell me. Eventually, she lets out a frustrated sigh through her nose.

"I want to get it right this time." She quickly takes a drink of her latte as if the words tasted bad coming out of her mouth.

I turn to fully face her. From this angle she has to look up to meet my gaze, but only a little. I want to reach out. Run my hands up and down her arms in reassurance. I settle for falling into her dark eyes. "You're doing the best you can," I reassure her. "That's all anyone can ask."

She looks pained as her gaze falls to the floor. "That's just it," she says quietly, almost embarrassed. "I didn't." She swallows audibly, then snaps her gaze to mine again. "I know how to write with heart, Trevor. I'm good at this. Or, at least, I used to be before..." she trails off, then shakes her head. "Let's just say a lot has changed. I've been skating by on good enough for a while now. I realized it as you were talking about your dad and that hole in the wall the other day. You have so much passion for that little shop that I didn't even bother to uncover for that first article, and it showed. People don't want to read dry articles about local shops. They want to feel the heart of the story. I want to give that to them. And to you. The heart, I mean." Her eyes widen slightly as if she realized what she said. "The heart of the *story*," she clarifies unnecessarily.

I know she meant the heart of the story, but if she felt the need to clarify, maybe she was thinking about her heart, too. At least, my own stupid heart seems to hope so, considering how hard it's beating. I'm so distracted that I'm nodding without even realizing it, and I don't notice that she's stopped talking until it's been silent for too long. I don't think she's ever given me this much of a peek into herself. I want to know more. I want to pry into that heart and see what she's holding back. I could listen to her talk all day. But she's stopped talking, and now it's getting awkward.

"I can show you heart," I offer, and try not to cringe at how weird that sounds.

But she glances at my chest, as if what she's looking for literally resides in my ribcage. "I believe you can," she almost whispers. She shakes her head slightly, as if waking up from a trance. "Anyway," she says much louder, "I was here working on some edits. I..." She trails off, meeting my eyes. Hers are infused with a fiery commitment that's so sexy, I have to remind myself to breathe. "I want to do it right this time," she finishes.

A smile stretches across my face. "I have faith you will, Emery."

She nods once, sliding her gaze away from mine. But, as I watch her, I'm sure she's hiding a smile.

BY FAMILIES, FOR FAMILIES: BAKER'S BLEND HAS HISTORY AND HEART

EMERY DARLIS

Welcome back to our special feature of Baker's Blend Coffee Shop.

When you walk into Baker's Blend, you're immediately greeted with the scent of coffee and the sounds of an acoustic playlist carefully curated to give you exactly the vibes you're looking for from a local coffee shop.

But if you look a little closer, you'll see the details that make this space truly unique: The floor-to-ceiling windows overlooking the street. The oak chairs and tables that are so well-crafted, they must have been handmade in a previous decade. The vintage tin ceiling that has been lovingly polished and restored. The bar-height counter where countless patrons have sat to enjoy coffee and a conversation over the years.

During one of those conversations, you might even find out a little more. Owner Trevor Kovacic might flash that brilliant smile at you and tell you about his father, David, who owned the shop before him. He might point to a slight imperfection in the wall behind him and recount the tale of his dad accidentally punching a hole in the wall. His grandfather, Marko, who first opened the shop in 1954, made a young David patch up the hole and perfectly match the paint on his own before he could see his girlfriend—the girlfriend who would later become Trevor's mom.

"He was an exacting man," said Kovacic with a sparkle of the memory in his eyes. He wouldn't have been born at the time of the ill-fated hole in the wall, but it's a story as well-worn and well-loved as the chairs and tables that fill the shop. And it's as comforting as the warm drinks and muffins Kovacic serves every day—the same ones his father and grandfather served before him.

But it's not the story that's important, though it does give you an idea of the heart of the place. This story is one of many. It's representative of the feeling you get when you walk in the door at Baker's Blend. You feel the family history like a comforting blanket. You feel relaxed and at home. You feel like Kovacic is welcoming you into his coffee family with every sip of your drink and bite of your pastry.

Baker's Blend Coffee Shop truly is a place with history and heart. Get your own taste of the history. And get a taste of the delicious coffee, too. You'll want to stop in soon and check it out as Kovacic gets ready for his grand re-opening in two weeks.

Come back to *Baker's Grove Living* next week to read even more about this historical shop.

Chapter Fifteen

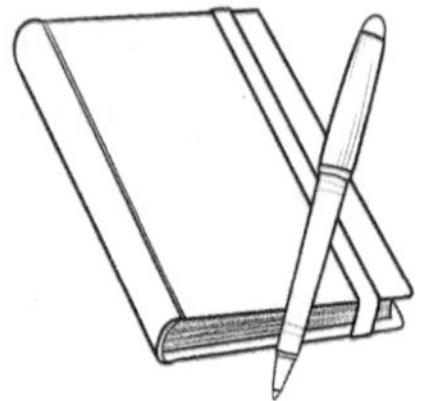

EMERY

I REFRESH MY BROWSER screen while chewing at a loose piece of skin on my bottom lip. If I'm not careful, it'll start bleeding, but I'm not terribly concerned with that right now. My second article about the shop should have gone live seven minutes ago, and conventional wisdom dictates that the performance in the first hour is a good indicator of how it'll perform for the rest of the day.

"Try clearing your cache," Ethan's voice floats between the cubicle walls. I grumble a little, then do as he suggests. I refresh my browser again, and there it is.

BY FAMILIES, FOR FAMILIES: BAKER'S BLEND HAS HISTORY AND HEART

It's not my best title. I was too busy writing the damn article to come up with a good pun, so I settled for alliteration. I hear Ethan hum disapprovingly on the other side of the cubicle wall.

"It's fine," I mutter. Then, I raise my voice so he can hear me. "It's catchy."

"I mean..." He drags out the word and trails off, implying that he doesn't agree.

I roll my eyes just as he pops up over the cubicle wall. He does it so quickly, the wall jiggles dangerously. One of these days, that thing is going to come crashing down. Maybe this whole place will come down with it. That'd be the day.

"Did you see the photo?" he asks, his eyebrows waggling suggestively.

I grimace in disgust. "You really need to stop objectifying him. It's starting to get weird."

He tilts his head. "Sex sells, honey. But if you don't want my help..." He shrugs and lowers himself back to his chair.

"I love you and need you and you're the best photographer in Baker's Grove," I call in a singsong voice.

"Think bigger, Emery," he singsongs right back.

"The nation? The world!"

"That's more like it," he says. It's really too easy to soothe that man's ego.

I scroll down past the bold headline and the first teaser paragraph of the article. Only because Ethan suggested I take a look. Not because I need to see what made him waggle his eyebrows like that. I certainly do not.

The picture takes up almost the entire width of the browser, and as soon as I see it, I gasp. Ethan lets out a satisfied "Mmm-hmm" from the other side of the wall. I want to scoff at him, but I can't even manage it because my heart is in my throat.

It's not hard to make Trevor look good. He's all glowy good looks and sparkly eyes. The man has a jawline that could cut steel and cheekbones that could touch the sky. On top of it all, his smile is easy and would look almost boyish if it weren't for the stubble gracing his jaw.

But somehow, Ethan has managed to capture Trevor at his absolute best. He's sitting at the table as he was doing while we were talking on Monday. The surface of the table is blurry, but his forearms are in focus, the shirtsleeves of his plaid shirt rolled up. His black slouchy hat rests atop his head, and his golden-brown hair pokes out of the hem at the front. He looks every inch the neighborhood hipster coffee shop owner.

But none of this is what's so intoxicating about the photograph. It's the complexity he exudes. He looks joyful, though his grin carries a tinge of nostalgia. He looks like a man who is completely and utterly at home in the chair he's sitting in, especially because he knows the history of it. It's the perfect photo to pair with this week's article.

But what really catches me off guard are his eyes. Those damn eyes of his are practically glittering as they laser-focus on whatever is across from him, out of the frame.

If I hadn't been there myself, I would think he was looking at something he adored. Something that piqued his interest, maybe even something he was infatuated with. But it's me he's looking at in that picture. I was sitting right there. And warm tingles that rise in my core at the realization.

"Never mind the world," Josie calls dreamily from her side of the office, having clearly eavesdropped on our earlier conversation. "You're the best photographer in the universe."

Ethan chuckles. "You know it."

I can't even pretend to protest because he really is. This photograph is stunning. Trevor is stunning. And he's looking at *me* like *that*.

If it were any other woman, I'd consider her one lucky bitch. I'd tell all my friends to find themselves someone who looks at them the way Trever looks at her.

But it's not any other woman. It's me. And I am not the relationship type. Not anymore.

I chew on my lip a little more as the picture continues to fill my screen. I should look away, but I can't. The image is practically intoxicating.

"I hate to say I told you so," Ethan sings after a few minutes. "But check out some of these comments."

That snaps me into action. I wheel forward so I'm as close to my desk as I can be and refresh the page again before I scroll quickly to the comment section.

It's Coffee Hottie Friday, ladies!

Is he serving those forearms along with the muffins?

I'd let him serve me literally anything.

I chew on my lip again as similar comments start rolling in. Who knew posting thirst trap photos would draw in the clicks? Well, Ethan and probably everyone else on the internet knew, but if this continues, my job is about to get a lot easier.

A nagging guilt gnaws at me, though. These commenters are interested enough to look at Trevor's picture—and I'm going to fully ignore whatever feelings I have about that—but are they interested enough to check out the shop in real life? If I win this bet with Randall but Trevor doesn't see any increase in business, will it be a hollow victory?

The pit that falls in my stomach feels an awful lot like a resounding yes.

I guarantee these commenters by-and-large mainline iced coffee during these summer months. They're always posting pictures of themselves with their trendy coffee cups on their social profiles. I lean in further and squint. Two of them even have an iced coffee in their profile picture.

They need a catalyst to get them through the door. Something more familiar to them than the call-to-action at the end of the article. Maybe someone who is just like them, suggesting they should pay Baker's Blend a visit.

Everyone knows you should never read the comments, but at a lifestyle magazine like this, engagement is what makes or breaks a writer's success. To that end, everyone here has at least one burner account to spur on a few more clicks. It's a dirty trick, but it's unfortunately the nature of the beast.

I log into my latest burner account and type out a few quick replies that I'm planning to stop by the shop on my way home from work to see if Trevor lives up to his photo, and maybe grab an iced coffee while I'm there. I post them before I can think better of it.

A few moments later, Ethan lets out a low, warning hum. "I sure hope you know what you're doing there, NewsJunkie814," he says.

Yeah, I think. *Me too.*

Chapter Sixteen

Trevor

It shouldn't be a surprise that the bell above the door dings at seven-thirty in the morning on Saturday. It should be a normal occurrence that any coffee shop owner might expect.

But this is my coffee shop. And no one ever comes in at seven-thirty in the morning. Or any other time.

So, when the door opens and three twenty-something women wearing leggings and loose-fitting tops and carrying rolled-up yoga mats appear, it takes me a moment before I realize I should probably greet them or something.

James is working today, but he's no help, either. He takes one look at the women and mumbles an excuse to go to the back office. It's probably for the best. These women don't look like the type to order black coffee, which is about all he can handle.

My eyes follow him through the back door. I'm definitely going to have to do something about that sooner rather than later.

Not now, though. Now, three women are slipping me surreptitious glances while pretending to eye the menu, and I need to focus.

"Good morning, ladies." I flash my most winning smile. The middle one—a blonde woman in floral leggings and a matching sports bra under her gray top—blushes and looks away. The tallest of the three, a brunette with a bobbed haircut, steps forward.

"Hi. You must be Trevor. We read all about you online. This... place... seemed so cute and we had to check it out." By the way she's eyeing me up and down, I doubt it's the place they're here to check out. I try not to grimace at the almost-blatant objectification. Customers are customers, and I can't afford to lose any because I can't handle a little gawking.

"Well, I'm glad you stopped in this morning. Can I get something started for you?" I widen my smile, which makes the third woman giggle.

"I'll take a skinny iced mocha with oat milk, please," the short-haired woman says. She eyes the case of baked goods next to the register, then rolls her eyes. "Oh, I might as well get a muffin, too. We'll burn it off later, right girls?" she asks her counterparts, who both nod enthusiastically.

I bite the inside of my cheek to avoid telling them that they don't have to earn their food. "Coming right up. Anything else for you today?"

The woman steps to the side and waves at her friends. "Whatever they want, too. It's on me, girls!" she says excitedly, then winks at me. She actually winks at me. I can't remember the last time a woman winked at me. I'm not sure how I feel about it. The other women both order muffins, a medium one-third decaf triple mocha with half the mocha, and a medium blended green tea latte with oat milk and three pumps of raspberry.

I'm once again grateful James excused himself to the back room. As it is, I consciously have to stop myself from making judgmental noises as they order.

Just as I start making their drinks, the bell chimes again, and a little thrill runs through me at the thought of more customers. "I'll be right with you," I call, my back to the door as I start pouring the half-third-triple mocha concoction into a cup.

I'm definitely going to have to figure out how to train James better if this continues. No, *when* this continues.

I had read Emery's article yesterday, of course. She wasn't kidding when she said she could find the heart of a story. The way she retold the details about my dad patching up the hole in the wall and wove it with details of the space here felt as if she was as personally invested in the story as I was. That story had been told to me a million times, and I've told it almost as many, but something about her description made it feel fresh and intimate. It was a nice article. I'm not surprised it drew people in today.

But when I turn around to place two of the drinks on the counter for the women to pick up, there's no one else standing there. My eyes scan the space as I turn to deposit the third drink next to the other two, knowing the bell would have rung again if whoever walked in had left.

That's when I see her. Emery. Sitting in the far corner, at the same table she sat the first night she came in the shop. She has her laptop in front of her and is staring at it as if it holds the key to understanding the universe. If I didn't know any better, I'd think she was trying to avoid looking at me.

The women take their drinks and muffins and sit at a table on the other side of the shop near the window that faces the street. They start chatting loudly, as if they want to be heard, but I don't have any energy to focus on them when the most beautiful woman I've ever seen is sitting in my shop.

I'm distracted for a moment by my phone buzzing in my pocket. I take it out to see a text message from my mom. I unlock the screen and open my messages.

> Mom: I read that article about the shop. Your aunt forwarded it to me. I had forgotten that story.

She had forgotten it? That story had been told to me so many times over the years, it's burned into my brain. I touch that spot every so often on my way into the back room, just to feel my dad's mark on this place. I guess she didn't grow up here like I did. She never worked here. She came here a lot, but she might not be as connected to the details as I am.

Another buzz pulls me from my thoughts.

> Mom: Anyway, thank that writer girl for me. It was a nice memory. She must be special for you to have shared that with her.

I'm starting to think "special" doesn't begin to cut it, but I am not ready to have that conversation with my mother. Especially when that writer girl is sitting right here, in my shop.

I laugh lightly to myself and shake my head slightly as she continues to stare at her laptop, clicking at the keys and clearly avoiding my eye contact. I quickly make her an iced hazelnut latte before poking my head into the back room to strongly suggest to James that he comes to the counter for a few minutes. Luckily, he doesn't need a ton of encouragement. I grab the latte on my way over to her table and slide into the seat across from her. She doesn't look up right away, so I push the drink across the table to her. She finally drags her eyes from her screen as she begrudgingly raises the straw to her pink lips and takes a sip.

Her features immediately relax. She pulls two earbuds out of her ears and sighs.

"Hi, Emery," I say, my voice a full octave lower than usual. I certainly didn't intend to sound so sultry, but it's out there now. And, if I'm not mistaken, Emery's cheeks grow rosy as her gaze meets mine.

"I just came in here to get some work done," she says as if she has to explain her presence in the shop. As if she's apologizing for being here.

"Yeah, of course." I can't take my eyes off her.

Her gaze, however, flicks to the giggling girls by the window. "Don't let me interrupt," she grumbles.

I turn in my seat to find all three of them looking at me. They titter when I notice them, then quickly avert their gazes. I face Emery again, shaking my head. "It would seem I woke up this morning and found myself back in high school," I joke. She huffs a laugh, and even that small sound emboldens me. "That article was good."

Her brown eyes snap to mine, and she shrugs as if this may or may not be true. "I just told your story." She eyes the women before meeting my gaze again. "I think you probably have more to do with your new customers than I do."

My eyebrows pinch together a little. "How so?"

She looks at me as if I'm a complete idiot. "They're here to see the hot coffee shop owner," she explains. "They..." she trails off, shakes herself a little, then continues. "They saw your picture and wanted to check you out for themselves, I'm sure."

I'm going to try very hard to ignore the fact that she just called me hot.

"And here I thought they came in for the excellent lattes," I tease.

She takes another long sip of hers, her tongue darting out to touch the end of the straw before her lips close around it. Watching her drink her coffee is doing things to me I'm also trying to ignore.

Almost as if she knows it, she doesn't break eye contact as she draws the straw further into her mouth and takes a long, slow sip. Some of the creamy coffee lands on her bottom lip as she removes the straw from her mouth. She smiles almost imperceptibly as she licks the drop and hums, satisfied.

This woman is burning me from the inside out. I force myself to look away just as she says something I don't catch in my haze of desire.

I clear my throat before turning my attention back to her. "I'm sorry, what was that?"

She eyes me as if she knows exactly what she's doing to me. To be fair, the entire world probably knows what she's doing to me. "I said, did you see the comments section of the article yesterday?"

"No," I respond. "I thought you were never supposed to read the comments."

She chuckles. "That's generally sound advice," she concedes. "But I'm trying to go viral, so I'm..." she trails off again, then recovers. "I'm monitoring it."

That seems reasonable. I nod as she continues. "Anyway, it blew up yesterday. Most of the commenters appeared to be women interested in meeting you." Her eyes sparkle a little as she regards me. The women by the window switch to more hushed tones, but the difference in volume is actually more conspicuous than if they had kept talking loudly. Emery gives me a pointed look, and I shrug.

"It's not like I've never had women check me out before."

"Well, I'd say you should get ready for more." She idly twirls her pen around on the table next to her laptop. "There were over four hundred comments the last time I looked."

My eyes practically bulge out of my head. "*Four hundred?*"

Emery nods as she bites her lip. God, what I wouldn't do to be that lip.

No, Trevor. Focus.

"So, what does that mean for clicks?" I ask, hoping that means she's a lot closer to her goal.

A slow smile spreads across her face. It changes her whole appearance. If I thought she was gorgeous before, she's absolutely stunning now, smiling at me, eyes twinkling with pride and mischief.

"Three hundred thousand," she says.

Overjoyed for her, I jump out of my seat and let out a whoop. The other women laugh, then stand to throw their trash away as two more women, a little older than the other three, enter the shop.

I turn back around to catch Emery shooting daggers at the newcomers until she realizes I'm watching her. She schools her face into a neutral expression, but I saw it. I'm sure I did.

Is she... jealous? She sure looked jealous.

I temper my smile. "So," I force myself to stay on-topic. "That brings you to, what? Three hundred and fifty thousand?"

"Yeah. Not as good as I'd hoped for at the halfway point, but not so far in the hole that I can't dig us out."

Us. Now that's something. Today is full of wins.

I catch James starting to edge his way toward the office out of the corner of my eye. Emery dips her chin toward him. "I think you're going to have to deal with this situation pretty soon," she suggests.

I scrape a frustrated hand down my face as the new women move toward the counter. "Yeah, I was thinking the same thing. Will you excuse me for a moment?"

Emery pops an earbud back in. "Take your time. I came in to work." She waves at her screen. "I thought it might help me set the mood to write here." She pauses with her second earbud halfway to her ear. "Is that okay?" she asks.

I grin at her. "That's a great idea. Stay as long as you like."

She nods and places the second earbud in her ear. She jiggles the touchpad on her laptop to wake it up, then starts typing.

"Uh, Boss?" James says, the trepidation evident in his voice.

"Yep. Right," I say to myself. Then, I address the newcomers. "What can I get you this morning, ladies?"

Chapter Seventeen

EMERY

I'M ABSOLUTELY SHAMELESS. I fully know it as soon as I walk in that coffee shop door on Saturday morning. The whole time Trevor is talking to me, I try to resist giving the stink-eye to those tittering idiots across the café with only moderate success. They're just here to check him out. Which is entirely NewsJunkie814's doing, I'm sure of it. Last I checked, half of the four hundred comments were about Trevor. And NewsJunkie814 responded to a lot of those. But considering we are the same person, I only have myself to blame.

What the hell am I even doing? And maybe more importantly, what am I doing *here*, in Trevor's shop, watching him sling lattes and flash his shiny grin at his customers? His almost exclusively women customers.

I try to tell myself at least he has people coming in now. It's not a stream, but there's a steady trickle of them throughout the time I'm there.

I thought coming to the shop this weekend to write would be productive. I thought I'd be able to soak in the ambiance of the space in order to better write about it. That's what I told myself, anyway. That, and the objective truth that his hazelnut lattes are the best I've ever had.

It has absolutely nothing to do with the fact that, ever since he dropped by the office Thursday evening, I haven't been able to stop thinking about how good he smelled as I was standing next to him—all coffee and vanilla and cinnamon. It certainly has nothing to do with the smile he was flashing me in that picture.

I try to get words on the page. I really do. Instead, what I get is an eyeful of Trevor every time I look up. He's wearing his mustard yellow beanie that complements the amber color of his eyes, and a yellow-and-gray plaid shirt, rolled up at the sleeves. I hate myself for noticing any of it.

Three hours later, all I have to show for my efforts is about fifty words on the page and a burning-hot nugget of jealousy in the pit of my stomach.

I really need to get it together.

When I've had about as much as I can handle of watching Trevor smile at giggly women, I snap my laptop shut a little more forcefully than I intend. I slide it into my bag and bring my cup to the bin where people have been depositing their ceramic plates and cups. As soon as I drop it in, James rushes over to bus it to the back room. Trevor watches him with his hands on his hips, then shakes his head slightly.

I chuckle. "Is he avoiding working the register?"

Trevor sighs. "No. He's avoiding making drinks. He's still learning."

"How long has he worked for you?" I ask.

"About five months."

I bark out another laugh, and Trevor smiles at me. This one is different than the smiles I've seen him handing out like candy all day. It's gentler, more genuine.

"Five months and he's still learning?" I'm unable to tear my eyes away from his smile—the way it crinkles around his eyes and creases the corners of his lips into dimples. It feels like a smile that's only for me, and it makes me all tingly.

Trevor slides his hand to the back of his neck to rub it sheepishly. I hate that I know exactly what that spot of soft, short hairs feels like. I hate it even more now I'm thinking about it.

"He may not have been the best person to hire. His mom used to be in my mom's book club, and she begged me to give him a chance."

"Ah," I say. I'm not sure why, but I continue to stand there awkwardly, just looking at him across the room.

His gaze turns earnest as he regards me standing there like an idiot. "Did you get some writing done?" His voice is quieter, caring. It's the voice of a long-term partner asking how my work is going when I come home after a long day.

And that's the exact moment I realize that I wouldn't mind having that in my life. I never felt that with Derek. I always told myself it was because we worked together. He knew how my day was already, so he didn't have to ask. But he never really asked me at work, either. In retrospect, that was probably a big red flag.

I clear my throat. "A little," I say, unwilling to admit more than that. "I was thinking. We should probably exchange phone numbers since we're going to be working together for a few more weeks."

Trevor's face lights up. "Yeah? I mean, yeah. Yes. Here, give me your phone, and I'll enter mine."

I hand it over, trying not to laugh at how excited he is to be exchanging digits. He quickly taps the screen to enter his number, then calls it so he has mine.

"Thanks," I say when he hands my phone back to me. "I'm sorry if I made that awkward. I don't... It's been a while since I've asked someone for their number."

He tilts his head as he looks at me, those gorgeous, amber eyes turning inquisitive. I could look at those eyes all day long. "Why's that?"

I shrug noncommittally. "I tend to stick to myself, mostly. I have my small circle. That's all I need."

"What about guys you meet when you're out?"

I laugh drily. "How it happened with you is how it generally happens all the time. Not that it happens a lot. Just, you know—"

"Emery," he cuts me off gently. "It's okay."

"Okay," I say, almost breathless. How does this man turn me on and make me feel so at ease, all in the same conversation?

He studies me for a moment longer, then squares his shoulders as if he's decided he wants to say something. "I'm surprised one of those guys hasn't made an honest woman out of you yet." He offers a slight, teasing smile.

There's no malice in it. No judgment. Maybe some curiosity, but his open expression is more interested than critical.

His voice reverberates in my mind. *It's okay.*

And, suddenly, it is. I was married once. An "honest woman," as he put it. Now I'm not. Sure, most men who have stuck around long enough to learn this about me have found some fault in it, but there's nothing about Trevor that makes me think he'll be the same.

Besides, we're just working together, right? My other colleagues know about Derek. Why not loop Trevor in?

I huff. "Been there, done that."

I know I shouldn't care what he thinks, but I do. I search his face for any sign of pity or disgust, and all I find is understanding. As if this explains me. And a small, upward tilt of his lips, like he's glad to be in possession of a piece of my history.

I linger in his soft gaze for another moment, but I'm torn out of it when my watch buzzes. "Oh shit. I have an interview in" —I check my watch—"Now, actually. I have to get going." I rush back to the table, grab my bag, and sling it over my shoulder. Just as I'm about to leave, I stop and rifle through my bag for my wallet.

"Crap. You made me like three lattes today, and I never paid you." I'm digging and digging in my bag but coming up empty. "Where the hell is my wallet?"

I dump my bag on the table so I can look through it more easily. I don't notice Trevor coming closer until he's right next to me and his hand is on mine, squeezing. It takes all my effort not to zero in on that slight contact.

His hand is warm and rough, and the skin of his palm is dry from constant hand-washing. It scrapes against the back of my hand and, *dammit*, now I'm remembering the way his hands felt against my hips, between my thighs...

"It's really okay," he says again. The soothing tone of his voice draws my gaze to his. We're almost eye-level, but he makes me feel smaller. Not in an insignificant way, in the way I assume a tinier woman might feel enveloped by the soothing presence of a man much larger than her.

He squeezes my hand again, almost as if he doesn't want to let it go. "You saw all these people in here today. We're talking at least a sixty percent increase of customers, just from your articles. The least I can do is make you a few coffees."

I swallow hard, his hand still on mine. I force a corner of my mouth to tip up casually, and I hope my face doesn't reveal the fact that my stomach is in my throat and a whole horde of butterflies has taken up permanent residence there. "We've been over this," I chide. "You need to stop giving things away for free."

"It's not free," he insists. "It's an exchange."

An exchange for what? For thirst trap photos and an artificially inflated comments section that essentially objectifies him further?

What am I even doing here? I mean, sure, he's hot as hell. And we shared a really amazing night together. But he's off-limits. I might suddenly want someone to talk about my day with, but that doesn't change the fact that my relationship era is over. And even if it wasn't, he's too *nice*. I'm the exploiter who will stir the pot on a meaningless article just to get more clicks.

I shouldn't even try. I'll be a cloud over his sunshine energy. And even if I could ignore that, I need to focus. He needs to focus.

We. All. Need. To. Focus.

But I can't focus with his hand on mine, so I carefully slip it out from underneath him. His eyes widen slightly in embarrassment, as if he forgot he had been touching me the whole time.

I glance in my bag one more time and decide I must have left my wallet at home in my rush to leave this morning. I blow out a frustrated puff of air through my nose. "Well, I suppose I'll have to get you next time. I have no idea where my wallet is, anyway."

"Next time," he repeats, and the way he says it has me looking up at him again.

It sounds like hope.

God, I should stop this now. I should leave here and never come back. I have enough to fill out two more articles. Who cares if I lose this stupid challenge with Randall? At least I won't lose my heart in the process.

But when my eyes meet his again, he smiles that same smile from the picture. The one that lights up his whole face and proves his singular focus on me. Just me. And for a moment, it's like we're the only two people in the shop. We aren't, and that in and of itself is a reminder that I need to keep digging deeper to put this place back on the map.

"Yeah," I breathe. "Next time."

***

I run from the coffee shop to the diner, already late for the interview I scheduled with Donna today. I can't believe I lost track of time. I hate being late, and I especially hate it when it's an interview I scheduled.

Luckily, Donna doesn't seem to care too much. She's set herself up in a booth near the door with a cup of diner coffee. There's one in front of my seat, too, which I push away as surreptitiously as I can once I'm seated.

"No coffee for you today, hun?" Donna asks. I should have known better. She misses nothing.

"I'm good," I tell her as I get my notebook and pen out of my bag. When I look up, she's eyeing me like she doesn't believe me.

"I was working at the coffee shop before I got here," I admit.

She smiles knowingly, her ice-blue eyes twinkling. She pushes back from the table and folds her arms. "Ahh. I never could compete with their coffee." She chuckles. "Never wanted to, actually. There's something about a terrible cup of coffee from a diner that has people all nostalgic or something." She winks at me, and I chuckle.

I set up my notes on a blank page, then tap the end of my pen against it. "I wanted to talk to you because you spoke passionately about the coffee shop the other day when I was in here. I've never heard you mention it before that day, even though I've been coming in here for years. Why's that?"

She turns her gaze upward and takes a deep breath. "Oh, I don't know. When David passed, it hit us pretty hard. Me and my husband, I mean. That shop and this diner are the only two original businesses left in this area. I'm closer to David's father's age than to his, and to see someone so young leave us so soon..." Donna trails off. She looks at me and shrugs as if I can fill in the end of that sentence myself. I can, and I can also tell that she doesn't want to continue, so I switch gears.

"Did you know Trevor's grandfather well?"

"Not terribly well, no. There were a lot of smaller businesses on this block when we opened. The tailor next door, the shoe shop next to that, then a general store..." Her face takes on an expression of nostalgia, and I smile softly at her remembering the good old days. But she moves her hand in front of her face, as if she could wave away the memories like smoke. "Anyway, all those businesses dropped off one-by-one. The buildings are still there, sure, but they're different businesses now. Marko had retired by then, thankfully." She kisses her knuckles and looks skyward, then back to me. "He would have had a fit seeing all those businesses close up shop. But David kept the place open despite these big businesses with their tall buildings cluttering up the block—probably in his father's memory. I stopped in there once or twice at first, just to see if I could help, but he seemed to have everything under control. He had his boy there with him, too. Things seemed fine. Until that big place opened up down the street. I honestly thought he had shut it down and moved on until I heard you talking about it the other day."

"What made you think that?"

Donna shrugs. "Never seemed to be anyone in or out of there."

"Yeah, I suppose that's why we're here." I smirk sarcastically, but Donna just studies me, all seriousness. I start to feel a little squirmy under her scrutiny.

Suddenly, she leans forward, and her intensity has me reeling back. "I read your articles, you know," she says. "Every one of them, since the day you started at *The Gazette*."

I nod. I absolutely do know this. She used to have one of my articles—my very first one from *The Gazette*—framed and hanging above the register, back when she thought for sure I was going to be famous or win a Pulitzer or something. When *The Gazette* downsized, I made her take it down. I'm positive she still has it somewhere. This woman has believed in me unconditionally since Cass, Vi, and I started coming in here a million years ago.

"The ones you write for *Baker's Grove Living* aren't as good." She leans back in her chair again, punctuating the sentence.

"Uh, thanks?" I frown. I came here to talk about the coffee shop and its history in the community, not be chastised for my inability to write a half-decent story.

Donna looks at me like I'm an idiot for not understanding her. "This last one, though. It was better." She says it as if she's spelling it out for a five-year-old. She regards me with a heavy gaze. "What changed?"

I laugh a little nervously. "I'm not here to talk about my writing—"

"I'll tell you what changed," she cuts me off as if I weren't even talking. I slam my lips shut. I'm actually kind of curious about what's coming next. "You've decided to care about this neighborhood." When I start to protest that I've always cared about this place, she waves it away. "Oh, that's not what I mean. I mean you've started to care about this city. Your home. You always thought you were made for bigger and better things, and who knows. Maybe you were. But I could see it in you when you got the job at the magazine. It was beneath you to write about the smaller comings-and-goings of people. But now, suddenly, it's not. You care. Why?"

"Jeez, Donna. I'm here to ask you questions, not the other way around." I don't exactly appreciate the way she's dressing me down, and I'm not quite sure what I did to deserve it.

"It wouldn't have anything to do with that boy, would it?" Now she's smirking at me, and I don't like that, either.

I open and close my mouth a few times, but I don't have words to respond. Eventually, I settle on, "No." Because it doesn't. "My boss gave me this... challenge, I guess. He's going to let me write something I want if this goes viral."

"And what you want to write is something bigger and better than what you're doing now." It's a statement, not a question. She crosses her arms again.

"Better than puppies and coffee? Yes," I snap.

Donna points her finger at me. "You'd do well to acknowledge that these things matter to some people, and they matter a great deal. That boy grew up in that shop. His father owned it, and his grandfather before that. His whole life is tied up in that place, just like mine is here. I'd like to hope someone takes over this diner after I'm gone and saves it from some bulldozer and a shiny new high-rise, but that remains to be seen. Trevor is doing that. He has probably used his own savings to keep that shop afloat for as long as he can. If I were a betting woman, I'd put money on it. Just because something doesn't matter to the whole world, doesn't mean it doesn't matter. And now, it's up to *you* to make that place matter to more people so he can keep his family legacy alive."

"No pressure," I mumble.

Donna dismisses that with a wave of her hand. "You've done harder things." She thinks for a moment, then a wide grin spreads across her face, wrinkling her skin even more in the best possible, joyous way. "You'll have a harder time evading that boy's charm than writing a few more good articles, I bet."

I arch an eyebrow and tap my pen against the table. "Would you put money on that, too?" I ask sarcastically.

Her eyes twinkle with mischief. "I would."

Chapter Eighteen

TREVOR

"UH, BOSS?" JAMES POKES his head through the door to the back office on Monday morning. I'm currently sitting in front of my ancient laptop and between piles of invoices and receipts. My hand is lodged in my hair, gripping it tight as I'm obsessing over a spreadsheet with numbers from the weekend's sales. Better. Not enough, but much better.

When I don't look up, James clears his throat. "There's a pregnant woman here to see you?"

"A what?" I ask, then shake my head to clear it. "James, you shouldn't assume a woman is pregnant."

"She told me she's pregnant," he insists.

"Why would she do that?" I'm not exactly sure why I'm even having this conversation instead of just going out to see what this person wants, but I'm too invested now.

"She said, 'I'm pregnant, and I need a muffin and to talk to Trevor. In that order.'" He looks up and to the left as he punctuates each syllable with a movement of his head as if he's trying to remember exactly what she said to him while he quotes her.

I sigh deeply and release the death grip on my hair. "Did you get her a muffin?" I ask.

"Of course I did," he says, offended.

"Okay." I don't bother reminding him that's not necessarily a given. Instead, I push my way past him and out into the store. Emery's sister is standing smack in the middle of the empty shop, her hands on her hips, and her baby bump protruding almost past her feet. Her eyes dart over every surface of the place, scrutinizing.

"Ah, there you are," she says when she sees me. "Are you ready to get to work?"

I frown and look around the empty shop. "There's no one here," I say.

Her eyebrows squish together, then she shakes her head. "Oh. No. Not that kind of work. I mean you have a grand re-opening event in a few weeks, and we need to get you ready."

I stare at her as if I wasn't standing in that exact same spot just a few days ago, looking at this place in almost the same way she is. "Do you have any experience in this?"

"No," she says slowly. "But I've watched a lot of restaurant makeover shows."

I tick up an eyebrow. "You can't be serious."

She narrows her eyes at me as if I'm clueless. "Of course I'm not serious. I mean, yeah, I've watched a lot of those shows, but I'm an investment manager. My job is dealing with money. You want to make money, right?"

"That would be nice," I say.

"Good. So, let's get to work." She plops herself down into a chair near the door where a muffin has been placed for her. "I'm going to need your profit and loss statements for the past year, and a cost breakdown of all your current menu items." I turn to leave, but she calls after me. "Oh, and I asked your employee for a half-caff iced mocha, too, but he's nowhere to be found. What's up with that?"

I face her slowly. "I'll get that for you right away."

"Why can't he do it?" Cass is incredibly imposing in a sweet and unsuspecting way, and I feel like she's drilling holes into my brain by the way she's regarding me. It feels a lot like being scrutinized by her sister, and the reminder of Emery has me feeling lightheaded for a moment.

"Uh..." I start, trying to regain my bearings. Probably no use lying to her. "It's complicated. He's good at a lot of things, but making specialty drinks isn't really one of them."

"What types of things is he good at?" She tears a piece off her muffin and pops it into her mouth. When I just stare at her, she nods. "Right. We will remedy that, too."

"I won't fire him," I say, suddenly defensive. "I believe he can be taught. I just haven't had a reason to teach him."

"Well, you have a reason now." She circles her hand in the air, as if to hurry me up. "Coffee, please. And statements."

Shit. She's so much like her sister, and I suddenly wish Emery was here. "Yes, ma'am." I salute good-naturedly, and she laughs as she takes another bite of her muffin.

I get started on her drink first, assuming that she is going to need some sustenance before looking at my bloody loss statements. She said "profit and loss," but, let's face it: there hasn't been a profit to speak of in a long time.

As I'm pumping mocha syrup into a cup, the bell over the door rings. I look up just as Emery walks in. She stops short when she notices her sister sitting right in front of her. Cass has turned around, but I can see just enough of her face to see that she is trying—not very hard—to hide a wicked grin.

"What are you doing here?" Emery demands. She looks beyond pissed. I guess I kind of assumed Emery sent her here, but it seems they hadn't discussed it. I pour in some espresso and decide to stay as far out of it as I can.

"I'm here to help. What are *you* doing here?" Cass doesn't sound angry. She sounds like she's holding back a laugh.

Emery's nostrils flare ever so slightly. "I'm here to write. How do you possibly think you can help?"

Cass scoffs. "I'm an investment manager. I know money. Trevor is trying to make money. Frankly, I'm offended you didn't ask me to help before now."

"I didn't ask you to help *now*." Emery looks as if she would give anything to fall right down into the floor.

"Well, I'm here. So, Trevor," she addresses me, as I stir the drink with a reusable straw, the ice clinking against the glass a little louder than necessary. "Statements?"

"Coming right up," I say as I step out from behind the counter to deliver the drink to her.

I quickly make my way to the back office. When I enter, James looks up at me, then he glances over my shoulder, his eyes growing huge. I turn around slowly to find Emery right behind me. I straighten up and pray to all that is holy that my hair isn't a rat's nest from all the grabbing it I was doing earlier. Her eyes flick upward to my hairline, and her cheeks color ever so slightly. It must be a mess, then. I busy myself by stacking some of the papers on the desk. I snap the laptop shut and add that to the pile for good measure.

Emery composes herself quickly as I avoid looking at her. "You're not going to let Cass do this, are you?"

"James, can you watch the front, please?" I ask without looking at either of them. He rushes out of the office, seemingly all too happy to escape whatever is about to happen. "Do what? Help?" I ask as soon as James is gone. I don't mean to sound bitter, but it comes across that way. I shrug, trying to lighten up a bit. "Yeah, I guess. I could use it, honestly."

When I finally look at her, she looks taken aback. "Are you…" she trails off, then stands straighter, tugging at the bottom of her cropped blouse. *She's nervous*, I think. What does she possibly have to be nervous about?

"Are you okay?" I ask, frowning softly.

"I don't like my sister in my business," she says unconvincingly.

I take a step toward her without even thinking about it. "Since when is this 'your business?'" I emphasize the words, my eyes not leaving hers. Dammit, I could drown in those warm, brown depths. I couldn't look away if I wanted to. And I don't want to.

"Since I have a vested interest in the success of this place."

"The success of your articles, you mean," I say quietly, taking another step.

She shakes her head. "If you succeed, I succeed." It's almost a whisper. She can't seem to tear her eyes away from mine, either. I can't say I'm mad about it.

"It's okay to admit you care about m—" I stop before I can say "me," but I'm dying to say it. Now that she's here again, and now that she's been so embarrassed to be caught by her sister coming to work in the shop, I have a sneaking suspicion she isn't coming here only for the ambiance. I want so desperately for that to be true. I want her lips on mine again, my hands tangled in her silky hair. Right now, I want to take three more steps and be pressed up against her, begging her to dive in with me again. "This place," I say instead before swallowing hard.

Her gaze slowly trails down to my lips. She lingers there, desire unmistakable in her shallow breathing.

Holy shit. She's thinking the same thing I am. I'm sure of it. My heart soars, and in that moment, I would give anything to kiss her. I'd even call off this whole project and walk away from this shop if it means I could be with her.

And, for a minute, I'm considering it. Until she says, "I talked to Donna on Saturday."

The shift in conversation throws me. I tilt my head, pinching my eyebrows together, trying to place the name. "Donna?"

"From the diner," she explains. "She says she knew your family. That your business is almost as old as hers, and she insists it matters to the neighborhood. I thought about it all weekend. She's right. So, yeah, I guess I care."

I clear my throat. "About the business."

She nods curtly and tugs at her blouse again. "Yes. About the business." I'm starting to think that tugging at her blouse and fidgeting with things is her tell that she's either lying or uncomfortable, but I let it go. That tiniest glimmer of hope from when she looked at me the way she just did is enough for now. I can certainly work with hope. I've been existing on hope for years.

"Okay then." I turn abruptly to get the papers and laptop off the desk. I feel more than hear Emery let out a long breath. When I try to leave, papers in hand, she's still blocking the door. She stands there, looking a little dumbfounded, until I indicate that I need to get around her. Instead of moving to the side, she turns on her heel and stalks out into the shop.

Her cucumber scent trails behind her, and I take an extra second to breathe it in. Even mixed with the overwhelming smell of coffee, it's refreshing.

I hold my breath to try and calm my racing heart. It helps a little, but it occurs to me that I'm falling a little more for this woman each time she's near me.

And all I want is to be near her more often.

So get out there, you idiot, I tell myself. I push open the door and make my way back out into the shop.

Emery has selected a table far away from her sister. Cass is glancing at her out of the corner of her eye. When she sees me, she chuckles darkly in the way of someone observant enough to know exactly what was said in the office just a moment ago.

Though, part of me thinks she doesn't have to be all that observant to figure it out.

Cass waves at the seat across from her. "Emery is going to pout in the corner while she pretends we're not here. She'll probably write all of twenty words before leaving in a huff of frustration. We might as well chat."

I glance over to Emery, but Cass says, "Don't worry. She has her earbuds in. She can't hear us." She lowers her voice and barely moves her lips when she adds, "Unless she's just pretending to listen to music. We'll find out soon enough."

"Okay," I say slowly as I slide into the chair and place the stack of papers between us.

She shuffles through them for a few agonizing minutes before she finally says, "I want you to know that I took the liberty of putting out feelers for investors for this place. I hope you don't mind, but it seemed like a logical next step." From the deep breath she takes at the end of that sentence, I know better than to get my hopes up. "But it seems no one is willing to take a chance on an old shop without a new plan. I'm sorry."

"It's okay," I assure her. "I've tried to get loans a few times, too. No one wants to take on a failing business. I get it."

Cass nods sharply, her lips pursed to the side. "That doesn't mean we can't get it there. It just means it's going to be harder." She picks up the papers and starts rifling through them again before glancing up at me. "You've been sinking personal money into this place." She's not asking, but I nod anyway. "Right. Okay. You're going to stop doing that right now."

I start to protest, but she glares at me, and I quickly snap my mouth shut. Damn, she's got the mom look down already.

Emery chuckles from her spot near the window. Cass shoots me a knowing look before she swivels around to scowl at her. Emery schools her face to seriousness. I get the sense this is an old song and dance between these two and resolve to stay out of it.

"If you're going to eavesdrop, you might as well come over here and make yourself useful," Cass challenges.

"I am being useful. I'm writing these articles to get people in the door, remember?" Emery points at her computer screen.

Cass turns back to the papers as she says, loud enough to be heard, "I think that photographer has gotten more people in the door than either of those articles." When no one responds, she raises her voice slightly. "Hotness is not a sustainable growth plan."

"I can hear you, you know." Emery sounds exasperated, but there's an edge to it. Like she's embarrassed of her articles, too, or she doesn't like being called out.

Cass rolls her eyes dramatically. "How many words did you get down in the past few minutes?"

Emery glowers at her sister without saying anything. James takes a few quiet steps toward the office door, but Cass snaps her attention to him next. "Oh, no you don't. You're going to start earning your paycheck here, too. No more dead weight."

"Damn, Cass. He's just a kid," Emery protests.

"Like I said," Cass addresses her sister. "You're welcome to help at any time."

Emery sighs and takes out her earbuds before snapping her laptop shut. "What do you need me to do?"

"Well, I need to go over these statements and come up with some kind of plan." She eyes me with a pensive look, and it makes me inexplicably nervous. "Your menu is... pretty basic."

"My grandfather insisted we never change the actual menu, though we do offer things off-menu, as you've seen. He never could understand giant coffees and to-go cups," I say sheepishly. I'm not embarrassed of him, exactly, but I'm starting to see that his refusal to change in any official capacity might be what got us into this mess in the first place.

"Right." She drags the word out as she gives Emery a sidelong glance. "You've seen an uptick in customers this weekend, I heard."

I try to ignore the excitement bubbling up at the knowledge these two were talking about me. "We have," I confirm.

"And have any of them ordered anything directly off the menu?" Cass raises her eyebrow.

I take a second to think, then deflate again. "Not many."

"Right," Cass says again, more forcefully this time. "Let's give the menu a little update then, yeah?"

Emery scoffs from her seat. "If I know you, nothing about this is going to be 'little.'"

"One or two signature drinks should do it, especially if they're unique. Something that big place down the street isn't offering. For now, at least. And thank you for volunteering to help him, Em!" Cass exclaims with fake enthusiasm. "I'm sure you're both just bursting with ideas."

Emery frowns, the creases between her brows deepening. "What the hell do I know about coffee?"

"Uh," I say, trying to get between these two before we stumble any further into whatever sibling thing is going on here. "I do have some ideas, actually. I'd love a taste-tester?" I direct the question to Emery, who immediately softens. "I mean, if you want. I've gotten the impression you like coffee."

"Sure." She straightens in her seat. "Yeah, I can do that."

I stand, suddenly nervous. I feel like a goddamn schoolboy trying to impress a girl on the playground, but when our eyes meet across the room, I grin. "Perfect."

Cass snorts, effectively breaking the moment. "Get a room, you two."

Emery's head whips in her sister's direction. "Cassandra Darlis," she hisses.

Cass rolls her eyes again. "Fine. Seriously, though, can you both go... somewhere else? I need to talk to..." she trails off, indicating James, who has been watching this entire exchange looking like a deer in headlights.

He points at himself, then looks behind him as if hoping to find someone else standing there. Cass nods, clearly irritated.

"Uh, this is James," I say by way of introduction since he's clearly not going to do it himself.

"James. Come sit," Cass says. I wince sympathetically at him as he comes around the counter to sit down by Cass. Poor kid.

I drag a chair over to the counter from one of the high-top tables and motion for Emery to sit. She carries her laptop and bag over and slides onto it, leaning her elbows against the countertop and putting her chin on the palm of her hand. I take a deep breath and force myself to think about something else—anything else—besides how breathtaking she is in her blouse, her black hair falling straight past her shoulders and her dark eyes trained expectantly on me.

"Allergies," I blurt out. She frowns, and I cough. "Do you have any allergies? Anything you can't stand the taste of?"

She shakes her head. "I'll put pretty much anything in my mouth," she says.

I just about choke on my own saliva, and she goes completely still. "Shit," she says. "I didn't mean that—"

I can't hold back my laughter. "No, no. I understand what you meant," I assure her, though my dick seems to have other ideas as I feel it press uncomfortably against my jeans. I grab an apron and quickly tie it around my waist.

"Iced or hot?" I ask, gathering cups and ingredients from under the counter.

"I feel like if I say 'hot' now, it'll sound like some kind of innuendo." She's teasing. I know she is. And *fuck*, it's sexy as hell to see her loosen up like this.

Should I tease her back? I want to, but I definitely don't want to push too hard. When I risk a glance at her, though, she's smiling this beautiful, radiant grin and her eyes are sparkling.

"Oh, I don't know," I say playfully, leaning closer and lowering my voice so Cass and James can't hear. "I've heard of some tricks people do with ice cubes, too."

She barks out a surprised laugh, and her hands fly to her mouth. "Will you not?" she whispers.

"You started it." I wink. But before I can start making the drinks for her, two young women come through the door, giggling and scanning the shop as if they're looking for someone. When they see me, their expressions turn playful, but they compose themselves enough to walk to the counter.

It almost pains me to have to look away from Emery, but I suppose paying customers deserve some attention, too. "Good morning, ladies. What can I get started for you?"

"Hi," one says dreamily. "Can I get a medium nonfat latte with three pumps of mocha?"

"Sure thing," I say, punching that into the register. Thank god my father updated this thing after Dida retired, because there's no way

I'd be able to handle these orders that have been coming in otherwise. "Anything else?"

"I'll have a large nonfat extra dry cappuccino with four sugars, please," the other woman says shyly.

I process their payment and get started on their drinks as they select a table with a clear view of the counter. I avoid looking at Emery because I know what her face will say: these orders are bonkers. She's not wrong, but I suppose in the age of the big coffee shops, I'll have to be able to make them to keep up. It almost seems wrong to make them on my grandfather's original espresso machine, but I tell myself he wouldn't mind so much if he knew it was keeping this place afloat.

I deliver the drinks to the two newcomers. They bat their eyelashes at me, so I shoot them a friendly grin for good measure, though I know it's strained. Something about their attention doesn't sit well with me, and when I catch Emery's eye on my way back to make the drinks for her to taste, I realize it's entirely because she's here. There's not a woman in the world who can hold a candle to her, and I have zero interest in even pretending to flirt with some twenty-somethings who are coming in to ogle me because of some pictures on the internet.

I could swear a look of apology flashes over Emery's face when I make my way back around the counter, but it's gone too soon for me to be sure. I get started on her drinks without thinking much about it.

I decide to make two of them iced and two hot for some variety. I set them in front of her in a very specific order. The first is a straight shot of espresso, just for fun. The second two are iced—a matcha latte with cucumber syrup and a coconut and banana latte. The last drink is a hot honey lavender latte with cinnamon and oat milk. I've topped that one with a lavender whipped cream I've been playing with in my ample free time.

"I want you to try them in this order," I say.

"Why?" she asks, narrowing her eyes at me in suspicion.

I lower my voice again. "Trust me," I say. When she looks at me dubiously, I change tactics. "Just do as you're told, then."

At that, she visibly shivers, and my jeans grow tight again.

So, she likes a little dirty talk. I don't know if I'll ever have a shot with this woman again, but I file that tidbit of information away for later.

She eyes the first, tiny cup as she clears her throat. "Espresso?" she asks. "I assumed you'd be a little more creative than that."

"There's plenty of creative drinks in that lineup," I assure her. My voice goes softer when I say, "That espresso is exactly how my dida used to drink it. I wanted you to try it."

She tilts her head in the way I've learned signals she's going to ask a question. "How do you drink your coffee?"

I huff, waving at the cup of espresso in front of her. "Usually like this," I say through a sudden emotion that sticks to the words in my throat. "Like he taught me."

Her entire expression changes as she registers the importance of what I'm sharing. It's like she lets the words settle into her. She lifts the tiny cup of espresso to her lips and takes a sip. "Oh wow." Her eyebrows raise. "That's actually really good."

"You don't have to act so surprised," I tease.

"I've never had straight espresso before."

I run a hand over the old machine behind me on the counter, then lift the corner of my mouth in a teasing grin. "I'm proud to have been your first."

"You are insufferable," she groans, but her cheeks flush again. Jackpot.

She wastes no time bringing the straw from the second cup to her lips. A soon as she takes a drink, her eyes flutter closed. "Cucumber," she breathes. "I love cucumber." And *fuck me*, she licks her lips.

"I had a feeling you might," I say.

She eyes me up and down, then grabs her phone to snap a picture of the drink. "Do you have social media accounts?" she asks.

"Yeah, but I'm really bad at updating them," I say.

Cass must have been listening, because she points at James and says, "You're young. How are you on social media?"

"My band's page has over six thousand followers." He's clearly proud of this fact.

"He's in a band?" Emery mouths to me. I shrug. I had no idea.

"Perfect," Cass says. "You're the new social media manager for the shop. Trevor, give him the login info, please." When I don't immediately move, she adds, "Now."

"Better do as you're told," Emery murmurs. I stumble over my next step on my way to type in the login information for James.

As she chuckles behind me, I know, without a doubt, that this woman will be the end of me.

Chapter Nineteen

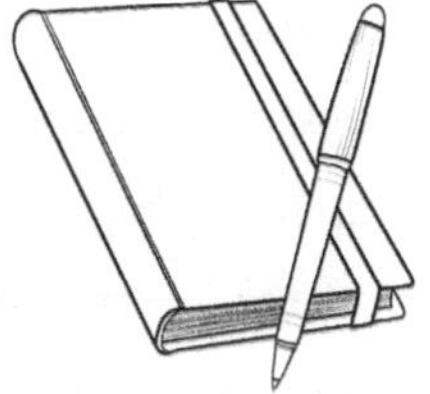

EMERY

ONE OF THE WOMEN who walked in earlier is now clearly checking out Trevor's ass, and I hate it. So, I know that when I tell him he'd better do as he's told, I'm stepping way over the boundary I set for myself, but I really can't bring myself to care.

And I take absolute delight in the way he stumbles when he hears it.

I'm awful. I know I am. But he is, too. He said the same thing to me not two minutes ago, and the flood of warmth to my core has me thinking he just unlocked a brand-new kink. Even when he's not teasing me, I can practically feel the heat of his gaze. Any time he looks at me, it's as if he and I are locked in some kind of vice that's squeezing us together.

That's not the only thing squeezing together, I note as I press my inner thighs against each other to relieve some of the pressure that's been steadily gathering there since I was here on Saturday. My vibrator wasn't even able to take the edge off this weekend.

Dammit, I need to get laid. And not by Trevor. No, that would be a very bad idea. I can't get any more involved with him than I already am without tipping dangerously over into relationship territory. Not to mention, these articles might suffer, and so will his shop. I'm already having trouble writing them, and judging by the giggling gals who have been coming in here for a few days now, I'm thinking anything that damages his single image is going to also damage his emerging brand.

No. I definitely need to find someone else to fixate on, and fast.

I stand quickly, almost knocking over one of the cups on the counter in my haste to shove my laptop in my bag.

"Where are you rushing off to?" Trevor asks. He's smirking, which only makes his godly cheekbones stand out more. His arms are folded over his chest, giving me an excellent view of both his pecs stretching his shirt and his forearms, bare to the world like some kind of softcore porn and—fuck—get me out of here.

"I, uh... I have this article to write, and I feel like I'm not going to get anything done here with Cass the Enforcer hanging around, so..." I shrug helplessly.

"You haven't tried the other two drinks yet." He deflates a bit, and he looks so much like a puppy I need to leave at home when I go to work that my heart skips a few beats in my chest.

This is why I need to *go*. And, incidentally, why I've never gotten a puppy. Which I told him the night we met, and the memory of that has me going all gooey inside. Again.

But he's right. I promised I'd taste test, and I haven't, so I slink back into my seat and grab the other iced cup. I take a sip and scrunch up my nose. "That tastes like a piña colada."

Trevor laughs as he comes to stand on the opposite side of the counter as me again. "I wasn't sure if you'd like that one. It's an iced coconut banana oat milk latte." He fills a glass with water and sets it in front of me. "To wash out the taste, if you need."

I shake my head. "It's not bad. It's just not my thing."

"Oh, I love piña coladas!" one of the newcomers exclaims. Trevor fights a smirk that seems to say, *Of course she does*. I have to look away from him to keep from laughing. "Can I have one of those?" she asks.

"Of course," he says, and it's laced with the tiniest bit of sarcasm. I catch it, though, so I take a quick sip of water to keep myself from falling out of my chair.

Trevor makes another drink like the one in front of me and delivers it to their table as I finish the water. He told me to try these drinks in this specific order, so there must be a reason. I want to wait until I have his attention again to try the last one. When he comes back, I tick up an eyebrow at him.

"This last one looks a little frilly," I say skeptically, swirling a finger in the whipped cream topping.

He hums. "I took a risk with that one," he admits.

"The piña colada wasn't a risk?"

"I figured someone would like it, even if it wasn't you." He barely resists glancing over at the table where the two women are trading sips of their drinks and cooing over them. Loudly.

I tip my head to him in concession. He certainly wasn't wrong. "Okay," I say. "So, what's special about this one, then?"

"It's special because it's for you." His voice is low and raspy, and the warning bells are starting to ring in my brain. They're telling me to get out of here before I find something else to fall for about this man, but the way the edges of his eyes crinkle at me again has me pinned to my seat.

"Why's that?" I manage to ask, though my voice is barely a whisper.

He runs a hand along the back of his neck as if he's embarrassed to say it, but his eyes don't leave mine. "Well, you always order hazelnut lattes. That tells me you like some flavor, but not too much. Sweet, but not too sweet. It's kind of a soft flavor, though it's edgier than a basic vanilla. Unique, in a way, but not flashy."

"This is definitely flashy," I wipe the whipped cream off on a napkin. Licking it off my finger feels a step too far given I'm pretty sure we have an audience. The whole shop has gone quiet aside from the soft, folksy music that's always playing.

"Just try it," he urges.

I bring the cup to my lips and breathe in. A soothing, floral scent greets me before my tongue darts out to taste the whipped cream and the coffee underneath.

"Oh," I breathe, setting the cup down carefully. "This is amazing." I wipe my lips with the back of my hand, ensuring there's nothing lingering there to embarrass me. "What is it?"

"It's a honey lavender latte with oat milk and cinnamon and lavender-infused whipped cream. I thought you might like it. It's floral, so not at all like hazelnut, but the honey adds a little earthy sweetness." He shrugs, as if that can't clearly express exactly what he was trying to do, but he also isn't sure how to convey whatever it is he's trying to say.

"It's wonderful," I assure him. And then, because my stupid heart doesn't know what's good for it, I say, "It's maybe my favorite drink I've ever had."

"We'll talk about the cost-effectiveness of having all those ingredients just lying around later," Cass mumbles. A smile stretches slowly across Trevor's face, twisting one corner of his mouth up a little more than the other, the imperfection making his features even more attractive without trying.

I can't look away. But I have to. Those warning bells are sounding at full blast. I take another sip of the lavender latte for lack of something better to do, but that's perfect, too. And it's something he did just for me. Because he thought I'd like it. I can't escape him right now, and I need to.

"That one, for sure," I say, pointing at the latte. I glance at Cass, whose eyebrows are pinched together slightly in concern. Now, I need to get out of here before she outs me for my inability to keep it together around this man. "Actually, can he afford to do all of them?"

"Can he afford not to?" Cass asks. "He needs something to set him apart from the competition. We'll just have to figure out what we can take off the menu to make room for the cost of ingredients."

"I'd come here solely for the piña colada latte," one of the other women chirps.

I throw my bag over my shoulder, then tug the bottom of my blouse back down, cursing how short it is. That'll show me for trying to be stylish. "Well, there you go. You're a latte genius, Trevor." I circle a finger in the air. "Add them all to the menu. I have to get going, but I'm glad to have been able to help. See you all... soon." And with that, I'm out the door before anyone can stop me.

Once outside, I take a deep breath of the humid, summer air. It's still before noon, but it's already hot and sticky outside, and the sun is beating on the downtown pavement. I'm wearing silk, and I don't want to get it all sweaty, but I opt to walk back to the magazine office anyway to clear my head. I have an article to write, and even though I'm positive Ethan and Josie will give me crap for going to the shop instead of coming in this morning, it's worth it to have some quiet time to work. And to not have Trevor hanging out in my field of vision all day.

Chapter Twenty

TREVOR

I STARE AT THE door Emery just ran out of until Cass clears her throat pointedly, which draws me out of my stupor. I wince in her direction, which is when I realize she's looking at me with a healthy dose of sympathy.

We stare at each other in silence for a second before the two young women who came in earlier take their lattes and leave in a flourish of giggles, their heads bent over one of their phones.

The whole energy in the place has shifted, and I'm not sure why. I'd say maybe it's the absence of the other women, but I fear it's me. I feel completely dejected.

James seems engrossed in his own phone, probably working on editing our social media profiles. I never could figure those out. Cass is still regarding me over his head as she chews on the side of her mouth. The scrutiny is starting to make me uncomfortable.

"What?" I ask.

She averts her eyes. "Nothing."

"Okay." I draw the word out as I start to clear away Emery's cups. I try very hard not to think about the fact that her lips were just pressed against their edges as I rinse them in the sink, but I run my thumb over a lipstick stain on one anyway.

I must be lost in my own thoughts again because I jump about a mile when I turn around and Cass is about a foot from me, leaning her elbows on the counter.

"I know you've got it bad for my sister." Her tone is matter-of-fact, though I think I detect some teasing.

I sputter a little, then raise my arms away from my sides in a shrug and let them fall. No point in denying it anymore, I suppose. She wouldn't believe me anyway.

She hums, propping her chin in her palm. "While I'd love to see her with someone again, you might be fighting a lost cause." Her eyes widen slightly as if she hadn't meant to say that, but she recovers quickly.

I don't want to show my hand, so I shrug a shoulder. I'm curious to see where this goes. If she hadn't meant to let it slip that Emery had been with someone seriously before, then she must not know Emery already told me—albeit briefly—about what I gather is a past marriage.

I sweep a hand to indicate the entirety of the shop we're standing in. "I'm a sucker for a lost cause, I guess."

She narrows her eyes as if sizing me up. "That's... it? That's all you have to say about this?"

"Doesn't seem like there's much else to say." I lower my voice, teasing as I lean forward on the counter across from her and meet her gaze head-on. "You'd love to see her with someone *again*," I emphasize the word, and she presses her mouth into a slit. "And you think it's not going to happen. Agree to disagree." I wink.

She circles a long, manicured finger in my direction. "Your charm doesn't work on me, young man. I'm not interested in you like some of the other people who have been in and out of here lately." She tilts her head and shifts her gaze to the side as if something just occurred to her.

I decide to press forward. "I know you care about her a great deal," I try. Her gaze snaps back to mine, and she bristles. I think I struck a chord, but maybe it's enough to crack this code. "And *I* know *you* know that I care about her, too. So why don't you tell me whatever it is you clearly want to say."

She suddenly goes languid, yawns, and rubs her protruding belly. "She's thirty-seven, Trevor. She's got some baggage, is all." Her air of nonchalance is forced. Her movements are stiff, and her voice is a bit robotic.

I regard her for another moment, but she's studying the counter in front of her like it's the most interesting thing she's ever seen. Her hand rests on her belly in a reminder not to mess with the pregnant woman.

Fine. She's won this round, I suppose. From what I have seen so far, she's stubborn as hell, and I'm not desperate enough to beg, especially because I think I already know what she's holding back. I grab the nearest dish towel and start wiping down the counter next to the sink unnecessarily.

"Well, I'm definitely not going tell you now," Cass taunts.

Oh, she wants to play? Well, two can play this game. I continue to wordlessly shine the counter.

"Anyone who wants to be part of Emery's life needs to try a little harder than *that*," she continues to provoke me, but I'm not taking the bait. I throw the towel over my shoulder and start reorganizing bags of coffee beans, my back still to her.

That's all it takes for her to groan theatrically. "Okay, fine," she says in exasperation. I try not to grin at having gotten Cass to give in so easily. "She got divorced five years ago."

I face her again. My turn to show my cards. "I know."

Her eyebrows lift, and the hand on her belly goes rigid. "What do you mean you know?"

"She told me when she was in here Saturday. I made a crack about someone making an honest woman out of her, and she said she'd been there."

"That's… huh." Cass chews at her bottom lip, her brow deeply furrowed.

"What?"

"That's so *unlike* her. She's deeply private. I don't think you fully realize the lengths she'll go to avoid telling anyone about her divorce."

I take a deep, satisfied breath. I had a feeling she was trusting me with a piece of her when she told me, and I was right. But Cass is still gnawing at her lip and staring at me.

"Isn't it a good thing she told me?" I ask.

"She never tells anyone because people make such a big deal about it. She hates that."

I shrug a shoulder and lay my palms flat on the counter. I'm determined to make her understand the truth in what I'm saying. "It's not a big deal to me." When her teeth still don't release her bottom lip, I continue. "You said yourself I have it bad for her. I won't deny it. A divorce isn't going to change that."

She laughs humorlessly. "She might have told you, but my guess is she bolted right after that." She raises her eyebrow and waits for me to confirm, which I do. "Right. So good luck proving to her that it doesn't bother you. She's practically made a career out of avoiding relationships since she left him. And no, I'm not going to tell you why," she adds before I can ask. "You'll have to get the full story from her when she's ready to share it. I was trying to save you from heartbreak, but it seems you're determined on that count."

"Would you want anything less for your sister?" I ask, half-teasing.

But she's all seriousness when she shakes her head. "No. I want that and so much more for her." She eyes me up and down, one corner of her mouth tipping up. "But that's a good start."

Chapter Twenty-One

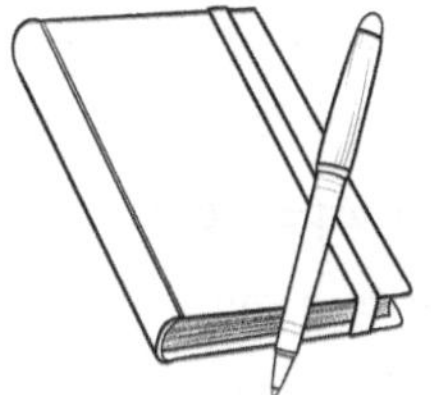

EMERY

TREVOR HAS ME PEGGED with lavender and cucumber and whispered innuendo. So much so that I run out of his shop feeling vulnerable and raw. Who knew coffee could make someone feel so *seen?* I'm entirely cracked open, and I don't like it. Those drinks feel distinctly like relationship drinks. His amber eyes dragging themselves over my face, lingering on my mouth or the curve of my jaw feel distinctly like relationship eyes. His raspy voice feels distinctly like a relationship voice.

It's special because it's for you.

This has gone entirely too far. I'm not a relationship person. Not anymore.

I mean, sure, I've thought about getting serious with someone else at times, but it's easier this way. No risk, no heartache, no husband and job and parents vanishing into midair in the span of a few months. No broken pieces to pick up. No heart to stitch back together. No life in shambles to try to rebuild.

But if that's true, then why do I feel like I want to crawl out of my own skin? My clothes are all itchy and too tight. Even when I try to sleep at night, I wake up with the comforter kicked onto the floor because everything feels so hot.

By Wednesday, I have the beginnings of a draft going—finally—after staring at the monitor in my cubicle for hours. It took a while for me to find the angle I wanted, but I am leaning heavily on my conversation with Donna and the community aspect of the shop. I want to couple it with the cultural history Trevor told me when we first met. I've made a few notes where I need to ask Trevor for some more history—and not just because I want to see him again. Which I do, even though I shouldn't. But I have to. For the article.

My phone buzzes next to my monitor. I glance down at it to see a message from Cass. It's when my phone buzzes three more times in rapid succession that I realize I haven't talked to her since we were in the shop on Monday, which is unusual for us. My pulse picks up with each urgent vibration until I push forward in my seat and grab the phone.

> Cass: Hi.

> Cass: So.

> Cass: This is awkward.

> Cass: Are you there? I don't want to text this to an empty room.

My body goes cold and my stomach drops. This isn't like her at all, and for a moment, I'm sure something is wrong with her or the baby. I type rapidly, letting autocorrect fix mistakes in my wake.

> Emery: Are you okay? What's wrong? Is it the baby?

> Cass: Oh. Shit. Sorry. I'm fine. Baby's fine.

I breathe a shaky sigh of relief and press my hand to my chest as the dots appear at the bottom of the screen, signaling she's typing again.

> Cass: I actually wanted to make sure you're okay? Vi told me to leave you alone about it, but we all know I don't leave you alone about anything.

> Emery: Leave me alone about what?

The three dots appear and disappear at the bottom of the screen a few times while I watch, frowning. Finally, her message comes through.

> Cass: It's a really long story, but Trevor and I got to talking and he said you told him about Derek.

My body goes cold again, but this time with barely suppressed rage at them talking about me behind my back. About things that are nobody's business but my own.

> Emery: How did that even come up?

> Cass: Like I said, long story. I haven't heard from you since Monday, so I had to check in.

> Emery: I'm fine. Momentary lapse in judgment. But I definitely don't love you talking to him about me.

I've mostly been too wrapped up in my own thoughts about Trevor, but she doesn't need to know that. Luckily, she messages again quickly.

> **Cass: Can I blame the pregnancy for my lack of judgment?**

> **Emery: No.**

> **Cass: That's fair. I'm really sorry.**

I slam my eyes shut and pinch the bridge of my nose. I take in a deep breath, letting the stale newsroom air expand my chest and slow my heart rate as much as it can. I stretch my neck back and forth as I try to recover from the whiplash of so many strong emotions. Cass is always a little chaotic, but this is next level.

After a few deep breaths, my head feels clearer. I'm not actually angry at her. My divorce is an objective fact about me, and I had already decided to share that with Trevor. She didn't know that, but she was probably only trying to help. She knows I hate it when people find out and look at me all sympathetically. The tilted heads, the drooped shoulders, the sad smiles, the raised eyebrows. All because he cheated. I don't need people's pity. And I certainly don't need them thinking anything is wrong with me for not being able to stay married longer than a couple of years. My parents have voiced that particular opinion enough.

But the fact that she was talking to him like he's my boyfriend or something is a clear sign that things have gone way too far. If the past two days are any indication, I'm more interested in him than I should be, and now the next time I see him, I'll have to worry about all of this all over again, and my panties will instantly dry up. Cass did me a favor.

Hoping this is a natural end to the conversation, I return my phone to my desk and try to focus my thoughts back on my draft. But despite everything I've told myself, a small tug of disappointment pulls at me that I'm about to bring whatever this is with Trevor to a crashing halt. It's not that I ever thought it could go anywhere. It couldn't. I am who I am, and he is who he is. And yet, his shop has started to become a balm to my soul in a way. Maybe he has, too.

I shake my head violently. Nope. Not going there. Time to get to work. I decide it's a good idea to grab the links to the shop's social media accounts, since they're now under new management. Though I chuckle quietly to myself at the idea of James' band. That bit of information sure explained a piece about him. I bet he's great at stuff he's passionate about and can't get the hang of the rest. It would make working in a coffee shop pretty difficult for him if that's the case. Maybe he can find his footing working Trevor's social media. That would be good for both of them.

Derek used to be like that. He'd spend hours upon hours poring over his writing. When it came time to pay the bills, though, he would always fail at the more menial jobs we needed for the money before we were both hired at *The Gazette*. After that, he flourished. We both did, even if he had to work a bit harder at it than I did. He never quite got over how easy it was for me to write the words, then leave the office. I always figured an editor was going to tear it apart anyway, so why spend hours trying to find the perfect words only to be disappointed when the editor changed everything you loved? But he insisted, saying it was better to have passion about something than treat everything as coldly as I did.

To me, it was just a job. One I loved, but a job, nonetheless. There are more important things than work. Or, at least, I thought that way when I assumed there was no possible way I'd ever leave *The Gazette*. Joke's on me, I guess, because he's still there, and I'm not.

And, on top of it all, when my parents found out Derek wasn't laid off, they used it as ammo for their litany of reasons why I should be thankful a man like him wanted to be with a woman like me. Without a job, husband, or kids, I was useless—their word, not mine.

I try not to think about it very often. Because it still hurts when I do.

Randall's office door swings open, and he saunters out. He catches my eye and nods briefly. "Darlis," he says. "Looking forward to this week's article." There's no malice or sarcasm in his statement. He even kind of smiles at me. It's so jarring, I don't know what to do but nod back.

Maybe Trevor was right. Maybe coffee really will help soften him up.

Against my better judgment, I click out of the shop's website and over to Derek's byline. I scroll through a few of the headlines. It's all his typical stuff—mostly political reporting. When we were together, I took a cursory interest in the nitty-gritty of politics because I felt I had to for his benefit. Not that he ever bothered to take an interest in my features. Now, I pay attention to politics as much as any good citizen should. Certainly more than the average citizen *does*, anyway. But it's always a relief when I can scroll past the analysis of the latest ruling of the State Supreme Court and the like, as I'm doing now.

"I don't know why you do that to yourself." Ethan's voice startles me out of my thoughts. I quickly minimize the window as if he hadn't seen its incriminating contents. He's standing behind me, holding a mug of something steaming. From here, it smells like chamomile.

I sigh. "I'm a glutton for punishment lately, I guess."

Ethan tilts his head, regarding me sadly. "What's going on, Em?"

"I don't know." I bury my face in my hands, then drag them down my face. The pressure of my palms feels good against my skin. "Believe it or not, I liked being married, you know? Maybe not to that prick, but in general."

Ethan leans over me to set his mug on my desk, then grabs a chair from an empty cubicle and pulls it up. He leans his elbows on his thighs and presses his hands together between them. He looks every inch his usual therapist role in his tailored slacks, vest, and glasses. I almost want to laugh.

"What is bringing this on?" he asks, and the transition to therapist is complete.

"I don't know."

He eyes me warily. "I think you do."

"I suppose you have a theory." I cock an eyebrow at him. "If you're going to suggest that this is because I'm now working with my one-night stand—"

"I'm not suggesting it," he protests. "You're suggesting it."

"I'm not marrying Trevor." My voice is flat as I try to convey how ridiculous it sounds. I'm not some middle school girl with a crush, doodling his name on my notebooks. He's hot. And funny. And really sweet. We slept together once. I need to get my hormones under control. End of story. "I'm not marrying anyone ever again," I say quieter. And I hear it, then. How sad I sound.

It sounded much more determined and logical in my head.

Ethan sighs deeply, his expression going thoughtful. It's not piteous. He knows how much I hate that. But he's known me long enough to know the whole story. How Derek systematically worked to make me feel as if I were cold and heartless. How he eventually cheated on me. How I left him feeling sad, sure, but every bit the empowered woman who wasn't going to stand for that shit. And then, a few weeks later, I was laid off as part of *The Gazette's* downsizing, even though Derek was not.

I wanted that marriage to work, despite seeing the writing on the wall probably earlier than I was willing to admit. I knew I wasn't cold or heartless, but I wanted *him* to see it, too. Desperately. Turns out, he was probably trying to make himself feel better about the cheating.

That particular joke's on him, though. I have one thing I absolutely will not tolerate in any relationship, and that's infidelity. I left his ass as soon as he came clean to me. Cass and Vi graciously cut him out of their wedding photos that night while we all got drunk on cheap wine and ate ice cream out of the carton.

Of course, none of that mattered to my parents when it was all said and done. They were so disappointed. When the layoffs came shortly after, they couldn't even look me in the eye the next time I saw them. I'm a big girl; I certainly don't need their approval, but it would have been nice to have their support.

No way am I chancing that again. Nope. And as I remember the giggling yoga girls streaming into his shop this weekend, I know without a doubt that I need to shut this down right now. My resolve is complete. I'm not opening my heart to the resident neighborhood hottie. Too many opportunities for heartbreak.

Even if it's my comments on that article that have been coaxing them through the doors. I almost laugh at the irony of it all—I've all but sabotaged my own feelings.

God, what a mess.

Ethan pulls in a deep breath through his nose and leans back in his chair. He gives me a sad smile, as if he knows exactly where my mind went. And, who knows, he might. He's never met Derek, but him, Josie, and I became very close, very fast when I started working here. He knows enough to know exactly how I feel about the whole thing.

"Only you know what you need," he says. "But it's not against the rules to open yourself up again."

"It's against *my* rules," I say quickly.

Ethan chuckles as he stands, lifting his mug from my desk. "Well, your rules are shit, so best of luck with that," he says as he starts to make his way back to his own cubicle.

"Stellar advice, as usual," I call after him, laying on the sarcasm. He doesn't answer, so I'm left to grumble all alone as I scoot my chair back toward my computer, which is still showing the social media pages for the coffee shop.

I stare blankly, trying to remember what I was going to do with that besides stalk it for pictures of Trevor. No, definitely not that. Links. I'm after links. What is wrong with me?

I highlight and copy the first link. It looks like there are some recent photos up, but what catches my eye is a new pinned post of Trevor at the top of the page. It's the same picture from the second article: Trevor in all his glory, his forearms on display and his brilliant smile directed at something off camera.

Not some*thing*. Some*one*. Me. It's the same look he directed at me all Monday, and seeing it in front of me again brings that too-tight, crawl-out-of-my-skin feeling right back.

I bury my face in my hands, careful not to groan too loudly. I do not need to explain all of this to Ethan, who I know can hear me on the other side of the thin cubicle wall.

The problem isn't necessarily that I'm embarrassed by how he keeps looking at me. The problem is that I like it. Way too much.

This has gone far enough. I need to get him out of my mind as fast I possibly can. I snatch my phone off the desk and open up a text message to Vi.

Emery: Going out tonight. Need a wingwoman. Geezer at 8?

Vi: It's Wednesday.

Emery: And?

Vi: You're right. Who cares? See you there.

I click my phone off, then shut down my computer, too. I need to go see what hot wardrobe items I can scrounge up because tonight, my plan is to let someone else—anyone else—help me get Trevor out of my head.

Chapter Twenty-Two

TREVOR

FOR TWO DAYS AFTER Cass leaves, I wait for word from either her or Emery, though none comes. Cass tasked me with developing a new menu and had said she'd come back with a plan. She had told James to document the process, take pictures of the food and drinks, and post daily videos to grow our follower count. It seems like a good plan, even if I can't wrap my head around social media in general.

Thankfully, James seems eager to get started, immediately pulling out his phone and setting up for pictures when he's back in the shop on Wednesday. I start making drinks, and James snaps action shots of me the whole time. I wish I had seen this untapped potential in him earlier. But, I suppose, what's done is done. Onward.

"Is this really necessary?" I ask, grimacing as he gets the phone too close to my face for my comfort.

He shrugs. "We don't have to if you don't want to, but those ladies sure seem to like looking at you."

I eye him sidelong and press my lips together as I make up another batch of lavender-infused whipped cream. I wish we had some actual lavender flowers to use as props for these photos. I add that to the growing mental list of things to buy. And to add to my budget report for Cass.

James stops taking pictures and backs away from me. "I get it. You don't want to be the front man."

"The what?" I ask as I shake up the whipped cream dispenser.

"The front man," he repeats. "Our lead singer is the perfect front man. He likes being in the spotlight. I prefer being in the background. That's why I play the bass. No one notices the bass. Until it's gone, that is." He pushes some of his curly hair out of his eyes.

"Why haven't you mentioned your band before?" I swirl the whipped cream on top of the purple mug I selected for this particular picture. A little on the nose, but without lavender flowers, it'll have to do.

James shrugs. "I don't really like to mix my two worlds, you know what I mean?"

I do know what he means. I wish I didn't. Right now, Emery doesn't want to mix our two worlds, either. She wants to keep our relationship firmly in the work hemisphere, even though I'm having trouble keeping things on this side of strictly professional. With the way she was talking to me the other day, I don't know how much longer I can stay the course. Never mind that we pretty thoroughly crossed that line before we started this whole scheme.

The thought of Emery has me pondering all I've learned about her past relationship. I want to be a part of her life, and this feels like something I need to get right. But I don't have time to contemplate that further. James is tapping the side of the phone impatiently and holding it up, ready to take pictures.

I slide the mug toward him, and he sets it up so the café is visible in the background. He walks around it, taking a few pictures. I squeeze a bit of whipped cream out on my finger and taste it. It's pretty good, if I do say so myself, but the sight of it triggers the memory of Emery with the same whipped cream on her finger, and me praying she was going to lick it off.

She didn't. It was probably for the best, but I can't say I wasn't disappointed.

The bell over the door chimes, and I look up to see Mike walking into the shop, his arms spread wide.

"Hey!" he exclaims. "You've had customers!"

"We have." I grin at him. "It was a good weekend, actually."

"And there has been a rush the past few mornings," James pipes up from where he's taking pictures.

"I wouldn't call that a rush." I frown. Though, I suppose I can see why James would. Having any kind of line makes him nervous. "But we had maybe ten or twelve people in here yesterday morning."

"That's great!" Mike exclaims again, his voice booming throughout the empty space. I'm not sure why he always feels the need to be so loud. "We need to celebrate."

"Uh," I start, looking around. "I mean, I guess this weekend—"

"Not this weekend," he interrupts, his tone suggesting I'm an absolute idiot. "Tonight."

I screw up my face. This man has lost his mind. "It's Wednesday," I explain slowly.

He walks over and claps me on the back. "So what? A drink or two won't keep you from waking up for the morning rush." When I continue to frown at him, he grips my shoulder. "You have to celebrate the small wins. It keeps you positive."

"According to you, I don't need help staying positive," I say drily.

"I'll pick you up at eight." He claps my shoulder again, effectively shoving me a step backward. "Drinks are on me."

***

I groan and slam my head against the head reast as Mike pulls his sports car up to the curb near The Tipsy Geezer.

"No," I say.

"No what?" he asks, as if he doesn't know.

"The last time we came here, it set this whole runaway train in motion. I'm not interested in revisiting that." Not to mention that, if I run into her again, I still have no idea what to say after talking to Cass.

Mike rolls his eyes. "It's a chill place. You liked it here last time. I picked it specifically for you."

I give him a condescending smile. "It's unlike you to be so thoughtful."

He presses his hand to his chest and drops his jaw. "I'm offended. This is your night, man! We're celebrating you. I wasn't going to take you to some dance club or something."

I raise an eyebrow. He absolutely would take me to a dance club even if it is my night, and he knows it. He's done it before.

He grumbles something unintelligible, then tips his head back. "I really was trying to take you somewhere you'd like, but if you want to hit up somewhere else, it's fine. I have ideas of other places we could go."

Mike's idea of a good time is loud and flashy, so I am positive I will not enjoy these other places at all. The Tipsy Geezer might be where I met Emery last time, but what are the odds she's here again, in the middle of the week, no less? I don't think karma is going to try to taunt me with the sight of her.

I let out a long exhale. "Fine. Let's go in."

Mike lets out a small whoop. He pushes his door open and jumps out before I have the chance to change my mind. I exit the car a little more slowly, trying not to grunt as I push myself up from the low seat.

When we get inside, we pause to look for a table. It's not packed, though there are more people here than I'd expect for a Wednesday. Not that I'd know with my limited frame of reference. Mike starts to make his way to an empty table toward the back, but my eyes snag on a few people sitting at the bar. Namely, the blue-black hair glinting in the low pendant lights hanging above her, and a flash of a red blouse.

I close my eyes and open them, but I'm not imagining it. Emery is sitting at the bar, her profile visible as she leans her cheek on her palm. I must have pissed karma off more than I thought.

Violet is sitting next to her, chatting with the bartender. It seems weird that she wouldn't be chatting with her friend, until I notice Emery's body is tilted slightly away from Violet and toward a tall, dark-haired man with tortoise shell glasses standing next to her chair.

Oh, hell no.

Mike appears back at my side. "Hello? Where'd you go?"

I'm still staring at Emery, trying to decide if I want to interrupt her conversation with Marty McGlasses.

Who am I kidding? Of course I want to interrupt their conversation. I just don't know if I should. Or how.

Mike chuckles darkly. I slowly slide my gaze to him.

He raises his hands, palms out. "I swear, I had no idea she'd be here. I mean, I hoped she would, for your sake, but I didn't know."

I don't respond. Instead, I look back to where she's sitting. She tips her head back and laughs at something McGlasses says to her. My stomach drops. I've never made her laugh like that. And now I desperately want to.

She reaches out and touches his arm, and that's it. I've seen enough. Time to go. Except what if McGlasses makes a move she doesn't like? I should stay. Just to be sure.

I turn on my heel and march straight to an empty table at the back of the bar. I slide into the shadowy booth where I can watch her, hopefully without her seeing me.

Mike slides across from me. "You're not going to let that guy take her home, are you?"

The very thought of it has my hands clenching and unclenching beneath the table. "If she wants to, there's not much I can do about it," I say through gritted teeth.

"Bro, she doesn't want to." He nods in their direction. "Look at her. That smile is fake. And check out her friend. She keeps shaking her head like she can't believe his douchebaggery."

I watch them for a second, and sure enough, Violet rolls her head back as if McGlasses has exasperated her beyond whatever tolerance she had left.

"How did you see that from all the way over here?" I ask.

Mike flashes a roguish grin. "It will probably shock you to know that I am used to getting that exact look from women."

I eye him sidelong. "It does not shock me in the least."

He shrugs. "Well, I don't know about you, but I could use a beer, and it seems the place is understaffed tonight." He stares at me pointedly, his eyebrows raised as if he's waiting for me to catch on. When I continue to frown at him, he takes some cash out of his pocket and leans in further, offering it to me. "Why don't you go grab us a few drinks at the bar?"

I shake my head slowly. "I don't think I should go over there. I can't guarantee I won't physically move that guy to the other side of the room."

"Dang, Trev. You're wound tight tonight. Relax, man. She doesn't want him. Go over there and get us some beers, casually say hi to your new friend, and see what happens. It would be rude not to at least say hello, and I can almost guarantee that once she sees a better option, she'll ditch that guy real quick."

I eye him warily, but he has a point. What's the harm in saying hi to a friend in a bar? It would be weird if I didn't.

He presses his cash into my palm as I slide out of the booth and take a second to roll some of the tension out of my shoulders. Mike is right; I am wound up tonight. I need to play it cool, or I'm going to scare her off for good. I take a deep breath and let it out before making my way to the bar.

I sidle up on the other side of Violet. When she notices me, I nod in greeting. A slow, mischievous smile stretches across her face as her eyes light up like things finally got interesting. I suppose they have.

"Well, hello there, Trevor," she says a touch too loud. Emery snatches her hand off McGlasses' arm and whirls her head around, her eyes wide and her ruby-red lips parted. I would claim those lips right now if I could.

"Hey, Violet." I try to keep the strain out of my voice, though I'm glad for the music and the noise of the bar to cover up the edge I feel creeping its way into my words. "Emery." I nod at her. I completely ignore McGlasses. I'm not interested in knowing anything about him. I'm only interested in him going away.

The bartender comes over, and I place my order, all the while aware of Emery's eyes on me.

"What are you doing here?" she asks. McGlasses shifts pointedly behind her, brushing his arm up against her back. She ignores it, her eyes searching mine instead.

"Mike insisted on celebrating the shop's moderate success tonight. I'm here to get us some drinks and wanted to say hi." I drop the cash on the bar as the bartender comes back over with our beers. "Keep the change," I tell him, then turn back to Emery. Her gaze is intense, her pupils dilated enough to make her already dark eyes seem completely black, even despite McGlasses clearly shuffling to try to get her attention back on him. Mike might actually be right. She doesn't seem to have any interest in him at all now that I'm here.

Amusement is practically radiating off of Violet, but I try not to seem overconfident as I take one glass in each hand. "Have a good night, ladies. I'm sure I'll see you later this week."

I try to walk as casually as I can back to the table. I make Mike switch with me so I don't have to look at Emery and that asshole while I finish this drink, which I resolve to do as quickly as possible so I can get the hell out of here.

Mike looks over my shoulder. "I'd ask how it went, but I think it went pretty well."

"What makes you say that?" I ask sullenly into my beer.

"She's headed over here right now." He stands from the table and takes his beer with him. "Good luck, buddy," he mutters, clapping my back. He greets Emery, then walks toward the bar.

She flops into the booth across from me, and her knees brush against mine as she slides further into her seat. To my surprise, she makes no move to break the contact, though her cheeks turn a pretty shade of pink. She drags her bottom lip through her teeth, smudging her red lipstick slightly. I wish it were my lips messing up her lipstick. My dick goes hard at the thought.

I take what I hope is a laid-back sip of my drink. "Hey," I say, and immediately do a mental facepalm. That's the best I could think of to say?

"Hi," she returns. Her brows pinch together ever so slightly. "Do you want me to leave? I don't want to interrupt your guys' night."

I huff, carefully setting my drink down on the table. She left that guy to come over here to talk to me, and the realization makes me bold. "Emery, I'm surprised you haven't figured out that I never want you to leave."

Her cheeks flush darker, but she doesn't protest. That's a good sign.

She rubs her palms together, which is when I notice she doesn't have a drink. But before I can offer to get her one, she blurts out, "I know you and Cass were talking about me."

I study her for a moment before I nod. "We were."

Her throat works against a hard swallow. "Aren't you going to say anything about it?" she asks quietly, and I think I hear some trepidation in her voice. She must have been working up to this question.

"What's there to say? You were married. Now you're not, which *you* more or less told me. Right?"

"Right." She drags the word out slowly. She takes a sharp breath in. "It's just that... well, most guys press for more information. You didn't. And they have this look when they find out."

"What look?"

"I don't know." She shrugs tightly and looks down at the table, as if she's uncomfortable in her own skin. "Like they feel bad for me, or there's something wrong with me."

I press my knee into hers, and she snaps her gaze back to mine. She seems to settle into it.

"Do you miss him?" I ask gently.

"Hell no," she answers quickly, then chuckles as if she's amused at her own speedy response. "No. He and I were not good together."

"Then there's nothing to feel bad about." I shift my leg, so my shin presses up against hers. I lean in and drop my voice an octave. "And there's definitely nothing wrong with you."

She gasps and her eyelids flutter. She looks equal parts turned on and relieved by my response. Her leg rubs against mine under the table as she eyes me playfully. I don't think I've played footsie with a girl since middle school, but fuck, that's hot.

Emery flashes a coy smile that tells me she knows exactly what she's doing. And it looks as if she likes it as much as I do.

That is when I'm certain I'm taking her home with me again tonight.

"I thought you wanted to keep things professional," I practically growl.

"I don't care about professional anymore," she whispers.

"What about Glasses over there?" I tilt my head toward where she was sitting at the bar.

She hums as her foot, which she must have slid out of her sandal, brushes up my leg. "Funny story," she breathes. "I was here to find a guy so I could stop thinking about you."

She bites her bottom lip again as her eyes ask a question. I'm not sure what the question is, but whatever she wants, the answer is yes.

"And you think Glasses was going to help with that?"

She hesitates, swallowing hard. "No," she says. "I don't think anyone could."

Her eyes find mine again, and she smiles self-consciously. God, she is so beautiful.

I take a breath, emboldened enough to ask her if she wants to get out of here when a man lumbers up behind her, leaning in to get a good look at her face. "Emery, is that you?"

She stiffens, and her eyes go wide. She slides back away from me, removing her legs from where they touched mine. I'm immediately cold in her absence.

What is with the douchebags here tonight? Is it a full moon or something?

"That *is* you," he slurs, then plops himself into the booth next to her, sloshing his beer over the side of his full glass.

That's when he notices me. He sticks out a beer-glazed hand and says, "Hey, man. I'm Derek, Emery's ex-husband."

Chapter Twenty-Three

EMERY

Fucking Derek.

He is absolutely not supposed to be here. I ran into him here once about a year after our divorce, which is when I demanded that this was my place first, and he needed to stop coming here. He threw his hands up and shouted this place was a dive anyway on his way out. I haven't seen him since.

Just being near him is making my skin crawl. He's clearly been drinking, and now I'm trapped in this booth with him blocking my only exit. I send up a silent prayer that Trevor won't leave me here with him.

Derek must realize Trevor isn't going to shake his hand because he retracts it and wipes it on his jeans. Trevor leans back and folds his arms, eyeing him up and down and clearly finding him wanting.

"What are you doing here?" I grind out. I don't know why, but I need Trevor to know this isn't a regular occurrence. I try to catch his eye across the table, but his gaze is trained on Derek. He's not shooting daggers, exactly, but he does not look happy.

"We were bar hopping. I thought it might be fun to visit the old haunt, you know?" he says, leaning over the table to box Trevor out of the conversation. It only serves to box me in.

I swallow heavily. "You were bar hopping on a Wednesday night?"

He shrugs, which effectively brushes his arm against mine. My lip curls of its own accord. This contact is unwelcome, and entirely different from the heat Trevor's leg gave me a few minutes ago.

"*You're* here on a Wednesday," he points out.

"I'm not drunk. I'm having an after-work drink with a friend." I indicate Trevor, who leans forward. His eyes haven't left Derek, and I would pay a million dollars to find out what he's thinking right now.

A few minutes ago, I was positive I was giving this a shot with him. I couldn't hold out any longer as my leg pressed up against his in the most sensual game of footsie I've ever played. Now, I'm not sure if he's going to run away or start a bar fight. Or, worse, if he's judging me for my obviously poor taste in men.

"I'm not drunk either, baby," Derek says. Trevor stiffens. I try not to gag.

"You only ever called me 'baby' when you'd had too much to drink," I mutter. Derek doesn't seem to have heard me, but Trevor's gaze flashes to mine. I try to send a telepathic apology, but he furrows his brow. His foot finds mine under the table with a reassuring tap.

He's not going anywhere. I'm more comforted by that than I expected to be. I give him a small, tense smile. The one he returns is soothing and genuine, and that previous warmth creeps back into my belly.

"I'm surprised you're out tonight." Derek obviously hasn't gotten the hint that no one wants him here. "I could never get you to do anything on a weeknight when we were together."

I scoff. "I was a different person then." I'm saying this for Trevor's benefit. I desperately hope he understands.

Derek leans in even closer to me, backing me into the corner of the booth. I hate how my shoulders are hunched as if I'm cowering, but I have no choice if I want to keep him from touching me.

"You were cold as fuck," he sneers. I can smell the liquor on his breath.

"Hey, man," Trevor's voice is placating. "What are you after?"

Derek snorts and turns away from me to face Trevor. He hooks his thumb in my direction and chuckles, suddenly chummy. "She was so cold, I'm surprised her pussy wasn't ice." He laughs heartily at his own joke.

Trevor's eyes darken as he stares Derek down. "Felt plenty warm to me," he says.

I gasp. Trevor flinches ever so slightly as if he didn't mean to say that aloud, but he quickly directs his attention to me. He flashes me his brilliant smile. I should be completely insulted by the way he defended me, but between the physical contact and this new confidence I'm seeing in him, my panties are soaked.

"What do you say, srećo?" he asks gently. "Should we get out of here?"

"Yes," I breathe. I clear my throat and try again. "Yes," I repeat with more solidity. I turn to Derek. "Move."

Derek is stunned silent, his eyes bouncing back and forth between us. He slides out of the booth, and I'm finally free. I waste no time standing. Trevor is right behind me, his hand protectively on my lower back. I lean into it as we start walking toward the door. Trevor signals to where Mike and Vi are chatting at the bar. Vi sees us and smirks, then looks behind us and spots Derek. She's out of her bar stool and on her way to me in half a second. Mike is on her tail, though I imagine he's pretty clueless.

Trevor doesn't rush me, but I can tell from the firm pressure he's placing on my back that he wants out. We are out the door quickly with our friends on our heels.

"What was that asshole doing at your bar?" Violet asks in a huff.

I pinch the bridge of my nose, trying to regain some control of my breathing. "I don't know, but he was drunk and embarrassing."

"Ew," Violet grimaces.

"What are we talking about?" Mike chimes in.

"I'll explain later," Trevor assures him. His hand hasn't moved from my lower back, and I like it. A lot. He steps into my line of vision, blocking out everyone else. He doesn't break contact when he drags his hand to my upper arm and gives it a gentle squeeze. He leans forward, searching my eyes. "Are you okay?"

I huff. "Yeah. Nothing I haven't heard before."

"That's a damn crime."

I shrug. All I can do right now is bask in the warmth of his intense focus.

"Do you want to go home?" he asks. "I can take you home if you want."

Home? So I can sit and replay the whole encounter on repeat in my head while tossing and turning alone in my bed? No. I do not want that. I shake my head.

He looks around as if taking stock of our surroundings. "Let's—"

The door opens behind us, and Derek stumbles out. He pauses when he sees us standing there, and an ugly sneer stretches slowly across his face.

"Friend, huh?" he asks. He walks over and claps Trevor on the shoulder as if they've been best friends for years. Trevor's control snaps as he violently shrugs him off.

"Let me save you some time," Derek continues, unfazed by Trevor's seething. "She's a pretty one, but if you're looking for someone to warm your bed, I'd look elsewhere."

"Back the fuck off, man," Trevor grits out.

"You seem like a nice guy." Derek tries to put his hand on Trevor's shoulder again, but he sidesteps, and Derek stumbles a step forward.

"Don't touch me," Trevor warns. He raises his hands, palms out.

"Whatever. Listen, I'm just looking out for you," Derek insists.

A muscle in Trevor's jaw ticks. "I'm a big boy. I can make my own choices, thanks." He turns to me, his amber eyes darkening in a different way. "Ready to go?" he asks me.

"Yes, please." I try not to go weak at Trevor's gentle treatment of me. I want to kiss him so badly—for the way he's looking at me now, for the way he defended me in the bar, for the way he doesn't seem to care about Derek. But I am not doing that in front of my ex.

I scoff at Derek, who has his arms folded and is wearing a scowl. "Go home and sober up. No one likes a sloppy drunk."

"No one likes *you*," Derek spits out. It's a stupid comeback, and I bark a laugh at the childishness of it, but before I can tell him so, he reaches out and grabs Trevor's shoulder again.

Trevor spins around, brushing Derek's hand off his shoulder, then uses both his hands to push Derek squarely in the chest. "Don't touch me," he grinds out as he pulls his hands backward in a clear I-don't-want-to-fight-you motion. But drunk Derek loses his balance and falls straight on his ass.

Trevor backs another step away with his hands still raised. "I don't want to start anything, man, but you can't talk to her like that."

Everyone else seems frozen for a second. Violet wears a smug grin. Mike looks like he's never been prouder. I'm not exactly sure what to feel, but I know I'm gaping at the scene.

Trevor turns toward me and puts his hand on my back, trying to lead me away. I all but fall back into his touch, happy to let him take me wherever he wants, but before we can get too far, Derek scrambles to his feet and grabs Trevor's shirt, effectively whipping him backwards and away from me. Trevor manages to spin and shove Derek off of him again, but Derek is ready for it this time and is able to stay on his feet.

"Back off," Trevor grits out, but Derek was never one to listen to reason. He runs at Trevor, barreling into his torso and landing a couple of hard punches to Trevor's ribs as the two men fall to the ground. Trevor grunts a few times as the punches land, and I wince at the sound of flesh meeting flesh.

Before I know it, Trevor flips Derek over and lands a punch right on Derek's jaw. Derek cries out as his arms fly up to cover his face, but Trevor doesn't seem to be making any more moves.

I've never seen a bar fight before, so I'm not really sure what to do. Luckily, Violet and Mike take the break in the action to jump in. Mike grabs Trevor under his arms and heaves him off Derek. Derek jumps to his feet looking like he's going to attack again. Vi stands in front of him, arms out to try to back him away.

Derek throws his head back and cackles. "She's a damn ice queen," he jeers. "Surely, you've noticed no one in her life but this bitch"—he throws a hand at Vi, who blocks it—"can stick around more than a couple years."

Trevor almost charges forward again at that, but Mike grabs his shoulders and drags him away.

"He's not worth it, buddy," Mike says in Trevor's ear. "Walk away."

"*She's* worth it," Trevor shouts. My heart wants to beat out of my chest. Somehow, even in the midst of Derek's absurd reminder that so many people have left me in the dust, Trevor's words mean more. I want to crash my lips to his and show him exactly what it means to hear that

I'm worth it, but while these two are both still foaming at the mouth, it isn't the time.

"I'm pressing charges!" Derek yells over Vi's outstretched arm. "You shoved me, you prick."

"I'm getting you out of here before the cops show up," Mike tells Trevor as he pushes him into the passenger seat of what must be his car parked nearby. Mike closes the door on Trevor's protests and jogs around to the driver's seat to start the car. He drives away quickly.

"That asshole shoved me first. I want his information, Emery. Give it to me, now!" Derek is pressing his hand against a bloody gash on his cheekbone.

I whirl on him. "Get a grip!" I scream. "Why can't you leave me alone? Or act like a grown man? We've been split for five years! Go home to Erika and get out of my life!" I don't like to think about the woman he cheated on me with, and I spit out her name with all the disdain I feel.

"Well, joke's on you because Erika dumped me." His sarcasm falls flat.

"She finally saw you for your manipulative ways?" Vi sneers.

"Fuck you," Derek seethes.

"Stop it, both of you!" I shout. "I don't need to know how much you hate me every time I see you, Derek. Grow the fuck up. Drink some water, and do not come back here again."

"I'm pressing charges!" he repeats.

"The hell you are," I say through clenched teeth. I take a few steps toward him, pointing my finger in his face. "You're lucky I don't do the same to you for harassment. Now *leave*."

He sputters for a moment, then sharply juts out his chin. "Fine. I'm leaving. But because I have a job to do in the morning, not because you told me to." He curls his lip. "A real job, unlike yours."

I stare at him flatly, unphased. "Good one. Get out of my sight."

Derek spits on the ground at my feet and turns his back on us, walking away. Violet looks like she's ready to land a punch, too, but I shoot her a warning glare. We stand there in silence until we're sure he's long gone.

Violet lets out a low whistle. "Well, that was more excitement than I was expecting tonight." She runs a hand through her hair. "You okay, Em?"

"Yeah." I take in a sharp breath. "Trevor said I was worth all that."

"He did," Violet confirms.

"I should..." I trail off, looking toward the direction Mike drove.

"He probably took Trevor home, would be my guess," Violet says suggestively. "He's going to be in a world of hurt in an hour or so."

I nod slowly. His place isn't that far, and I remember exactly how to get there. "I'll call you later, okay?"

Violet's smile is wide and knowing as I turn on my heel and start walking in the direction of Trevor's apartment.

Chapter Twenty-Four

TREVOR

MIKE PEELS OUT OF his parking spot so fast, I'm surprised his tires don't squeal on the road.

"We shouldn't leave her alone with that asshole." I uselessly twist in my seat to look behind us, but they're well out of view.

"She's not alone. Violet is with her." Mike chuckles darkly. "I have a feeling that woman could land more punches than you. Besides, the last thing you need is someone calling the cops."

I grumble something incoherent. I don't like it, but he has a point. I shake out my right hand, pumping it open and closed a few times. I rub my knuckles, which causes me to suck in a breath through my teeth. "That fucking hurt," I announce.

Mike chuckles. "You've never punched a guy before?"

"You know I haven't." I wiggle my fingers, hoping to relieve some of the pain.

"Well, that's not the only thing that's going to hurt once the adrenaline wears off. That guy landed some punches before we stepped in. What was his deal?" Mike turns the corner onto my street.

"That was Emery's ex-husband," I say.

Mike whistles. "Glad he's an ex. What a douche."

"Yeah." I can already feel soreness starting to creep into my ribs. I shift in my seat and rub at a spot on my side. I wince. "I don't think he broke anything," I mutter.

"Nah, he didn't have a chance. But you're going to want some ibuprofen and ice pretty much immediately."

I eye him sidelong as he parallel parks in front of my building. "You sound like you're saying this from experience."

He shrugs. "I go out a lot. Put a bunch of guys in a bar, and it's bound to happen occasionally. You want me to come up? Tend to your wounds?"

"Don't patronize me." I grimace again as I shift to unclip my seatbelt.

"I'm not. I'm proud of you. That was epic." Mike slowly bobs his head at the memory of the fight.

"Felt more stupid than epic," I grumble.

"Fights like that always do. It's not like in the movies," he assures me.

I stare over the dashboard at the yellow streetlight. It flickers a few times before it brightens slightly. "Do you think she thought it was stupid?"

"Probably. A girl like that isn't going to swoon over misplaced chivalry," he muses.

I deflate. "A *woman* like that doesn't need me to defend her honor." I wince again at the pain in my side. It's growing sharper by the minute. "He had her cornered in that booth. She looked like she was folding into herself as he insulted her. After watching her with that other guy when we first got there... I don't know. Something snapped."

The leather seat squeaks as Mike shifts toward me. "I don't think she'll hate you if that's what you're worried about. The way she was looking at you outside would suggest she was trying not to swoon. I think you should get inside, get some meds, ice, and sleep. And then you should talk to her in the morning. Communication, bro. Solves a lot of problems."

I shoot him an incredulous look. "What do you know about communication?"

He scoffs, offended. "I'm an excellent communicator. Now, get out of here. I'll stop by the shop tomorrow."

As much as I hate to admit it, he's probably right. I open my door and carefully swing my legs out. I grab the edge of the door to heave myself up, and it doesn't hurt as bad as I was expecting. This feels promising.

I close the door and wave to Mike as he pulls out into the street and disappears around the corner. I try to sigh, but expanding my chest brings the ache back to my ribs. "Shit," I say sharply. Meds, ice, sleep. It seems like sound advice, so I pull open the door to my building and make my way upstairs.

Once inside my tiny apartment, I down some pain medicine and search for a bag of frozen peas or something. That's what people use for bruises, isn't it? But I don't eat peas, so I don't have any. I don't think frozen broccoli has the same effect, and I'm pretty sure the food would be spoiled if I used it as an ice pack, so I grab a handful of ice and wrap it in a towel instead.

I strip down to my boxers and check out my side. It's purpling already, but it doesn't look too bad. I get settled on my bed and press the towel of ice against my skin. It almost immediately starts to get wet as the ice melts, but I don't want to get up again, so I let it seep through the towel. I'll leave it on for a few minutes and dump it before my sheets get soaked.

As soon as I'm finally comfortable, a knock sounds at my door. I freeze. Oh, shit. Is that asshole really pressing charges? Would the police come to my door that quickly? Am I about to be arrested?

The knock sounds again, more urgent this time, which springs me to action. I grab my jeans and throw them on, and then remember the towel of ice. Maybe if I hold it against my bruise, they'll take pity on me and skip the handcuffs. Is that a thing that happens? I wouldn't know.

I start to take a fortifying breath before opening the door, but then I remember it's going to hurt to breathe deeply, so I stop myself. I press the ice to my side and try to look as innocent as possible as I pull the door open.

But it's not the cops on the other side of the door. It's Emery. Her black hair is falling over her shoulder, her dark eyes are wide, and she looks uncertain. She's holding a six pack of beer in one hand and a plastic grocery bag in the other.

Her gaze travels down my face and over my bare torso, and she clears her throat. When she notices the ice I'm holding, she winces.

"Peas," she says.

"What?"

"Peas," she repeats, holding the plastic grocery bag out to me. "I think they're better than ice. Less cold and wet."

"You brought me peas?" I ask, pursing my lips against a smile. This might be the cutest thing a woman has ever done for me.

"Well, yeah. I didn't know if you had any. Is that weird? I'm kind of new to this physically-defending-my-honor thing."

I can't fight the smile anymore. I let it spread wide across my face and thank my lucky stars I didn't get punched in the jaw so I can still smile at my Emery.

My Emery.

Is she mine? She might not know it yet, but if she's bringing me frozen peas after my very first bar fight—a fight about her, no less—she's definitely going to be.

I remind myself to play it cool. She's here, and I don't want her to run away again. "I don't have any peas, and I think you're right. They are better. Though I'm pretty new to this, too." I chuckle, but wince quickly as my side starts to hurt. "It's not an experience I plan to repeat."

Her face hardens again. A little crease appears between her eyebrows, and she looks fierce. It's the most adorable thing I've ever seen.

"Yes. Good. I do not need you or anyone else to stand up to my slimy ex for me. I've handled him before, and I'll handle him again."

I try to reflect her seriousness. I really do. But I'm thrilled she's here, and she's so captivating, standing there. I fear my happiness is written all over my face. "Noted. Should I apologize for punching him?"

She tilts her head, considering. "Are you sorry?"

"Not particularly," I say drily.

That's when she lets a little smile escape, and I have to fight not to run my thumb over it.

"Good," she says. "I'm not sorry either."

Well, that solves one problem. I'm glad she doesn't hate me after that primal display. Next problem: how to get her inside my apartment. I nod toward the beer in her other hand. "You brought beer, too?"

She shifts on her feet, uncertain again. "Oh. Yeah. I felt bad you didn't get to finish yours, so..." She holds it out to me, and I take it in my free hand.

No time like the present to shoot my shot, I guess. "Do you want to come in and have one with me?"

"Oh, um..." She slides her weight to the other foot, then seems to realize she's still holding the bag of peas. She sets that on the ground just inside the door. I catch a whiff of her cucumber shampoo and inhale it deeply, pain be damned. It's worth it. As she straightens, her gaze snags on my bare chest again. She swallows heavily as she shakes her head. "No, I'd better go."

I try to be understanding, even as my heart falls. I'm sure this evening has been much more than she bargained for, and we probably all need some time to process. But I don't hide my disappointment when I say, "Okay, srećo. Thanks for the peas. I guess I'll see you... soon."

She blinks a few times, nods, and turns to leave. I'm sure I detect some regret in the shuffle of her feet, and the knowledge of that will have to be enough for now. I shut the door quietly behind her.

I take the frozen peas out of the grocery bag and discard my now-sopping towel in the sink. I'm hit by a sudden wave of exhaustion. That towel will have to be tomorrow's problem.

A knock sounds at the door again. Maybe it really is the cops this time, but I don't even care. Emery came to see me, and that's enough to carry me through a lot worse.

I open the door again and am beyond relieved to see Emery standing there. Her red lips are swollen like she's been biting them, and her cheeks are pink. She looks flustered and unsure.

"Hi again." My voice is unintentionally husky, but I can't hide it anymore. She's so beautiful. And she came back.

"What does srećo mean?" she asks, the word falling clumsily over her tongue.

Not what I was expecting, but I suppose I can roll with it. I reach a hand up to rub the back of my neck. I knew I'd have to explain it eventually, but now that the time has come, it feels a little awkward to be doing it in the hallway of my apartment building. While shirtless. "Why don't you come inside?"

She doesn't waste any time brushing past me and into my apartment. I close the door and pick up the six pack from the floor to bring it over to the small counter in my tiny kitchen. I twist off two tops and hand her one of the bottles. She takes a generous swig, then sits at the table next to the bed. I start to follow her, then think better of it. "Let me grab my shirt."

"Why were you answering the door shirtless in the first place?" she asks.

"Funny story," I say, gingerly sliding my shirt over my head. The meds must be working, because the pain is dull as I pull it down my torso. "I thought you might be the cops, and I thought I could get some sympathy points if they could see my bruise."

"He's not going to call the cops." She takes another sip of her beer. "He was drunk and disorderly. He'll sleep it off and wake up to the realization that he was a dumbass. I wouldn't be surprised to get a text from him in the morning apologizing."

"Does he text you often?" I ask, carefully lowering myself into the seat across from her.

She shakes her head. "No. Never. I haven't seen or heard from him in years. From what I gathered, the woman he cheated on me with dumped him, and he was looking for something to fill the void."

My mood sours. "He cheated on you?"

She eyes me warily. "Don't get all defensive again. He's not even here, and what's done is done. Yeah, he cheated on me. He had me convinced I was emotionless and... well, you heard him. Cold. He wanted someone warmer. But I think he was trying to make himself feel better about his shitty behavior."

I take a sip of my own beer to calm myself before responding. "You're not cold."

She laughs humorlessly. "Well, I'm no ray of sunshine."

I shake my head slowly, leaning into the table. "You don't have to be. You're confident. Collected. Determined. All good things."

She holds my gaze as a slow smile spreads her red lips. I'm seconds away from pulling those lips to mine when she clears her throat and asks, "So. Srećo. What does it mean?"

I huff. "You want the long story, or the short story?"

Her eyes light up. "I'm a journalist. I always want the long story."

I give her a wry look. "Are we on the record?"

"Depends on how juicy it is." She's teasing, and I like it. I lean back in my chair, the picture of casual confidence.

"Okay. Well, my grandfather immigrated here from Croatia after World War II, which you know." I pause for her to confirm. "My father was born here in the 60s. Dida—my grandfather," I add for her benefit. She nods as if she put that information together already, so I continue. "He taught my father Croatian. Baba, my grandmother, was from Croatia, too. They were proud of their home country. To hear Dad tell it, he might as well have grown up there with Croatian church, Croatian Sunday school, Croatian neighbors..." I trail off, and she chuckles. I pause to take a drink and study her. She's leaning forward slightly, her eyes trained on me. Enraptured. Taking mental notes, I'm sure. I like this look on her. I like telling her about my family, my history. I like how interested she is. I like *her*.

"Anyway," I can't help but smile. "That's not really the story. My dad grew up speaking Croatian, but my mom didn't. She's not even Croatian at all, actually. So, I never really learned. I can understand it, more or less, but I don't speak it well, and I certainly can't write or read it. I knew enough to understand what my grandparents were saying, and that was about it. But my dad used to call my mom all sorts of pet names in Croatian, and she'd always laugh. And then they'd kiss, and I'd pretend to get all grossed out." I chuckle at the memory. "But srećo was always my favorite name he had for her. I think it was hers, too."

Emery swallows heavily and takes a shaky breath. "What does it mean?"

"Literally, it means 'luck' or 'happiness.' In the language, happiness and luck are intertwined," I say, but that's not quite it. "It's also used for something sweet. She joked that they were lucky to have each other. That his muffins were what made her fall in love with him in the first place, and he liked to say she was his sweet inspiration."

"The same recipe you serve in your shop?" she asks quietly.

I nod. "Passed down from him." I pause, regarding her. "So, when you said you had a sweet tooth the night we met"—I shrug—"It felt right. I felt lucky. And you, uh..." I rub the back of my neck again, suddenly embarrassed. "You made me laugh. Of course, I didn't know you were going to leave me in the middle of the night," I tease.

She glares playfully at me. "I'd shove you, but I don't want to hurt you further."

"You should absolutely take pity on me," I pout, clutching my bruised side.

"That's beautiful, though. Thank you," she says on a breath, her lips parted and her eyes shining.

"You're beautiful," I return quietly, and she doesn't protest. "Are you going to use that story in your next article?"

She shakes her head, her eyes locked on mine. "No. That one's just for me."

I stand, drawing her up with me. I reach a tentative hand up to cup her cheek, and she leans into it. I thread my fingers through her silky hair and force myself not to moan.

"I'm going to kiss you now," I whisper.

"Please do," she whispers back.

Chapter Twenty-Five

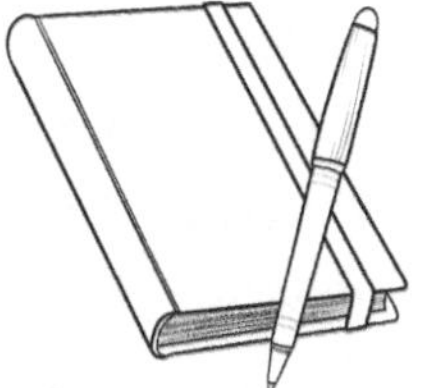

EMERY

THIS KISS IS ENTIRELY different from the one we shared the night we met. It's soft, though it's no less passionate. It's not as hurried, but equally as intense. His facial hair scrapes the skin around my lips as I press closer to him. He smells like rich coffee and tastes like tangy hops. His entire presence envelopes me. And just like that first night we spent together, I want more.

I slide my hands up his waist and under the hem of his t-shirt, pressing my palms into the skin of his torso, like I've wanted to since the minute he answered the door. I can't believe I almost walked away from this. I'm so glad I came back.

He's everything. And when his tongue meets my lips, asking gently for me to open for him, I do without hesitation. It slides sensually in to meet mine, hot and wet and full of promise.

It's the kind of kiss that ruins you for all other kisses. I'm hazily aware of this fact when he breaks it and presses his forehead to mine. His hand is still cupping the nape of my neck, keeping me close. I would do anything to have that hand explore the rest of my skin the way his fingers are exploring my hair.

"Stay," he says. It's a command and a question. No, not a question. A plea. And it opens something in my chest the same way his mouth opened mine a few seconds ago.

"Okay," I reply, tilting my head to kiss him again, but he pulls away enough to meet my gaze. His amber eyes are almost entirely black. Smoky. Steamy. Obsessed. With me, I vaguely realize, and something tight releases within me.

"No," he breathes. "I want you for the whole night. I want to touch you and taste you and fuck you and sleep next to you and wake up to do it again."

Holy shit, that's hot. I don't make a habit of staying the night at guys' places. But, then again, none of them have asked me to. And, frankly, none of them have kissed me like *that* either.

I laugh breathily. "Way to put it all on the table upfront," I joke.

A corner of his mouth ticks up, creasing the skin there. It's my favorite look on him, and it registers that I can run my thumb over that little crease if I want to. I do, the course hairs scraping against the pad of my finger.

His eyes go hooded. "We can do it on the table, too, if you prefer."

I giggle again, suddenly nervous. "I think the bed will do just fine."

"So, you'll stay?" He's so focused on me that it takes a moment for me to fully catch my breath.

"Just one night?" I ask, and I'm surprised to find that I'm not sure which answer I want.

Something flashes in his expression, but I can't decipher it. He leans in and kisses me again, as if this moment of separation between our lips has been too long. As if he needs to fill up with me before he can move on. "Let's start with one." As he talks, he slides his other hand under my blouse and cups my breast over my bra. He squeezes, and my knees go weak. "We can see how it goes." He draws the fabric down and pinches my nipple. My head falls back, exposing my neck to him. He leans in and presses a hot, wet kiss on the column of my throat. "But I'm open to more than just the one," he says, kissing my throat again. "If you are."

"Okay." I moan as he flicks my nipple with his thumb. He withdraws his hand from under my blouse to undo the buttons. His fingers make quick work of them, but they're light as feathers when he brushes the fabric off my shoulders, fully exposing the red lace of my bra.

Trevor's eyes darken again, and his breath hitches. "You wore this to pick up another guy tonight?" He slides one strap off my shoulder and kisses down to where my nipple is exposed. He draws it into his mouth and sucks on it, hard. Almost punishing, but oh, so wonderful. My skin is on fire. I want his mouth and hands everywhere, all at once.

"We all made some foolish mistakes in the past few hours," I say.

He chuckles darkly, gently pushing me back to the bed. I collapse onto the pillows, propping myself up enough so I can watch as he hovers over me, careful to avoid pressing his injured side against mine.

"I suppose we did, srećo." He lowers his mouth to my neck again, his chest barely grazing mine. I shiver at the nickname and its new, added meaning.

He kisses my collarbone. "I won't fight your ex again," he continues, "but you'd better not show this lingerie to anyone else, either."

"That sounds like an even trade."

Apparently satisfied, he reaches a hand down to cup between my legs. I roll my hips to chase the pressure of his palm, but it's not enough. I want every inch of his skin against mine, and I want it now. I reach for the hem of his shirt and pull it up and over his head. He helps me get it off and tosses it on the ground. He kneels over me to undo the fly of my jeans, and he pulls them off to expose matching red lace panties.

He runs a hand down his face. "Fuck, Emery."

I trail a finger lightly over my torso to the waistband of my panties, my eyes never leaving his. "Yes, please," I say with a knowing smile.

He's on me fast, claiming my mouth with a fiery kiss. His hand finds its way between my legs again. It's better with my jeans out of the way, but still not enough. I press myself into his palm, and he hums.

"Want something specific?" he asks, his tongue teasing the skin under my earlobe.

"Anything. Everything," I say, breathless. "You decide."

"Dealer's choice, huh? Okay." He backs away, hooks his fingers under the waistband of my panties, and they join the rest of my clothes on the floor. "Spread your legs," he commands, and my name sounds like chocolate on his tongue.

I'm so surprised by it that I do what he asks without question or comeback. He looks at me, smiling approvingly.

"Of all the things you could choose, this is it?" I ask. My skin heats in anticipation for whatever is coming next.

"I told you," he says. "I want to touch you." He drags a finger through my wetness and circles my clit slowly, lazily. Watching my center the whole time.

"And taste you." He leans over before I can protest and presses his tongue right where his finger just was. I tip my head back and moan in pleasure and surprise as the hot wetness of his tongue circles exactly where I need it to.

He presses a finger to my entrance, and in one swift motion, it's inside me. My hips buck against his tongue completely against my will. Trevor moans, the vibrations heightening the sensation. He sprawls out on the bed in front of me, then presses his hips into the mattress, seeking his own pleasure.

He's enjoying this. And somehow, that makes me enjoy it even more.

But no, that won't do. I want him inside me. I want him to feel what I'm feeling.

"I believe you also said you wanted to fuck me," I grind out.

He looks up at me, his finger still working in his tongue's absence. "We have all night for that, remember?" He licks up my center again, lapping up my arousal. "Mmm," he hums. "So sweet." He licks again, and the pressure is building in my core. "Perfection."

"Trevor," I whimper. "I'm so close."

"Then come, Emery. Use me." He presses his tongue to me again. I reach down and grab his hair, holding him right where I need him as my hips meet his mouth in exactly the right rhythm.

I come apart, my hips bucking wildly into his face. His tongue and finger continue their movements, drawing the pleasure out of me until I'm spent. My limbs collapse into the mattress, and my breathing is heavy.

Trevor kisses his way up my torso. My skin is still tingling from my release. He stops, hovering his lips over my mouth.

"Can I kiss you? I can clean up if you'd rather not—"

I cut him off by pulling his lips to mine. I can almost taste what he did—sweet and sour, mixed with his own taste of coffee and beer. I moan, and he swallows it with another claiming kiss.

"I know you said we had all night," I say between kisses. "But I'm going to need you to fuck me now."

"I wouldn't want to keep a lady waiting." He smiles against my lips before jumping off the bed to remove his boxers. I hear the foil of a condom wrapper tearing, and then he's back, kissing and touching and pinching and bringing me higher again.

"Can I..." I trail off, not sure how to ask for what I want. I push him off me gently, then roll to my hands and knees, my ass in the air.

"Oh." He sounds surprised. His hand grips my ass, hard. "I wouldn't have guessed this was your favorite."

My head falls between my arms, and I moan at the pleasure of his fingers digging into the soft flesh. "It is. But we can do something else if you want."

"Mmm-mmm," he says, lining himself up with my entrance. "This is perfect." He thrusts once, then again, and again before he's fully inside me.

"Oh," I cry out. "Trevor, it's... god." I can't even form a full sentence. The pressure is so exquisite. "Give me a second."

"I wish you could see this, srećo." He traces my spine with a soft touch. "You're taking me so well."

My arms give out. He leans forward, pressing himself further into me. He brings his hand under my throat, drawing me up off my arms and pressing my back into his bare chest. He reaches his other hand between us and unclasps my bra, letting it fall to the bed. His other hand doesn't move from my neck, though he doesn't apply any pressure, just keeps me upright.

"Is this okay, Emery?" he asks softly into my ear.

I try to nod, but I can't with his hand on my neck, so I say, "Yes. Fuck me, Trevor. Please."

He draws out and presses in again. His thrusts are like his initial kisses, slow and sensual. Like he wants to enjoy every inch of me.

I rest the back of my head against his shoulder. He kisses my cheek. His breathing is heavy and hot against my skin. I grab his hip behind me with my left hand and dig my nails into his skin. I remember he liked that last time, and I'm rewarded with a few hard, erratic thrusts.

"Mmm," I hum approvingly.

"You like that?" he asks. "You want me harder?"

"Yes," I breathe.

He pumps harder a few times, and I fall forward onto my hands. "Oh," I say. "That. More."

He grabs my ass again, using it for leverage as his cock goes harder and deeper inside me. For a while, the only noises are those of our slick skin and the sounds of pleasure we each make.

Then, unexpectedly, he reaches his hand between my legs and presses his fingers to my clit. I come undone around him again, shuddering and crying out. I bury my face into the mattress to quiet myself. Trevor presses himself into me twice more, and then follows me over the edge.

We both stay right where we are until our breathing slows, unwilling to break the moment. Eventually, though, he pulls out of me, and I roll to my side as I watch him disappear into the bathroom to dispose of the condom. He turns out the light on his way back to the bed and tugs at the comforter to pull it out from underneath me.

We both crawl under it, on our sides, facing each other. He reaches up to brush a wet strand of hair off my cheek.

I make a noise of disgust. "I'm sorry, I'm sweaty and—"

"No," he insists gently. He scoots closer to me and presses a kiss to my lips. "You're perfect."

I reach up and rest my palm on his stubble. "Are you okay?" I ask. "I didn't even check to see if your side was hurting." I flush a little, and I'm grateful for the dark so he can't see it. "I was too... It felt too good."

He nuzzles into my hand, then kisses my nose. "Didn't even notice it. I can feel it now, though. A little."

He flips over onto his back and slides an arm under me. He uses it to bring me in tight. I rest my head on his chest and sigh contentedly.

"I... like this," I admit.

He squeezes my shoulders and I nestle in even closer. "Good," he says. "Me too."

Chapter Twenty-Six

TREVOR

THE SUN ISN'T EVEN a whisper in the sky when my alarm goes off the next morning. I roll over to quickly shut it off and suck in a breath through my teeth when my bruised side meets the mattress. I carefully shift to my back to relieve the pressure, which is when Emery stirs beside me.

Emery. She's still here. Like she promised.

I can't be too surprised. We spent most of last night and into the early hours of the morning exploring each other's mouths and bodies. I hadn't wanted to fall asleep at all, but her eyelids started drooping. I kissed her nose and told her to sleep. She curled up next to me and was out in minutes.

Now, she stretches out her long legs and sinks further into the mattress, her eyes still closed and her breathing still deep. Neither of us bothered with sleep clothes, so I allow myself a moment to brush my fingers against her smooth skin. She's so *soft*. I could run my hands over her skin all morning.

If only. I have to get to the shop to get muffins and cookies in the oven in time to open up. I've never cursed my choice of employment, but I'm coming close right now. I'd give up any potential income for a few more hours in bed with Emery.

I press a light kiss to her forehead. I can't resist it. I don't mean to wake her, but her eyelids flutter open.

"Good morning, srećo," I whisper.

She searches my face, sleep clearing from her eyes after a moment. A smile stretches across her features, completely lighting up the room.

Who needs the sun? Emery can smile at me like this every morning, instead.

Every morning? The realization gives me pause. Up until last night, I hadn't thought I had a chance with her again, let alone the possibility of a real future. But, yes, I want to wake up every morning like this. Of course I do.

"Mmm," she stretches again. "It doesn't look like morning."

I chuckle, lightly tracing circles on her bare back. "Well, it's a little after four o'clock."

She drapes an arm over me. "That's an oddly specific time for wake-up sex, but I can make it work." She kisses my shoulder.

I groan, scrubbing a hand over my face. "I wish I was waking you up for that, but I have to get to the shop."

The smile falls from her face as she eyes me warily. "At four in the morning?"

"Those muffins aren't going to make themselves," I tease as I lean. She lets me kiss her, but then pulls away, her eyes wide.

"My breath has to be awful."

I shake my head, kissing her again. "Everything about you is sweet, srećo. Even your morning breath."

"That's such bullshit," she says, rolling to her back. Her perfect breasts peek out of the top of the comforter, and I have to clasp my hands together against the urge to touch them. She rubs her eyes with her palms. "And speaking of bullshit, why am I awake at four in the morning, again?"

I laugh heartily. "I didn't mean to wake you. You can go back to sleep if you want. But I do need to get going."

She stiffens slightly. "I..." she trails off, staring straight up at the dark ceiling. Her head flops helplessly in my direction.

"You don't have to if that's weird," I say quickly.

"It might be a little weird," she admits. "I'm sorry." She's silent for a minute before she laughs lightly. "You probably don't want to leave a journalist alone in your apartment, anyway. I'm very good at snooping for information."

"What about journalistic integrity?" I play along. It feels like I'm part of a special club of people she jokes around with now, and I like it.

"Doesn't apply here," she counters. "I wouldn't use it in a story, so it's really just a transferrable skill."

I chuckle. "Transferable to what? Finding dirt on your partners?"

"Yes," she says, as if it's the most obvious thing in the world. Then a laugh bubbles up out of her, like she had been holding it back through that whole exchange.

"Well, I guess I'll have to find better hiding places for all the illicit items in this place before I allow you here unattended." I kiss her again. "Come with me, then."

She kisses back. "To the shop?"

I run my tongue along her bottom lip, drawing a gasp from her. "Yes."

"At four in the morning?"

"It's very quickly going to be not-four-in-the-morning if I don't get moving."

"Hmm," she hums. I'm a little surprised to find myself holding my breath, awaiting her answer. I don't want to leave her. But if I have to leave this apartment, the next best thing would be to tuck her into me and take her with.

She stifles a yawn, then laughs again. I want to record that sound.

"I'm going to hate myself for this, but how about I meet you there? I need to work on this next article anyway, but I could use a shower. And a change of clothes. And my laptop."

I kiss her collarbone. "Why would you hate yourself for that?" I ask, looking up at her.

She glares down at me. "Because it's before the crack of dawn, Trevor. And I... we..."—she smirks at that—"barely slept. I don't think there's enough caffeine in the world to make this a productive day."

"Lucky for you"—I punctuate it with a kiss—"I know a guy."

***

I'm not anxiety-baking per se, but I might be over-stirring the muffin batter, and the cookies look a little lopsided. I don't want to admit it, but there's a small part of me that's afraid she won't show.

Forty years old, and I'm giddy like a high school kid waiting for his prom date. Absolutely ridiculous.

But when a knock sounds at the window and I look up to find Emery waving at me in the dark, I get even more giddy at the sight of her. I almost drop the mixing bowl in my haste to rush and unlock the door.

She slips by me into the shop, and I catch her cucumber scent, stronger now because she just showered. She's wearing a loose, white t-shirt and cutoff shorts that are going to haunt my dreams for years. Her dark hair is piled on top of her head in a giant bun. She's summer personified.

She looks amazing.

"What?" she asks, and it's then that I realize I'm standing there, holding the door open and staring at her.

"I've never seen you this casual," I say, locking the door again.

She frowns, and her shoulders slump forward slightly. "Oh. I figured I wouldn't be going into the newsroom today, so I didn't see a reason to look professional." Her voice ticks up at the end like a question.

I turn to find her fidgeting with the hem of her shirt. She shifts her laptop bag higher on her shoulder and twirls an escaped strand of hair between her fingers.

"Don't get me wrong, your professional clothes are hot," I say, taking a step toward her and catching that strand of hair in my own fingers. "But you..." I don't even have words. I swallow hard and tuck the hair behind her ear. "I like this look more."

Her dark eyes meet mine as she leans slightly toward me. "Oh." Her eyelids are hooded, and she drags her bottom lip through her teeth.

I catch her bottom lip with my thumb and drag it over the spot where her teeth just were. "Are we at the point where I can kiss you in public?"

Her gaze flicks around the empty coffee shop and the equally empty street outside. "This looks pretty private to me."

"Good," I say as I replace my thumb with my own lips. She drops her laptop bag on the ground and circles her arms around my waist, pressing her torso against mine. I force myself to break away sooner than I'd like. She makes no move to step away from me, so I don't either.

"I'm not in the business of hiding things, but maybe you can give me a few days to fill my sister in? You know, in case she randomly shows up here again." She considers something, then adds, "And maybe to sort out what's appropriate when we're dealing with the magazine for the next few weeks."

"Can I get you all to myself again sometime soon?" I ask, my eyebrow ticking up in question.

She hums. "I can't be functioning on three hours of sleep every night this week." She bites down on her pink bottom lip again. "But, yeah. How did you put it? I'm... open to more than one night."

I press my lips to hers again, filling up in case this is the last time I'm able to kiss her until closing. I am so far gone for this woman, but I don't even care. If it were up to me, I'd shout from the rooftops right now that she's mine. But she needs time, and I want to respect that.

Doesn't mean I can't kiss the shit out of her while I wait.

The oven timer sounds, but I ignore it, my hands skating over her body and finding a place on her ass. I squeeze, my fingers reaching under the torn hem of her shorts. She's the one who breaks the kiss this time, a breathy laugh tickling the hair on my face.

"Sex in the shop is surely a health code violation," she teases.

"Health code violation is probably the best-case scenario," I return.

"A fire is the worst case, I imagine." When I look at her in confusion, she clarifies, "The oven?"

"The oven. Right. Okay, I'm going to get another batch of muffins in. You go ahead and get set up. I'll get you some caffeine. Anything special?" I ask as I put some distance between us on my way to the back-room kitchen. I have to, or I'm going to be kissing her all morning.

"Dealer's choice," she winks. I almost growl at the reference and take her on the counter right here, but she drags her lip through her teeth, suddenly bashful. "Actually, no. Can I have the lavender latte?"

My heart feels like it might actually burst. She wants the drink I made especially for her. I don't have words, so I cross the space between us and pull her lips to mine again.

"You sure you don't want hazelnut?" I ask when I pull away. My voice is raspy and thick.

"Don't get me wrong. I love hazelnut. But that drink was... special. And I didn't get to finish it."

The oven timer dings again. "Okay, coming right up."

I tear myself away from her and duck into the kitchen to quickly get the muffins out of the oven. Luckily, they're not terribly overdone. I slide the trays onto the counter to cool and grab two empty muffin tins. Normally, this is a much smoother operation.

I spin around the kitchen area, looking for the mixing bowl, but then remember I left it on the counter because I didn't want to miss Emery when she got here. I give myself a mental facepalm as I toss the empty tins on top of the oven, but before I can go back out, Emery appears in the doorway, holding the bowl.

"I thought you might need this?" she teases, her voice feigning innocence.

I pretend to play it cool. "Uh, yeah. Muffin batter would be helpful, I guess."

"Can I help?"

"You want to help me make muffins?"

She shrugs a shoulder. "You seem flustered."

I laugh humorlessly. "Not going to lie, srećo, having you back here is not going to make me less flustered."

Her features light up at my use of her nickname, and my stomach flips. She likes that name. She likes the name I've given her.

I am in so much trouble.

She doesn't say anything as she walks to the muffin tins. She lines them with the paper cups on the counter, then sprays them with cooking spray. She takes the scoop from the counter and fills each space, then slides the tins into the oven.

It's like she belongs here. With me. Baking muffins for my shop.

I come up beside her and set the oven timer, then lean a hip against the counter. I fold my arms and study her, still in awe of how she fits so well in my life.

She shoots me a little smile as she takes some of the cooled muffins to the front. "I believe I was promised bottomless coffee," she calls on her way to the counter. "And I'm taking a muffin. Someone got me out of bed before I could have a proper breakfast this morning."

I shake my head as if to clear it. "Coffee. Yes. I'm on it," I say. Lattes and pastries feel completely inadequate as an offering to this incredible woman, but if that's what she wants, that's what she'll get.

Chapter Twenty-Seven

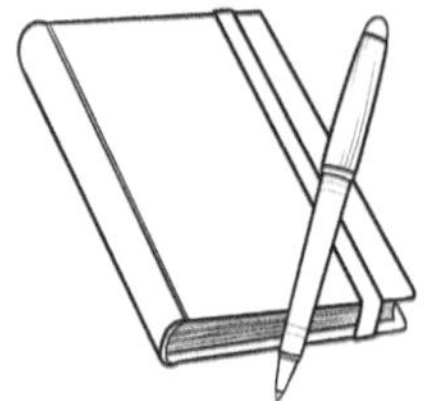

EMERY

THANK THE UNIVERSE AND all that is holy that I finished a draft of this article yesterday because Trevor is larger than life. His entire presence dominates my senses, even from across the room. When he opens the shop, there's a trickle of people who come in even in the early hours. Some, he greets by name and with that warm smile that crinkles the corners of his mouth. Most of them are elderly, and I realize they must be regulars his grandfather would have known.

Something about that strikes me square in the chest. These people have likely been coming in this shop for decades. What would they do if it closed? Where would they go in the morning? They surely wouldn't visit that shop down the street to sit and enjoy their espresso for an hour or so before going about their days.

But there are newcomers, too. Trevor greets them with the same warm smile, though it's more guarded than the one he uses for the people he knows. Not much, though. If there's one thing I'm learning about Trevor, it's that he's open to almost anyone and anything.

He's so unlike me in that way. I'm wary of everyone. It's refreshing to be near someone so genuinely welcoming, but it still tickles something in my brain that tells me maybe we're too different to have anything serious. Eventually, he'll realize I'm not a relationship person, and we'll go our separate ways.

But when he catches my eye over the shoulder of one of the younger customers he's serving, his smile changes. It becomes tender, almost giddy, but no less intense. His amber eyes hold mine, and I break out into a smile of my own before he turns back to help the next person in line.

I'm equal parts completely at home and not of this world in this shop, tapping at my laptop with the clink of porcelain and the hiss of the espresso machine as the soundtrack to my work, but it doesn't take long for me to sink into the comfort of the space. The lived-in ease of the laminate counters and over-loved tables and chairs seeps its way under my skin, loosening something in my chest. It had been wound so tightly for so long, I hadn't even registered the tightness until it was gone.

I close my eyes and breathe deeply. That heady scent of coffee and sugar and vanilla fills my lungs, easing its way into the tight spaces between my ribs and around my heart. It's the same scent Trevor carries with him wherever he goes. He wasn't kidding when he said this place is in his veins. I don't think he'd rid himself of this smell if he was away from here for twenty years. I don't think he'd ever want to.

It smells like being wrapped up in him. Like burying my face into the soft fabric of his plaid shirt, or tangling in the sheets and waking up to a kiss to my temple. It's a warm hug. Like coming home.

Home. That's what this place is. It's a realization, one that's been sitting patiently at the edges of my brain, waiting for me to call it to the front. All I had to do was settle into it rather than try to run from it. This place is home for the old man sitting at the counter, pushing his tiny, empty espresso cup away from himself and placing a gray cap on his head before shuffling to the door. It's home for James, awkwardly pouring drip coffee into to-go cups and carefully checking that the lids he places on top are firmly secured. It's home for Mike, who stops in to grab a latte on his way to work and looks around at the people in the space before winking at me on his way out. It's even home to the twenty-somethings who giggle before placing their orders as they try not to swoon when Trevor smiles at them.

I suddenly realize exactly what Donna was trying to tell me about a shop like this being important to the community. It's the same as her diner—it's a gathering place. Somewhere for people to feel whatever it is I'm feeling now. Something warm I didn't know I needed. Something loosening I never realized was tight. Something settling I had no idea was restless.

I want to belong here, too. And that's a much stronger realization than my earlier one, because I didn't understand until just now that I was lacking a sense of belonging elsewhere. But, I suppose it makes sense. I lost my husband, my job, and my relationship with my parents. I've been adrift ever since.

And the memory of that crashes into me like a bucket of ice water. Of course I don't belong here. I'm someone people leave, not who people settle with. I wonder how long before Trevor realizes it.

I sip my lavender latte and bury my fingers in my messy bun, turning my attention to the words on my screen. I don't want to engage with whatever that was. Not yet, anyway. There's no reason I can't enjoy Trevor for as long as he'll have me, even if it means watching him smile and chat with the young women coming in for their iced matchas and raspberry macchiatos. Even if it means living with the fact that it was

NewsJunkie814 who enticed that particular clientele. The memory of typing out those comments sours the bit of latte I was holding in my mouth. I swallow hard. I push that away, too. I didn't know then what I know now.

Now, I know that Trevor doesn't keep peas in his freezer. I know his grandfather saved up money to buy the espresso machine he's currently cleaning. I know that he's ticklish just to the right of his belly button. I know that, when he blushes, it starts at his chest and works its way up his neck. I know the little, passionate noises he makes when he's close to his orgasm.

I dig my fingers further into my hair. I'm a mess. This is why I don't have serious relationships anymore. It's too convoluted.

But I catch Trevor's gaze briefly again, and he looks so damn happy every time he sees me. It makes me want to be worthy of that happiness. Worthy of the name he gave me.

I skim my draft again. This isn't worthy of anything. I'm trying. I really am, but this feeling is so foreign to me that it's hard to do it justice.

If I want to be worthy of the way he looks at me, I need to try harder than this. I'm sure of at least that much. I highlight everything on my page and, before I can think too hard about it, I hit *Delete*.

***

The shop has completely cleared out and the sun has risen above the top of the floor-to-ceiling windows by the time I have the skeleton of a new draft. It needs a lot of fleshing-out, and it still sounds stilted as hell in my head, but I'm feeling better about the new version. It's at least headed in the right direction.

I arch my back over the back of the chair, popping some vertebrae in the process. I stretch my neck back and forth, trying to release a kink in it from bending over my laptop for so long. It's been a while since I've been that engrossed in a piece, and I'm feeling every year of the thirty-seven I've been on this Earth. I'm also feeling every hour of the three or so I slept last night. I press the heels of my hands into my eyes to rub the tension out of them.

When I open them, Trevor is standing across from me, his hand on the empty chair on the other side of the table. There's a towel thrown over his shoulder, and his apron is smudged with coffee stains.

One corner of his mouth tips up as he studies me. "Hi," he says. "Come here often?"

"I found this place recently, actually," I play along. "It's nice. The lattes are pretty good."

He raises a golden eyebrow. "Pretty good, huh?"

I give him a casual shrug, furtively looking around as if to make sure no one is listening. "Don't tell anyone, but I'm coming here because I'm sleeping with the hot barista."

He tips his head back and laughs, and it feels like I won a game I didn't even know we were playing. The long column of his throat is exposed to me, and all I want to do is trail a line of kisses upwards on my way to his lips.

When his laughter calms, he slides into the chair across from me. He glances at my hand resting at the table, and I turn my palm up to give him permission. He takes it, weaving our fingers together over my notebook, his thumb making gentle circles over my palm. "You looked like you were concentrating hard for a while there. I didn't want to interrupt."

"Hmm." I stretch my neck again, and I don't miss the way his throat bobs as he watches me. "I didn't realize how deep in it I was. I started over."

His brow furrows in question. "Really?"

"Yeah." I look around the now-empty shop. "I guess you could say I was inspired."

He smiles at that, and I think I won again. "Do you need to get back to it?"

I snap my laptop shut. "Nope. I need to walk away from it for an hour or so and come back fresh."

"What I'm hearing is you have an hour to kill," he says suggestively.

"What did you have in mind?"

Before he can answer, the bell over the door dings and in walks a woman with shockingly red hair piled in a mess on top of her head. She's wearing short, green running shorts and a yellow tank top that's sticking to her with sweat. She looks around the shop, then furrows her brow as if she's disappointed in what she sees.

Trevor stands. "Hi there. What can I get for you?"

"You haven't seen a broody writer-type come in here, have you?" she asks.

Trevor eyes me sidelong and tips his head in my direction. "Just this one," he teases. "But something tells me you aren't looking for her."

The woman shakes her head. "No, mine is of the male variety. And if I would have known he was going to be late, I would have gone back to the hotel to shower." She rolls her eyes. "Sorry I'm stinking up the place."

He waves that off. "Not at all. Can I get you a water or something?"

"Water would be great." She smiles and wipes her brow, then wipes the sweat from her hand off on her shorts. "It's a hot one out there."

"Looks like you went for a run," I say as Trevor pours a glass of water.

The woman sits at the counter and chugs half of it before responding. "I did."

"Oh no." I reel back. "Why?"

She chuckles. "I actually love this heat. It's cleansing, in a way." She twists in her seat to look out the front windows. "This is a great town for running, too. I didn't want to pass up the trail that follows that creek on the other side of town."

"You're not from around here?" Trevor asks, wiping at an invisible spot on the counter and slinging the towel over his shoulder again.

The woman shakes her head. "Chicago suburbs," she says, then finishes off her water.

Trevor takes the glass to refill it and returns it to her. "What brings you out this way?"

"My husband"—she pauses to check her watch and sigh—"is here for a book signing. I'm just tagging along while I'm still on summer break."

"Teacher?" I guess.

She nods as the bell over the door chimes again. She turns to face the door. "You're late," she says, but there's no malice in it. Her smile is positively radiant as a lean man with dark hair and piercing, gray eyes enters. He's wearing an impeccably tailored navy suit, white button-down shirt, and bright purple tie. He looks vaguely familiar, though I can't put my finger on why. His wife said he was doing a book signing. Maybe I've read one of his books or something.

He crosses the shop in a few steps and pulls the woman into a side hug so he can kiss her sweaty temple.

"How was your run?" the man asks into her hair.

"Great." She leans into him. "But it is hot out there. Were you able to set up the space for your signing?"

"The whole thing was a mess." He sounds exasperated. "It took longer than expected. You want to grab some coffee and go back to the hotel to shower?"

The woman closes her eyes and inhales deeply. A small smile appears as she exhales, as if she just breathed in her very own sense of calm. "Yes, but I wish we could stay here." She opens her eyes and looks at Trevor. "We prefer smaller coffee shops, so we were delighted to find this place when we searched on the internet. We read a couple of articles about it and had to check it out."

Trevor's smile widens and he glances in my direction. If I'm not mistaken, his chest puffs up with pride. "Those are Emery's articles. We're working together to try to get more people through the doors."

The woman purses her lips, her eyes bouncing back and forth between us. She has the look of someone who knows a thing or two about a workplace romance.

Is that what this is? A workplace romance?

"Really." Her skeptical comment snaps me back to the conversation.

I clear my throat. "That's the idea, anyway," I say sheepishly.

The man looks at each of us in turn, then chuckles. "Well, we'll order and leave you to it, then," he says, clearly amused.

My stomach rolls with embarrassment or anxiety, I can't tell which. Are we that obvious, even to complete strangers? His wife saw us holding hands when she walked in, but he didn't. I'm suddenly uncomfortable with the idea of people knowing we're sleeping together. I had hoped to control that information a little. At least until this project is over, or until I can get a better handle on my feelings.

"I'll have a medium coffee. Black," the woman says.

"I don't suppose you can make a sugar free caramel latte, extra shot, extra whip?" the man asks. His wife rolls her lips between her teeth as if she wants desperately to tease him but is trying very hard not to.

"No problem." Trevor springs into action. As he works, the man whispers something into the woman's ear, and she laughs. She looks up at him, and he looks down at her. It's so painfully obvious how in love they are, how comfortable they are with each other.

I used to think I had that with Derek. I remember his arm slung around my shoulders, him whispering what I thought were sweet words into my ear.

How did I ever think anything he ever said to me was sweet? Why didn't I hold out for someone like Trevor, whose words and actions are sweeter than all of Derek's combined?

Sreća.

If only I had met Trevor first. I could have fallen for him so easily. It wouldn't have been tainted by everything that came before. Now, there's a tug-of-war going on inside my heart. Protect it at all costs, or put it in Trevor's hands and hope he takes better care of it than everyone else has.

Trevor places the couple's drinks on the counter. They take them and wave to both of us on the way out. "Good luck with your articles." The woman's green eyes sparkle with amusement. "And good luck with your shop," she says to Trevor. "It really is a wonderful place."

He beams in gratitude as they leave. As soon as the door is closed behind them, he turns that huge smile to me. "Out of town visitors!" he exclaims. "And they found your article. That's amazing, isn't it?" He slides back into the seat across from me.

"It's pretty cool," I admit, though with less exuberance.

"And they came here for the coffee," he says, still excited.

"Why else would they come here?"

Trevor levels a you-know-why look at me as he says, "I'm pretty sure most of those young women have been coming in here to see if I look anything like my picture."

A nugget of regret settles in my heart. "You are objectively, ridiculously good looking." I scramble to keep it light, but he shrugs. I can tell by the way he tries to play it off that he's at least a little bothered by the ogling.

"But they *stay* for the coffee." I am trying to keep his spirits up, even though I know this was at least partially my doing.

He visibly straightens, then nods once. "You're right. Doesn't matter how they get in the door. They got here, and they will hopefully keep coming back."

He threads his fingers through mine again, and I muster up what I hope is a reassuring look. But I can feel it already. I hurt him without even knowing it. I want to make it right with these next few articles, but it nags at me, nonetheless.

And this, I tell myself, is why I wasn't built for relationships.

COFFEE AND COMMUNITY: A HOME AWAY FROM HOME

Emery Darlis

I'm excited to be back with another installment of *Baker's Grove Living*'s month-long feature of Baker's Blend Coffee Shop.

Some people feel at home curled up with a good book on their couch. Others feel at home when they are with friends or family. Still others feel that sense of belonging at school or work.

For Trevor Kovacic, home is the Baker's Blend Coffee Shop.

When you talk to Kovacic, the first thing you notice is the scent of warm coffee and sugar. The shop has been passed down to him from his father and grandfather, and, as he says, the coffee is "in my veins."

But there are more people who feel at home there, too. If you come in during the early morning hours, you'll see patrons—new and old—coming in to stay a while with their coffee. Regular customers who knew Kovacic's grandfather, Marko, still enjoy the routine of waking up early and sipping their espresso at a counter facing the barista, taking in a quiet few moments before going about their day. Young people on their way to yoga classes stop by to share an iced matcha with their friends. Even I am writing this from a table in the corner, basking in the early-morning sunshine and letting the ambient coffee shop sounds inspire me.

We've made no secret of the fact that Baker's Blend Coffee Shop is in trouble. It can't compete with larger shops opening in the area. But maybe it shouldn't. This shop is in a different category all together. Yes, both serve coffee. But Baker's Blend serves a different kind of warmth: a home base for people who need somewhere to sit, sip, and savor their drinks. A friendly face and a conversation.

Baker's Blend is a staple in the community, and to see it fail would be a tragedy, indeed. "A downtown needs a diner and a small coffee shop. It just does. It's not about the food or the coffee. It's about the community," says owner of Donna's Diner, Donna Fitzpatrick.

And it's not only about the community at large; it's about the community inside the café doors. There's a missing link in our days, one that used to be part of a simpler time. It includes coming together more than moving apart—finding common ground. And a step toward that world we want is sharing an espresso with a friend.

"These things matter to some people, and they matter a great deal," insists Fitzpatrick. She's right, of course, as only a woman who has welcomed countless others into her doors over the years can be. Baker's Blend Coffee Shop matters. It matters to the community. It matters to the people who come through its doors every day. It matters in a way a big box coffee shop never can. And it matters to Trevor Kovacic and his family.

So, what are you waiting for? Come to Baker's Blend Coffee Shop for coffee and community. It's an experience you won't find anywhere else.

Be sure to join us for the grand re-opening celebration next Saturday. It'll be another great chance for the community to come out to support the shop. And come back in a week to see the last installment of this feature.

Chapter Twenty-Eight

TREVOR

"SHE IS IN LOVE with you." Mike lets out a low whistle as he slides the laptop back to me.

I practically spit out the espresso I had been sipping. I wipe the corner of my mouth with a finger while trying desperately to tamp down the blush I can feel creeping up my neck. "What makes you say that?"

"You read this, didn't you?" he asks as if it's obvious.

"It was a really nice article."

"'Really nice.' Sure." He slides the laptop back toward himself to consult it. "'When you talk to Kovacic, the first thing you notice is the scent of warm coffee and sugar.'" He shoves it back to the middle of the table, an eyebrow raised. He folds his arms and leans back in his chair. "Dude."

"I think love is a pretty strong word," I counter half-heartedly.

Mike appears unconvinced. "You can call it a hyperbole if it makes you feel better, but let's be real. That girl—sorry, that *woman's*—got it bad." He corrects himself.

"She's trying to get clicks on an article so she can write something she is passionate about," I say, but even I'm not convinced. Or, I hope she's not writing this for clicks anymore.

I know how to write with heart, Trevor.

I remember exactly how her eyes sparkled when she said that to me in her office a few weeks ago, like she was begging me to give her a chance. Like she wanted more than anything to find the heart of her work again. And when I read this week's article, I knew that if she hadn't found it yet, she was close. My own stupid heart dares to hope that she found it because of the night we shared together, even though I know it's foolish to jump to conclusions so soon.

Mike's loud snort cuts through my thoughts. "She's passionate about you, Trev. You can deny it all you want, but I saw her in here yesterday morning. Maybe punching her ex really did it for her. She was watching you like a hawk."

I wince. "That would suggest I'm prey of some sort."

He waves this away. "A hawk in heat, then. Do hawks go into heat?"

I gape at him. "Stop. Now."

"Whatever, man. All I'm saying is she wants you. Where is she today?"

"She... uh..." I rub the back of my neck, which shifts my slouchy hat forward a bit. "She was tired."

Mike's smile turns downright naughty. "And how would you know that?"

Emery had asked me to give her a few days to sort things out, but I'm a terrible liar. And from the look on Mike's face, he already knows exactly how I know how tired she is.

"After that thing with her ex, she stopped by," I offer, knowing that won't be enough.

"And...?"

"And she stayed the night."

"And she came here with you the next morning, which is why I saw her shooting you glances hot enough to heat my latte?" he guesses.

I nod.

Mike lets out a whoop. James fumbles the porcelain mug he was holding, and it crashes to the counter.

"It's okay, Boss! Nothing broke," he says after a moment.

I grimace in Mike's direction. "Can you please cool it?"

"The woman of your dreams runs by this very shop window on a day you've hit rock bottom—"

"I didn't hit rock bottom."

"You run into her at a bar that same night and take her home with you," he continues, unfazed. "She leaves your apartment while you were asleep for no apparent reason—"

"Well, I wouldn't say *no* reason."

"And she shows up in your life *again* to save your ass. You win her over with muffins and coffee, and she *stays the night* at your place and comes to work with you the next day. No, bro, I cannot cool it. I'm excited for you. This is, like, all your little optimistic dreams come true in the span of a month."

I try to hold my smile back. I really do. But it forces its way across my face. "I'm pretty excited, too."

"She was tired because you both barely slept, and then you woke her up at the crack of dawn to bring her here, didn't you?" he guesses again.

"Basically," I admit.

Mike smacks the table with his open palm. Porcelain clinks again on the counter, but there's no crash. I eye James sidelong, but he seems engrossed in the list he has in front of him. The kid is determined to learn how to make some of the new drinks on the menu. I don't know what lit the fire under him, but if he can figure it out, I'll be glad for the help.

"You need a day off to spend with your woman."

"I can't take a day off. Things are just starting to pick up, and I don't have managerial staff." I say the last sentence quietly to avoid offending James. The poor kid is trying, at least.

Mike leans forward, flattening his palms on the table. "I can do it."

"Do what?"

"Manage the shop for a morning," he says. "I practically work here. I used to work here in the summers while we were in college. It'll be like riding a bike."

I shake my head slowly. "You work all week. I can't ask you to do that on your weekend."

"You're not asking. I'm offering. And, on that note, you really need to figure out a way to take days off. You're going to work yourself to the bone. Emery deserves someone who can spend some time with her."

He's not wrong. Emery deserves that and so much more. I'd love to hire more staff, but until things turn around, I can't afford it. Which highlights another problem in his little plan.

"I can't pay you." I shrug apologetically. As much as I'd like to take him up on this offer, it's not in the budget.

"I'm doing it pro bono. I mean, I'll be drinking free coffee all day, so we can call it even."

"That's not even," I counter.

"Who cares?" He looks around the shop as if he's worried someone will hear him. There are, miraculously, a couple of people sitting at various tables, but all of them have headphones on. "You're my best friend. You've put up with a lot of my shit over the years. Let me do this for you."

It's the most sincere I've ever seen him. I'm touched. And a little wary, if I'm being honest. I'll probably owe him big time, and he'll most likely cash in at a really inconvenient time, but right now, I can't think of anything better than a lazy day with Emery, exploring and learning about each other.

"Okay," I say slowly. "Yeah. I would really appreciate that."

Mike flashes me a goofy grin and rubs his palms together. "Awesome. Yes. This is great. I've always wanted to play Cupid. You know, without the diapers. Anyway, text your woman and see what she's doing this weekend, because you've officially got your very own love hero ready to make shit happen."

Chapter Twenty-Nine

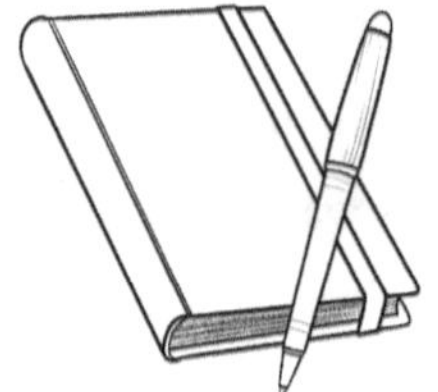

Emery

On Friday evening, I arrive at Cass and Vi's house promptly at five o'clock carrying a homemade lasagna for a pregnant woman with a craving.

Once today's article had been published and I made sure it was posted without a hitch, I had snuck out of the office. I thought about going to the shop to see what Trevor thought of it but decided to go home and pass out instead. With little sleep on Wednesday night, then burning the midnight oil with final edits on Thursday, by this morning, I was barely functional. I slept like the dead for about five hours before my phone rang. I answered it to Violet's forced calm, begging me to make a lasagna and come over for dinner because Cass said she couldn't rest until she had one made with mom's recipe. Cass was crying because mom wouldn't be making one for her. I heard her sobs in the background, and it damn near broke my cold, black heart. So, I dragged myself out of bed, made the lasagna, put on something that passed for clothing, and now I'm standing here—on time, I might add—waiting for someone to answer the door.

When the door finally opens, Vi is standing there in sleep shorts and her shirt on inside out. Her hair, which is now bright pink and shaved on the bottom half, is standing on end at the top. Her skin is flushed, and she seems a little out of breath.

I shake my head slightly. "You invited me over."

Violet nods. "I did."

"You begged me to make a lasagna." I hold the casserole dish up so she can see it.

"Yes."

"But you're going to answer the door like that?" I wave a hand up and down, encompassing her disarray.

Vi shrugs, opening the door wider and motioning for me to come inside. "Cass was sad. I was trying to make her feel better." She bounces her eyebrows suggestively.

"Oh my god," I groan.

She winks. "It worked, I think."

I turn my head and fake gag into the lasagna as Vi makes a noise of protest. I raise an eyebrow. "Don't talk about my sister that way."

Vi chuckles and takes the lasagna from me. I follow her to the kitchen where she sets it on the counter. She opens the fridge to grab three cans of sparkling water and sets them out on the table with plates.

Cass waddles in just as I'm sinking into one of the kitchen chairs. She's wearing a shirt that has seen better days. It's stretched almost to breaking over her belly, and she's paired it with sleep shorts with the waistband folded under. Her hair is significantly less matted than Vi's as if she had run a comb through it before coming downstairs. But her eyes are rimmed with red, and it's clear from her dejected posture that she's not feeling much better at all.

Vi shoots an empathetic glance in Cass's direction as my sister slumps into the chair next to me. She puts her head in her hands and groans.

"Fuck these hormones," she bites out. "There is no reason I should be losing it over lasagna."

I scoot my chair closer to her and wrap an arm around her shoulders. "You're not losing it over lasagna. You're losing it over our parents being shitty. I happen to think that's a valid feeling at a time when having your mom around would be comforting."

She curls even further into herself, but I hold on to her shoulders. I rest my forehead near her ear. Vi comes over to her other side and makes it a group hug.

"I called her," Cass whispers. "I couldn't help it. I thought maybe..." she trails off.

I bristle, but don't let her go. "Did she answer?"

She shakes her head, then lets out a sob. Vi catches my eye over Cass's shoulder, a pained look on her face. She looks like she desperately wants to fix this for Cass, so I shake my head. There's nothing we can do but let her experience these emotions. Though I do believe Vi would leave right now and stand on my parents' porch to shake some sense into them if she thought it'd work.

It won't. It just sucks. And all we can do is hold her until it passes.

Cass sniffs a few times, her nose plugged from the crying. "I smell lasagna." Her voice is tiny and muffled by her hands.

"I made some for you," I say. "Vi asked me to."

This sets off another round of sobs as Cass howls, "You're so nice to me! Why are you so nice to me?"

"Wish I knew," I tease.

Cass's shoulders start shaking again, but this time it's because laughter is bubbling up out of her. "You're such an asshole," she says between fits of wet giggles.

"An asshole who made you lasagna," I point out.

She laughs quietly for a few more seconds before shrugging. "Okay. It's getting hot under here. And I'm really hungry."

I give her one last squeeze before Vi and I release her at the same time. Vi starts serving the food, and I slide a can of sparkling water to Cass. She opens it and chugs half of it before letting out a giant belch.

"Sexy," Vi deadpans as she sets a plate and a fork in front of each of us.

Cass shrugs. "You knew who I was when you married me."

"Speaking of which," Vi says as she stabs her slice of lasagna with a fork, "we read your article today."

I cringe. "What the hell kind of segue was that?" I've known Vi a long time, and she's trying to change the subject. I'm grateful for it, for Cass's sake, but I can't let her get away with that monstrosity of a transition.

"In my mind, the transition worked because *holy shit, Emery*." Vi takes a bite of her lasagna and chews it with vigor.

"What?" I say around my own mouthful.

Cass levels me with a look. "What happened with Trevor to flip that switch?"

I let out a laugh that is humorless and edged with nerves. "What switch?"

Cass points her fork at me. "That was the best article you've written since you left *The Gazette*. It was all sensory detail and thematic possibilities. It was pulled together. Dare I say, it was *hopeful*."

I narrow my eyes at her. "You take that back."

Cass waves this away. "You can pretend you're some hard-ass all you want, but you're getting soft in your old age. That article was love personified."

I practically choke on my bite of lasagna. I cough and sputter as Cass and Vi look on disinterestedly. Some friends they are.

When the coughing fit has passed, I take a huge gulp of water. "That's a strong word, don't you think?"

"What, 'personified?'" Cass bats her eyes at me, feigning innocence.

I drop my fork on the plate and fold my arms. I'm suddenly not hungry. "No."

Cass shakes her head and lets out a triumphant, "Ha!"

"I think what my beautiful wife is trying to say," Vi jumps in, clearly sensing this conversation going off the rails, "is that it was a departure from your more recent work. And given the events of the other night..." she trails off and leans forward, clasping her hands on top of the table. I glance at Cass, who doesn't flinch. She's looking at me expectantly, which means Vi came home on Wednesday and told her all about the fight Trevor and Derek got in.

"Well," I start, then drop my gaze to the table. I study its black surface, pockmarked from years of wear and tear. I imagine little toddler hands fisting utensils and banging on it, giggling, and driving their moms up a wall. It tugs at that thread around my heart. The one that had loosened itself yesterday while I observed the shop. I objectively know that these two are about to become three. I have been aware of this for months, but this sudden and very specific image of their family life throws me. This house, with its manicured lawn and view of downtown is about to become a home with a real-life baby. A manifestation of their love for one another.

I don't want that. I don't. I've never wanted kids, and little baby Darlis-Jacobsen isn't going to change that. But there's a life here. A vibrancy I haven't had in my own life since... well, since ever. Not even with Derek. As much as I wanted to believe it was there, it wasn't.

But they're right. Writing that article opened something in me that has been closed off for a while. I felt it sitting in the shop. I felt it when

Trevor laced our fingers together on top of the table. I even felt it when he woke me up at four in the damn morning.

Ugh, maybe Cass is right. Maybe I am getting soft in my old age.

I draw in a deep breath and turn my gaze to the ceiling. I let it out through puffed cheeks. "I might have spent the night at Trevor's on Wednesday."

"I knew it!" Cass is victorious again, pumping her fist in front of her. She takes a giant bite of lasagna.

A slow smile stretches over Vi's face. It's so almost relieved, which is a strange emotion to express about a sleepover. I furrow my brow in question, but she shakes her head slightly. We'll talk about that later, I guess.

"It wasn't anything, really," I say, though I'm not sure I believe it. It didn't feel like something, necessarily, but it didn't feel like nothing, either. I'm not sure how to explain that.

Cass rolls her eyes dramatically. "You, Emery Darlis, are your own worst enemy. You know it's okay to be happy, right? You've got to let go of this notion that the way your life looks now is the way it's going to look forever."

I flip my hair over my shoulder as my body tenses. "What is that supposed to mean?" But before she can respond, my phone dings three times from where I left my purse in their entryway.

"Hold that thought," I say as I rush to grab it and bring it back to the table. Two messages and an email blink on my screen. I push one. It's an email from Randall.

FROM: Randall Skinner <rskinner@bgl.com>
TO: Emery Darlis <edarlis@bgl.com>
SUBJECT: <no subject>
BODY: Meeting RE: coffee articles. Monday morning. Plan to be there.

That's ominous. I square my shoulders and straighten in my chair. He agreed to this and has essentially given me free reign to write what I want. If he doesn't like it, that's his problem.

I flip over to my text messages and see the group chat with Ethan and Josie lit up. I press it, hoping for some explanation.

> Ethan: 350,000 clicks since noon. Bitch, you're gonna do it!

That would definitely be an explanation. Randall is likely pissed I'm actually doing something successful. His pride has always been worth more than the reach of any given article. As I'm thinking of how to respond, Josie's message comes in:

> Josie: Randall is in a sour mood. He was looking for you this afternoon. I'll gladly respond to Letters forever if it means seeing him agitated like this.

When I look up, my smile stretching wide, Cass and Vi are looking at me expectantly. "Three hundred and fifty thousand clicks since noon," I say. "With those numbers, more will see it over the next few days, I'm sure."

They let out whoops and cheers. While they're busy celebrating, I click on the next message.

> Trevor: Mike decided to be decent and open the shop for me tomorrow.

My smile turns secretive as I reply.

> Emery: That's nice of him to let you sleep in.

Trevor's response is almost instant.

> Trevor: He may have suggested WE sleep in.

I chew on the corner of my lip. I wasn't kidding when I told him I was open to more than one night. As I study Cass as she and Vi toast their cans of sparkling water to my success, though, I don't think I can leave her. She's grinning like a fool, but her eyes are still rimmed with red, and her posture is still slumped slightly. What kind of sister would I be if I bailed so soon after a crisis for a booty call?

> Emery: I'm with Cass. She was upset, so I came over. I don't feel great about leaving her tonight.

> Trevor: Is she okay? Everything okay with the baby?

> Emery: Yeah, she's fine. Baby's fine. Just some family drama.

I touched briefly on my parents a few times, but I've kept it intentionally vague. Now, over text message, doesn't seem to be the time. Luckily, he doesn't seem phased.

> Trevor: Good. Well, not good about the drama. You know what I mean.

I grin at his awkwardness as three little dots appear at the bottom of the screen.

> Trevor: Mike says he can open Sunday instead. Unless that stuff about Cass was a polite way to tell me to take a hike.

I suddenly realize the room has grown silent. I look up from my phone again to see Cass and Vi staring at me wearing matching, goofy grins.

"Who are you texting now?" Cass asks in her singsong voice.

"Would you believe me if I said Ethan and Josie?" I ask.

"Not a chance," Vi chirps. "Not with that look on your face, anyway."

I sigh through my nose. "Trevor says his friend Mike will open the shop for him so we can sleep in on Sunday," I say cautiously.

Cass doesn't miss a beat. "Yes," she says. "Do it."

"Let me think about it for a minute," I protest.

"What is there to think about? You like him. He's hot. You've slept with him more than once, so the sex must be good."

I drag my hands down my face. "Please do not."

"Go." She drags out the O and widens her eyes. "What do you have to lose?"

My heart? The tenuous hold I have on whatever is left of my dignity? But I know what Cass will say if that's my response, so I just swing an arm around her shoulders again and squeeze. "Fine, if it'll make you happy. But tonight is about lasagna, and I fully expect to make popcorn and watch a terrible movie, too."

She leans her cheek against mine, and I can tell she's about to cry again. Vi gets up to get another piece of lasagna, giving us a minute. I can worry about Randall and respond to Trevor later. Right now, this is where I need to be.

Chapter Thirty

TREVOR

A QUIET KNOCK SOUNDS at my door at six-thirty on Saturday night. I try to play it cool and walk slowly to the door, but I'm too excited. I've been giddy since she texted me Friday night agreeing to come over, so I end up bounding to the door in a few steps. I pull it wide open to reveal Emery. She's wearing a purple satin tank top and the same cutout jeans she was wearing the night we met. Her dark hair falls over one shoulder in waves. It grazes the top of her breast that's peeking out over her shirt.

My mouth goes dry at the sight of her. She's the most beautiful woman I've ever seen.

"Hi?" Her voice tips up at the end like a question, and that's when I realize I'm staring at her and leaving her standing in the hallway.

I clear my throat and step back from the door into my cramped entryway. "Hi. Sorry. Come on in."

She steps through the door, not even trying to avoid brushing against me. Her cucumber scent greets me like a breath of fresh air. Something in me snaps apart at the easy contact, and I twirl her into my chest. I press my lips to hers almost desperately. One day without kissing her has been too long. For a moment, she melts into me, her lips parting for me to taste her. But then she laughs breathlessly.

"Can I at least put this down first?" she asks.

I pull away and look at her hands, which is when I realize she's holding a bag of takeout in one and a bottle of sparkling wine in the other.

"I suppose that can be arranged." I drag my fingertips down her biceps, over her forearms, and down to grasp the things she's carrying. She visibly shivers, and it fills me with a desire to make her do it again. I take her things from her and move them to the kitchen counter as she kicks off her sandals and follows.

I peek in the bag. Whatever she brought smells bready and sweet. "What's this?"

"Dinner?" she asks again.

"Why are you phrasing everything as a question?" I return.

She huffs and looks everywhere but at me. "I don't know. I don't... I'm nervous, I guess? I don't do this. Date. Dating? Is that what we're doing?" She winces and finally meets my eyes. She lets out a frustrated breath and starts again with more confidence. "It would seem I cannot stop myself from being awkward. I brought waffles."

"From the food truck? From the night we met?" I can't take my eyes off her. She's so cute when she's nervous.

"Yeah," she says sheepishly.

"That's fucking adorable."

"Well, good." She laughs again, and it's a little looser this time. She runs a hand through her hair and tosses it behind her. Now, I can see both of her gorgeous shoulders, and my dick springs to life.

I start taking cartons of waffles out of the bag and stacking them on the counter. "What are we celebrating?" I indicate the wine.

"Four hundred thousand more views in total from Friday until now." She says this with much more confidence than she had when she spoke about the waffles.

I meet her steady gaze. "That's amazing. That's two hundred and fifty thousand left."

She nods.

My grin is wide and openly excited. "You're going to do it."

"I don't want to get ahead of myself, but yeah, it would seem so."

If my damn apartment weren't so small, I'd pick her up and twirl her around. But, since I don't want to injure anyone, I settle for crossing the room in two long strides, cupping her face with my hands, soaking up her gorgeous and triumphant smile, and kissing her.

"Your last article was really good," I say against her lips.

"So I've been told," she responds drily, our breaths mingling in the sliver of space between us. It makes me wonder who told her what about that article, but I don't want to pry. Instead, I plant a kiss on her nose. "Waffles?" I ask. I feel her body relax under my fingers, as if she's glad I changed the subject.

"Yes. I'm starving." She walks to the counter and opens one of the boxes. She pouts and opens another. Her frown deepens.

"What's wrong, srećo?"

"They forgot the whipped cream." Her voice is almost a whine, exaggeratedly childish, though I can tell she's truly disappointed. "How are you supposed to have waffles without whipped cream?"

Now it's my turn to be coy. I reach around her and pull open the door to the refrigerator. I take out a stainless-steel whipped cream dispenser that I had filled at the shop and brought home so I could make her some fancy coffee in the morning.

She flattens her lips together and raises her eyebrows. "Is that what I think it is?"

"If you think it's a whipped cream dispenser, then yes."

She wiggles—actually wiggles—in excitement. My heart swells to see her happiness at such a simple thing, and even more to know I did this for her.

"You're a life saver," she laughs as she turns toward the counter.

Her back is to me, and I don't even try to resist touching her. I come up right behind her and press my chest into her back. She leans into me as I gently brush her hair to the side, fully exposing her shoulder. I squirt a bit of whipped cream onto her bare skin, then lick it off. The sweet taste of the cream mixed with the salt from her skin is a feast for my senses. And, to top it off, she moans and lets her head fall back against my chest, giving me access to the long column of her neck. I squeeze a bit more right where her neck meets her collarbone and lick that off, too.

"Oh, Trevor," she breathes. The thin strap of her tank top falls off her shoulder, and I practically growl as I lightly bite the skin there. I am feral for this woman. I breathe her in. Cucumber and sugar and cream.

"You're so sweet, srećo. You taste like you were made for me."

"I..." she trails off as if she can't form the words. Her hand closes around mine on the dispenser. "Can I?"

I chuckle darkly. "I thought you'd never ask."

She turns to face me, taking the dispenser and setting it on the counter behind her. She pulls my shirt over my head and tosses it to the ground. Her fingertips lightly graze the valley between my pecs, and it's my turn to shiver as they descend slowly to the button of my jeans. She deftly undoes it, and they quickly join my shirt on the floor.

To my surprise, she also tosses her clothes to the side to reveal a purple strapless bra and matching panties.

"I like that shirt. I don't want to get it messy." She shrugs a shoulder.

I laugh, a breathy sound full of desire. "Do you always wear lingerie that matches your clothes?" I ask, remembering the red set she wore under her red blouse the other night.

Her tongue darts out to wet her bottom lip before she drags it through her teeth. "Sometimes," she admits. And I don't know why it escaped me until just now, but I realize she must have chosen her clothes and underthings today specifically for me. Because she knew I'd see them. The knowledge sends a wave of desire through me and straight to my dick, which is now pressing almost painfully against my boxer briefs.

Emery notices it, and she laughs lightly before meeting my eyes again. "You like that?"

"Very much." No point in denying it. My desire is written plainly on my body for her to see.

She takes the dispenser from the counter and holds it between us. She squeezes a dollop of cream onto my shoulder, then licks it off. She hums approvingly as she pulls away. Some of the cream remains on her upper lip and she licks it off. I groan and brace myself against the counter behind her, boxing her in.

Her eyes flash. She uses the dispenser to squeeze small swirls of whipped cream from my collarbone down to my navel. She places the dispenser on the counter behind her, then uses a finger to take some from the spot at my collarbone. Her eyes meet mine as she slowly licks the whipped cream off her finger.

"Emery," I breathe.

"Mmm." She licks her finger again, then presses her hot tongue to my chest to taste the rest there. "The nickname is nice, but hearing you say my name is hot, too." She continues licking and tasting down to the top of my abdomen.

"Emery," I say again, just to hear her moan as she continues her slow descent down my torso. I thread my fingers through her silky hair and tug. She tilts her face up to me, a sexy smile playing at her mouth. She watches my expression as she leans in and licks the last spot of whipped cream below my belly button clean, swirling her tongue there again for good measure.

"You're beautiful like this," I breathe.

Her eyelids flutter as she leans her head into the pressure of my palm. When she opens her eyes again, there's a hunger in them that wasn't there before. She loops her fingers into the waistband of my boxers and tugs them down. I spring free, and she wastes no time taking me into her mouth.

I loosely hold her hair back as she bobs her head, sucking and licking and tasting the length of me. I watch as she works, her eyes closed and an expression of bliss painting her pretty face.

It's too good. I'm going to come apart, and I don't want to. Not yet. I gently grip her hair and pull out of her mouth. She starts to make a little noise of protest, but it turns to a yelp of surprise as I scoop her up and set her ass on the counter.

"Trevor, we can't," she laughs.

"Why not?" I pull off her panties and fall to my knees in front of her. She's lined up perfectly with my face, and I lean forward for a little taste. "Like you, I prefer an appetizer before the main course."

She lets out a gravelly laugh even as her head falls back to the cabinet above her. Her hands find my hair as I lick her center again. She's already dripping wet for me, but I tease and taste her anyway. She's so sweet all on her own.

"I need you, Trevor," she says. "Please."

"Hmm. I do kind of like it when you beg." I stand and open a drawer next to her to pull out a condom. She giggles, and my gaze snaps to hers.

"Did you plan to do this here?" Her laugh is a tinkling sound that wraps itself around my heart and squeezes.

"No," I reply honestly as I work the condom over myself. "That's where I keep the ones that don't fit in the nightstand."

"Hmm," she hums skeptically, but I don't give her a chance to think more about it. I cup under her knees and spread her legs wider for me. I line myself up with her entrance, and in one thrust, I'm inside her.

She wraps her legs around me, drawing me closer. Deeper. It takes us a second to get our rhythm, but once we do, it's magic. She's wrapped so tightly around me, and I'm watching her face in real time as she falls apart in my arms.

Her gaze drops to where we're joined, and she moans. "Yes. Trevor," she breathes in time with my thrusts. Her head falls back against the cabinet again, and she squeezes her eyes shut.

I skate my hand up her side and cup the back of her head, tilting it toward me. "Eyes on me, Emery," I demand. She keeps her eyes pressed closed, and I can't be sure, but I think I see her imperceptibly shake her head. I try a different tactic. I slow my rhythm and press a soft kiss to her mouth. "Please, srećo," I say into her skin. "Let me see those pretty eyes."

They finally flutter open, and her lips part on an inhale. She looks almost lost, as if looking into her lover's eyes isn't something she does often.

"Are you okay?" I pause my movements.

"God, yes. Please don't stop," she whimpers, but she keeps her gaze on mine.

She doesn't have to tell me twice. I move harder and faster, our eyes locked the whole time. When she starts to shake, I know she's close. I swallow her breathy moans with another kiss as we come together.

***

Emery takes some time cleaning herself up in the bathroom. I quickly wipe the sticky remnants of whipped cream from my body and clean up the counter, and then I pull on my gray sweatpants and a white t-shirt. While she's still in the bathroom, I plate the waffles and top them with more whipped cream, smiling at the memory of it as I do.

When she emerges, she's wearing one of my t-shirts and a pair of my boxer briefs. She fills them out perfectly, her gorgeous hips curving under the waistband and her perfect breasts pushing against the fabric of the shirt.

She notices me staring and tugs on the hem of the shirt as she laughs. "I'm sorry. I should have asked before stealing your clothes."

I shake my head. For a moment, that's all I can manage. "No," I croak out. I clear my throat and try again. "You don't ever have to ask. That's... you're..." I run a hand through my hair.

She smiles flirtatiously. "Speechless?"

"Yeah," I admit. I close the distance between us and kiss her deeply.

"I was disappointed that this fits me like a normal shirt because I'm so tall, but seeing that look on your face is pretty worth it," she teases.

"It fits you exactly as it's supposed to fit."

She kisses me then, and that's when I know beyond a doubt that I could do this every day. That I want her around me all the time. That I want her to be mine.

"I smell waffles," she says. "And I'm still starving."

I lace our fingers together and pull her toward the bed. "Then let's eat."

She eyes me skeptically. "I need actual food before we eat other things again."

A big, spirited laugh escapes me. She's so unassumingly funny that it catches me off guard. "I thought we could eat breakfast in bed. For dinner."

"Oh, say less." She scoots herself up toward the pillows, angled sideways and facing the room. I bring our plates to the bed and sit. She lifts up her feet and puts them in my lap. It's the most natural movement, but it's so intimate. I pause for a moment before setting my plate down beside me to adjust to this new side of Emery. I like it. A lot.

We eat our waffles as we chat about things big and small. We laugh so much, and I hang on every word she says. It's close to midnight by the time her eyelids start drooping, and as she curls herself into my side to rest her head on my chest, I know one thing with a surety I haven't felt in a long time.

I'm falling for Emery Darlis.

Chapter Thirty-One

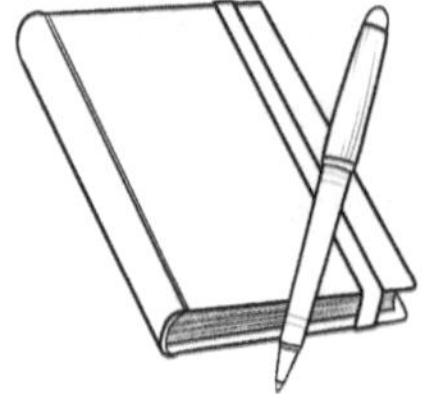

EMERY

I'M FALLING. A COMPLETE free-fall through thin air, and I'm jolted awake with a gasp when I hit the bottom.

I breathe hard, letting my heart catch up with itself. Letting myself remember that I'm in Trevor's apartment. In his bed. That I didn't just plummet off the side of a cliff.

I scrub my hands over my face and breathe deeply. Other than the fact that the sun isn't even peeking through the curtains over the window, I have no way of knowing what time it is. Trevor's long body is between me and the nightstand where my phone rests, and he isn't showing signs of waking up. I absently register that it isn't like me to sleep between someone and the wall. I never really thought about it before, but I guess I like an escape route, or at least an opening to the bathroom.

Then again, I guess it isn't really like me to sleep next to someone in the first place.

I sigh quietly, my heart finally beating at a more manageable pace. I roll my head toward the dark window and wonder if I'll ever be able to get back to sleep.

I hate those falling dreams. They feel so real, and the only way out of them is to be jolted awake when you… die, apparently?

Falling is such a terrible thing. We don't want to fall off a cliff, obviously, and we don't want to fall down the stairs. We don't want to fall out of someone's favor. We do fall all over ourselves to do things, but even that can be embarrassing. And yet, we use the word for wonderful things, too. Falling asleep. Falling into good luck. Falling in love.

I suck in a quiet gasp. That's not what has brought this on, surely. I've known Trevor for, what, three weeks? And, besides, I'm not doing a relationship right now. I'm doing… I don't even know what I'm doing. But it's not a relationship. It's not that for him, either. It didn't escape my notice that, when I awkwardly asked him about us dating last night, he skipped right to talking about waffles. Which is totally cool. I'm just having fun, anyway. I had only wanted to be sure.

"I can practically hear you thinking over there," Trevor says, his voice raspy with sleep and muffled by his pillow.

I startle and let out a brittle laugh. "Sorry, I didn't know you were awake."

He turns his head so he's facing me and slings an arm over my torso. He tugs, pulling my side into his chest. It's a completely natural movement, an innocent point of contact between two people sharing a bed together. But I'm still feeling the raw edges of that dream.

I don't mean to stiffen, but he must sense something is off because he asks, "You okay?"

"Yeah. Just a weird dream."

"Hmm," he nuzzles my neck, and I can already feel the edges blurring. "We're supposed to be sleeping in."

I huff. "I think you've messed up my sleep schedule," I joke. I need more stable ground, so I grab at anything that will get me there.

"I'd say I'm sorry, but I'm not." He kisses my neck as his fingers rub delicate circles right above my belly button.

My eyelids flutter closed as those edges grow even more dull. I turn my head to his. His amber eyes are clear and bright even in the dark, as if he's already shaken off whatever was left of sleep. He looks at me like he's taking me in, drinking me up. My skin heats under his gaze, and a small smile escapes me. He takes that smile for himself with a long, deep kiss.

He flattens his palm on my torso, but I guess I have a ticklish spot, too, because I break into a fit of giggles and curl into a ball on my side.

"Way to ruin a moment," I say between breathless laughter.

"I'm sorry!" he moans on a half-laugh. "I wasn't aware the unassailable Emery Darlis was ticklish. I'll be cataloging that piece of information to weaponize later."

It's like my breath is forced out of me. Like all the air is sucked out of the room. I must be the only one who feels it, because my laughter stops in its tracks, whereas Trevor's continues for a few more beats.

"'Unassailable.' That's a ten-dollar word. What am I, a fortress?" I try to keep my tone light, but even I can hear a sharpness in it.

"No. You're flawless." He chuckles again and kisses my cheek, which makes me think I'm overreacting. Of course I am. But words are my business. The right one matters. And I've had words like that thrown at me before.

He keeps peppering me with kisses until I'm giggling again and pushing him off of me. "I don't think you know what 'unassailable' means if you think it means 'flawless.'"

He rolls away and shrugs as he checks the time on his phone. "Words are your thing, not mine."

That's true. They were definitely Derek's thing, too. He knew exactly what he was saying when he said stuff like that. Maybe Trevor truly doesn't. I try to shake it off.

"It's almost six. I guess we did sleep in," he's saying.

I groan. "Still early. Need coffee."

He rolls over and kisses my temple again. "You came to the right place. Believe it or not, I happen to have some."

"Coffee is *your* thing." I say it as much for my benefit as anything.

"That it is." He throws off the covers, swings his legs over the side of the bed, and pulls on his sweatpants which had somehow made it to the floor in the middle of the night. He turns on a light, then stands and looks at me, hands on his hips. His golden-brown hair is standing on end, and the scruff on his jaw looks slightly unkempt. He's standing there shirtless and in sweatpants, looking all sexed up and happy. It makes me wonder if this is another dream.

He winces and rubs the back of his neck. "Uh, I might have brought that whipped cream home from the shop to make you some fancy coffee this morning."

"Oh yeah?" I sit up, letting the comforter pool over my lap.

"Yes. And we might have used it all last night." A blush starts at his neck and creeps toward his jaw.

I can't even pretend to be disappointed after the events of last night. "I'm a simple creature. I can handle normal coffee."

His face lights up as he drops his hand to his side. "I have an idea." He turns and crosses the small space to his kitchen and starts pulling things down from a cabinet.

Unsure of the level of clothing appropriate for the moment, I tug on my jeans and tank from yesterday before I join him. I lean my hip against the counter and fold my arms across my torso. "What's all this?"

"Turkish coffee," he says, pulling a set of measuring spoons out of a drawer. "This is how my grandfather made coffee before he scraped together enough money to buy that espresso machine for the shop. He still made it this way on his rare day off, or if he wanted some coffee after dinner."

He lines up two tiny cups, a bowl of sugar, a carton of milk, and a red package of what I assume is coffee on the counter next to a small, copper pot with a long handle.

I study him for a moment, arms still folded over the middle of my body. He fills a kettle with water and puts it on the stove before he notices me watching him. "What?" he asks.

"Trevor isn't a Croatian name," I say.

He laughs heartily. "You've been thinking about the origins of my name?"

"Well, yeah. I'm curious. Job hazard," I add with a wink, hoping he recognizes the phrase from our first kiss. He beams at me, and I smile right back. "So, where does the name come from?"

"It was my mother's maiden name. It's an old Welsh surname, actually. She insisted that, since my dad's family got my surname and middle name, she got to pick my first name. My grandparents hated it, but my dad insisted it was fair. I don't think he ever liked it either, but it made my maternal grandfather so happy. And Dad loved Mom so much. He probably wouldn't have batted an eye if she had wanted to name me Dick. Or worse." He's wearing a soft smile as he pushes all of his coffee ingredients into a perfectly straight line.

"What's your middle name?" I ask quietly.

He still isn't looking at me when he says, "Marko."

"For your paternal grandfather?"

He nods as he finally raises his gaze to meet mine. I know this is supposed to be a moment where we connect, where I find something deeper between us than was there before, but I'm struck by that feeling of standing at the edge of a cliff again. And, worse, I'm already off-balance.

"You sure are a medley of your ancestors, aren't you?" I say as a joke.

Trevor blinks, his eyes burning through me. "Aren't we all?"

An image of Cass flashes through me unbidden. She's hunched over the table, red-eyed and head in her hands with sobs wracking her body. All because our mother couldn't answer a call from her pregnant daughter. All because her daughter married a woman.

My parents come next. My dad is red-faced as he throws Cass's belongings on the front lawn. My mom stands behind him, her arms crossed. Vi and I hold Cass up as her knees give out.

I snap back to the present. My laugh is cold and harsh. Almost a bark, but I'm suddenly too tired to add that kind of bitterness to it. "I fucking hope not."

Trevor flinches. That's it. One flinch, and my heart cracks a tiny bit. He must have remembered that my parents are out of the picture, and I guess he didn't like that bit of information.

He takes a step toward me. The space is so small that all it takes is one step for our bodies to be close enough for me to feel the heat coming off his bare chest. He cups my jaw with a warm hand and presses a soft kiss to my lips.

I want nothing more than to melt into him, to go back to last night when being here felt more like an escape from the evening we spent trying to cheer Cass up than a reminder of it. So, I try. I part my lips and taste him on my tongue, and it feels like almost enough.

The kettle squeals, and he pulls away from me to press his forehead to mine. "I promised you coffee," he says.

"Yes. Please." I lean into him for one more second before he moves away to take the kettle off the heat.

He tears open the packet of coffee and adds three giant teaspoons to the small copper pot. He adds a teaspoon of sugar, then the hot water. He uses a small spoon to stir it quickly.

I raise my eyebrow as I lean against the counter again. "Hard to believe that tiny thing is going to make enough coffee for one person."

He smirks, eyeing me sidelong. "It actually makes enough for two. They're small. Espresso-sized."

I flatten my lips and frown skeptically. "I hope you're ready to make several of these."

Trevor laughs. "If you like it, I'll make you as many as you want." He holds the small pot over the burner on his stove that the kettle was on. After a few moments, the coffee starts bubbling up and he quickly removes it from the heat. He evenly distributes the coffee into the two small cups on the counter, then rinses the pot out in the sink. He comes back to the cups and adds a bit of milk into each one, then stirs them carefully.

"You don't filter it?" I ask, wrinkling my nose.

He chuckles again. "No. It's unfiltered. You really only drink about half the cup and leave the grounds. Some people swear you can empty them on a plate and have someone tell your future from them, but I don't have that particular skill."

"Like reading tea leaves," I say as he hands me one of the cups.

"Exactly."

He watches me expectantly as I breathe in the scent of the coffee. It smells rich and almost ancient, like dark chocolate and earth. I sip a bit of it and, sure enough, the flavor is dark and earthy, but sweet and creamy from the sugar and milk.

"Mmm," I hum. "It's different. Sweet."

"Like you, srećo."

I snort. He might be the only man in the world who thinks I'm sweet, even if I secretly love that he does. "I like it. Still kind of weirds me out that I'm drinking coffee grounds, though."

He takes a sip of his own then puts it down on the counter. "You're not. They're settled at the bottom. It's not meant to be guzzled like American drip coffee, or even a latte. It's meant to be sipped over hours with a pastry and a glass of water."

I frown at him over my cup as I take another sip. "How is anyone supposed to get an appropriate amount of caffeine that way? And who has time in the morning to do that?"

"Dida would roll over in his grave to hear you say that." His eyes once again burrow through me even as his humor still plays at his lips. "It's not about the caffeine. It's about the company."

I swallow hard. We hold each other's gaze for a moment longer before my phone dings from where it lays on the nightstand. I turn on instinct, and the spell is broken. I feel more than hear the woosh of air leave his lungs as I move out of his space and over to the bed. I sink down on the edge of it as I unlock the screen.

Ethan: You might want to check your email.

I type out a quick, *Why?* before I realize I could just check my email and find out. My heart jumps into my throat like it always does when I get cryptic messages like that. My thumb is shaking as I press it to the email icon and, there it is, an email from Randall right at the top.

FROM: Randall Skinner <rskinner@bgl.com>
TO: All Staff <as>
SUBJECT: Monday pitch meeting
BODY: It has been a while since Emery Darlis has graced us with her presence at our weekly pitch meetings, but I have asked her to be present to update us on the end of

her experimental series. I expect everyone to clear their calendars to attend.

I frown at my phone. I knew he wanted a meeting, but I don't remember him specifying it would be with the entire staff. I close the email and look at the next one down. Sure enough, another email from Randall sits below.

FROM: Randall Skinner <rskinner@bgl.com>
TO: Emery Darlis <edarlis@bgl.com>
SUBJECT: Tomorrow
BODY: I think our staff would benefit from an update tomorrow, as your series is coming to a close. Be prepared to present to everyone.

Randall is not a verbose man, but even this is sparse for him. Present what? A slideshow of numbers and reach? An overview of Ethan's pictures flashed on a screen like vacation photos? A dramatic reading of my articles?

I open the thread and type back to Ethan.

> Emery: That was cryptic.

> Ethan: He was in a mood on Friday. That's all I know.

> Emery: Why? Because his magazine is getting actual views? Seems like a strange thing to get upset about.

Across the room, Trevor's phone dings, too. He picks it up as he slides into a chair at the table set up close to the bed.

Ethan: Who knows. Better find those stone ovaries though, just in case.

I chuckle and lock my phone, only for it to sound again. I unlock it to read the message.

Ethan: You think he figured out who NewsJunkie814 is?

Emery: So what if he did? It's not against the rules to leave comments on my own articles.

I glance at Trevor, who is smiling like an absolute fool at his phone screen. It may not be against the rules, but I've never felt great about the comments I was leaving that week, and the reminder throws me off-kilter again.

I run a frustrated hand through my hair. This morning is so far from the cozy one I pictured having with Trevor when I arrived last night, and he's sitting over there, completely unaware of my inner turmoil.

I wonder if he knew how unsure I really was, would he still want to be around me?

He looks up from his phone, still grinning from ear to ear. "Check this out," he says, turning his screen to face me. I lean forward to see a picture of the shop taken from behind the counter. Every table has someone sitting at it, and a hand making a thumbs up is poking in from the side of the frame.

"Mike sent this." His voice is almost giddy. "He says it's been like this all morning. People are excited about the shop again." He puts his phone down on the table and leans forward, placing his hands on my knees and squeezing. "This is because of you. You did this."

The look on his face is one of awe and gratitude, and I can't deny that it makes me feel good to know he appreciates me, but the truth of the matter is that I didn't do much. I wrote a couple of shitty articles, left some comments to stoke the flames, and scrounged up one measly piece I was halfway proud of. And all the while, he's been working his ass off to create new menus, pose for Ethan's photos, and start up his social media. And punched my asshole ex in the face, to boot.

He thinks I'm something I'm not. Even he thinks I'm "unassailable." He might have pretended he didn't know what the word meant, but his subconscious must, at the very least.

I'm surprised her pussy wasn't ice.

What am I doing here? I'm an idiot who tried to ask him if we were dating last night. Who brought the same waffles we ate the night we met as some kind of romantic gesture. I should have known when he didn't quite answer me. I should have seen the forgotten whipped cream as some kind of omen.

"I didn't do anything," I manage to choke out. I want to try to let all of this go. To get back to licking whipped cream and moaning each other's names into the night air. But I can't get away from the edge of that cliff again, and I'm so completely thrown off, I don't think there's anything left to do but finally let myself fall.

He squeezes my knees again. "What's wrong, srećo? Is everything okay?"

I search his eyes. They're laced with concern. The edges of them crinkle together as he bounces his attention around my face, looking for cracks he can't see.

Whatever this is with him has gone too far. That's probably what that dream was trying to tell me. Get away from the edge or die. And suddenly, I'm so embarrassed about how I misread all of it. My mouth has gone dry, and my heart is pounding again. "I guess that's not entirely true," I start. "I did something. I wrote a couple of crappy articles and went in the comments section and told everyone how hot you are."

He reels back, and his hands slide off my knees. "What?"

The skin on my knees is cold where his hands used to be, and I shiver. This is a stupid thing to bring up, but I've jumped now. "I wanted so badly to win this awful game with Randall. I saw the girls fawning over your pictures, and I went in to respond to a few. Well, more than a few. I was poking around that comments section on and off for the better part of a week. That's when the yoga girls started coming in. Because I suggested they should check you out." I shrug helplessly, but it's twitchier, like even I can't stand being in my own skin. "We all do it. The writers, I mean. We have anonymous comment accounts to drive engagement."

Trevor runs a hand over his jaw, and I hear his palm scrape against the rough hairs. I search his face for something, anything, but it's carefully blank as if he's trying to decide how this new information feels inside his brain. And then hurt flashes over his features. It's quick, but it's unmistakable.

I hurt him.

I stand quickly. "I'm sorry. Like I said, it was stupid. It was before..." I sweep my hand, silently encompassing him, me, the bed, the waffles, the coffee, the entirety of everything between us, whatever it was.

Trevor stands, too, his features hardened in a way I haven't seen before. "I don't get it. Why are you bringing this up now?"

"You keep saying I'm helping you." I shake my head slowly. "And maybe I am, but it's not as altruistic as you think it is. I needed to win that bet, Trevor. I was drowning in that office."

"What happened to 'hotness is not a sustainable growth strategy?'" he asks, putting air quotes around my sister's words from earlier.

"I..." I swallow hard. "At the time, I wanted to win at all costs. I figured..." God, why is this so hard? "I figured sustainable growth was your problem, not mine. That changed, obviously, but..." I throw my hands up in a useless shrug. Words are my thing, but they're failing me now.

He runs a stiff hand through his hair as his other hand still rests on his hip. "Let me get this straight." He crosses the room and grabs a t-shirt to pull on, then faces me again. "You reduced my life—my father's and grandfather's lives—to a thirst trap. For clicks."

"When you put it that way—"

"Did you ever intend to take this seriously?"

I stand there, gaping. My mouth opens and closes a few times, but I don't have a good answer. I didn't, at first. Or, I did, but only seriously enough to win. I don't know when the switch flipped, as Cass put it, but it did. But I'm afraid if I tell him that, he'll take it the wrong way.

"That last article you wrote." His voice is shaky, almost pleading. "All that stuff about feeling at home and being part of a community? Finding common ground? Was all that a show to get more clicks, too?"

"No," I answer, almost too quickly. "I had written a half-hearted article before that. I deleted it. I was actually proud of the one that went to print."

He studies me for a moment, his eyes burning through me. His face is completely impassive. I wish I could tell what he's thinking, but I can't. All I can tell is that something has shifted between us. Inside me. And not for the better.

"I should go," I say slowly.

"This is my life, Emery." He sounds resigned. Almost flat. "I can't just go get a job somewhere else."

Sure, he could. He has a whole portfolio of skill sets the coffee shop has given him. How is it any different than me being laid off and finding my job at *Baker's Grove Living*? "Why not?" I ask. "I did."

He releases a frustrated huff, running his hand through his hair again. "Yeah, and you're super happy there." His voice is laced with sarcasm.

I reel back. "It's just a job. Having a job isn't necessarily about being happy. It's about paying bills."

"My grandfather would say otherwise," he snaps back.

I laugh humorlessly. "You're stuck in the past."

"And you're stuck in the present."

I bite my lip so hard I think I taste blood. "I really need to go."

Trevor shakes himself as if coming out of a trance. He steps forward and cups my elbows. "What is going on here?"

"What do you mean?" I ask. "I'm a shitty web reporter for a shitty lifestyle magazine, and I did a thing that's, at best, of questionable journalistic integrity. At worst, it hurt you. Now I'm leaving."

"You don't have to leave. We can talk this out," he insists. When I shake my head, he frowns. "People have feelings, Emery. I am allowed to feel something about this. That doesn't mean we call it quits."

His amber eyes are stormy and intense. His fingers press gently into the skin at my elbows, as if he can keep me here with him. But I stiffen and step back, even as he grips harder to keep me there.

People have feelings. I've heard that before, too. People have feelings, but I don't.

We had fun together. I stepped out of my comfort zone and stayed a few nights with him. I may have toyed with the idea of wanting something more. But it doesn't change the facts. I'm cold, and he's warm. I'm adrift in the present, and he's anchored by his family's past. I'm willing to do anything to win a workplace bet, and he's just trying to keep his work afloat. And I hurt him in the process.

Everything goes fuzzy at the edges, and I can't think. I can barely breathe. I squeeze my eyes shut so I don't have to see him anymore. So my eyelids can keep the tears at bay. "Please. Let me go." I sound pathetic even to myself, but he must hear the plea in my voice because his grip on my elbows loosens, and his hands fall away.

I look at the tiny, half-empty cups of coffee, the rumpled bedsheets, the light finally streaming in through the singular window in his small apartment. Anywhere but at him. My movements are robotic as I put my phone in my back pocket, slide my shoes on, pick up my purse from the ground, and leave Trevor in his stunned silence.

As the door clicks behind me, it sounds like a finality I'm not quite ready for. I stand there for a few minutes, praying the tears won't start to fall. I could go back in there and talk it out like he wanted to. I probably should. For a moment, I convince myself of how good it would feel to lay it all on the table for him. To tell him that this is me, that what you see is what you get. And beg him to want me anyway.

But I don't. What's done is done, and I don't think I could handle the rejection if that's where it led, anyway. I take a deep breath and let it out slowly, the tears receding. And as I make my way outside, I have myself at least halfway convinced that this is the way things are meant to be.

Chapter Thirty-Two

TREVOR

"I HAVE ABSOLUTELY NO clue what started it." I'm sitting at the counter of the shop, and not even the sounds of porcelain clinking and conversation flowing around me is enough to soothe the ache in my chest.

After Emery left, I didn't know what to do, so I went to the shop thinking I could get to work. But Mike sat me down at the counter on the other side of the espresso machine and told me I was, under no circumstances, to lift a finger to help. James brewed me up a surprisingly decent latte, set it in front of me with a look of pure sympathy, and Mike has been letting me fill him in on the events of the last twelve hours while helping customers ever since.

"That must not be entirely true," Mike says as he pours steamed milk over espresso in a large, red mug. "Something must have happened, even if it wasn't obvious. Did she seem off today at all? Or last night?"

"Not last night." I'm miserable all over again at the memory of her hot tongue on my body, and the thought that it might never happen again. "Maybe this morning. She woke up early and said she had a weird dream.

She got a couple of messages before we started talking, too. She never told me what they said."

"You think they were from her sister? About whatever the crisis was the other night?"

"I have no idea. Maybe?" I perk up slightly. "Do you think that's what happened? She got freaked out about something totally unrelated and used those comments on her article as a reason to pull away?"

"Hard to say unless you talk to her." He shoots me a pointed look as he hands off the red mug to James for him to deliver it to a table. He leans against his elbows on the counter between us.

"She doesn't want to talk to me."

"Were you upset about the comments?" he asks, clasping his hands together.

"It's not the comments so much as what they mean. I was under the impression she was taking this seriously, and she wasn't." I chew on the inside of my cheek, suddenly unsure. I don't know if upset is the right word, exactly. I wasn't happy about it, but I wasn't going to break up with her about it, either. I meant it when I said I wanted to talk things out.

Mike considers the question. "Did you tell her how you felt?"

"I was honest," I say. "Learning someone you're falling for didn't have your interests at heart doesn't feel great."

"But you said that third article—the one where she turned a corner—that one was real?"

"She said it was."

"Do you believe her?"

I take a sip of the latte James made for me. "I want to. Hard to say for sure when she wouldn't talk to me about it." I sag in my seat. Even parroting his own words back to him doesn't bring me the joy it usually does.

My phone buzzes on the counter next to me, and I grab it quickly, hoping it's Emery. It's not.

> Mom: Hi, sweetie. Wanted to wish you luck with your event this weekend. Sorry I can't make it up there to see you. Love you.

I run a hand through my already-messy hair. In the midst of everything, I had all but forgotten we're having this grand re-opening this weekend. It's not supposed to be a huge thing, but Cass and I did message back and forth a few times about specials to offer and a banner to hang. James suggested his band do an acoustic set and said he could handle setup. Thankfully, there's not much left to do except pick up the new menus from the printers since we opted to keep the original menu board over the counter as a nod to the origins of this place.

"Say hi to Mama K for me," Mike says, reading my phone screen across the counter.

I nod distractedly as I type out a quick message to her. I wonder briefly if she could help me decode Emery's behavior but decide against looping her in. Not right now, at least. I'm still processing it myself, and I doubt she could do anything other than try to soothe my wounds over the phone.

A high-pitched giggle drifts over to us from the corner by the window. I glance that way and smile delicately at a little boy sitting with his mother. He has completely demolished a muffin, and there are crumbs everywhere. His mom is tickling him while also trying to get the crumbs into some kind of order.

"James, can you—" I start, but he's already seeing what I'm seeing.

"On it, Boss." He grabs a broom and heads over to their table.

I turn my attention back to Mike, who had been watching the exchange with a satisfied smile.

"Kid's got some potential," he says. "When he wants to, that is."

"Did you all have a little heart-to-heart this morning or something?"

Mike tips his head back and forth. "I guess you could call it that." When I frown at him, he leans back on the counter as if he's conspiring with me. "I told him you needed someone around here who could pull his weight. Maybe even become a manager of this place someday. You know, so your best friend doesn't have to open the shop to give you a break. Seems he's interested in a promotion." He steps back again and folds his arms over his puffed-out chest. "He even got a couple of the orders right today."

I narrow my eyes at him. "Getting a couple right would imply he got more than a couple wrong."

"Baby steps, Trev." He sweeps an arm, encompassing the entirety of the shop. "This Sunday crowd put a pep in his step, I think." Then, he looks at me, more serious. "I hope these new customers will eventually give you back that optimism, too. You believed in a miracle, and it's happening for you. However, you got here, that's incredible."

I drop my gaze to where my hands are clasped together on the counter. My knuckles are practically white from how hard I've been gripping them together without even realizing it. I take a deep breath and let it out slowly. Is this crowd worth what Emery did to help it get there?

I wish I could feel even an ounce of optimism right now. But I can't escape the fact that the shop is full because of her, sure, but I also feel like shit because of her. Just when I thought I could have everything—the shop running at a profit and Emery fitting into my life—it turns out I can't. I guess I can only have one at a time.

The universe sure is a stingy bitch.

Mike's gaze snags on something behind me, outside the windows. "Your day might be about to turn around."

I straighten quickly, but I'm afraid to turn around and look. "Emery?"

"Her sister."

Sure enough, when I look, Cass is coming through the door. When she sees me, she stops in her tracks, and her eyes widen in surprise. "Trevor. I didn't expect to see you here." Then she shrugs and comes to the counter. She hoists herself into a chair next to me. "But, I'm actually glad you are. I have a new financial plan for you to get this place back on its feet and keep you from spending any more of your personal money. I've budgeted for the things we need for next weekend as well, and created one-, two-, and five-year growth plans to help you hire more staff, so you can do it all without burning out." She slides a large, purple binder toward me and nods at Mike. "A muffin and a half-caff iced mocha, please."

Mike doesn't immediately move. He stares at her, then shifts his eyes to mine.

Cass tilts her head slightly and pinches her eyebrows together as she looks between the two of us. "What?"

I clear my throat. "Have you talked to your sister today?"

She goes completely still, her confusion morphing into concern. "No. Should I have? Is everything okay?"

I shake my head slowly. "She got a couple of messages this morning, and we got into a fight. She was upset and told me about some comments she had left on her own article." I shrug helplessly. "She threw me for a loop."

Cass cocks an eyebrow and leans back on her stool, crossing her arms over her belly. "She broke things off with you?"

"It would seem so," I say miserably.

She draws in a huge breath through her nose and tips her head to the ceiling to let it out the same way.

"Well," she begins, her tone completely and utterly exasperated. "You'd better get me that muffin and then tell me the whole story."

Mike springs into action, crossing over to the pastry case.

I look at Cass in bewilderment. "Isn't this something you and her should talk about? Like sisters?"

She laughs humorlessly as her gaze meets mine. So much like Emery's, those dark eyes, though Cass's are a little rounder. It's almost disconcerting.

"Oh, I'll talk to her." She sounds almost menacing as Mike puts the muffin in front of her and goes to work making her drink. "But if I know Emery, she won't give me even half the details. So, spill it, lover boy." She takes a huge bite. "From the top."

Chapter Thirty-Three

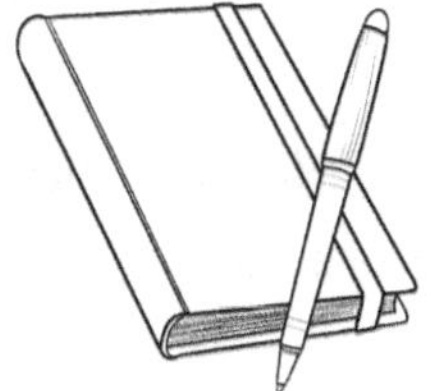

THE REST OF SUNDAY passes in a blur. My phone has been off since I left Trevor's apartment. When I get home, I toss it in my work bag and don't think about it again. I wander aimlessly for the rest of the day. Opening and closing the fridge and finding nothing I want to eat. Doing some laundry but leaving it in piles on my bedroom floor because I don't feel like folding it. Trying to read a book, but realizing ten pages in that I have no recollection of what has happened on any of those pages. Eventually, I fall asleep on the couch, wake up when it's dark out, and drag myself to bed.

Monday morning isn't much better. I wake up, shower, and get ready for work. When I look at myself in the mirror, I appear normal. Navy ankle-length pants, white blouse, red loafers. Hair falling in loose waves over my shoulder. Makeup looking natural and put-together.

My reflection squints back at me. What would I see if the mirror could show me what's inside, not just outside? Sadness, probably. But not only from yesterday; from years of people determined to convince me that I wasn't good enough to stay in their lives. Frustration that I can't fix our family for Cass, and that my little niece or nephew might never know their grandparents or have large, family parties for their birthday. Trepidation about this meeting today, writing the last article, possibly seeing Trevor again.

I square my shoulders, take a deep breath, and unnecessarily straighten my blouse. One thing at a time, I suppose. First up: the meeting.

When I arrive in the conference room about ten minutes early, everyone but Randall is already there. *Baker's Grove Living* doesn't have a huge staff, but since he told everyone to clear their schedules, the room is full. People line the walls, and there is no shortage of sympathetic glances as I enter. Ethan and Josie flank an empty seat, as if they're sentinels standing watch over me.

As I slink into the chair, Ethan slides a mug of breakroom coffee toward me. I can smell the burnt edge to it from here, and my stomach rolls over. I don't look at him as I shake my head slightly and push it back in his direction.

"Break room coffee isn't good enough for you now that you've had a taste of the good stuff, huh?" he teases.

I shoot him a sidelong look. "Break room coffee has never been good enough for anyone." The words come out more acidic than I intend.

He frowns at me, tilting his head to the side as he moves the mug out of the way. "This is not the attitude I'd expect from someone who is poised to win a bet."

"Breakroom coffee isn't a celebratory drink. And besides, don't get ahead of yourself. The invitation to this meeting was cryptic at best," I counter. "It's a classic power play. Randall wants me off-balance. He's probably about to make up some ridiculous rule or find a loophole out of spite to keep me from succeeding, even though I've done what he asked and then some."

Ethan leans in and lowers his voice so only I can hear him. "If he wants you off-balance, the best thing you can do is stand tall and straighten your crown."

I deflate a little and face him. "I'm too tired, Ethan." And that's the moment I realize it's true. I'm so tired of all of it. Of fighting for something better from this dead-end job. Of wishing my life wasn't such a goddamn mess. Of being a woman who had to turn herself to stone to withstand blow after blow from job, husband, and family.

And you're stuck in the present.

That was a blow yesterday. I can't pretend it didn't land square in my chest, right next to my heart. But he was right. I'm stuck. I have been for a while.

Then again, look what happens when I try something new. I get my heart handed back to me on a platter next to a waffle and a Turkish coffee.

As if he can see everything I've encompassed with that one statement, a corner of Ethan's dark lips lift in a sad smile. "Well, then," he says softly as he reaches up and adjusts an imaginary crown on my head. "Good thing you have friends here to do it for you."

Josie, who must have heard the whole conversation, puts a reassuring hand on my knee and squeezes briefly.

My eyes sting, and Ethan's face goes blurry as the door opens behind me. By the way the room silences, I know Randall has entered. I take advantage of the time it takes him to walk around to the head of the conference room table to pack my emotions into a little bag and set them to the side for later. I won't be able to ignore them forever, but I can keep it together for the length of this meeting.

Randall sinks into his chair and steeples his fingers in front of his thin lips. "Good morning," he says smoothly. A few mumbled "good mornings" are returned, but the tension in the room is palpable. No one knows exactly what he's going to do.

"Monday mornings are normally pitch meetings, as you know, but we have a unique situation this week. Our very own Emery Darlis has been working on a new type of piece for the magazine. Darlis, will you fill everyone in on what you've been doing this month?"

This is completely unnecessary. All the staff has a decent handle on what everyone is working on week to week, but I clear my throat. I may not know the rules yet, but I'll play his game. "Um, yes, sir. I've been writing a series of articles about a local coffee shop, Baker's Blend, that has been doing poorly in the current economic climate."

Randall nods. "And how have those articles been doing?"

The urge to break eye contact with him is strong, but I resist. I look right at him all the way on the opposite side of the table as I say, "The goal was to have one million unique visitors to the site over four articles. So far, the first three articles have driven approximately seven hundred and fifty thousand new clicks to the site."

Ethan is practically vibrating with pride next to me, but I resist the urge to punctuate my statement with a smug smirk. I'm still not sure what's going on.

I don't think I'll have to wait long, as Randall pushes back from the table. His chair creaks as he leans back in it and opens his gaze to the rest of the room. "Anyone else seen an uptick in visitors to their articles over the past few weeks?"

I tear my eyes from Randall to look around the room. There's some affirmative murmuring and a few uncertain nods.

Where is he going with this?

"I will admit, I was skeptical that this could work," he says as the room falls silent again. "It's not every day that a staff writer directly disregards the way things have been done for a pitch."

It takes all my effort not to grimace at the slight jab.

Randall addresses our data analyst. "Burkholm, can you tell the staff why they've been seeing an uptick in page views over the past few weeks?"

"It would appear that, when people click on Darlis' articles, they have a tendency to click on others in the *Suggested Articles* section," he replies.

Randall nods again. He clearly already knew this information. "So, you're telling us that Emery Darlis and her web series is the reason the site is doing better this month than it has in a while?"

Burkholm clears his throat. "It would appear that way, yes."

Randall locks eyes with me. He gives the tiniest nod of approval before addressing the room. I'm struck by the realization that he did want people off-balance today, but not me. His cryptic invitation was for everyone else.

"I don't love being proved wrong"—there's a smattering of nervous laughter—"but it would be foolish not to lean into this and see if we can make it work for us. We want to shift our focus to include more local interest series going forward rather than one-off pieces. We will, of course, still include singular stories, but I want to reschedule our pitch meeting for tomorrow to give everyone a chance to bring some of these new ideas to the table." When no one moves, he huffs frustratedly. "Dismissed!" he barks. The staff scatters. Even Josie jumps to her feet and shuffles out as she waits for the bottleneck of people to leave the conference room.

Ethan remains, and I turn to him wide-eyed. "What?" I mouth.

He smiles and shrugs. "You did it, queen."

I did it. And the normally gruff and cranky Randall admitted it in front of everyone. Before the deadline. And he didn't only admit it; he wants others to model their pitches after mine. That's *huge*.

I reach for my phone on instinct. I want to text Trevor to tell him all about it, but I remember it's still off and buried in my work bag. Because I hurt him and walked out on him. And suddenly, the victory feels completely hollow.

As the room empties out completely, Ethan stands. I move to follow him, but Randall calls out my name.

"Darlis. Stay back, please."

I sink back into my seat. Ethan pauses to squeeze my shoulder, then leaves the room, shutting the door behind him.

"I know I'm speaking prematurely, but it would seem you'll likely come out on top of our little challenge. I'm comfortable trusting you to run your piece on… what was it again?"

"Misallocation of local school funds, sir," I choke out around a tightness that gripped my chest right around the time I reached for my phone.

"Right. But don't lose sight of the fact that we want to try to keep our positive tone as much as possible." He dips his chin to look at me over his wire-rimmed glasses.

"Yes, sir."

He regards me for another moment before waving me away with a flick of his fingers as he looks down to make some notes on a notepad sitting near his elbow. "That'll be all."

Okay, then. I rise and push my chair in, but I stand there and grip the back of it. "If I may, sir?"

He looks up at me over his glasses with a pinched expression, his fingers tapping the notepad. "Yes?"

I swallow hard. I'm pushing my luck here, but I'm a journalist, even if recent events have called my integrity into question. My curiosity has gotten the better of me, and I need to know. "My original pitch was out of left field. It was a desperate attempt to win a bet."

He raises an eyebrow. "You know I could still pull the last article."

"Yes, sir. I know. I just..." I trail off and regard him for another moment. Some of his hard edges have softened, and I'm pretty sure his threat is empty. "Why did you accept it in the first place? You couldn't have known it would work."

He sets his pen down carefully. He folds his hands in front of his face and presses them into his lips. Then, he drops them to the table. "I've been to Baker's Blend. Years ago. Nice little place."

I pinch my brows together and squeeze the back of the chair. "Forgive my forwardness, sir, but that can't be why."

He huffs. Then he smiles. Actually *smiles*. I almost can't believe my eyes.

"My wife and I had our first date there," he admits. "It felt like a sign."

I have to fight not to let my jaw drop. All these years here, and I never thought Randall Skinner could possibly be even a little bit of a softie. Yet, here he is, talking about first dates and signs like it's the most normal thing in the world.

As if reading my mind, he says, "I know you don't think of me like that. No one does. I have a reputation to keep up here. Don't go spreading any rumors."

I try not to chuckle. "I won't, sir."

"Turns out trying to keep a local lifestyle magazine afloat in the middle of the collapse of journalism as we know it is tough to do. Makes a man rough around the edges. But you've bought us some wiggle room this month, Darlis. I won't forget it."

It's a clear dismissal, so I nod. "Thank you, sir," I say.

As I leave the room, Randall says to my back, "I can see how you were probably a great reporter at *The Gazette*."

The compliment doesn't go unnoticed, but it does little to assuage the tightness in my chest. "Thank you, sir," I repeat, quieter this time, without turning around.

I make my way back to my desk, but as I wait for my laptop to power up, those words weigh on me. Randall may have turned rough around the edges, but Trevor has been trying to prop up his shop for years, and he's remained one of the most hopeful men I know. I loved his optimism, even if I could never match it. It might have even started to rub off on me a bit. Why else would I agree to spend the night? Or bring him waffles?

Against my better judgment, I fish my phone out of my bag and turn it on. I hold my breath as the screen lights up, hoping there's a message or voicemail from him. I scroll quickly through the pitifully few notifications. There's only a couple from Cass and Vi. Nothing from Trevor.

I toss the phone back in my bag. Suddenly, my cubicle feels too tight. Too stark. Too constricting. I've been spoiled by the warmth of Baker's Blend, but I know I can't go there either. If Trevor hasn't even tried to contact me, he must still be too hurt. I'm not going to bother him.

I send a quick text to Cass and Vi letting them know I'm alive and I need to throw all my energy into this final article, which is probably true, but not for the reasons they think. Once it's sent, I power down my phone again and throw it back in my bag. "I'm working from home for the rest of the day," I call to Ethan over the cubicle wall as I pack away my laptop. "Let me know if you need me."

"Don't forget your crown," he calls back.

Chapter Thirty-Four

TREVOR

Monday and Tuesday pass, but I'm not sure how. I don't know what happens those days, or how to feel about any of it. I know I should be overjoyed that the steady stream of weekend customers seems to transfer into the next few mornings, but I can't muster up more than a minimum amount of excitement. I am happy, don't get me wrong, but what is the point of any of it without her here to celebrate?

I know the original goal was to help the shop. We did that, and I don't want to discount it. But, at the very least, Emery's success was always woven into it. She wanted to succeed more than anything, it seems. Maybe more than she wanted to be with me, at least at first. Can I continue to hold that against her? I refuse to pretend I wasn't hurt. Sex might sell, but objectifying me for her own gain was wrong.

But things changed between us. Somewhere between that second and third article. Somewhere between a coffee tasting and me punching her ex in the face. I can't escape the truth of it now. I miss *her*. Her laugh, her dark eyes, her cucumber shampoo, the way her skin tasted, how her fingertips felt as they explored my body. Without meaning to, she had become such a giant presence in my life, and then, *poof*. Vanished.

I'd call her right now if I thought it'd do any good. I wanted to talk it out. She didn't. I guess that's that.

The sun is dipping below the taller buildings behind the shop on Tuesday evening when James pulls up to the curb. He had been tasked with collecting items we'll need for the event this weekend. Mike is close behind him with boxes of more stuff. I told him he wasn't technically a paid employee, so he doesn't have to help. He looked at me like I was an idiot, reminded me that I had paid him in lattes for working here Sunday, and snatched the list of things we needed out of my hands.

I'm grateful for the help. And the company.

Mike gets to work unfurling the banner. We hold it up to be sure it'll fit in the window. It does. We put it away until the weekend, and he starts hanging string lights over the canopy and around the windows. Cass told us it'd add a bit of a festive air, and I'm too afraid not to listen to her. James unloads extra flavor syrups, milks, and pastry ingredients into the back room before setting himself up at a table to video chat with his band mates about Saturday's event.

I jam my hands in my pockets and walk outside to chat with Mike and give James some privacy. Even though we're all there, the shop is technically closed, so there isn't much for me to do. I grab a string of lights and start lining a window.

"You hear anything from her yet?" Mike asks around a couple of nails perched precariously between his teeth. He shifts on his ladder for better access to the building.

"Nope."

He starts banging a nail into the window frame. "She still writing that last article?"

"I wouldn't know. I haven't talked to her," I say through gritted teeth.

Mike hums and nods, unfazed. "Well, she probably has to," he says after a pause.

I drop my arms to my side, and the lights fall at my feet. "Do you have a point, man?"

His eyebrows shoot up, but he doesn't lose his grip on his string of lights. "Just making conversation."

"Well, can you make conversation about literally anything besides the woman who broke my heart?" I pick up the lights that I had dropped in a huff.

"The wound is still a little fresh. I hear you. Message received." He pounds another nail into the window frame and hangs a section of lights, then does it again. "Have you called her?"

This time, I throw the lights down on the ground like a child having a fit. "Do you want me to punch you in the face?"

He shrugs, which manages to piss me off even more. "If it'll help." Then, he smirks. "I know you're capable of it now, bro."

"I swear, Mike. You're my best friend in the whole world, but do not test me today. I just want to get through this godforsaken week and move on with my life, hopefully with some more money than I had before."

"No worries, man." He hammers again. "I'll back off."

"Back off what?" A woman's voice comes from behind me. I turn around to see Cass standing there, hands on hips and belly pointed at me like a weapon.

I try not to groan. I knew she was coming back, but it's so hard to see her when she shares DNA with the only woman I want here right now.

I must not have hidden my reaction to her arrival very well, because she hums disapprovingly. "Nice to see you, too," she deadpans. "I take it you haven't heard from my sister either."

I shake my head. "She hasn't called you?"

"She messaged once to say she needed to focus on this last article and was going dark. That was yesterday morning. Nothing since then. She could be dead in a ditch somewhere, and I'd have no idea."

"She's not, though," I say. "Dead."

She pins me with a look that says I must be even more of an idiot than she thought. "No, Trevor. She's not dead. She's hiding behind that article and pretending like she's not exactly as sad and lonely as you are."

"Hey—" I start to protest, but Mike claps a hand on my shoulder to silence me.

"Let's call a spade a spade." He squeezes, then releases it.

I look between the two of them, both staring at me expectantly. When they make no move to talk, I scoff. "Fine. But there's nothing I can do about it. She hurt me. She doesn't want to talk. I'm giving her space. And these lights aren't going to hang themselves." I turn my back to both of them and start vigorously pounding tiny nails into the window frame.

"You two have more in common than I thought," Cass mutters.

I pause my hammering. "What do you mean?"

"Well, you're both going to hide behind menial tasks and pretend like you're not broken inside and pining for each other."

I tilt my head, regarding her for a second. "You think she's pining for me?"

"I wouldn't know. I haven't talked to her," she reminds me pointedly. I go back to hammering as she adds, "Once, when we were kids, she borrowed my favorite necklace. It looked like an amulet. It was purple, my favorite color. I loved that thing. But she had a purple sweater that matched it, and she wanted to wear it. So, I let her. The clasp broke, and it fell off. She had no idea she even lost it until right before the end of the school day. She sat far away from me on the bus. Ran upstairs and closed the door to her room. Stayed in there for days, pretending to be sick, until our mom made her come out and tell her what was wrong."

She stops there, and her gaze falls to the ground. She takes a moment before she shrugs her shoulders and bounces her head back and forth as if shaking off something, then looks back at both of us.

When it's clear she's not going to continue, Mike frowns. "I assume there was a point to that story?"

"Obviously." She taps her foot and folds her arms. "Emery is the type to hide away when things get a little uncomfortable. Or when she knows she's wrong. And I have a feeling this is a little bit of both."

"I hope you're right," I say quietly.

She crosses the distance between us and puts her hands on my shoulders. She's much shorter than her sister, so she has to look up at me, but I meet her intense gaze all the same. "Patience, Trevor. I'll try to talk to her, but you have to let her come to this conclusion on her own, or she'll dig in further."

"Didn't you just say your mom dragged her out of her room to get her to talk to you?" I wince.

Cass laughs bitterly, but it turns into a giggle as if she remembers something funny. "Yeah. What I didn't tell you is she sat at the kitchen table in silence for three hours before finally coming clean, and then she didn't talk to our mom for three days afterward as punishment for making her tell me before she was ready."

"What makes you think she won't ice *you* out for days?"

"Because, unlike our mother," she spits the word out as if it tastes bad, "I am doing this from a place of kindness and love. She was annoyed Emery had locked herself in her room and hadn't done her chores. And unlike that necklace," she pauses and eyes me up and down, "she stands to gain something from figuring out her shit this time. Now, will one of you boys please help me carry the box of menus from my car? I had to park two blocks away, and they're heavy."

Mike jumps in front of me. "I got you," he says. "I think our guy here could use a minute."

As I watch them walk away, I wonder, even if Cass is right, maybe I should extend an olive branch. Maybe Emery really has realized her mistake and does want to be with me. Maybe she needs to hear from me to know it's okay to talk. I could save Cass the trouble by just calling her.

I take my phone out of my pocket and pull up Emery's contact info. Before I can think too hard about it, I press her number and bring the phone to my ear.

And I try not to let myself sag too much when it goes straight to voicemail. I hang up before I hear the beep.

Chapter Thirty-Five

How the actual fuck am I supposed to write this article? I can't write at my apartment. Even with music, it's too quiet. I can't write at the office because it's too cramped and sterile. And if this process has taught me anything, I do my best writing where I can observe my surroundings. The only place I really want to go to write is off-limits, for obvious reasons.

I pace around and feel sorry for myself for the rest of Monday. On Tuesday, I fall into a cycle of writing a few sentences, deleting them, writing more, deleting them, rinse, and repeat. On Wednesday morning, I realize that, not only is this process absolutely futile, but I've run out of coffee.

This is how I end up at Donna's Diner.

Donna tries to poke good-natured fun at me like she usually does. I try to smile and jab her right back, but everything feels flat. She gives me some space after that, but when she comes to refill my coffee and tells me, sincerely, that my last article was more like the stuff I used to write, I can only muster up a half-hearted thank you.

I don't see her again after that.

I put in my earbuds and turn up the music. I sit there for about an hour with my cheek resting on my palm, my elbow propped on the table. I mostly watch my cursor blink. My coffee grows cold, but I don't feel like making the small talk required if I wave Donna over for a refresh, so I sink my cheek further into my hand and close my eyes.

I don't think I can do this. After our little moment yesterday, I am pretty sure I could tell Randall I can't write the fourth, and he'd be okay with it. But I want to write it, and I want to do it right. Trevor's grand re-opening is this weekend, and I want to help him turn the corner. I want to do it for him.

Because I like him. A lot.

And that admission starts the 80s movie montage behind my eyelids. I am powerless to stop it. His smoldering, amber eyes, focused on me. The picture Ethan took where I'm out of frame, and he's smiling at me like I am the only thing worth smiling at. His forearms peeking out under his plaid shirts. The scent of him, all coffee and sugar and vanilla. His hot tongue on my skin, chilled by whipped cream. The sweet taste of him when his lips part and my tongue slides inside.

Srećo.

Happiness. Luck. Something sweet.

Somewhere in the back of my mind, I consider the idea that I could write this article as some kind of love letter to him. That it could move him so deeply, he would forget the hurt I caused on Sunday, or, at least, forgive it.

I inwardly chastise myself for fantasizing like I'm in some kind of romcom. An article in *Baker's Grove Living* can't be a love letter to Trevor. It can barely be an I-tolerate-you letter to this city.

And I berate myself even further for entertaining the idea of some kind of relationship with him in the first place. That's how we ended up here, and I'd do well to remember it. I'm not a relationship kind of person, and I don't know how many more red flags need to go up before I convince myself once and for all that this is for the best.

I sigh deeply, trying to let my music and the ambient noise of the diner soothe my nerves. It only grates on me. I pull out my earbuds, drop them on the table, and open my eyes.

And jump about a foot in the air.

"Holy shit," I shriek. "What the hell?"

I clutch at my chest as my breath comes in gasps. Cass and Vi, who are now sitting across from me, are barely controlling their laughter.

"Dammit," I curse. "How long have you been sitting there?"

"Like five minutes," Vi wheezes between fits of giggles. She clutches at her birthstone necklace as she folds over herself into another fit of laughter.

"You were really in the zone there. We didn't want to interrupt." Cass is doing a much better job of keeping a straight face, but her eyes are sparkling, and her belly is bouncing silently.

I take in a few more big gulps of air as my heart slows down. "And you thought scaring the shit out of me would be a better idea?"

Luckily, it's noon on a Wednesday, and there aren't many people in the place. I hear Donna's chuckle from the front, which must mean she was in on the whole thing from the start.

"Eh," Vi says. "You could probably use a little kick in the pants."

"Little do you know," I taunt, "I've already had several in the past seventy-two hours."

"Yeah." Cass draws out the word as if this statement does not surprise her one bit. "That's why we're here."

They must have talked to Trevor. I don't know why I hadn't calculated that into the possible scenarios I've been mulling over. I'd feel betrayed, but I'm the one who has had my phone off since Sunday. I could have headed this off, but I decided to isolate myself instead.

"Don't you two have jobs or somewhere else you need to be?" I try deflecting, even though I know it's useless.

Vi shrugs. "Perks of freelancing."

Cass points to her belly. "I called off for a doctor's appointment this morning. Good timing."

I groan, defeated. "Can I at least see an ultrasound picture?"

Cass reaches for her purse, but Vi holds out a hand to stop her. "Only if you're a good girl and talk to us about whatever made you go dark this week," Vi says.

"Ohh, tough love. Good idea." Cass beams up at Violet, who looks down at her with googly eyes.

I'm pretty sure they're about to kiss, which is a step too far for me in my current mental state, so I clear my throat loudly. They both snap their heads in my direction.

"Can you please say what you came here to say and leave me in peace?" I beg.

"Right." Cass leans forward, her belly tucked underneath the table. "What happened between you and Trevor?"

I level a glare at her. "Since you're here, I'm pretty sure you already know."

"I know his side of the story," she admits. "But I want to hear yours."

"What's there to tell?" I ask bitterly. "I said some stuff, his feelings got hurt, I left. It's over."

"I think he wants to see you," Cass suggests gently.

"What's the point? It was inevitable. This is what happens when you bang before getting to know each other. You end up finding out stuff down the line that you don't like." I grab my mug to take a self-satisfied sip, but I remember it's cold and put it down.

"So, let me get this straight. You told him you left some thirst trap comments on an article, and you think that's grounds for never seeing him again?" Cass seems incredulous. "It's not that big of a deal."

"Not necessarily. I'm saying it's indicative of how these things go for me. I wasn't meant to be with someone. Derek proved that. Hell, Mom and Dad proved that. *The Gazette* didn't even want me in the end. It's not who I am. I'm not like you two. I wasn't built for long term."

Cass's features pinch and she slowly shakes her head. She looks at Vi, and the two of them share a look that contains a whole silent conversation. It's the type of look only two people destined to be together can share.

Way to rub it in, ladies.

The glance ends with Cass tipping her head in Vi's direction. Vi leans forward. Her turn to take over, it seems. I steel myself for Violet's tough love.

I'm completely unprepared for what comes out of her mouth. "Cass and I hit a rough patch once."

I frown and look back and forth between the two of them. Cass is nodding.

"Really?" I ask. "When? And why didn't either of you tell me?"

"The most important part was the promise we made to each other when we decided to be together." Vi traces a line on the dark tabletop. "That you and I would always be friends no matter what happened between her and me. You two would always be sisters, and you and I would always be friends. Always."

I let the word settle into the tiny cracks in my heart. *Always.*

"What happened?" I whisper around the knot of emotion in my throat.

Vi shrugs. "Oh, I don't know. I got too intense too fast or something."

I laugh, and I'm surprised to find it's wet. "You? No."

"Funny," she deadpans as her eyebrow ticks up.

Cass leans in. Her turn. "Let me put this in terms you can relate to. You've pitched yourself this story. The one where people leave you, and you'll never be good enough to keep people around. That's been your angle for years. But let me pitch you another angle. The one where the people who really matter stick around. Where you're more than enough for the people who think you're worth it."

She's worth it.

I can barely hold the tears back when it's Vi's turn again. "You've got to see it, Em. Not everyone abandons you. Cass didn't. I never will. And maybe Trevor wouldn't either, but in your insistence that people do, *you* left *him*. You may not like being the feel-good reporter on the block, but you made him happy. That was clear."

Sreća.

The tears are really coming now, dropping onto the table one after another like little reminders. *People feel things.* I guess it's okay if I feel things, too.

"He made me happy." My voice is shaky, but the words are no less true for it.

Cass's shoulders sag in relief. "So talk to him," she urges gently.

"I will." I wipe my eyes with a diner napkin and take a deep breath to steady myself again. "I promise, I will. But I want to write this article first. I need to do it right. I owe him."

Cass and Vi share a smile. "Can we help?" Vi asks.

"No." I reach into my bag to power on my phone. I have to send a text to Ethan. There's a photo I need for this article, and I think he can make it happen. "I know exactly what I need to do."

AN ANCESTRAL CUP: MARKO AND DAVID KOVACIC LIVE ON IN BAKER'S BLEND'S LEGACY

Emery Darlis

Thank you for joining me for this month-long feature of Baker's Blend Coffee Shop. It's our last article today, and I'm proud that your interest in the shop has made a real difference. Baker's Blend has seen more and more customers over the month, and I'm happy to report that it seems the shop will be able to remain open.

I did not have the pleasure of knowing Marko and David Kovacic, the previous owners of Baker's Blend Coffee Shop. They both tragically passed before the writing of these articles. And though I grew up in this city, and Baker's Blend has been part of Baker's Grove since well before I was born, I didn't know about it until I started this series.

It seems a shame that I was never introduced to Baker's Blend nor its previous owners. The truth of it is that my family was not integrated in the community. Growing up, we were more isolated than I realized, not venturing out into the city to try new things or meet new people. And though I can't get enough of it now, coffee was not a part of our daily routine.

I wish I had met Marko and David. It would have been a treat to hear Marko talk about the beauty of the Croatian coastline. To listen to his stories about coming to America with his wife and a dream. To sip an espresso made with the original machine he saved up to buy shortly after opening the shop. To watch David make his signature blueberry muffins—an item still on the menu today—while he told me how he sourced his ingredients and where to find the best blueberries.

But they are gone now, and Marko's grandson, Trevor, remains as the sole owner of Baker's Blend. He is a man holding his father's and grandfather's legacy in his hands. He is committed to coffee, of course, but it's more than that. Coffee, to him, is about community. It's about sharing something special with the people around you.

I may never have met his father or grandfather, but to know Trevor Kovacic is to know his ancestors. His grandfather's smile is reflected in his own. He has his father's eyes. And he embodies their passion for bringing people together over good coffee.

To know Trevor is also to love him. You cannot talk to him and walk away unhappy. His brightness and optimism are contagious and can soften even the hardest of edges. His coffee and company are warm and hearken from ancient traditions. To love him is to love his ancestors. They are as much a part of him as they are of Baker's Blend itself. They are woven into the fabric of the shop and into everything Trevor does. They represent a permanence that is missing for so many of us—at least, for me. Through the coffee and conversation that fills Baker's Blend, his father and grandfather are eternal. They live on in every smile and every cup.

When you visit Baker's Blend Coffee Shop, you're doing more than buying a latte. You're supporting a rich history. You're supporting our community. And we hope the community comes out to show how much it means tomorrow for the grand re-opening of Baker's Blend.

Chapter Thirty-Six

TREVOR

On Saturday morning, James and I barely get the banner hung before our first customers arrive. I don't even have time to register any emotion at the *Sponsored by Baker's Grove Living* featured prominently in the corner. It's for the best.

I've been able to keep myself distracted enough for the past few days that I haven't thought about Emery too much. Only when I bring the extra whipped cream dispenser back to the shop. Or when someone orders a hazelnut latte, which is surprisingly frequent. Or when I wake up in the morning and wish she was next to me. Or when I go to sleep at night and wish the same. Or when I bump James out of the way to make every single drink someone orders on Friday so I can avoid looking at the *Baker's Grove Living* website.

So, I guess maybe I have been thinking about her a lot. I haven't heard from Cass. I tried to call Emery a few more times, but her phone is still off. The closest I get is when Ethan comes in on Thursday and asks if he can take a picture of me holding my framed photos of my dad and Dida.

He said Emery hadn't been in the office since Monday but had asked for this specific picture to run with her article. Someone must have told him something, though, because when I asked if I should roll up my sleeves, he smiled sadly and shook his head.

After Ethan left, James suggested I should hang the photos behind the counter. I nailed them up on the wall, above the patch my dad made when he was a teenager.

On Saturday, the customers come in a steady stream. James is doing great, but it doesn't take very long to realize we need more help. I text Mike an SOS, and he arrives about thirty minutes later with extra provisions. He jumps right behind the counter and gets to work. For a moment, it feels like the summers he'd spent working here during college. I almost expect my dad to walk out from the back room and throw on an apron.

A swell of pride bubbles up over the ever-present numbness of the past few days because I'm sure he'd be proud of me. I'm proud of the work I've put in here, too. But also because I'm proud of Emery. Whatever she wrote, it has had some effect. The amount of people pointing out the photos hanging on the wall would suggest most of them are here because of her articles.

During a lull in the action in the early afternoon, James dips out to touch base with his band members. Mike starts to clean up while I man the front. When he comes out of the back room, he catches me looking at the pictures.

"Did you read the article?" he asks.

"No."

"Why not?"

"Couldn't do it." I shrug. "It felt too final, you know?"

He folds his arms and comes to stand next to me. We're both facing the photos, now, taking an unintentional moment of silence.

"I miss them," I say quietly.

"I know," he responds. "I do, too." He's silent for a second before he says, "They'd be proud of you, though."

A sudden swell of emotion blocks any words trying to come out, so I just nod.

"You know," he says slowly, "I don't think it would have felt final if you had read it."

I look at him out of the corner of my eye. "What do you mean?"

He doesn't take his eyes off of the photos when he says, "She gets it, I think. What this place means to you. To all of us. To them." He nods at the photos before turning to face me. "Just read it, Trev. She wrote it for you."

Because I am who I am, and I can't help it, hope starts to worm its way up through the numbness, through the pride. It settles itself right on top of my chest.

Mike's smile spreads slow and wide as he pulls his phone out of his back pocket. He taps it a few times, then hands it to me.

I read it slowly, letting each word register. By the time I reach the end, I can barely see the page. I look up at Mike, and he's blurry, too. I swipe a hand at my eyes, and it comes away wet.

To know Trevor is also to love him.

"Do you think..." I don't have words to finish the sentence. The numbness is gone. I'm all nostalgia and pride and hope.

"I think," Mike says slowly, "you should take a look outside." He winks, then tips his head toward the windows that face the street.

I almost don't want to look. If Emery's not standing out there, it'll crush me.

Mike sees my hesitation. He claps both hands on my shoulders, then nudges me ever so slightly toward the front of the shop.

Chapter Thirty-Seven

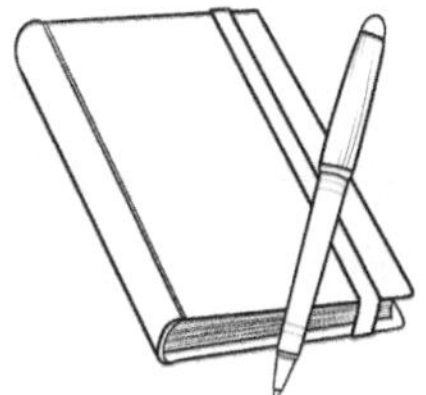

I RESTLESSLY SHIFT FROM foot to foot, praying I don't sweat through my pink blouse in this late-summer heat. Trevor is standing there, on the other side of the glass, staring at the wall. Mike comes out from the back room, and I glance to my right. Cass gives me a thumbs up while Vi taps out a message on her phone from where they stand, out of the guys' sight. Mike takes his phone out, taps a few times, then hands it to Trevor. He glances up, sees me, and nods once before turning his attention back to his friend.

I had set aside time yesterday to stalk Mike on social media since I didn't have his number, but he was shockingly easy to find. I needed to know if Trevor had read the article. When he said Trevor hadn't, I told Mike he had to read it before I talked to him. Mike came up with this ridiculous plan, and I roped in Cass and Vi for moral support.

And now, I'm nervously standing outside Baker's Blend Coffee Shop, hoping Trevor understands what I was trying to say in that piece.

"This is stupid," I mutter. "I should just go in there."

"It's a big moment," Cass insists. She's been practically giddy about it since yesterday. "Let it happen."

Trevor finally, *finally* looks up from his phone. His jaw is slack, and he wipes at his cheeks.

Panic starts to rise from my chest through my throat. "I think he's crying. Oh, shit. That is not what I wanted."

"It's an emotional piece, Em," Vi assures me. "He's feeling things. Let him."

I shift from foot to foot again, shaking my hands out like a boxer entering the ring. "Right. Emotions. Got it."

Mike puts his hands on Trevor's shoulders and slowly, gently, turns him to face me.

Time stands still. The edges of my vision go fuzzy, almost like I'm in a tunnel. The only thing I can see is Trevor, his amber eyes shining and an achingly slow smile spreading across his face.

I let out a half-laugh, half-sob and try really hard not to jump up and down to release some of this nervous energy. Luckily, I don't have to wait too long. Trevor, with all the professionalism expected of the owner of this establishment, comes out from behind the counter, crosses to the door in six measured steps, pulls it open, and stops a few feet in front of me.

His back is to Cass and Vi. I'm not even sure if he saw them or if he only has eyes for me. Probably the latter, because Cass loudly clamps a hand over her mouth to muffle a squeal, and he doesn't bat an eye.

"Hi," he says breathlessly. It sounds as if he ran a mile to get to me. His cheeks are wet, and I have to curl my hands into fists to keep myself from reaching out to brush the tears off them.

"Hi," I return. "Trevor, I—"

"You don't have to say anything," he interrupts me. He leans toward me a little but doesn't take another step. "I'm just glad you're here."

"No. I planned this whole thing. I need to say this." I shake out my hands again. I don't know if I've ever been this nervous in my life.

Trevor's expression turns indulgent. "Okay," he says, his voice husky. It rumbles through me and pools right in my middle. "Go ahead."

"Okay," I whisper. I clear my throat. "Okay, listen. I might have started this project with entirely selfish motivations. I'm sorrier than you can ever know that I hurt you because of it. I didn't realize it at the time, but I was closing myself off to new possibilities. Running from my past. Trying desperately not to make the same mistakes and fall into the same traps. But you were right. I've been stuck. In an effort to not repeat the past, I've inadvertently made myself afraid of the future."

Trevor starts to shake his head, but I press on. "And you... you have never been afraid of any of that. You embrace your past and your history. And because you can do that, you can also see ahead of you. I admire that about you."

I pause to take a deep, shaky breath. "I meant every word of that article. I wrote it for my job, I guess, but I really wrote it for you. Because you're more than just your forearms." I laugh nervously, hoping the joke lands.

He chuckles, and it's the best damn sound I've ever heard. Another little knot loosens in my chest. I close my eyes briefly to soak it in, and my own breathy laugh escapes me. I open my eyes to meet his, still intensely focused on me.

"But my forearms are pretty great," he insists, finally taking a step toward me.

"That goes without saying," I assure him.

"'To know Trevor is also to love him,'" he quotes, his eyes never leaving mine. "Did you mean that, too?"

My heart skips a beat. Here we go. "I told you I meant every word." I search his face for any sign that he is either going to return the sentiment or run away screaming. "Unless that's a lot. Then I meant it in a very universal sense. Strictly platonic. Like I love hazelnut, or whipped cream." I can't help the smirk at that last one.

Tears have been escaping over his long lashes and running unchecked down his cheeks this whole time. He's looking at me as if he wishes he could drink me in. "Is it my turn, now?" He waits for me to nod. "It is a lot," he says, and my heart just about falls out of my chest and to the ground. He takes that last step to close the distance between us and brings a hand to cup my cheek.

I had been holding my breath, but I breathe him in now. I'm completely enveloped by coffee and sugar and vanilla. A smell at once so new and so old. Sweet and bitter. I let him fill my senses and spill over into any of the remaining cracks in my heart.

He leans his forehead against mine. "It's a lot," he repeats, his lips an inch from mine. "But I've been feeling a lot for you for a while now. To know you is to love you, too, Emery Darlis. And I plan to spend every day from now on proving it to you."

"Oh," Cass whisper-shouts. "They're the perfect blend! Get it?"

Vi groans. "Will you just let them have a moment?"

I laugh, the sound lighter than it has been in a while. "We have an audience," I tell him.

"We have more of an audience than that," he says, looking sidelong at the café windows.

I glance in that direction out of the corner of my eye. I can clearly see a crowd of people trying to pretend they're not looking at us.

"You'd better kiss me, then," I say.

"Happily, srećo." He closes the distance between our lips, and my heart soars.

There's cheering—both muffled from inside and loud and high-pitched from outside. But I don't register it. Trevor is here, kissing me in front of his crowded shop and our friends and family, past and present. It's a kiss that's sweet and bitter. Ancient with hints at a future, all in one.

Cass is right. It's the perfect blend.

Epilogue

Trevor

Two Months Later

"Drive faster!" Emery shouts from the passenger seat. She's white-knuckling my hand, and her knee is bouncing erratically.

"I'm going as fast as I can, srećo. We'll get there soon, I promise." I try to keep my voice measured and calm for her benefit, but her excitement is contagious.

"I can't believe I had my phone off for that pointless meeting. It should have been an email. How much longer?"

I lift her fingers to my lips and kiss her knuckles. Her knee stops bouncing, and she looks up at me. Her cheeks are flushed, and tendrils of hair have escaped her messy bun. She's wearing a yellow cardigan over a white shirt and navy slacks. If I thought summer Emery was gorgeous, fall Emery is in a whole different league. She's beautiful inside and out, and I am so lucky to call her mine.

"Soon. Just a few more minutes," I assure her, but the words don't seem to do as much as the kiss to her hand did. Her knee starts bouncing again as she turns her attention back to the road.

"I'm sorry you had to leave the shop," she says. "I know you were in the middle of training your new hire."

"I'm not sorry about it. She'll be fine with James there, now that he finally has a handle on things." I kiss her hand again and watch as a small, nervous smile graces her lips. Better than the grimace she's been wearing since we got in the car, but she remains silent.

"She's your family. I'm happy to be with you." I give her hand a gentle squeeze. "Maybe someday she'll be my family, too."

"Mmm," she hums as she chews the corner of her mouth and stares distractedly out the passenger window. I turn the corner and wait for the words to sink in as the hospital comes into view ahead of us.

Sure enough, her head whips in my direction. "What did you say?"

"I said"—I kiss her hand again—"maybe someday she'll be my family, too." I glance sidelong at her and raise my eyebrows in question.

"Slow down there, Romeo. We've been dating for like two months."

I chuckle heartily. That's exactly the reaction I was expecting.

"But yeah," she says quietly, her head turned back to the passenger window. "Maybe someday."

I would try to catch her eye if we weren't pulling into the hospital parking lot, but my chest swells at the possibility she admitted to. It's more than I expected, and everything I've hoped for.

She unbuckles her seatbelt before I've even put the car in park. As soon as I have, she jumps out and starts walking toward the building. I catch up to her quickly, but I have to work a little to keep up with her pace. Once she enters, she walks straight past the desk and makes a series of turns until she gets to an elevator. We go up to the fourth floor, where we stop at a desk in front of a series of rooms.

"Cassandra Darlis?" Emery asks. I reach between us and thread our fingers together. She squeezes my hand without looking at me.

"Room 403," the nurse informs us with a smile as she indicates a set of rooms behind her. Emery nods once and walks in the direction the nurse is pointing.

When we find the room, she stands outside it for a second. From inside, we can clearly hear a tiny wail and some gentle cooing.

Emery turns to me, her eyes wide as saucers. "I just realized. I don't think I've ever held a baby before."

I press my lips together to keep from laughing. I don't want her to think I'm laughing at her. "They're sturdier than you think. Just support their head."

She nods again, turning back to the door. "It's real," she breathes.

"It's real," I confirm.

"I'm an aunt."

"You are."

"I'm going to be the best fucking aunt that baby could ever hope for."

"I don't doubt it." I lean in to kiss her temple. "Might want to start by watching that language, though."

"Right. No swearing. Got it. Okay. Ready?"

"I'm with you," I say. Her gaze meets mine as her other hand flutters up to her chest.

I knock lightly on the door, and when Cass's voice floats out to us that we should come in, I hold the door open for Emery to enter first.

Cass and Vi are both laying in the hospital bed. The lights are off in the room, but sunlight streams in, casting the scene in a natural spotlight. Cass looks exhausted, but she's glowing from the inside out. Vi's now-green hair is tousled, and she has dark circles under her eyes. She's glowing, too. Cass is holding a small bundle in her arms, and Vi is completely enraptured by the small little face peering up at her.

Cass looks up at us with a tired, beautiful smile. It's so much like her sister's that it still takes my breath away.

"Hey, sis. Want to meet your niece?"

"It's a girl?" Emery breathes. From the set of her shoulders and the waver in her voice, I can tell she's trying not to cry.

"Mmm-hmm. Auntie Emery, meet Iris Emmeline."

Emery drops my hand and takes a few steps to stand at Cass's side. She peers down at the baby in her arms. "Iris Emmeline?"

"Yeah. I grew her, so she's a little bit me. Iris is a little bit Violet. Em is a little bit you." She looks up at her sister, waiting to see her reaction.

"A little bit of all of us?" Emery says, choking back a sob. Her gaze meets mine.

"She's a medley of her ancestors," I offer, and I wonder if this is how my grandfathers felt when they saw me for the first time. "She's beautiful."

Twin tears snake their way down Emery's cheeks. She doesn't bother wiping them away as Cass hands her baby Iris. Emery cradles the baby in her arms, stiffly at first, but gaining confidence after a few minutes.

"You're so perfect, Iris Emmeline. I love you," Emery coos as she traces a finger over the baby's tiny hand. She looks up at me. "Will you help me pick a nickname for her? In Croatian?"

I look to Cass and Vi, who both nod their approval. "I'd be honored," I say.

"She can be a little bit of all of us. And a little bit of herself, too," Vi offers, the pride already shining in her voice.

Emery and Cass's eyes meet. Emery cocks an eyebrow. "The perfect blend?"

Cass groans. "Are you ever going to let me live that down?"

"No." Emery devolves into a fit of giggles. Baby Iris evidently doesn't like being jostled because she lets out a surprisingly loud wail. Emery stops laughing immediately and hands the baby back to Cass.

We stay for a little while longer, but we leave when it's time for the baby to feed. When we're back in the car, the sun has set, and the fall air is cool.

Emery's hand immediately finds mine. "I'm so glad she's here."

"Me too, srećo." I lean over to kiss her sweetly. "They're getting ready to close up the shop. What do you say we grab some waffles and go home?"

"Mmm," she hums. "That sounds great."

I start the car and pull out of our spot. As I drive into the night, I send up a little thank you that this wonderful woman is part of my life. When we're home, after we eat waffles and share whipped cream, I show her exactly how grateful I am. We talk late into the night about our future, and how sweet and happy it will be.

Trevor's Latte Recipes

Honey Lavender Cinnamon Latte

(Makes one 12-oz latte)

Ingredients:

- 1 oz of espresso (light roast recommended)

- 2 tablespoons of lavender syrup

- 1 tablespoon of honey

- Cinnamon to taste

- 12 oz of milk (oat milk recommended)

Directions:

- Put 2 tablespoons (2 pumps) of lavender syrup, 1 tablespoon of honey, and a dash of cinnamon in cup

- Pull 1 oz of espresso

- Pour espresso over syrup, honey and cinnamon, swirl to

melt and combine

- Steam milk to desired temperature

- Slowly pour milk over espresso

- Top with lavender infused whipped cream and sprinkle of cinnamon, as desired

- Serve with love

Hazelnut Latte

(Makes one 12-oz latte)

Ingredients:

- 1 oz of espresso

- 3 tablespoons toasted hazelnut syrup

- 12 oz of milk

Directions:

- Put 3 tablespoons (3 pumps) of hazelnut syrup in cup

- Pull 1 oz of espresso

- Pour espresso over syrup, swirl to melt and combine

- Steam milk to desired temperature

- Slowly pour milk over espresso

- Serve with love

Tip: Enjoy either of these iced! Just melt the syrup and honey with the hot espresso, add ice and cold milk. Stir to combine.

Want More Mike?

Baker's Grove, Indiana is not a real place, and unfortunately, neither is Baker's Blend Coffee Shop. The city is based on several midsized Midwestern cities I've had the pleasure to both live in and visit. I tried to keep it as realistic as possible while also keeping it completely separate from any real place. Any likeness to a real town is purely coincidental, and is most likely a result of my deep love of all things Midwestern.

Not ready to leave Baker's Grove? Sign up for Allie's newsletter for free bonus chapters and behind-the-scenes content at https://alliesam berts.substack.com.

Acknowledgements

Wow. My fourth book. It's incredible to think that, just over a year ago, I was releasing my first. Thank you, from the bottom of my heart, for being on this wild ride with me.

As with any huge undertaking, this book has been a group effort. I am so lucky to have such an incredible team in my corner. When I say this book wouldn't be in your hands without them, I mean it.

First and foremost, a huge thank you to my husband. He's given me the best love story in the world—better than these books because it's real. He puts up with my late nights, takes the kids out of the house when the muse is yelling at me to finish a scene, talks out plot points, helps me come up with jokes, and is the first to hug me after I type "the end." You're my favorite, and I love you.

A giant thank you to my alpha reader and critique partner, Hannah. This story brought me a lot of joy, but it was a hell of a lot better with your suggestions, and I don't think I would have made it over the finish line were it not for you dragging me there. I'm so glad we crossed that finish line together.

Massive thanks to my early readers. Your feedback and cheerleading has been invaluable. Thank you to: Jillian, Alexis, Stefanie, Caitlin, Jessica, Elizabeth, and Sandy. You're the absolute best readers out there, and I'm so grateful to have your comments—critical and unhinged.

Thanks also to my street team! Anna, April, Ashley, Ashley, Brooke, Cami, Catarina, Courtney, Hana, Hope, Jen & Victoria, Kae, Kathy, Katie, Kayla, Laura, Lindsey, Meg, Mindy, Sav, Sidney, Trish & Ash, and Victoria. A lot of you have been with me since the very beginning, which is so amazing. Thank you for your ideas and your help spreading the word about my books. You've gotten me unstuck more times than I can count, and I'm so grateful.

A big thank you to my agent, Katie Monson at SBR Media. Thanks for helping me bring my stories to new readers and believing in me.

That beautiful artwork I know you love so much at the front of the book and in the chapter headings? (And on the awesome swag you can buy on my website?) That's all because of the amazingly talented Lorissa Padilla. She designed the Baker's Blend Coffee Shop logo, too. Thank you for sharing your art with me. I am forever in your debt.

And of course, this gorgeous cover. Jillian Liota of Blue Moon Creative Studio has done it again. Thank you for this amazing cover design—it inspired the book!

How do I even start to thank Megan Carver? She has worn so many hats on my author journey—editor, audiobook narrator, confidante, sounding board, punching bag—but most importantly, she has been a friend. And, look! I included some extra em dashes in this paragraph, just for you.

I did a lot of research for this book. A lot. I wanted to do everything justice and frame it with authenticity and sensitivity. My dear friend, Katarina, helped me so much with her knowledge of Croatia and its history, what it is to be a descendant of Croatian immigrants, and their coffee culture. She even went so far as to walk me through preparing Turkish coffee so I could experience it myself. Katarina and I have been friends since elementary school, so she also unknowingly helped me with the sense of nostalgia I wanted for this book, too. It was so wonderful to dive deeper into not only her history, but our shared stories, as well. Thank you, friend.

Thank you to my family and friends who not only were completely unsurprised when I said I wanted to do this author thing, but who have been cheering me on the whole way. Your support means the world to me. Thanks, especially, to my mom, dad, and brother who were tortured with my very first stories when I was a kid. Hopefully, I've come a long way. And to my sister-in-law who has been endlessly supportive. I still have that Christmas wrapping paper.

And last, but not least, thank you to my readers. Thank you for every message, every review, every post. Thank you, most of all, for reading my words and loving my characters.

About the Author

Allie Samberts is a romance writer, book lover, and high school English teacher. She was voted funniest teacher of the year for 2023 and 2025 by her students, which is probably her highest honor to date. She is also a runner, and enjoys knitting and sewing. She lives in the Chicago suburbs with her husband, two kids, and dog. You can follow her on Instagram @alliesambertswrites, TikTok at @alliesamberts, sign up for her newsletter at alliesamberts.substack.com, and get other updates at www.alliesamberts.com.

Also By Allie Samberts

Leade Park

The Write Place

The Write Time

The Write Choice

Standalones

Common Grounds

Love Out Loud

Novellas

Pumpkin to Talk About

Christmas by Design

Love in the Time of Conversation Hearts (with Hannah Bird)

Coming 2026 from Page and Vine

Not a Strong Enough Word

Not on the Same Page

Not the Way it Ends

Stay up to date on new releases and grab some bonus content! Subscribe to Allie's newsletter at https://alliesamberts.substack.com